Knee Deep in Thunder

KNEE DEEP IN THUNDER

SHEILA MOON

ILLUSTRATED BY PETER PARNALL

Guild for Psychological Studies
Publishing House
Fall, 1986

Published in the United States of America by
The Guild for Psychological Studies Publishing House
2230 Divisadero Street
San Francisco, California   94115

Illustrations: Peter Parnall
Cover Design: Dorothy Nissen
Typesetting: Pan Typesetters
Printing: Braun-Brumfield, Inc.

This book is the first title in a trilogy. The other titles are *Hunt Down the Prize* and *Deepest Roots*.

Library of Congress Cataloging in Publication Data

Moon, Sheila 1910-
  Knee-Deep in Thunder.

  Reprint. Originally published: First edition. New York: Atheneum, 1967.
  Summary: An unusual stone provokes a journey into an underground world of fantasy where Maris is guided by a dog-sized beetle.
  [1. Fantasy] I. Parnall, Peter, ill. II. Title
Pz7.M778Kn 1986   [Fic.]   86-19534
ISBN 0-917479-08-4 (pbk.)

To E.J. and R.R. who,
wherever they might be,
would be joyful

Starflower
Burn

Marsh

Lagoon

Beasts
Stockade

Contents

The timid folk beseech me, the wise ones warn me,
They say that I shall never grow to stand so high;
But I climb among the hills of cloud and follow vanished
lightning,
I shall stand knee-deep in thunder with my head against
the sky.

(FROM "*Climb*", BY WINIFRED WELLES)

PART I

The Beginning

1

I CAME RUNNING OVER THE PALE SPRING HILL AND HALF STUMBLED, half slid into the hollow to sprawl in disorder on the damp grass. Except for the remote sound of the sea, the hollow held silence as a cup holds water. I felt as if I floated there softly, which I liked. But Scuro hadn't come, so I sat up and whistled. Only sea and silence. He was probably still concerned with that desolate gopherhole. I whistled again and he came flinging over the hollow's rim, a smallish black eccentric mixture of dog. He sat beside me, head and tongue lolling.

"Silly Scuro!" I said, pulling his ear, scratching under his chin, and rubbing the top of his head. (His name was the silliest thing about him; it came to him from a cousin who'd been to Italy and said *scuro* meant "dark.") Anyway, I always called him "silly Scuro" when I was feeling bothered. So I sat and he sat and I went on rubbing his head and thinking.

I loved this special scooped-out piece of ground high above the long beach. It was far enough from the small town where I lived that I felt secure; it could be reached only by a steep, thin path that few people knew about and fewer ever climbed. I had found it by accident one day while Scuro and I were exploring. So now I came whenever I needed to be with myself and to feel— well, pulled together, I suppose. Sometimes the place seemed alive, or as if I shared it with some live thing, though nothing grew in it but short wild grass, sparse and burned most of the year. Finally I stretched out full length on the ground, my face to the sunlight, and tried not to remember.

But the wretched morning scene paraded back and forth, Mother's tension, Dad's awkwardness, my own frustration as I slammed the kitchen door on the perennial bickering about money. It would be nice if we could have just a little more money, so Mother wouldn't have to work, and Dad wouldn't have to look so small and distressed when shopping times came around. Like today.

Excited yelps from Scuro brought me sharply back. Knowing how urgent he could be about nothing, I merely turned my head to see what he was about. He was undertaking an assault on a small beetle ducking under a smallish rock. His eagerness as usual spoiled his accuracy and the beetle flew in one direction, the rock in another, while Scuro dug frantically to enlarge a hole that contained nobody.

The rock Scuro had flung lay near my left hand. By reaching, I could close my fingers around it; and for some odd reason, I felt compelled to do so. The rock was about chestnut size, and my finger ends found it surprisingly like velvet. I picked it up to see it more closely, almost dropping it because I hadn't expected it to be as heavy as it was. I began to be fascinated by it. Its color was a dark blue-green, not merely on the surface but through the entire stone, which was not quite translucent but almost, and marked with pollen-colored, swirling striations, which made it appear to be moving inside itself.

As I stared at it, it became like a pool, and I seemed to be in it, and it was of my substance and I was of its substance, neither place nor time anywhere, only a queer empty stillness surrounded by invisible motion. And then the pool was gone and I was myself, and myself was looking at the stone. Slowly, I lifted myself from my prone position and propped myself on one elbow, looking outward, seeking my familiar earth.

What I saw was earth surely, but, not mine; it was earth of the deepest of browns, a shadowy, purpled mahogany soil lying under me and beyond me. I was in a hollow, not mine but one whose sides rose at least fifty feet above a fair-sized valley with brown earth in the center and with some sort of silver-green trees around its circumference.

Later on, when I thought back to this scene, I wondered why

I hadn't been terrified, and knew that those purposes I later came to know were already at work. Quite calmly I decided to learn where I was, if possible, or at least to get my bearings before night came. Already it felt surprisingly close to evening. My only worry was about Scuro. He was nowhere to be seen, and although he was quite used to wandering off alone and poking into his own mysteries, he was not always sensible about them. I got up, dropped the stone into my skirt pocket, took a deep breath, and shouted. "Scuro! Come Scuro, Scuro, Scu-u-uro!"

"Here now," said a small, precise voice from close behind me. "Stop that! You have just arrived and you have no right to disturb our silences with such noises!"

I spun around to see a very large black beetle staring at me as if I, and not he, were the insect. No usual beetle, he was about Scuro's size (maybe a bit smaller) and was waving his antennae angrily. Before I could say anything, he spoke again.

"And if your noise is related to that most monstrous and impolite creature who knocked me down, he is being cared for!"

"He's very young and awkward, and I'm sorry he hurt you. He didn't mean to, really."

"That may be, that may be. It still needs to learn manners. And They will teach it when They have time."

"They? They? Are there people nearby? And can I go to them and get Scuro? They mustn't punish him, please." I was feeling upset now, having visions of Scuro being tied up and whipped by strangers. I stepped toward the beetle.

He raised a front leg in a gesture of command. I halted. In a slower, less angry, still precise voice he said, "It will not be hurt." After a pause, as if he were considering whether to say more, he continued. "They are not exactly people. They have been called by many names. I prefer to say Them, and to call Their home the Place of Them. You are, I suppose, an earth person. Though whether or not you are a part of the dreadful events that have been happening here recently, I cannot say." He sighed. "Too many have disappeared, and They are troubled." He stopped as if considering whether to say more. "Well, come along. It is growing dark, and we must move with matters as they happen."

"But Scuro will be—"

"Do come along, please!"

Although I wanted to ask all sorts of questions, for some reason I did not then understand I followed him obediently as he started plodding over the rough ground toward what seemed, in the dim twilight, to be a hole in the valley's nearer side.

By the time we had crossed the center of the valley, it was quite dark. No moon shone; a few stars appeared in the remote, cool sky. Then I felt turf under my feet. Walking was easier, but it got harder and harder to see the beetle and follow him. I was about to say as much when the beetle stopped.

"Put your hand on my back," he said firmly. "I wouldn't want to lose you."

Somewhat tentatively I leaned over and touched him, having to bend far to reach him. Contrary to my expectations, his back was not cold and brittle but solidly comfortable and even reassuring.

We moved on slowly and very clumsily. After what seemed a long time, I sensed that we had left the outside and were now inside. Inside what, I couldn't tell. The air smelled of earth, and I could even hear a faint clicking of the beetle's several feet, so I guessed we might be in a tunnel. The blackness was almost feelable it was so black, and I pressed my hand more firmly on the beetle lest I lose him.

We went on in this awkward way for so long that I began to ache in every part of me. I was about ready to say I couldn't go on unless I stood straight for a while when the beetle halted. The sudden silence was a shock, I had gotten so used to the sounds of his clicking feet and my shuffling. Then I heard from somewhere not too far away the trickle of water.

"Just around the corner," the beetle advised, "and we will have arrived."

So we clicked and shuffled around a bend in the darkness, and then all at once the curtain of black was raised. We had come into a cave where a central fire burned. Soft reddish shadows and lights played about, and red glinted here and there from the surface of a little stream running through the cave.

All that was visible then was the stream, the well-built and steady-burning fire, and the beetle, who climbed up on a large rock nearby. There might be movement in the shadows beyond the fire, but I couldn't be sure.

"I'm hungry!" I said before I thought, and wished at once I hadn't.

The beetle eyed me coldly. However, his voice didn't sound annoyed as he replied in his formal fashion, "Quite so, I am certain. There is, first, a matter of ritual to be undertaken to establish something about you. Then you shall be fed."

The rock on which he stood gave him added height, so that he was nearer my level. As he spoke I saw how luminous were his many-faceted insect eyes—luminous and, to my surprise, beautiful in a strange way.

"I will ask you, please," he continued, "to walk a few paces to your left. There you will find a pool. Look into it until I call you."

I obeyed him as I had never obeyed anyone else in my life, sensing somehow a profoundly meaningful adventure at hand. Four or five paces left brought me to a place where the stream widened and slowed to stillness, before running imperceptibly onward into the dark. When I bent over slightly and peered into the pool, I could at first see only faint outlines of myself, but the longer I looked the clearer the image grew. What a sight I was! My denim skirt and jacket were very dirty from the crawl through the tunnel, my blue blouse half out of the skirt and mud-streaked. My hair was falling limply about my face, its usual mouse color seeming drabber than ever. My nose, which I'd always felt was too large, was not made any smaller by mud on its tip. Altogether the sight was quite discouraging. I wanted to turn away. But remembering the beetle's words, I stayed. Maybe the mouth was not too bad. It was full and well curved, although the lines on either side, like parentheses, made me look older than thirteen years. The vivid blue of my eyes I really (although secretly) liked. How very strange to be staring into my own eyes as if I were somebody else! Was I perhaps somebody else? Maybe everyone was also someone else somewhere? Maybe—

"You will return to me now." The beetle's quiet voice interrupted my inner conversation, and I was glad because I was beginning to feel frightened. When I once more stood facing the beetle, he spoke slowly as if every word were important.

"Tell me your name, and why you are here." As he asked the question—or, rather, gave the command—it sounded like the first day of school, and I almost giggled.

"My name is Maris." I stopped. The full weight of the second part of his command filled me with confusion and anxiety. "My name is Maris," I repeated, not knowing where to go next.

"So you said. Now what really brought you to this place? Or perhaps I should say, what do you think led up to this?"

"Well, I guess it was kind of an accident."

"Nothing," said the beetle gravely, "nothing, my dear Maris, is ever an accident. All events and circumstances in a life are conjoined, in ways known or unknown, to each other as cells in a living body. Let us not then speak of accidents!"

"No," I said, "no," though I was not clear at all as to why. "Well, I wanted to be by myself, to be let alone."

"Why?"

"Because I feel all mixed up and scattered whenever Mother and Dad are having problems! I love them both and I can see both points of view, and then I get mad at both of them for being like they are!"

"And you, Maris—what is your point of view?"

"I guess I want everyone to be happy!"

"Although perhaps a meritorious sentiment, that is hardly a point of view." He sighed. "I had in mind something rather more individual. But I greatly fear that you are not yet individual, and we must begin where you are and not where I might hope you were."

I wasn't sure I understood, but I got the idea that I wasn't very desirable, and the only reply I could think of was, "That's where I am even if you don't like it!"

"So you are. Of course." A quality of amusement came into the dry, grave, quiet voice. "Come along, then." He climbed down from his large rock and went toward the fire. I followed. The fire burned in a round depression in the ground. Over it, I could see now that we were nearer, hung a little sooty pot swung between two green sticks. Beyond it, gnarled-looking in the firelight, sat an old woman, out of sight in the deep shadow until now. Her clothes were strange and hard to define, for their color and texture seemed continually shifting, now sombre, now luminous, now rough and worn, now rich as finest velvet.

"Grandmother!" The beetle whispered in a voice conveying both awe and love. "O our Grandmother!"

The old woman turned her face full toward us. I caught my breath at the dramatic and ancient beauty, great dark eyes set deep in a maze of wrinkles, a mouth that had smiled at all beginnings and grieved at all endings since life began. When she arose her shadow was gigantic behind her, and she herself seemed very near and tree-tall, yet far off and diminishing. Involuntarily and quite unconsciously I bent my head, closed my eyes, and let my arms drop. As I stood so, I felt my right hand being lifted, and something like a crude bowl was put in it.

When I raised my head again, I saw only a bent and nobbly crone, busy about the fire. In my hand was an earthen bowl of poor workmanship, no larger than a child's cereal dish. The old crone ladled into it from the cooking pot a steaming portion of a mealy-looking substance and silently handed me a wooden spoon. She pointed to the bowl, then to the spoon, and disappeared into the darkness. I turned to protest to the beetle, but he was nowhere. I tried a spoonful dubiously. It had a pleasant nutlike flavor and fragrance. Hungrily I spooned it from the tiny bowl, eating and eating as if it were a large plate filled with choice food. As I began to be satisfied, I realized that the food in the bowl hadn't grown less.

When I was satisfied, without thinking—for thought had no space to exist in this timelessness—I laid myself down, curling like a child. Just as I gave myself over to sleep, I fancied I saw the beetle nearby looking at me compassionately, and I almost saw a hand, wrinkled but strong, reaching from the darkness to cover me with some soft thing. I wasn't certain of either sight; then I was asleep.

2

I WAKENED WITH THE GURGLE OF THE STREAM SOUNDING FRESH AND clear and a soft light from an unknown source bringing day into the cave. Only ashes remained where the fire had been. Not far from me stood the beetle, waving his antennae thoughtfully while he watched me.

"Come," said the beetle. "We must leave. We have a journey to try, and a work to attempt." I was reluctant to leave this mysterious shelter, and there was a hunger in me to stay near the old woman I had seen in the night. As if he guessed this, the beetle said, "Someday you will see her again. She said that herself, while you slept. Please don't ask questions of me yet. I will explain when it is time. Hold within you silently whatever you have seen. You will have need of the memory because They have need of us. Now let us go."

The procession of the previous evening (if two make a procession) repeated itself in a reverse direction, with me again stumbling through the tunnel after the beetle. The tunnel was not quite so black nor did it seem so long as it had before, and soon we emerged into the valley.

At once I was dazzled and excited by a covering of blossoms I did not remember from the day before. But the beetle plodded on, pushing aside blossoms and tipping bees from their work as he went, and I knew I must follow despite the day's loveliness. I knew it with the same compelling sense that had made me respect the beetle and his words from the moment we met, though where he had come from and why, I do not know.

Eventually he spoke without stopping his pace, tossing what he said over his antenna as if it were quite casual. "In the event that you had wondered," he said, "my name is Exi. Short for Alexaminander."

It was a nice friendly thing to be able to call him something. He seemed warmer. I was about to tell him so when I saw that we had reached the central area of bare ground, and to my alarm I saw that it now sloped quite steeply toward the center. Actually Exi had already begun to slide down and, though he was obviously trying hard to stop himself, he could not. "Watch yourself!" he cried out. But by this time, I too was slithering and slipping down the slope faster and faster, into a giant cup of earth with a hole in the bottom. I saw Exi's black body disappear, then I was flung into an abyss of darkness and was falling through space feet first.

The surrounding air was alive with things I couldn't see. My skin was aware of them and my ears caught quick flickers of sound. Once a flash like invisible lightning caused the air to quiver, and I had the sensation of swimming in a sea of dark space rippled with phantoms. If I'd been falling head over heels over head, as one is supposed to fall, it would have been more dizzying but less terrifying; but to fall so straight, always feet first, sliding down the palpable darkness . . . What should I do? Where was I? Who was I? What was where? Who was where? I twisted my hands together and they were wet with the sweat of fear. Rubbing them against my skirt in unconscious preparation for action, I felt a lump in the pocket. It was the stone, the small, velvety, nut-sized, blue-green stone I had picked up and put there, ages past, when Scuro had found the beetle. As my hand closed about the stone I felt inwardly quieted, and a line from a poem stood clear in my mind: "the still point of the turning world."

The plunge did not actually end, it just ceased to exist. One minute I was fearfully in it, the next minute I was sitting on softness in a silence unbroken by sound. There was no visibility, no light and no darkness. Nothing was absent, nothing present; I was there resting on and surrounded by invisibility. It was so sudden, this ending, that for a while I sat stunned. Then thrusting my arms out into the invisibility, I moved them in slow arcs about myself. One hand touched something hard, smooth for a distance and then regularly ridged; now a larger bump, then a long, flexible extension which my fingers began to explore very cautiously.

A familiar voice snapped, "Oh, stop it! Stop pulling my feeler! Things are confused enough without destroying my only means of orientation! Please!"

"Exi! Exi! Exi, it's you!"

"Maris, my dear, do control yourself! And *please* let go of me!" Despite his words, Exi sounded glad not to be utterly alone. "And if we are to get out of this—this—this thing, whatever it is, we will need to be calm and to use all our wits." As an afterthought, he asked absently, "Are you all right?"

"I guess so. I don't hurt anywhere. But I'm blind."

"Not blind," Exi said, irritably. "It is only that you cannot see."

"Aren't they the same?"

"Of course they are not the same! If you are blind, really blind, there is no way at all to see. But if you cannot see, there *is* a way but you have not yet learned it. Is that clear?"

Already frustrated, tired, on edge, I was irritated by his scorn, and began to protest. "But I don't see—"

"You don't see! You don't see!" he mimicked. "Truly you don't! If you did, you would sit quite still and remember something important and this might help us to get unstuck! But no! You give up, and complain, and, I am sure, hope someone else will come to your rescue!"

Half angry, and yet wondering what he meant, I did sit quietly and tried to remember something. But what was there to remember? My pulse was loud in my ears, beating against the dense nothingness around me. Then it came to me. Of course! The stone! I had shoved it back into my pocket when the falling had ceased. Now I put my hand in and found it, warm and alive, and was ashamed that I had so soon forgotten it.

I drew the stone out and let it rest in my left palm. At first I could only feel its warmth and heaviness and velvet softness; slowly it began to become visible, and, as when I had first held it, its blue-green depths moved with currents of pollen swirling here and there. From itself it was dissolving the invisibility, making a small area of visibility with itself as center. I could see my left hand holding the stone. Little by little the circumference within which things could be seen widened, until I could see quite a bit of myself, and almost half of Exi. And Exi made himself wholly visible by stepping toward me.

At Exi's suggestion, we began again to explore the unknown place. The ground was black, hard, and rough. Finally we reached a wall. It resembled marble, very black, very highly polished, and with a discouraging permanence about it.

I was less confident than my words sounded when I told Exi to stay touching the wall, not moving, while I worked my way along it to see if it came solidly around us. He agreed with a nod of his solemn beetle head, and I left him behind, his luminous eyes watching until the invisibility closed around him.

The farther I went along the wall, the lonelier I became. Had it not been for the stone lying limpid and alive in my hand, and for the knowledge that Exi was waiting for me, I would have stopped. Sliding my right hand along the wall, I moved after it. Slide, follow, slide, follow, slide, follow, on and on into eternities of time and distance.

Then, on one slide forward, my hand felt a space beyond the wall. "It isn't true!" I said it aloud, startled. I reached forward again. It was true. I moved my left hand and the stone, and saw by its light that the wall was broken by a vertical opening about a foot across and reaching from the ground upward out of sight.

"Exi! Exi! Where are you?"

"Here! Right here!" His voice was so near I jumped. I must have come almost full circle.

"Exi! Keep touching the wall and come toward my voice. Maybe there's a way out." With me calling and him answering, in a very short time he was there, his delicate antennae waving before the opening.

"It feels safe." He spoke confidently. "Shall we try it?"

I knew I must go first with the stone to illumine the way, ominous though that way might be. "Yes," I said, and entered the narrow passage.

3

NOT EVEN A WREN FEATHER COULD HAVE BEEN SLIPPED BETWEEN the massive marble walls of that passage and me. I soon found that there was only one way to proceed—sideways, left hand and stone going first and the rest of me sliding after. Exi followed. From time to time I spoke his name, and he answered. Occasionally I heard the click of his feet on the rock floor. There was no other sound.

Suddenly Exi said, "Stop! I hear something." We ceased moving. I couldn't hear a sound, and was about to start forward again when Exi cautioned, very softly, "Shhh. There *is* something ahead of us. We must take care. Put the stone away."

I did as he said. Momentarily I was sightless, but then some distance ahead I could just make out a difference in the texture of the invisibility, a faint lightening of it. I still could hear nothing.

Again Exi whispered. "Let me climb around your feet and go before you. My methods of knowing will be much better than yours." I didn't protest, although I was slightly hurt at his attitude. I pushed my heels back against the wall as tight as I could and stood very still. I felt his scratchy little feet march over mine and his body brush my legs. Then after a time a small voice, so small I could barely make it out, spoke from the other side of me. "Come very, *very* slowly. And quietly. Now!"

What lay before me when I turned the same corner made me want to back away, and left no doubt as to the reason for Exi's hesitation. It was a world of twilight where everything was visible but colorless. And everywhere, hurrying back and forth, carrying, lifting, setting down, pushing, and pulling large pieces of stuff, in nightmarish activity, were ants, enormous ants, half again as large as Exi.

He was hiding behind a mound of large-grained sand, looking quickly out and then pulling his head back as quickly. He turned and again motioned wordlessly with one wing that I should join him. It was not as simple for me to remain hidden as for him, I realized, and I dropped flat and wriggled forward on my stomach until I was stretched beside Exi, my face level with his. By raising my head slightly, I could see over the mound and watch the ant-beings. They seemed to be building storage heaps rather than dwellings, for some of them carried seeds and piled these into small pyramids, while others came along with grains of sand and carefully covered over the seed piles. What made the scene so dreadful was the absolute impersonality of it, the machinelikeness of it. The ants seemed neither human nor animal, but went at their frantic work like automatons in the perpetual twilight.

I lowered my head behind the inadequate hiding place. Exi edged near, voicing in a faint whisper what I was already thinking. "They are bound to discover us sooner or later, and we cannot go back. We must be prepared for them. I believe they will not hurt maliciously, so we must not fight them nor resist them but must try to be as relaxed and as honest as we can. I believe this is best." His voice dwindled away; then he added, "I do hope it is best. I do hope so!" I nodded, fearing that a whisper would be too loud.

Without any warning, a red hot stabbing pain went up my leg. I flopped over to a sitting position with a loud yelp, and quicker than one could imagine, Exi and I were surrounded by giant ants. Ants were fastened to all six of Exi's legs, while a ring of them, pincers open, closed him in. Because I was so much larger, the ants circled me but kept a wary distance except for the one still clinging to my ankle. Evidently he had tried to pick at this foreign substance unaware that it might be alive. He looked wobbly as he let go and limped away; and I felt pleased over his discomfiture, for by this time my ankle and leg were hurting fiercely.

Exi had obviously followed his own advice and had utterly relaxed; consequently the ants loosed his legs and stood around him as if they were not sure how to proceed. I tried to relax, too;

but it was not so much my partial success at this as it was my greater size, I decided, that kept the ants at a respectful distance.

More and more ants kept coming. And I grew conscious of a high-pitched shrilling, which increased in volume as the number of ants increased.

Exi spoke finally more deliberately than I had ever heard him. "We mean no harm," he said. "We mean no harm." All sound ceased and all movement, except at the periphery of the mass where newcomers were still crowding in. "Please let us go. Or at least take us to someone who can help us." Exi waited. The ants waited. Exi carefully took one step with one leg. Immediately all the ants nearest him opened their pincers threateningly. Exi relaxed and spoke again in the same calm voice, addressing his words to me while acting as if he were still talking to them. "They do not understand our language," he explained. "At least, I do not think they do. Therefore I will try to say what I have just said in the ancient insect tongue. Perhaps some of them will know it."

I watched him with my heart beating hard. His body was, if anything, more still than ever, while from him there came a new kind of penetrating sound, like a tiny kettle boiling in syllables and phrases.

When he stopped, I turned my head slowly so as to alarm no one and surveyed the massed ants on all sides. At first I had the dismal impression that there was absolutely no comprehension in any of them, and I hated them. Then one ant, slightly smaller than most, began pushing his way forward till he was directly in front of Exi. One leg was partly gone, so he moved more haltingly than others had, although with a certain confidence. After a few seconds he began making sounds similar to Exi's, but higher pitched. He stopped frequently, as if hunting for a word or a phrase, then continued. Exi replied. The ant spoke again. I sighed in relief as I realized that quite a conversational stream was bubbling between them.

When the interchange stopped for a moment, Exi quickly murmured, still not looking at me, "This is an old one, and he does understand. From now on just follow me, do as I do, and I think we are safe. I will explain later on." The old one, despite his missing leg, shrilled at the crowd authoritatively. With some tangling of legs, and some subdued sounds of dissent (I supposed), gradually the ants opened a path for us.

We moved cautiously forward—the old ant leading, then Exi, then I walking as carefully and precisely as I could so I wouldn't by accident tread on any ant's feet.

Certain of the ants had formed a sort of guard around us so that we proceeded in a rectangle of moving oval shapes. The land changed as we went on, I noticed, and the sand-covered granaries were replaced by strange spearlike plants, as tall as I, growing in clumps. But the same twilight was everywhere. I just avoided bumping Exi when the marchers suddenly and with no warning halted.

Before us was a huge pyramid-shaped mound rising so high that its summit was invisible in the twilight. The mound was made of a hard claylike material. Surrounding it on all sides were clusters of the spearlike plants. An arched entrance, flanked by antguards, faced the massed company; the height of the archway was at least four and a half feet. The old one who led us went up to the entrance, made shrill talk, whereupon one guard turned and entered the mound. Everyone waited, with very little moving about. Soon the guard returned, took his place by the arch, and another ant came out. He was larger than the others, fuller in body, richer in color. Evidently he was someone of importance, for the other ants were hushed and stepped back a few paces, leaving the old ant, Exi, and me to confront the newcomer.

The old one spoke first, in the odd sounds of the language Exi had used earlier. Then the important ant made a short reply, and Exi moved forward so that he and the two ants were all facing each other in an intimate circle. Exi, in his most considered tones, spoke briefly in human language to me saying, "The one who brought us here is called Grandan. He is old, wise, and knows of our journey. The other is Prince Urfang III, second in rank to his mother the queen. We will be talking the ancient tongue, but I am permitted to translate to you when it is relevant. Please sit down and rest, as I am sure we are in no danger."

Thereafter, for what seemed to me an interminable time, Grandan, Prince Urfang, and Exi talked back and forth in their weird boiling-kettle language, with Exi at long intervals giving me

a very brief summary. Prince Urfang asked our names. Exi gave
them. He wanted to know where we had come from, and Exi tried
to tell him. Prince Urfang seemed fascinated by this, and the
talking went on and on. I was almost drowsing when I heard
Exi say, "Come! We are to enter the castle. And do walk carefully!"

Preceded by Prince Urfang and Grandan, and flanked by two
ant guards, we went under the arch into the mound. I had to
bend my head and shoulders to pass through, but once inside, I
could stand erect again, and was amazed at the spaciousness of
the great chamber in which we stood. There were no straight lines
in it. On all sides, except where we entered, were arches leading
into further rooms, with ants quietly coming and going on mysterious errands. I could scarcely tell where floor left off and walls
and ceiling began, the curves of the room were so soft and flowing.
In the center was a sculpture of an enormous grain of wheat, and
from it the entire chamber was illuminated in delicate golden
light. I found it beautiful and said as much to Exi, who conveyed
my feelings to Prince Urfang. The prince turned toward me and
spoke.

Exi said, "He is pleased. And now he would like you to go with
a servant to a guest chamber where you will be bathed, your wound
will be cared for, and you will be prepared to meet the queen."
He went on. "No need to be afraid. All is well, and I think you
will be better treated than you know." He turned away to follow
Prince Urfang out of sight into another room.

I saw that several smaller ants had drawn near me. I had no
alternative but to go with them, although I did so somewhat
reluctantly. They preceded me through one of the arched door-
ways into a small chamber, whose floor was covered with literally
thousands upon thousands of flower petals. On the other side of
the chamber the ants who had conducted me, lifted, shook out,
and folded a mass of soft material like the most delicate of silks.

Later on I recalled Exi's words—"I think you will be better
treated than you know"—and realized what truth he had spoken.
Never before had I appreciated the real significance of bathing
until I had undressed and stretched out full length amid the
fragrant petals. The ants moved about me piling petals over me,

washing me with petals, drying me with petals.

At last the ants indicated it was finished. They pulled all the petals away, then stepped back. I arose and looked for my clothes. They had vanished. Suddenly I was frantic as I remembered the stone, the precious stone in my pocket. How could I ask for it? Where could I go to find it? As I was about to rush out of the room, naked and distraught, one of the ants touched me with a foreleg and then tugged at my foot with its pincers, gently but insistently. Remembering Exi's advice, I let the ant direct me to the farther side of the room and there, on a mat of wheat blades, all my possessions had been deposited with care. Side by side were a wrinkled and not-too-clean handkerchief, Scuro's leash, four pennies, a broken seashell, and the stone, as ordinary as if it were nothing at all.

My ant attendants were awaiting me, all eight of them holding the silken cloth I had watched them preparing. It fell about them in drifts as delicate as mist, yards and yards of billowing pearly mist, and I knew that somehow I was to wear this. I got onto my knees so that they could reach me; and they draped and folded and pulled and tied and worked with the silk until I began to feel like an Oriental princess. I wished I could see myself when at last I got to my feet to be conducted back to the great hall.

Exi and Prince Urfang were there to greet me as I entered, surrounded by my attendants. Exi had been polished until his tidy beetle body gleamed like ebony. Prince Urfang was regal, with a russet cape flung over him and with a golden circlet on his head.

"You are quite lovely, Maris," said Exi. Both he and the prince bowed their heads in tribute. It made me put up my hands to caress the silk as it lay in graceful folds across my shoulders, and to wish again for a mirror, a thing I usually shunned.

Prince Urfang and Exi spoke together briefly. Then Exi told me, "We go now for an audience with the queen. I am sure I need not emphasize to you how important, even how vital for our further safety, this meeting is! Bring everything you have of graciousness, sensitivity, wisdom. As I, too, will do." Then he added, "But do not try *too* hard. Just be your own person rather than someone else."

While I was pondering this difficult piece of advice, the procession moved slowly around the great hall. A single ant went first, bearing upright a particularly symmetrical leaf from one of the plants that grew outside the mound. The leaf waved above its bearer like a golden-green royal banner, heralding the approach of Prince Urfang III who followed, escorted by a company of ants marching in well-disciplined lines on either side of him. Exi came next, also flanked by ant escorts, and then I with my attendants.

The procession seemed to be going ever farther into the interior of the mound. The corridor down which we passed was subtly serpentined, and thus its truly great length never became tiring to contemplate. And at intervals were wheatseed lamps sending their soft radiance into every inch of space.

The procession halted eventually before a very large and very high arch, closed by rippling curtains of delicate antsilk, almost imperceptibly lavender in hue. Contrasted to this fragility were two fierce-looking ant guards who stood at either side of the curtain, their extra large sharp pincers upraised. Prince Urfang gave a penetrating shrill. The bearer stepped aside and the prince moved forward, the curtains were quietly pulled back until the entrance was large before us, and we entered the place of the queen.

4

I TRIED MY UTMOST TO BE MY "OWN PERSON" DURING THE ROYAL audience, and later I felt I had partially succeeded. The room we entered was starkly white and even larger than the original entrance hall. When, led by Prince Urfang, our company drew up in a semicircle and stopped, I saw that the whiteness was from hundreds, probably thousands, of tiny spherical objects laid like mosaic tiles over every part of the enormous room except on the floor, which, however, was highly polished and reflected the walls and ceiling brilliantly. It was like standing inside a vast egg. And with this image the truth hit me. Of course! The tiny spheres *were* eggs, ant eggs, hundreds upon hundreds of ant eggs!

Exi's voice saying, "Maris!" in a sharp whisper broke my contemplation, and I became aware that the others were bowing before a sort of dais, also formed of eggs. I managed an awkward curtsy, trying hastily to recall anything I might have read about queens and how to treat them. Nothing came to mind, so I decided I would have to do whatever seemed right. I raised my eyes to see the dais. Exi, the prince, and the members of the retinue had straightened from their bows and were gazing expectantly before them.

Resting rather than standing on the dais—for her legs were very short—was the queen. Billowing masses of silver silken cloth surrounded her, but from what was visible of her she was almost as white as the eggs. An exquisitely made crown of silver sat upon her somewhat bulbous head. The overall effect was not quite what I had anticipated, yet in some unaccountable way this grotesque being was majestic.

Prince Urfang was addressing her. Exi told me later that Prince Urfang informed the queen of the events involving us and our attempted journey, and also presented to her the problem of how to get us out of the ant country. (For it was clear even to me, ordinarily not so astute in affairs of this sort, that Exi and I couldn't remain here. I would be too big, too different, too hungry, and, as such, would be intolerable.) The queen in her shimmering robes was so impassive during Prince Urfang's tale that she seemed not to be listening. Yet when he concluded, she replied at once, in a low monotonous voice, and spoke at considerable length. The audience ended when the queen stopped speaking; the entire retinue backed silently from the awesome, gleaming birth chamber.

As soon as we were outside in the corridor with the curtains drawn, I turned eagerly to Exi. "What did she say?" I whispered.

"Wait," said Exi, "please wait until we are alone." He would say no more. As the procession returned along the corridor no one said much, except for an occasional exchange between Exi and the prince. At last we were ushered into a room where there was a good-sized heap of grain and, beside it, a waxen dish filled with liquid. Fresh-cut leaves covered the floor. All the ants, including Prince Urfang, departed.

"It would be better if we ate before we talked, I think." Exi reached toward the grain pile, grasped a seed in his mandibles, and began nibbling. There was no quarreling with him, I realized, and remembering the goodness of yesterday's queer food, I popped some of the grain into my mouth. It was crisp and nut flavored, really not too bad. We went on eating until the grain heap was gone, and then both of us drank from the wax cup. Whatever the liquid was, it was cool, fragrant, and refreshing. Only when we had both had all we wanted, did Exi begin.

"We have a difficult task, a most difficult task," he said, shaking his head sadly. He told me that neither Prince Urfang nor the Queen had been of any real help in suggesting ways out for us, although both of them—and especially the queen—had left no question in Exi's mind about our leaving. We could not use any of their regular up and down passages. Most of them would take us nowhere anyway. The queen, he said, had alluded to some ancient and dangerous lost passage that might be usable by travelers, but she didn't seem to know more. Prince Urfang had suggested talking to Grandan about such a route. "So here we are," Exi concluded, "having to get out but having no real idea of how to go or where to go. So I think we had best find Grandan. It may be he does remember some old tale that could give us a clue." At that moment Grandan limped quietly into the room.

Exi bowed and launched at once into the ancient language. "He has some clue," Exi finally said; "he will take us to a secret place and show us a beginning. He knows something about our journey, but he does not know what we will find in the dark corridor we must travel. The way will be dangerous and hard, if indeed it still remains. Are you willing to trust him? And to try?"

I said I guessed I was. "After all, there's nothing else, is there?"

"No," Exi stated, "nothing." Grandan spoke again, and Exi added, "He says you must get your own clothes. He will take you."

Led by Grandan, I returned to the bathing room, and entered alone. The petals had been removed, though their perfume remained in the air. My familiar old clothes, clean and neatly folded, lay beside my small heap of belongings. Regretfully I took off the lovely silk cloth and dressed in my own things, leaving the silk a soft pile on the floor. I put the stone and the other items in my pockets. Grandan and I returned to where Exi waited, and together we set out along the same path we had followed to go to the queen. Soon, Grandan turned left into a branching corridor, narrower and apparently unused, for we met no ants and the floor did not have the smoothness of the main corridor.

Gradually the way grew less light. Soon we were walking in semi-twilight, and there was an increasing number of twists and bends. Grandan was becoming less sure; frequently he would stop and touch the walls of the corridor questioningly. No one spoke. There was really nothing to say.

The slow, hesitant pace of Grandan allowed me to turn many thoughts over and over as we went along. I pondered our situation, and the question suddenly arose as to whether our present situation was a choice or an accident. This was followed by the frightening thought that I couldn't run away but had to endure this journey Exi kept referring to, no matter where it went.

When Exi spoke my name I was grateful and said, "Yes"

very quickly.

"Don't go on too long with your thoughts." His intuitions about me were unerring. "It is good to ponder, but then to let go. It will come clear at a later time."

His words quieted me somewhat, though Grandan seemed ever more uncertain in the tortuous corridor. He and Exi discussed something while Grandan was again questing along a certain area of wall with his feelers.

"Grandan hopes," Exi told me, "that in here somewhere is an ancient opening, which, if he remembers true, was sealed up many periods past by a previous queen." I wanted to ask why the queen had had it closed but I was sure that the answer, if Exi either knew it or would give it, wouldn't be pleasant.

"He thinks he has found it!" Exi's voice translated Grandan's exclamation in tones as nearly urgent as Exi ever was. "He needs you to help him!" Guided by Exi's terse commands, I found the wall beside Grandan and inch by inch went over an indicated area, pushing against it with both hands and considerable force. There was an almost imperceptible yielding of wall at one place. I pushed harder, leaning all my weight forward; a small crack showed. Pushing and panting, while Exi and Grandan could only give silent encouragement, I finally managed to force the door far enough to get one arm through. Then little by little I was able to make an opening wide enough for us to get through, at which point I sat on the floor to rest.

Grandan spoke and Exi translated. "He says you are intelligent and helpful. Which, by the way, is a rather large tribute from him. He says he must leave us here and return to his people. He cannot go with us further. He tells us to have courage, to hold to our natural possessions, and to remember that all great power is not necessarily evil—some is, and some is full of light."

I was deeply moved by Grandan's words, though I didn't wholly comprehend them. I said good-bye to him. And though he didn't know my language, he seemed to know what I meant. He bowed, turned, and walked away from us. We watched until his limping body passed from sight around a bend in the dim corridor. We waited a few minutes wordlessly, then turned toward the unknown way.

With Exi going first, we forced our bodies through the narrow opening. It was obvious that we were in a further extension of the same corridor we had been in, and that those who had plugged the way with the great rock door had acted in haste and fear. On this farther side, the stone was roughly shaped. The floor was littered with debris—rocks, chips of granite, desicated wheat kernels, and several abandoned and broken knives. I was depressed and chilled by the disorder, for it smelled of danger, and I was in haste to move on.

Exi insisted that first we reclose the opening, for he said he had promised Grandan we would do so. Most of the work of forcing the heavy door back into its place had to be done by me. Exi helped as much as he could but he was not strong enough to do much. I wondered how the ants had done it in the first place.

"Let me go ahead," said Exi. "I have keener senses, and we need the best we have now." As we started out, for no reason I could explain, I selected one of the old and broken knives lying among the rocks and thrust it into the belt of my skirt. I also gathered a handful of the dried-up wheat kernels and put them in my pocket. You never could tell what you might need.

The corridor continued to twist this way and that, and I gave up all attempts to determine direction. It was my skin, not my ears nor eyes, that first registered a change in the situation. I began to feel warmer and warmer, until there was no doubt that the air was actually hot. I took off my jacket, careful to carry it so that nothing would spill from its pockets. The air grew even hotter. Sweat began running down my forehead, my neck, the backs of my legs. Breathing was more and more difficult. "Exi!" I gasped, coming to a stop, "I'm not sure I can keep on!"

"I am not sure either of us can," Exi replied. "We have reached the end of something."

I wiped my face on my arm and was about to say that this was no time to make jokes when I realized that Exi's statement was a literal one. The passage ended abruptly in a dead end, stifling and imprisoning.

My first panic was overcome by a fierce anger, first at the inhuman ants for abandoning us to this suffocating terror, then at Exi for being so prosaic. He should be concerned with finding a way out.

"Blast and damn everything!" I shouted. "I hate all of it, all of it!" (I found the "it" vague but comprehensively satisfying.) "And I just refuse to take it any longer!" With that I banged my hand against the blank wall before me, and as I stared stupidly the wall swung away from us and we looked into a vast and ominous landscape.

In the middle of a desolation without end, burned a gigantic fire, its flames leaping to heights of fifty feet or more, rising, falling back, rolling upward again in dreadful splendor. The heat was intense, although the air was more breathable now that the passage had opened. We stood where we were, reluctant to make the move we knew we must make, forward into this inferno. Once or twice, when the billowing fire pennants parted, I fancied I saw a gray mass within the flames but I couldn't trust my vision. When I asked Exi if he saw anything, he only shook his head, and suddenly I was struck by his fatigue. How much harder this must be for him! His beetle armor, enviable in certain situations, would be a miniature bake oven in this temperature! But I tried to keep the concern from my voice when I asked, "Exi, are you all right? Can I help you?"

He didn't answer. His usually alert antennae were drooping alarmingly. Hastily I fumbled in my pocket for my grimy handkerchief and began fanning him as vigorously as I could. Before long he began to revive, and finally he said, in a weak but very Exi sort of voice, "Thank you, my dear Maris, thank you! I feared for a time that I would not make it, I really feared."

I started to cry. "Oh, Exi! Exi!" I reached down and patted his hard back, and some tears plopped onto him. I wiped them off gently and fanned him again. He tried to protest but it was apparent that he needed it.

"I have an awful feeling that we've got to go out there." I pointed toward the leaping flames. "But why? Why must we?"

"I think that is the inevitable way," Exi said weakly. "A bit more air, please."

After a short silence for fanning, he went on. "Must there always, for you, be reasons? And why should you assume that I would have them, any more than you? Sometimes, you see, we must act on unreasons." He paused to gather strength. "We cannot go back, except to destruction. We cannot stay here forever, or we suffocate. We must proceed, whenever and however that is possible, because, as I have said before, we are needed."

The long reply had tired him, and I hated myself for having put an extra burden on him. Even so, I thought, waving my handkerchief wearily up and down, even so, it was somehow a relief to know that neither of us knew. We each had to use an instinct for survival and this was all we had. Nothing more. Nothing more. Maybe not even that. Not that. Not . . . that . . . not . . .

With a convulsive jerk, I roused from a state of exhaustion so great that it was beginning to make me numb, almost paralyzed. I had stopped fanning Exi and hadn't been conscious of it! My head and shoulders sagged and I couldn't seem to straighten. Exi again appeared to be wilting noticeably. It was all too terrible! And what could I do? What could I do? Slowly, slowly as a nightmare, I pushed and pulled Exi back into the corridor, out of the direct heat of the great fire, he neither resisting nor helping. I leaned against the hot wall, hands flattened on it to keep myself upright, being certain that if once I let myself slide to the ground I'd never get up and we would both die. I must fan Exi, I kept telling myself, I *must!*

So incapable was I of focusing on anything that it was some time before I sensed coolness near my thigh. My first response was to ignore it; my second was to think that I was imagining it; only with my third thought did it occur to me that the coolness corresponded to the area of a skirt pocket, and in that pocket was the stone.

With what small energy I had left I drew the stone forth and held it tight lest the violent trembling of my hand make me drop it. I couldn't muster any enthusiasm over its coolness; it seemed too late. Yet I managed to get onto my knees and very carefully set the stone close to Exi's still form. Then I collapsed on the hot ground. Lying inert and mindless, I was swept by fierce winds and invaded by misty dreams. Mother and Dad appeared, disappeared, as elongated ghosts shouting words I couldn't hear. Strange, sinister forms crowded and rushed about me, over me, through me, as if I weren't there. I tried to cry out, but couldn't, and felt my-

self becoming less and less substantial until I was only a minute
prick of light in a vast darkness.

And that light was almost out.

Very thin, very far away, I heard what seemed my own identity
calling, "Maris! Maris!" The tiny light held against the dark, pushing it back ever so little but pushing nonetheless. Would the light
stay? Could it stay? Who would tend it? Who? Faintly came the
call, "Maris!"

"Yes," I whispered, "Yes," and reached out in the nothing to
grasp a lone thread of meaning bearing my name. My feeble fingers closed around something fragile and thin. It was thus that I
found myself as I came slowly back to awareness—holding Exi's
leg while he stood close beside me where I had fallen. His voice
was saying, "Maris."

5

NEITHER OF US KNEW OR TRIED TO KNOW THE DURATION OF OUR almost-death. We had been too deeply shaken to express anything except the wordless love that joins sufferers together. I never said, and Exi never asked, how the stone had come to be where it was, how I had known to use it. It was enough that it had revived us and that it lay between us, its mysterious liquid beauty giving us coolness and an air to breathe.

The physical effects of the heat were more severe for Exi. One wing was quite sunken in, giving him a lopsided appearance, and what was worse, his middle leg on that same side had withered so as to be useless. When I wept over this, Exi replied, "It is better for me than for you, for I have five left and you would have had but one."

I felt little bodily damage other than a bruise on one elbow and a pounding headache, but physical weakness and the strain on my spirit made me feel ages older than I had felt when we left Grandan. At some moment I remembered the dried-up grain from the abandoned ant tunnel, and we each chewed up a few kernels. This gave us a small lift in energy. Water was the great need. Both of us craved water almost beyond endurance.

Finally Exi said, "We must go forward now, to find water and a way out." Forward meant out into the flame-crowned landscape, meant going toward a destructive power greater than any I had ever faced. But if the stone kept its magic, at least we could try. I insisted that Exi carry the stone, and he agreed reluctantly, knowing that he couldn't survive without it near him.

We moved slowly. Exi would lug the stone as far as his strength
allowed and then put it down. At each pause I would lie prone and
get my head and shoulders inside the cool area. It was rather like
a grim game of leapfrog, bringing us closer and closer to the billowing fire.

The closer we came, the more all-pervasive was the sound of
the burning, growing and expanding into a low roar that filled our
ears and pulsated against our bodies.

At last came the moment when we knew that the next stage
had to bring us either into or through the fire. No other possibility
existed and there was no reason to discuss it. Taking an extra long
rest period, we stared silently at the roaring, boiling, rising and
falling flames. Exi, as he picked up the stone to begin the final
move, had no need to look at me, nor I at him. Each of us knew
how desperate this final move was.

I have never had clear in my mind what happened next. Exi
went forward, I followed close to him. Noise, glare, heat, confusion, filled all space, encompassing us and the world in a volcanic
nightmare. Every breath was an agony, every step a pain. We
seemed to be rushing and stumbling and creeping and pushing
through an endless furnace, terribly and futilely on and on and on,
when in quiet suddenness the bottom dropped from under the
roaring and the flaming and there we were standing in a small
canyon beside a pool of delicately blue and very still water. Slowly
I lowered myself to the moist gravel and immersed my face in the
water. Lifting my face out, while the wonderful cool drops fell
about me, I drank greedily. Exi, too, moved directly to the pool,
only just in time remembering to set down the stone. He stood up
to his six knees in water, touching its surface with his mouth, his
antennae moving in delicate delight.

I watched Exi and with a laugh plunged my arms, head, and
shoulders in the pool.

"Isn't it beautiful!" I said. Finally abandoning all reasonable-
ness, I slid completely into the pool. I rolled over and lay with just
my head above the surface, letting my body rest in the water while
I looked curiously about me.

A great gray mountain towered above the scooped-out hollow
where we bathed; there was no visible break in its conical symmetry

except the place of the pool and a small canyonlike cleft leading into the mountain. A stream came from somewhere in the cleft, a bit of powder blue water trickling into the upper end of the pool. The sky—well, there was not actually any sky, but space, soft, gray space that was strangely disturbing.

"What happened to the fire?" I asked.

"It is still there." Exi waved an antenna vaguely.

"Where?"

"Look the other way, back of you."

I did and was startled to see a wall of flames leaping and spiraling in unbroken intensity. "But how did we get through? And why don't we feel it here?"

"I really cannot say. Courage helped us through. And the stone. The rest is mystery."

I arose, splashed from the pool, and sat on a large boulder nearby, smoothing my wet clothes against my body so they would dry with as few wrinkles as possible. "Aren't you thankful?"

Exi's reply was blurred because he was combing his head with a front leg, but I knew it was affirmative. I'd asked the question more for companionship than for reassurance anyway. We stayed beside the water until Exi had finished his grooming and I was dry and clean. We looked at each other then, knowing without hesitation that we should go on. "Shall we?" Exi said, turning his black body toward the cleft beyond the pool.

"Yes." I picked up the stone, put it in my pocket, and followed.

The diminutive canyon we were approaching seemed only a dimple in the mountain's unbroken side, a dimple shaped like an S. Soon our pool was out of sight and we were enclosed in the meander of the little canyon.

"I wonder where we are going," I said.

"Wherever the way is going," Exi replied calmly.

"But where do you suppose the way is going?"

"Wherever we go."

"That doesn't really make sense, does it?"

"Oh, yes. Quite good sense."

"Why?"

"Do you know any method by which you can go one way and your path another? Not the path, but *your* path?"

"Well—" I hesitated. "Well, if you put it that way, I guess not. But what about crossroads? Couldn't you choose the wrong one?"

"I suppose you could. However, if it was the wrong way you chose, it would still be *your* way, wouldn't it?"

"Yes," I answered, "yes, it probably would." I decided not to say any more.

During this conversation we had passed the first bend of the S-curved stream and were rounding the second bend when a curious noise broke the quietness. We stood listening. Again it came—high, sweet notes like a soft, distant trumpet. No trumpeter of any sort or size was visible. After a pause we moved forward. Once more the sound halted us, and after the fourth repetition we decided that we were being called. But by what? Or whom? Exi stood in characteristic solidity, his antennae asking questions, while I sat down on a sloping rock and peered ahead of us, upstream, where I saw the ravine widen slightly to end against the smooth base of the mountain. The stream itself seemed to be coming from an opening in the mountainside. A more concentrated inspection revealed a gray-silver bush beside the opening, and on it something bright moved and flashed in the sunlight. Then to my surprise whatever it was came gliding through the air to settle on my shoulder.

I could only see out of the corner of my eye that it was gray-black with somewhere a patch of scarlet. There was no doubt that it was the owner of the sound we had heard, for the voice in my ear had the sound of a tiny muted trumpet.

"Not many come through the fire," the voice was saying. "You are brave. And welcome! Very welcome! Maris, and Exi, welcome!"

I was enchanted with this piping friendliness and wished that I could see the little creature face to face. As if sensing this, it flitted from my shoulder to Exi's black back. "My name is Hatch," it piped. "I am a messenger. Welcome!"

Hatch was even smaller than I had thought, not much bigger than a big dragonfly and not unlike one in shape, except that his body was feathery, gray in color, and his wings gossamer thin and covered with down. His head had a pert scarlet crest, giving him an expression to match his voice.

"How do you do, Hatch. We are glad you knew us and are honored to meet you." Exi could be exceedingly, almost excessively, polite when he wished.

"Oh, I do a great deal! A great deal! Messenger, you know. Actually it was *I* who met *you.* But honored, of course!"

When I asked for what he was a messenger he replied, "Messenger for Them, of course! Who else sends real messages?"

I couldn't think of any possible answer.

"I was sent by Them," Hatch continued, flicking his wings and staring at us unblinkingly. "Must be off, you know. Others are waiting for us. Must be off!" He left his place on Exi, flew to the bush, sat for a moment uttering his small trumpet sound, then returned to hover just ahead of us.

Exi turned and began to follow toward the mountain base and the opening. I did likewise, although I was considerably confused as to whether the "others" were "Them" or somebody else. However, Exi's silent acceptance of this odd messenger made me feel comfortable about following.

The stream's source as we approached it was a contrast to the bare smooth landscape surrounding it. Water bubbled up as if from the depths of the mountain. Where it came out there was a grotto with a silver bush beside it, a grotto large enough for us to enter. At the entrance we halted.

"Is there," asked Exi of Hatch who was perched on the bush, "is there anything we should know before we go on?"

"Much to know, always! Always! But only at the proper time, you see." His crest was a flame above his owl eyes. "Now Dark One pushes from earth through fire to water. And the spiral stair and more companions are waiting for you that is enough, you know!"

The air in the cavern reminded me of the scent of a sweet grass basket given me by my grandmother when I was very young. I had loved to bury my face in it and sniff. Here the very same fragrance was everywhere; it surrounded me as though I were walking into my grandmother's basket. I was lighthearted and lightfooted in the way of a very young child. So I was quite unaware that water was rising, until I was suddenly ankle-deep and my skip became a slosh. I returned to the present to hear Hatch speaking.

". . . and when a thing is lost, up comes the water! Up it comes! Dark Fire, they say, does it. He makes the rising! Doesn't like lostness at all!"

"Is it because we, Maris and I, seem to have lost ourselves awhile back?" Exi was asking.

"No! Oh, no! That's not lost! That's looking! It's not knowing about looking that's being lost!"

Exi's measured tones and Hatch's rapid horn sounded odd in this echoing grotto, but odder still were the words they spoke, which they seemed to comprehend though I didn't. There was no time to think about them, because the water was rising rapidly. It didn't gush or boil or make any different sound. It only bubbled away softly inside the vaulted cave, more and more and more of it. In fact, it was already well above my ankles and Exi was quite deep in it. Obviously we'd have to go somewhere else or be drowned.

"Hurry now!" Hatch's little trumpet voice hit a higher key. "Hurry! We're nearly at the stairs! Come!" He flitted his gray and scarlet body ahead, with us making the best progress possible after him. It was not long—although it seemed forever—until I looked up from my submerged feet, to see immediately ahead a huge shaft rising upward from the floor of the cavern to the cavern's roof and apparently on into the substance of the mountain. It looked much like a gigantic reed growing from a pale blue marsh.

Hatch was urging us forward. A door opened just above water level. We clambered through into the shaft, and at once a babble of voices greeted us; a large group rushed toward the door, and everybody, including us, pushed and shoved to close the door before the waters could enter. It was a frantic and breathless scramble. I couldn't distinguish in the mass of movement anything more than a blur of faces of variegated sorts, furred or feathered or masked, and hands and feet and antennae and beaks all mixed up together. After the door was closed, we all hurried after Hatch toward a spiral stairway in the middle of the shaft. We pushed and urged each other up and up until we reached a small opening. Everyone squeezed through, and the last one in slammed a trap door.

I felt as if I'd been caught in a miniature tornado, and was more than glad when I saw everyone sitting down to rest. We had come into a spacious circular room. In the center was the closed trap door and rising above it in curves was another flight of spiraling stairs, which ended at the ceiling where there was a second trap door. There was no furniture of any sort in the room. All those who had rushed here in such disorder were now seated around one side of the room in quiet orderliness.

Exi was on my left, Hatch on my right. Beyond Exi were two other beetles, one brown and about Exi's size, one a deep bottle green and somewhat larger. Next to them was a fire-red ant, vaguely like Prince Urfang but slimmer in the waist. Hatch's nearest neighbor was a sort of puppylike field mouse about as big as a full grown kitten. It sat up on furry haunches and surveyed the room with enormous eyes set in a wizened little face, its mouse whiskers and absurd pointed ears giving it a permanently startled expression. A very large caterpillar, its terra-cotta fuzz marked with black stripes, leaned against the wall in the next place, its fierce visage out of keeping with its relaxed body. The eight of us comprised half of the circle. The other half, opposite us, was occupied by eight robed and masked figures. An invisible air surrounded them, not unlike heat waves rising from August earth, so that they seemed to be continually changing shape and color. All I could see was that the robes were dark and full and that the masks gave to the wearers an awesome mystery.

In the silence one of the masked figures stepped forward. My heart missed a beat and my throat tightened. Surely it was she, the old woman, the wonderful old woman who had fed me beside the fire. I was certain and not certain, eager and apprehensive, all at once.

"Grandmother, Grandmother." Whispered voices in manifold pitches and resonances echoed and sighed. The solitary figure seemed to grow and diminish, to shift and glimmer, to be heavy and transparent. Once it was as if the mask fell away, revealing briefly the beautiful wrinkled face and the great dark eyes that I remembered, eyes of tragedy, pain, laughter, life, fulfillment.

Then the Grandmother stepped back in the circle, indistinguishable from the others, and all was as it had been before. Not quite the same because now a small clay bowl was being passed along, each one eating from it before giving it to the next one. (I recalled how scornful I'd been of this bowl when I first encountered it.) Exi handed it to me, as full as when it had started, and I ate gratefully and hungrily. It was long since we had had any food. When the bowl had made its rounds, it disappeared as unexpectedly as it had appeared, and the masked figures with it.

Then the quiet was broken by several conversations beginning simultaneously. Each one seemed to have been mysteriously drawn from his usual life to struggle toward some unknown goal, and each one (except the voiceless little mouse) gave some clues to his previous life and how he had come here.

"Carabus," Exi was saying to the brown beetle, "Carabus is not a name that was used in my family, as far as I know. Now—"

"Not *nearly* as distinguished a history as *mine*." The green beetle spoke loudly and aggressively. "The name of Mr. Green, Mr. Calosoma Green, is *very* well known in many parts! Which is why I was brought here, I suppose. May I introduce myself?"

He shouldered Carabus aside and planted himself in front of Exi, who seemed to be, for the first time since I had met him, momentarily rendered speechless. So I turned my attention to others while the big fellow continued, "The Greens, you know, are . . ."

Seeing the fire-colored ant standing alone, I went toward him. "I'm Maris. What's your name?"

"Red." His voice was soft and hard to hear. "My real name is too hard." He was embarrassed, almost apologetic. "Just call me Red. They all do."

"Do you know Prince Urfang? Or Grandan?"

"No, they are very important ants. I'm not. I only know their names. I come from the servant class, you might say. Just a soldier. But I am usually helpful." In his painful shyness, his voice became virtually inaudible.

"What was the last word?" I asked.

"Helpful." Red drew a needle-sharp sword from a sheath hanging at his side, then replaced it and looked embarrassed.

Meanwhile Hatch was flitting nearby, obviously waiting to introduce the remaining strangers, so I beckoned to them to join us.

"You are to be friends, you know." Hatch was excited as always. "Chosen because you're willing to try." He lit on my shoulder. "That odd one is Locus. She loves living! Very happy about it, she is!" At this, the tiny mouse face blinked its huge eyes, while its whiskers quivered, its delicate pointed ears twitched, and a laugh of such true joy came from its mouth that I found myself laughing and being flooded with a sense of exuberance. Before I knew it, I sat down and reached out my arms, and Locus settled into them as if she'd been there forever.

Engrossed in stroking Locus, I forgot the other stranger. Finally responding to Hatch's flutters, I looked up. The caterpillar had curled around, head to tail, and if I hadn't seen it earlier I would have thought it a black and orange woolly hassock. Hatch hovered over it, his trumpet voice calling, "Isia! Isia! Wake up! Wake up!" Slowly the hassock uncurled, stretched lazily, and raised half its length off the floor to peer at me in an absurdly benign way.

"Why, you really aren't fierce at all, are you!" I exclaimed, confronted with his round, placid, honest face. It must have been only those two horns atop his head that made him seem fierce.

"No, I really am not fierce at all, my dear. I sometimes practice fierce faces just for the discipline. It keeps me from getting too fat, occasionally keeps me from going to sleep in the wrong situations, and rarely frightens even those I'd like to frighten." He sighed, yawned, and started to curl up again, but stopped just before his head reached his tail and added, "Oh, yes, one thing I forgot. I would appreciate it if you'd call me Isia. This is my right name. Unfortunately too many call me Woolly, which I find most undignified." He completed his curl and fell asleep.

Woolly was a better name for him, but I resolved always to call him Isia if it mattered so much to him. I glanced down at Locus, who had fallen asleep on my lap and whose tiny laughter was very faint but still going on. Hatch had disappeared, doubtless about his business of being a messenger. Nearby stood Red, one forefoot on his sword, ready to guard something or someone whenever orders were given. Exi, Carabus, and Mr. Green were still talking—or rather, Mr. Green was still talking to Exi and Carabus, I gathered, about "great-uncle Calosoma," and "original Greens."

Feeling tired and in need of sleep, I said, loudly enough for everyone to hear, "I think we *all* need some rest, don't you?" It didn't occur to me—or seem to occur to any of us—to question that we were en route together. Grandmother had fed us. We had shared something of our past. And we seemed to be "willing to try," as Hatch had told us.

"Yes, to be sure." Exi and Carabus replied simultaneously, and shushed Mr. Green when he kept on talking. Soon the great circle of the room was quiet, with all creatures in it falling asleep.

6

I WAKENED QUICKLY WITH A SENSE OF ALARM. THE SCENE WAS exactly as it had been before I fell asleep. Or was it? Something had changed. After an interval of listening, I knew what it was. The purring of Locus's joy had stopped, though she still slept warmly in the curve of my arm. Another sound was there instead— the ominous sound of rushing waters. I leaped to my feet, dropping Locus. No one else was awake yet, but water was spraying out furiously from the edges of the closed trap door.

"Exi! Hatch! Everyone! The waters are rising!" I wasn't too surprised to see Hatch appear from nowhere and add his trumpet call. "Yes!" he piped. "Yes! Come to the stairs! Quick now!"

Up the spiral stairs we went, I first with Locus bouncing around my feet, Exi and Carabus next, Mr. Green and Isia straggling behind, the beetle because he considered it undignified to be rushed, the caterpillar because he was lazy. Red, at Hatch's command, acted as a shepherd, prodding Mr. Green and Isia with his sword whenever they protested too much or gave evidence of stopping. It was an orderly flight, though toward the top it got crowded and confused, with everyone pushing to get through the next trap door.

Hardly had we arrived, however, when Hatch called out, "Can't stay here! Waters coming faster! Dark Fire is really pushing!"

The ensuing scramble up the next flight of spiraling stairs was even worse than the first, if that was possible. This time we could actually see the flood following, covering step after step; and then we all were packed onto the last few steps below the next trap door and I, being strongest, pushed on the door. It was stuck! I shoved

harder with no effect. Again! Again! It was firm as rock! At this
point the two unlikeliest members of the company began to help.
While Locus dug away with her tiny paws at the trap door's edges,
Red probed with his sword, and the door was loosened. I flung it
upward and we all exploded through, not into another room but
into the out-of-doors.

There was scarcely any opportunity to examine our surroundings because the water, at our heels on the stairs, was overflowing,
boiling through the opening with a force that made closing the
door impossible. It was clear that something must be done.

"Maris and I were given to understand, when we first met
Hatch, that a loss had occurred." Exi's voice was loud and authoritative, more grave than usual. Everyone listened with full attention.
"I do not know what this means. But it seems reasonable to ask
who has lost what. Or who has what someone else has lost." He
paused to allow his words to be considered. "Has anyone here lost
some valuable thing?" There were a few sharp noes and a general
shaking of heads. "Very well," he continued firmly. "Who then
has a thing that someone else owns, or at least that is not his?"

No one spoke. Each of us was pondering the question in search
of an answer that might save us all. Meanwhile the water was
flowing over the ground, making a shallow but spreading lake in
which we stood uneasily.

"Well?" Exi pressed. "Someone must have something."

It was the "must" that pushed me. I had in my pockets the
dried seeds and the rusty knife from the ants' kingdom, and the—
no! It couldn't be the stone! It must be one of the other things.
But I turned to Exi knowing it was the stone. "What must I do?"

"I am not sure. You might try applying it where the greatest
danger is."

As always, I understood Exi even when I didn't know what he
meant. I waded out into the deepening flood toward its center
where the water was gushing upward in a small geyser. When I
could reach out and touch this fountain I stopped. The water was
above my knees. One by one I took out of my pocket almost all
the seeds and the knife, tossing them into the water. Nothing
happened. If anything, the geyser was stronger. Then reluctantly,
I drew out the beautiful, strange, magic stone. I let it rest for a

moment on the palm of my hand, gazing into its pulsating mystery. Finally with a cry I dropped it into the fountain and turned away. I had given all I had, and it seemed cruel to me that I must sacrifice such a fine and helpful thing. We probably would drown anyway. Probably some fool like Mr. Green, or some dullard like Isia, really had the lost item and was too stupid to see!

"Hurrah! Hurrah!" "That's done it!" "Oh good!" "*Should* have been done *before!*"

Roused by the voices of my companions, and by Locus tugging at my wet skirt, I looked back. The geyser had ceased and the waters were returning to their own proper abode. So it had been the stone! My treasure had been demanded of me for the sake of these ill-assorted strangers! But then maybe it wasn't really mine. It belonged to them too. And to Exi, whom I already loved. And yet apparently it belonged to none of us but to another or others, maybe to Dark Fire and to Them.

Exi affirmed this immediately. "That step has been taken. Good. If only the greater difficulty could be as quickly healed." He told us then that some of the inhabitants of the land had split off from the rest, and that destruction and death were abroad. Somehow we were necessary to Them in Their attempt to heal the split. This, in short, was our mission. But what we were to do, and how, even Exi did not seem to know. We were all speechless for the moment.

I held out my arms and Locus leaped into them, burying her furry face in my neck as I hugged her close. Then I knew I hadn't lost my treasure, and knew that some matters were all right because in my ears was the delicious sound of Locus. Even if Scuro was somewhere else.

With the fear of flood removed, we could begin to be aware of what the country around was like. We had emerged out of the mountain, not on a mountain top, but on a plain. As far as sight could penetrate, in all directions from the muddy clearing were trunks of trees, enormous trees towering upward, their branches interlaced some twenty-five or thirty feet overhead to form a tangle of great shiny leaves. From many of the branches pendulous vines, as thick through as a man's wrist, twisted downward. Giant plants, resembling ferns but each one bearing a waxy green-white blossom the size of a wagon wheel, grew here and there among the irregular aisles of huge trunks. It was not really an ominous landscape, but it was so big, so lush, so endless that it dwarfed everything else. Anything we might have seen beyond the forest was hidden by the forest itself.

After a brief debate as to which way to go, we set out on a path to the left. I couldn't decide just what determined the choice, but Exi and Carabus led off with such firmness that it seemed right. Mr. Green followed the other two beetles; then I came with Locus dancing beside me. Red, having prodded Isia into movement, came last. Before long we grew used to the vast corridors, the tangle of vines, the enormous blossoms in the green shadows, and could recognize other smaller growth.

Exi and Carabus seemed to know where they were going, or at least knew what they wanted, for they were unhesitating in leadership. After about an hour we saw ahead of us a gradual rise. At closer view it was a smallish wooded hill in a place where the giant trees were less crowded and there was almost the possibility of sunlight breaking through the foliage. Up the hill we went. When we reached the top, Exi and Carabus stopped and we gathered around them.

"Here," said Exi confidently, "is where we must begin to make something to live in while we wait to learn how we are needed. Now what will each one do?"

"I," said Mr. Green, "will not stoop to gathering and building! The Green family—"

"You," Exi interrupted with great authority, "you, Green, will go out and gather fuel for a fire. You are the strongest, next to Maris, who has other tasks. If you do *not* cooperate, there will be no place for you here and you will have to go on alone! With the aid of the Green family!" This last was added with unexpected fervor. Mr. Green, also unexpectedly, said no more. From then on he gave his best to his work, apparently fearful of being abandoned.

Isia and Red formed a team. Isia said he would cut leaves and Red said he would carry them back. Carabus would dig a fire pit as soon as a site was chosen. Exi and I would work together to assemble some sort of shelter out of whatever was brought, and Locus and I could tidy it up and prepare food. Nobody knew what food yet, but that wasn't the first order of business anyway.

Our building site was lovely as well as functional. It was on the crest of the knoll, slightly to the left side of a grassy flat. Numerous vines hung down from the surrounding trees. With Exi's eye for precise detail and balance and my more agile hands and fingers, we looped vine tendrils around and over a small willowlike tree, to serve as tent ropes. The leaves Red kept bringing were then placed like waxy green shingles over the tree and its vine ropes, the shingles secured with sharp-needled grass we discovered. Four or five feet from the entrance to our shelter Carabus completed a smooth, round, deep fire pit, and beside it Mr. Green built up a very adequate fuel supply.

At last Exi gathered all of us together and said that everyone should go food hunting except Locus and me, who would get the shelter ready inside, and Red who would stay outside as a guard. Nobody objected to Exi's commands, for he was never dictatorial and always did his full share. The food gatherers departed in various directions. Red stood near the fire pit, his back to the shelter, his sword drawn, and Locus and I were alone.

It was comfortable and cozy to be occupied for a while with house things. In our green bower, cool and fresh, with Locus happily sweeping at the earthen floor with a pawful of long grass, I felt contentment. I sang as I swept and pounded the floor solid and then constructed beds from waxed leaves of the kind we had used for our shingling. It was very important to me to have the inside fresh and clean and inviting. Since there were no utensils or furniture, and at the moment no way that I could see of making any, I had finally done all I could do. I crawled out and went down to a stream that wound about the base of the hill. Locus sat close, chewing on a blade of grass and purring.

It hadn't occurred to me to wonder how a fire could be made. Red apparently had no doubts. I could see him above in the lingering twilight busily arranging material in the hole dug by Carabus. Then he took something—I couldn't tell whether it was his sword or some other similar object—and twirled it rapidly. Soon I could see faint reddish sparks inside the fire pit, and it was not long before a fine blaze was pushing back the darkness. I laughed aloud to see Locus trying to take hold of the flickers of fireglow.

Sounds of familiar voices brought me quickly to my feet. The food gatherers were coming back into the firelit circle. In the uncertain illumination they looked like especially gnomish gnomes with dozens of legs, marching along carrying grotesque bundles— that is, all except Isia, who looked like a small, legless burro with several bundles fastened to his undulating back.

"Welcome home!" I shouted, rushing up the hill to help unload them.

"We are glad to be back." Exi sounded tired but pleased. "We have brought many things we hope you can use." And they began piling things up near the fire.

Suddenly I knew that the "you" meant me, and my happiness faded when I realized how useless I was even in my mother's kitchen where everything was available. I stood by the heap of goods, whatever they were, waiting for Exi to tell me what to do. But he, Carabus, and Mr. Green had walked to the stream to drink, and Isia had curled up to rest. So there I was, alone, with things I knew nothing about, and there was nothing for me to do but try. With Locus near me, I sat down by the pile of possible foodstuff my companions had brought and began to sort it. When I finished, I had three small piles: the first contained six midget ears of multicolored corn; the second, a fair-sized mound of what appeared to be nuts; the third, at least twenty large oval leaves. I contemplated this assortment in a dismay tinged with dim amusement at having utterly no notion where or how to begin.

It was Locus at play who gave me sudden insight; for as she began putting an ear of corn into the curve of a leaf, I recalled a childhood camping trip where an uncle had wrapped corn ears in wet corn husks and laid them in the fire's coals. It was at least a possibility. Taking the leaves to the stream, I soaked them thoroughly. Then I wrapped each ear of corn, together with a few of the nuts, in a roll made of several wet leaves and laid the rolls carefully in the fire pit, poking coals around them with a piece of wood. Soon the sweet fragrance of roasting grain filled the air, and even Isia awakened to join the eager group about the fire. It was a moment of rich satisfaction when I extracted the steaming bundles from their primitive oven, laid them before my friends, and knew the meal was good.

Mr. Green, who had not spoken for some time, was sounding officious again. "*I think we are not being properly organized! I think—*" He stopped suddenly, realizing that all the others were staring at him in silent censure.

"We would be as safe, and more comfortable, inside, don't you think?" Exi spoke quietly. "Red and I will sleep across the entrance." And he led the way into the house.

It was like a nest as each one of us settled into, or onto, or under, the leafy beds I had made—a dark, warm, cozy nest almost overflowing with nestlings. Exi and Red tugged their beds to the entrance. After a few more rustles, scratches, and shifts, sleep and silence filled the world.

7

EARLY THE NEXT MORNING, WITH SLIVERS OF PALE LIGHT JUST visible through openings in the green walls, quietly so as not to disturb anyone, I stole from the shelter. I needed to be by myself. Locus, of course, came too. Softly we went to the stream banks where I washed my face and hands and drank from the cold rippling water. On all sides the aisles of forest stretched away, and there was a subtle scent of dew on grasses mingled with the almost imperceptible smell of wood smoke from the previous night's fire. The windless air held a profound silence, and it seemed as if we were at the beginning of time, a time waiting for us to walk into it. So we did.

We crossed streams, wandered through dells prodigal with lilies, picked a few more of the nutlike fruits we had eaten the night before and found them palatable raw. By the time I realized that we had been gone much longer than I knew, we were quite, quite lost. I came to a dead halt, joy replaced by confusion.

Locus, however, tugged at my skirt insistently until I gathered I was to follow, whereupon she trotted off down one of the aisles as though she knew precisely where she was going, stopping now and again to see if I was coming. We had taken several turns, and I felt I was being led through a bewildering maze by one of the three blind mice, when quite unexpectedly a clearing opened before us. It was bright with sunlight, and we paused at the forest edge in the shadows. When my vision got adjusted to the light, I saw that one of the great trees had fallen in the middle of the open land. On this trunk someone was either seated, or kneeling—it was

48

difficult to tell from my distance.

The someone was large, and Locus rushed across the clearing and up to the log in positive eagerness. I went nearer. Soon the figure looked like a monk in a pale green habit. As I went quite close, I distinguished an extraordinary figure, large as myself, the lower half of him resting quietly on four angular insect legs, the upper half, tall and giraffe-slender, raised up with two bent and thorny forelegs clasped in an attitude of prayer. His head, on a long neck, was itself strangely elongated, and his eyes were glowing garnets of wisdom.

"My child," he was saying to Locus in a deep, rich baritone, "it has been long since I saw you. The spirit remains abundant in you, I see. May They bless you always." He turned gravely to me and bent his head in greeting. "And you, my child—who are you and why do you come? I know you are to be trusted or the little one would not have brought you. But who, and why, remain relevant questions, do they not?"

I agreed that they did and proceeded to tell him my story. He listened attentively, his body in absolute repose, his eyes watching my face as I talked. "And now," I concluded, "I've gotten us lost!"

"If you had not gotten lost you would not have found me. Or perhaps I should say, you would not be here if you were really lost."

"You mean you intended me to find you?"

"Intended? No, not intended. One cannot 'intend' life's purposes. To do so is to try to force life into our plans. But profound intention underlies all honest acts. Whose intention, I am not sure we can say with certainty, but what issues from truth is always right. Don't you think so?"

"Maybe. I don't know." I tried to be as honest with him as possible, because I felt that nothing less would be enough. "I don't know. I don't even know if I understand you. I don't really understand why we're all on this journey for Them. I only know that when I get lost, or seem to, then I'm afraid. And when I'm afraid it hurts!"

"You believe that what hurts is necessarily wrong?"

"Well, isn't it?"

"Have you had hurts so far in this new journey of yours?"

"Of course! Lots of them!"

"Were they wrong? That is, to put it backward, did good ever come from them?"

"Well—" I began to glimpse what he was telling me. "Yes. Usually, I guess. The stone, and Exi—and Locus. And cooking. Yes."

"Well, then," he said, "I must tell you that to be alive is the same as pain, and so everything that lives is in pain. Pain of love and loss, pain of solitude, pain of beauty." Even Locus sat very still, as the voice seemed to penetrate the air in ever-widening circles of sound. "Try not to dispel pain but rather to see for your-self, and others, how it purifies, sets free, blesses. Pain is the most vivid of colors brightening the world of Becoming." The last words hung suspended for a moment, then faded away. He reached with a front leg back to his long body, plucking a piece from what I now realized were long and graceful wings folded against him. With a courtly bow he handed to me the bit of wing. "In this, my child, is the wisdom and blessing of the Mantid—as much of it as you are able to use. When you are in doubt or afraid, look through it. It may help you and others." He turned back to the contempla-tive state in which we had found him, clearly dismissing us.

Even Locus walked rather than scampered to the forest's edge, though once there, she darted off into the trees and back again several times. I stood for a long while before entering the trees, gazing toward the great fallen log and the quiet, pale green figure seated upon it. Then I looked closer at the gift of the Mantid. Such a frail bit of nothing it was, like very thin glass tinged green, but soft and pliable. Not so frail, either, for I found I could pull at it or even roll it up with no visible effect. I put it in my pocket with the three remaining wheat grains, then turned and entered the forest, not seeing Locus and wondering if anyone knew where anyone was, when a gray and scarlet flash lighted on my shoulder.

"Hatch!" I cried. "It's so good to see you! Where have you been?"

"Being a messenger! That's my work, you know. Being a mes-senger." The clarity of his delicate trumpet sounds echoed sweetly down the forest ways. "Always They have much for me to do! Much!" Then he went on, "So you've met the Mantid. Not many do. Only the choosing are chosen! Now off we go!" And he flitted ahead of me into the shadowed trees.

I followed, turning to look over my shoulder toward the clearing once or twice as I went. I couldn't see the colossal tree or the monkish figure of the Mantid, and if I hadn't felt the gift in my pocket and the gift of words in my mind, I might have doubted his existence. But I had no doubts. Outwardly my feet went right, left, right, left, and my eyes stayed with the figures of Hatch and Locus. Inwardly I wandered in a far land filled with mists of many colors and shapes whose outlines I could not discern. Thus I arrived back, not really aware that I *had* arrived until Exi spoke.

"I knew you could find them faster than we could," he said to Hatch, who had perched roguishly on Mr. Green's back.

"I *say* now, you cannot—" began Mr. Green.

"Yes, he can!" exclaimed Red. "And just you be quiet. Hatch belongs to Them. I'd be proud to have him on me!" Red looked both angry and surprised at his own temerity.

Hatch bowed his thanks in Red's direction and went from Mr. Green's offended back like a small red-tipped arrow, disappearing into the trees.

"Well," said Exi, planting himself before me, "well, where have *you* been?" His brevity sounded indignant, and I didn't really blame him. I told him I was sorry, not for having gone but for causing him worry. I tried to say why I'd gone, but found myself stammering for want of words, so I quit.

"Next time," he said, not angry now, but surprisingly sympathetic, "you might leave some sign somewhere, at least indicate whether you have gone up, or down, or around, or in!"

I nodded, and then to change the subject went busily to the fire pit and took from its cold maw the leaves, nuts, and corn left over from the night before. When we had finished everything, down to the last kernel of corn, the last leafy stem, Exi called us together.

"You and I," he looked at me, "have come furthest together. The rest of you—" He stopped, reached out suddenly, and poked Isia into reluctant attention. "The rest of you have not been with us many days but, for such time as we have had, we certainly have been a chosen company. More or less unified." At these words, I squirmed guiltily and noticed that Mr. Green, too, seemed uncomfortable and gazed fixedly in another direction. "Now," Exi continued, "I think we must become a better company. As long as They apparently chose us to help somehow, it seems to me we should choose to be together. What do you feel?"

I said I felt the same.

"Yes." Isia startled us by speaking up so soon and by sounding so wide awake. His eyes were bright in his woolly face. "Yes indeed," he said in his deep, slow voice, "I would like to be part of this. I will work at staying awake, I will practice activity, I will resist my passiveness, I will try to be fierce. I—" A great yawn interrupted his words. He shook his head sadly. "It won't be easy, but I will do my best."

Carabus said he wanted whatever Exi wanted, and the conviction in his quiet tone carried far beyond his words.

"Me, too." As usual Red's speech was quiet. But then he drew his sword and said almost loudly, "Exi is captain."

"Thank you, Red." Exi turned toward the one member of the group who had not yet spoken. "And you, Mr. Calosoma Green? What do you feel?"

"Well, I should think *everyone* has abilities! My grandfather was a *splendid* commander, and this trait has been noted in my family. For *my* part, I think we should *share* leadership!"

"Oh, I quite agree about abilities," Exi replied calmly, "and I too believe we should use them all. Also, because I think we will have dangers to meet soon, I hope we can all share in the full responsibilities of decisions."

"Splendid! Splendid!" Mr. Green spoke loudly, stepping forward. "Now then, I propose—"

"Shut up!" Carabus sounded ready to explode.

"Yes," put in Isia, who had remained amazingly present, "do come off the platform, Green! You know you're incapable of proposing anything. And even if you did we probably wouldn't do it."

Mr. Green began to splutter, but Exi said in a voice that was deceptively gentle, "As a matter of fact, I am pleased to learn that military skill runs in the Green family, because Red and I cannot carry the burden of guarding day and night. We would be overjoyed to have you, Mr. Green, take the long night watch and lead some of the food forays. Your great strength will be a fine deterrent to enemies."

"Well, now," began Mr. Green, his bluster considerably lessened.

But Exi went on as if he did not hear. "So it seems we are all in accord. Good. I don't know what our task will be, but I have reason to believe we may need our resources soon. May I suggest that we devote the rest of this day to gathering and storing food and strengthening our shelter?"

We dispersed to go about our tasks with a deepened sense of purpose. Somehow Exi had welded us closer together. Even Mr. Green, subdued and cooperative, seemed more a part of us.

Red proved his ingenuity by constructing a storage space around the tree trunk just under the roof's highest point; and by late afternoon this was filled with neat piles of wood, corn, leaves, and nuts, which Red had hauled up the trunk as the others had brought them back.

The day had begun to dim into twilight when the last loads were stored away, with just enough set aside for supper. Red started a fire burning in the pit while Locus and I prepared the food to go into the coals.

The night settled upon us blacker than I could ever remember. Had it not been for the firelight on tree trunks, we might have been at the bottom of a black pit. We drew closer to the fire and to each other, and nobody had much to say. Deepening anxiety touched us all, increasing the sense of closeness among us.

Finally Exi spoke matter-of-factly out of the darkness. "Let's build up the fire tonight and take turns keeping it burning and standing guard while others sleep." Red said he'd be first, but Exi said we'd better work in twos, a suggestion that convinced me he was worried.

"That seems excellent!" Mr. Green startled everyone with his loud voice. "Excellent! And I will stand with Red."

If Exi wondered about Mr. Green's courage or ability, he didn't show it. "Good," he said. "Then Carabus and I will relieve you later on. And Isia can guard the entrance. Inside. And *not* curled up!"

"I will," said Isia. "I promise, really I promise. And if I should fall asleep—which I probably will because I do it embarrassingly often—if I should fall asleep anything climbing over me will awaken me."

When at last I lay on my pallet of leaves, with Locus beside me and with Exi and Carabus nearby, I couldn't sleep. I tried for the sake of the others not to toss about. Not once but many times I slid my hand into my pocket and fingered the strange gift of the Mantid. My mind kept repeating his words about pain as a condition of existence. For a while I hung between sleep and non-sleep; then despite myself I dropped into a world of dream.

I was running after Scuro down a long, long hill covered with gigantic boulders. I was also running away from creatures who pursued me in a frenzy, yelling and screaming at me. I tried to hide behind the boulders but they were hot and untouchable and I had to keep running under a brazen noonday. Then I was on Exi's back as we swam and floundered through gelatinous seas whose thick waves folded over us without sound, and finally Exi sank from under me and I was alone in a waste of quivering waters. Now I was on land again, but in an endlessness of tree trunks, bare and dead, and I could glimpse shadows of things everywhere, but nothing was there when I approached. Vast and terrifying loneliness overcame me. I began to run, faster and faster, crashing into dead trees, falling, rising, falling, finding no exit. I saw a light and ran toward it in wild longing, and it became a cavern of fire; then I saw it was the maw of some great beast opened wide. And it was waiting for me! And screaming flames!

I came awake to hear a scream tearing into the night and to see Exi and Carabus scrambling out of the entrance. My heart pounding, my body covered with sweat, I struggled to my feet, clutching Locus in my arms; and I knew at once that the creatures who were the destroyers were at hand. Locus was utterly silent.

PART II

Rescue

8

I STUMBLED AFTER THE OTHERS AND WOULD HAVE GONE OUT IN A blind panic if Exi had not commanded, "Stay where you are!" I stopped at the doorway. Again the hideous scream tore the night into fragments. I saw that five of my companions were standing very close together between fire and dwelling, staring into the darkened forest beyond. Nothing was said until the screaming ceased. "You should have called us!" Exi said sharply.

"That would have been impossible before," Mr. Green replied, "because Red and I only just *now* saw the eyes, and then this—this—this unholy thing began and then you were *here!*"

"Is that right?" Exi's question was not meant as insult, only as request for confirmation.

"It's true." Red moved nearer Mr. Green, almost protectively. "We're a good team, you see. Balanced, if you know what I mean. No talking. No sleeping. Eyes appeared all around, then the noise. Then you."

During the whispered council that followed, I strained to see what lurked outside our circle of light, but the fire prevented me. A thin whimper brought me back. Locus too was afraid. Locus needed me, and I gathered her closer to me and began to sing softly the first thing that came:

> "*Sing a song of sixpence,*
> *A pocket full of rye . . .*"

I became so absorbed in this maternal act that when another

scream shattered the night, I was able to keep on singing although I couldn't hear myself. It was well that the full fury of sound had not broken over us all at once; I at least wouldn't have been ready. But when the worst of all screaming finally came, setting the world utterly on edge (so it felt to me), a hurricane of noise beating against us, I found resources new to me, and in them I had the needed strength.

A brief lull in the terrible noise let me hear Exi say, ". . . and build up the fire! Keep it up! I will return as soon as I can!"

He came quickly inside. "Maris, take Locus and get up in the storeroom! At once! It is the safest place. Don't come down until I come for you!" I said I would, at once. He hurried out, not looking back to see if I obeyed. He knew I would.

I acted at once by going to the tree trunk supporting our shelter. The further actions were not so simple, because Exi had not told me how to climb up with someone in my arms. None of my companions would have found it difficult because they could just walk up. But I suffered through some frantic trials and errors before I finally put Locus on my back, paws clutching my collar tightly, and then shinnied up boy style, arms and legs wrapped around the trunk, pulling and pushing myself and my load slowly away from the ground.

Another problem arose when I reached the storage platform and realized it was far too flimsy to hold our weight. However, by going a bit higher I reached a fairly good-sized branch. Sitting astride that, my head above the roof top, my back braced against the trunk, Locus in my arms below the roof top, I could at least rest. Though we were far from secure, there was a feeling of tentative safety. Thus I spent the endless night surrounded by the screaming frenzy of sound. Mostly I kept my eyes closed, lowering my head to sing to Locus, through the hole in the roof, every song I could recall. I knew Locus didn't rest, for her paws never relaxed their tense grip on my arm, but somehow the singing was a small flag on the mast of a storm-swept ship. My body ached, my throat was sore, and my sight blurred when dawn felt its way into the forest. With a suddenness equal to its onset the screaming ended. Absolute silence was everywhere, shocking to my ears. Exi's voice, calm and welcome, called us down.

Seated near the the dead fire, I munched wearily on some cold leftovers Isia offered me, while the night's events were discussed by the others. The five had remained on guard all during the long hours; the screams had come from many directions and had also changed location; each of the watchers had seen eyes, huge shining eyes; whenever the watchers added fuel to the fire the eyes had gone farther off, coming closer again as the flames fell; almost all the wood had been used up.

It was frighteningly clear to every one of us that several questions had to have immediate answers, answers not easy to come by. We agreed that whatever They needed us for, it was somehow related to these evil creatures who had to be faced. But beyond that we didn't know. Should we stay where we were or try to find a safer shelter? If we stayed, could we get more fuel without being caught by—whom? What was out there? What did it, or they, want? Finally we decided the sensible first step was to rest, or no further steps would be efficient. All of us except Red, who declared he was quite wide awake, went into the shelter and were soon asleep.

Some while later Red roused the company to gather outside. Expressions were more cheerful and voices more confident. The general opinion was that we should stay where we were at least a few days if we could get more wood. Exi said we'd better try because fire seemed to keep the creatures at a distance. So we spent the afternoon gathering.

Dark came quickly. The very trees seemed to breathe and whisper of danger, although the night was windless and our fire leaped unwavering into the black air. With more courage and foresight than usual, I asked Exi if it might not be a good idea for Isia to take Locus up to the storeroom. I could be more helpful somewhere else, maybe. I waited for Exi to disagree, but he didn't.

So we did it that way. Locus, though a bit reluctant, seemed to understand what was required and clung to Isia for the upward climb. When they were settled, Isia called down, "We *do* make quite a furry nest, you know, really we do!"

I went out to take a place by the fire. I selected a stout stick from the woodpile as a weapon in case I needed one, and, seated where I could look beyond the flames into the invisible distances of forest, I felt right about being there. There was no denying that I was frightened. Nor could I say that no part of me was wishing I were somewhere else. Balanced against this, though, was the ever-increasing awareness of a destiny, and a sense that my particular being was necessary to a resolution of problems larger than I.

"Pain is the most vivid of colors brightening the world of Becoming." I began to comprehend what the Mantid meant. Touching his gift in my pocket, I wondered if I should use it. "When you are in doubt, or afraid," he had said. Was I afraid enough? Or confused enough? And he hadn't promised it would help, but only that "it may help." It wasn't time yet, I decided, and went back to watching.

The hours crept deeper into the night. Periodically I or Mr. Green would add wood to the fire to keep it blazing. Otherwise nothing. Truly this was a silent night, touched by none of the usual noises of night. Utterly soundless, until the silence became so thick, evil that when the first scream struck at us it was almost a relief. Closer to it now than before, I turned my head in the direction from which the scream appeared to come. Gleaming through the blackness were two enormous fiery eyes staring with an expression of patient malevolence. Even as I sat stunned by the shock of the scream and the awful eyes, the eyes disappeared. Another scream joined the first, then another and another, and the suffocating silence was transformed into an equally unbearable chaos of noise. Without thinking, I leaped to my feet, brandished my club, and shouted into the din, "Keep away, you devils! Keep away! Keep away!"

This produced a momentary lull. And when the screams came again, they seemed to have moved farther off. I had found my work! The rest of the night was a sequence of screams advancing, shouts, the fire built up, screams retreating, and on and on and on. The gleam of eyes appeared and disappeared, now closer, now farther off, but never did any shape manifest itself. My own eyes ached from trying to see what I couldn't see, and my throat was raw from shouting, when day finally came. I dragged myself indoors to drop onto a bed, so utterly tired that I didn't even look for Locus but plunged at once into heavy sleep.

The forty-eight hours that followed were a blur of fatigue and tension. Everything was unnatural. We slept by day, always being sure that someone stood guard. We ate cold food when we could because we knew we should, but without any desire for it. Dispositions were irritable, and conversation was limited to the minimum needed for some sort of organization. We seemed incapable of action. Fortunately our supplies, except firewood, were enough. And always there was the fear. It seemed to spread through the surrounding landscape not only at night but by day as well, so that the trees in the forest beyond our shelter began to be ghost creatures watching, and the stream curving below had an evil song, and the silence was not peace but a cruel waiting.

"I don't see how we can stand it much longer!" I said to Exi in the late afternoon of our fourth day, while we chewed tasteless corn and waited for nightfall. I hoped he might say some word of comfort, or perhaps suggest some new course of action.

"No, I don't either," he replied.

The darkness encompassed us more ominously than ever that night. After Isia and Locus were settled, the rest of us huddled by our fire. My hand was a tight knot around my club and my ears already hurt from the unheard sound that I knew would soon crash the silence. Exi's limp was accentuated as he walked periodically away from the fire to peer into the black distance. Red drew his sword in and out of its sheath, and Mr. Green constantly cleared his throat. Only Carabus was a quiet and unmoving silhouette in the firelight.

Into this agony of expectation nothing came. This was the worst horror of all—that the horror did not manifest itself, that neither sound nor sight happened. Time lost all meaning as the night grew deeper. Our tension acquired almost the quality of trance, until we stood immobile in the awful emptiness. And then what we had not, in fact could not have, prepared for fell upon us from several directions.

Our world was split apart, not only by screams right beside us but by the sound of our shelter being ripped open from the back. I spun around and had just time to see a great paw raised against the side of our house before the fire was snuffed out. Because

my vision could not accommodate suddenly to such a total loss of
light, I floundered about in my desperate attempt to reach the
shelter and Locus and Isia. The others, too, were trying to find
their way, stumbling over each other, colliding, uttering small
noises of pain and urgency. But it was all quite useless. Only
when at last dawn light allowed us to see, did we know what had
happened. It was evident then that our home had been completely
destroyed, our storeroom pulled to ruin.

It was Exi who gathered us together from the places we had
found in the dark. "Come! Do come as I call you, for we must
know just how things are!" We came in from our scattered spots,
Carabus, Mr. Green, and I, each saying he was all right.

"The storage room is gone, so obviously the enemy found
Locus and Isia and took them. But where is Red?" Exi asked.
"Was he with any of you?"

There was no answer.

"Red? Are you there?"

Still no reply.

"Red? Red!" Exi shouted.

"I *must* find him!" Mr. Green spoke with more emotion than
I had thought possible. "If he is here, I must find him. He is my
friend!" He moved hurriedly away and began to pick his way
through the snarled heap that had been our house.

"Carabus and I will help," said Exi. "You stay here, Maris,
unless we call."

The call came soon. I was dreadfully afraid as I went to where
the three searchers were and saw them trying to clear away some
of the wreckage.

"He's under there! Please go gently!" Mr. Green was crying as
he pulled at the tangle.

I had to hold myself to keep from rushing headlong into the
confused mess. Yet I succeeded in going quietly about the work
of lifting torn branches and twisted vines until I could get to the
inert body. When finally I lifted Red in my arms and carried him
to a grassy space near the stream, the sky was beginning to grow
bright with dawn. I laid Red gently down. He was limp and still,
and we stood helpless beside him wondering what to do. The
loss of Locus, Isia, our home, and now Red, seemed to me to be

too heavy to bear.

Suddenly Mr. Green, who had been standing in pathetic disbelief beside Red's body since the moment I had laid it on the grass, cried out in a cracked, almost hysterical voice. "He isn't—he isn't—oh, it can't be—oh, Exi, Carabus, Maris—he isn't dead! He isn't!" We crowded forward together and saw at once that Mr. Green was not imagining things. One of Red's front feet, despite his terribly lifeless appearance, was twitching.

"Quick!" said Exi. "We must keep him from getting cold!" To me he said, "Your jacket. Wrap him in your jacket." And to Carabus, "Bring some leaves and grasses for a bed."

While Carabus hurried about gathering fresh grass and leaves, I removed my jacket. Emptying the content of its pockets into my handkerchief, I very carefully put Red onto the jacket and wrapped it about him. Soon we had him on the makeshift bed, and Exi and Carabus were searching through the ruins for any stray bits of food they could uncover. I didn't feel too sure that our efforts in Red's behalf would save him. He seemed so lost and far away from us already. And I couldn't bear to look at Mr. Green standing there, his great eyes fixed on Red's face, his right forefoot stroking Red's head.

In order to escape both Mr. Green's suffering and my own doubts, I decided to see if a fire could be started. The enemy had used wet greens to fill the fire pit and quench the fire; these had to be scooped out. It was a messy task, but one on which I could concentrate. It gave me satisfaction to find, deep under the ashes, a few smouldering coals that glowed when I blew on them and broke into flames when I added dry leaves and sticks. Despite all the havoc created by the marauders, whoever they were, it would yet be possible to have a bit of warm food.

For a long time after we had eaten, not with any real appetite, we stood around silent and preoccupied. Red gave no indication of consciousness although occasionally a convulsive spasm shook his body. Carabus had discovered Red's sword half buried near the base of the old center pole and had put it beside the couch of greens where Red lay. It looked as forlorn as we felt.

For a second time it was movement by Red that shook us from our gloom.

"Where is it? Where?" The whispered words were almost inaudible, but Red's head moved slightly as the words breathed out. Mr. Green leaned listening over his friend. "It's lost! Lost! Where is it?" The feeble voice was urgent. Mr. Green sensed the need sooner than any of us and lifted Red's sword and held it where Red could see it. "Where is it? Where—oh, there it is!" New hope same into the whisper. "I was afraid . . . just tried to get one, but too late . . . Locus caught, and tree fell . . . be all right . . . later . . ." Red's voice faded off into nothing, but we were much relieved, believing now that he would live.

"And what about Locus and Isia?" I asked the question for all of us.

"Well," Exi said, very kindly, "we can't do anything right now for them, can we? If they are alive," he added reluctantly. "Red is our immediate concern. And also ourselves. We need rest too."

We coudn't seem to think of what we could do, until Carabus remembered a cave he'd seen on a food-gathering expedition.

"Yes! Of *course!*" Mr. Green was excited. "Of *course* you are *right!* Down the hill where the stream has cut a deeper bed and the trees are much closer together. It's a *big* hole in the river bank, a *truly expansive* hole. Let's investigate!" And he started off at once, Carabus following.

I turned to Exi after the others were out of sight. "Exi, do you think we'll get out of this, and that Red will get well, and that we can find—" My voice broke.

"It may be. It may be. Since the day we met, something has been at work, although in the beginning I was not at all sure what it was. I am not sure now; but we must take whatever way opens up to us, must we not, if we are to do whatever we are to do?"

When Carabus and Mr. Green returned, they had found the cave. It was big enough and quite dry, they told us. If I'd carry Red ("Very gently, please!" urged Mr. Green), the others would bring what they could. As I picked him up, Red whispered, "So tired," and then lay quietly in my arms.

Mr. Green took an enormous heap of leaves and led off downhill and along the stream. Carrying wood and the food we had salvaged, Exi and Carabus followed. We picked our way along the stream's rocky edge until we reached a place where the banks were easily six feet or more above the water. Here, its opening quite disguised by reeds and a bush growing over it, was a cave.

I had to go in on my knees, holding Red carefully. Once inside I could stand up, although I had to bend head and shoulders a little to do so. Mr. Green arranged leaves into a bed far back in the cave, and Red was placed there in the dim quietness. I prepared what food we had and we ate silently, each one occupied with his own thoughts and feelings.

"If the rest of you," Exi said at last, "are as tired as I am, wouldn't it be well to get some sleep now? The day has still a long way to go before dark, and I think we can rest until night."

We withdrew into our new earthen house and collapsed onto the several heaps of grass provided by Mr. Green. I had only time to note that Red's breathing sounded quite regular and that the reeds outside the door made a good screen, before exhaustion overcame me.

9

THE FOLLOWING AFTERNOON I SAT AT THE CAVE'S DOOR, LOOKING out at the water flowing past, each ripple of it winking gaily in the light, and wondered what was to come next on this fearful adventure. We had all been so unutterably tired that we scarcely noticed the peace that had prevailed during the previous afternoon and night and so far during this present day.

Now I sat and gazed at the stream and was troubled deeply. Mr. Green had gotten Red to take a few swallows of food, and Red had recognized him. Therefore presumably Red would get well, though perhaps slowly. What appalled me was what I did *not* know. Where was Scuro? Where were Locus and Isia? Why had the creatures not come again last night? What must we do next? What *could* we do? And why was it happening this way? How could this suffering and loss help Them to do whatever They needed to do?

When Exi came to stand beside me, also peering out of the cave as if hoping to see something that was not there, I turned to him and said, "Why? And what?"

"Exactly," he replied. "That is what I have been asking myself. What are we going to do?"

"Don't you have any answers?"

"No, not really. Answers must be much more certain than I. I have a knowledge (as we all do) that something is waiting for us to solve it, or that something wants putting right."

"Or wants to be found?"

"Perhaps that as well. Perhaps." He was silent.

It was then that I decided to do what I had long postponed doing. After Exi, Carabus, and Mr. Green departed to gather up more food, I went to the back of the cave and got the little collection of things I'd wrapped in my handkerchief. Opening it, I picked up the gift of the Mantid. Instinctively rather than deliberately, I seated myself in the middle of the dim and quiet cave, facing away from the entrance. I cupped my hands around the gift, closed my eyes, and waited.

At first I was agitated and beset by a tumble and rush of doubts and questions. During this crowded state of mind, it became clear to me that the use of this gift involved me in choice to a far greater degree than the use of the magic stone had ever done. The stone had seemed to seek me out, to remind me of itself, to choose the time for its use. Now I must choose to seek the mystery of this thing and not know if it would reveal itself to me. What had the Mantid said? "It may help." Only that. But he had told me, too, that the gift held in it "the wisdom and blessing of the Mantid—as much of it as you are able to use." That put a definite limit on it, for certain! Yet who could be sure what was possible when the need was so urgent? Anyway, I could only try. Having reached this point, I realized I had also become quieter, emptier. Again I waited.

The cave grew more and more still; the darkness behind my eyes expanded to encompass all space, with myself a dot at the center of it. The piece of delicate Mantid wing stirred in my hands. Then it began to pulsate and to flutter until I felt as if I had a diminutive bird imprisoned with me in this center of darkness. Slowly and with great care I lifted my hands and their contents to my closed eyes. For a time nothing came; only a deeper darkness closed around me and I diminished to a breath and faded away. Nothing existed. Nothing. No. No, not quite. A dim shape moved into and out of space. Was it the Mantid? The Grandmother? It pointed. Or was it flinging itself out of space? It was gone. Without warning a huge bubble of fiery liquid appeared, grew monstrous, and burst open into a sea of boiling orange-red lava that grew slowly calmer, finally rolling back as a giant curtain to reveal a landscape at first blurred and filled with undefinable forms flowing into each other, then becoming clearer so that the

forms separated into gigantic primeval plants growing in frightful
profusion; and among these stalked enormous ugly Beasts, restless
and searching. And their eyes! The awful eyes of the nights of
terror! These were the eyes! These were the paws too, the tearing
and destroying paws! The landscape grew misty and blurred again.
Now one huge tree came into clearness. High, high up in its
massiveness was some sort of structure, and on it, behind a
barricade or wall, were several creatures. Who? What did they
want? For it felt as if they wanted something. I strained to penetrate the mystery. I could see an outstretched and pleading arm,
and then faces that immediately started to fade from sight, but
not before I recognized the fierce face of Isia and startled expression of Locus. They lived! Yes! I held fiercely to the vision, not
wanting it to go, as I knew it was beginning to do. It kept
receding. My will kept following. Just as I felt my strength could
no longer hold out and my inner sight could go no further, another
face was manifested before me, instantly gone. The sad face of a
boy, with large dark eyes, dark hair, a pallor in the skin, lips
parted to speak, an open hand reaching toward me—and that was
all. It was gone, everything gone, and I sat in the cave's darkness
with the gift of the Mantid lifeless in my hands.

My surroundings were unchanged; the dim light was almost as
it had been; Red was still sleeping, the others not yet returned.
It did not matter. The "wisdom and blessing of the Mantid" had
imaged events far beyond and unutterably different from anything
I could have imagined. In one sense, I knew little that I hadn't
known already, except that my friends were alive somewhere and
that the eyes and the paws belonged to Beasts of fearsome powers.
I also knew that a boy was there, and a prison, and some far
strange land to be found and searched. This was a lot to see all
at once.

When Exi arrived to call me, he had to speak to me three
times before I heard him, and I went about preparing supper in a
state of absent-mindedness. Exi helped unobtrusively. He recognized that my mind was elsewhere. Supper was a quiet meal,
marked by the happy fact that Red not only ate what Mr. Green
fed him but also whispered a thank you before falling to sleep
again.

"Exi," I said, after the others had left, "Exi, we must go on now."

"We must? How do you know? How can you sound so sure?"

"I just do."

"That is not good enough, Maris my dear." He sounded both hurt and annoyed. "We have traveled a great way together, and I have always been honest with you. Usually—" and he paused on the word—"*usually* you have been honest with me. Our situation is too precarious now for us to move forward on less than the truth. And we have all been singled out, not you alone. Don't you agree?"

I was ashamed, realizing I had hugged a secret to myself instead of sharing. So I told him of my encounter with the Mantid, of the gift and my decision to use it. I described my experience and what I had seen through the gift of the Mantid. "Do you see now why I said we must go on?"

"Yes. Yes, I do! The gift of the Mantid is a rare thing. My great-uncle called it the Mantid's Mirror. It comes only to those who have the courage to choose to go on the path chosen for them." Exi continued thoughtfully, "I wonder in which direction we should go? Of course we cannot go until Red is able to travel."

"We can't—" But I bit off my protest unfinished, knowing we must wait. "Yes. Red must go with us." I shut my eyes and tried to visualize the landscape I'd seen. "I'm not sure why—and I may be wrong—but it feels to me that we have to go south. It's silly to say this! But it's how I feel."

"Well then, it shall have to be south—if the others assent. But how? That is, we could wander in the forest, as you and Locus did, and we might be as fortunate as you were, or we might not. We could get hopelessly lost."

"I guess that's right. I hadn't thought of how." Against my closed eyes I could almost catch again the vision of the place I'd seen. "Exi!" I exclaimed. "I don't know why, really, but I think we'll have to go on the water. Down the stream, wherever it goes."

"It is too small."

"Not for long," I replied, amazed by my certainty. "I'll explore tomorrow."

The next day held several matters of consequence, not the least being a decided improvement in Red's health. All of us felt a renewed vigor, both because of Red and also because, since we'd had no fires, the enemy was not harassing us at night.

Exi had told the others of my vision, and Carabus had spoken for everyone when he said, "Well, we'll go to them as soon as ever we can!"

I held to my resolve to explore the stream's course. Reluctant to let me go, Exi had to agree that it probably would be safe enough by day if I didn't go too far. I felt a strange excitement rise in me as I started downstream. But the farther I went, the less navigable the stream seemed. Each time I rounded a bend I hoped to see a change, and each time it showed the same rapid, rocky, narrow course.

Yet excitement persisted; and it was at least two hours (and more turns than I could count) before weariness made me realize I must stop, eat the food I'd brought, and decide if I should go on. Just one more bend, I thought, just this next one and then I'll halt. And, coming around, I saw my hopes realized.

There was a cascade of white water where two other streams merged with mine and then a clear, deep, still pool of considerable expanse which, at its farther end, flowed peacefully on as a river between banks green with grasses, with thickly wooded land on either side. Surely this was the place to begin our river journey.

It was a long way from the cave, of course. But I could carry Red, and the other three could walk, even if it took them more time than it had taken me. Food of some sort was available, as we had learned already. A boat and safety were the major problems to be solved. I spent almost too much time trying to see some answer, and suddenly realized the afternoon was passing and I'd better get started back or night might catch me out.

Walking as fast as possible, I made the return journey in good time, arriving at the cave well before dark. Exi and Carabus greeted me as if I'd been gone for days. Exi looked relieved, and in his reserved way pleased, at my description of what I'd found. "Tonight, after we are inside with Red—who is, by the way, much improved—let us discuss plans," he said.

It was evident that Exi was right about Red. His bed had

been moved near the entrance so that he could look out, and even in the thin light that came in I could see that his odd bulbous ant face was eager and very much alive. I said how fine it was to have him better.

"Thank you, miss." He touched my jacket which still served as a blanket and gazed at me sadly. "But I didn't save them, I didn't save them."

"Oh, Red! You did all you could do, and more than anyone else! We're just grateful you're here and getting well!"

"*That*," said Mr. Green as he entered, "is *precisely* what I have been saying to him the *whole* day. Our friends were *not* lost through any fault of his. He has been *most* courageous. And he will continue to let his bravery serve us as we go forth to rescue them. I am *sure* you will agree."

Exi and Carabus came in then, and we decided we would discuss plans before the evening meal so that Red could get to sleep early. Sitting there in the dusk, I told of my trip downstream, of the pool and the river beyond the pool, and of my conviction that we must go that way to find Locus and Isia. When I'd finished, the others were silent and thoughtful.

"If we assume your hunch is correct, Maris—" Exi said finally, "and we have no reason not to—then we must follow it. But—" he paused—"how can we go down the river?"

"A raft?" Carabus suggested. "Some sort of raft."

"Yes," Exi replied, "that is the obvious thing. But how are we to get a raft? We are hardly equipped for such construction, are we?"

It was Red who found the answer. Having listened quietly, he said, "What about those flowers?"

"What flowers, Red?" Exi was not quite certain if Red was feverish or not and thus not sure whether to take his statement seriously.

But Red answered lucidly. "Remember those big flowers, green and white, great big ones, bigger than Exi—we saw them on the way from the flood place to our house, quite a lot of them, remember?" We all nodded, and I could visualize the huge wheel-like blossoms. "Well," Red continued, "they're sort of bowls, you might say, shiny bowls that would maybe float. Several bowls—"

Then I got excited. "And they were thick and waxy, and I don't think they'd leak!"

"Also," Carabus put in, "they could be fastened together by their stems, tied with wiry grasses or something."

"Now, just a minute!" Exi was realistically cautious. "Those flowers were away back, when we first came to this land. Miles and miles away. We absolutely cannot go that far, and you all know it."

"Don't have to." It was Red again. "I saw one or two last time we got food in our other place. Maybe there are some nearby. Shouldn't wonder." He seemed tired from his effort. So we decided to wait until the morning to see if the idea would work.

10

Restless and eager to be about the business of boats, I expected to be awake all night, but the day's traveling had wearied me and I slept dreamlessly. I rose, however, with the first wash of light, whispered to Exi, and stole quietly from the cave. Carabus, evidently at Exi's request, went with me.

We wandered through the twisted corridors, often taking right-angled turns or reversing directions. It was quite a time before I spied a blob of white in the shadowy distance. I hurried toward it, and when I came near I was delighted to see one of the greenish-white waxy flowers suspended from its fernlike stalk. It was all of three feet across and at least half an inch thick at its outer edge. Its five petals were not separate but grew seamed together tightly. It appeared to be thoroughly floatable; but would it be too heavy? It was not. When Carabus had cut it from its stalk, taking care to leave several inches of stem, I found it light as a piece of balsa wood despite its diameter and thickness. I didn't see how anything could be more suitable for raft-building.

It took considerably more time than we had thought it would for us to find enough of the blossoms. We had decided we should have six of them, and I had to carry them all. It was well into mid-morning when we arrived back at the stream's edge below the cave and deposited our find. Mr. Green and Exi came to meet us, while Red watched in pleased silence from his bed, which had been moved outside onto the ledge by the cave entrance.

A long discussion, almost an argument, followed. I, of course, wanted to get at the boat building right away. I was rather stub-

born about it. But my three beetle friends patiently pointed out
that it was foolish to build a boat there and then have to carry it
all the way to the lake. And furthermore, we needed to be all
ready to go, with as much food as we could collect, before we
launched the boat. After all, the Beasts might return any time.
It was astonishing that they hadn't before now. Finally I agreed
and we began preparations.

Being sure that someone always stayed with Red, we made in-
numerable foraging trips back and forth along the stream, and
into the woods and out again. The heap of food grew larger and
larger. Soon we were ready to go; each loaded with an appropriate
burden.

The path along the stream was harder and longer for the group
than it had been for me alone and unencumbered. Added to the
weight of the burdens being carried, was the fact that we dared not
stop. Darkness must not find us still on land, or at any rate must
not come before we were well prepared to set forth on the river.
We pushed ourselves forward as fast as Exi's lameness permitted.
Occasionally he stumbled when his deformed wing and his one
withered leg upset his balance, and I ached for him but said
nothing. Over particularly bad bits of the way, Mr. Green could
he heard grumbling to himself. Otherwise we didn't talk, con-
serving our energies for the matter at hand.

When at last we had reached the shores of the wide pool, I
put Red carefully down in a soft grass clump, then untied and
removed all my bundles and burdens, piling them in a heap
nearby. I removed the beetles' bundles. I stretched my cramped
muscles, and exclaimed, "Wonderful! Oh, wonderful!"

"It is, miss, it is," Red answered. "Do you think—would it be
all right—please couldn't I get up for a little and just try my
legs? And maybe get a drop of water?"

I was touched by his pleading, and as long as the air was soft
and warm, I said I didn't see why it wasn't all right if he felt
like it. He pushed back the jacket-robe, and together we walked
to the shore where the others stood knee-deep in the lake. Red
proceeded slowly but without much shakiness. He was greeted
joyfully by his companions.

Building the boat was easier than we had anticipated. The

waxen flower disks were laid out with the five largest ones in a circle and the smallest one in the center, making a giant blossom about eight feet or more in diameter. Then the disks were turned over and the stems lashed together securely with lengths of extremely tough grass fibers. Red, eager to be of some use, prevailed upon Mr. Green to let him braid grass into a strong rope. This was fastened to the lashed-together stems, then brought up into the boat, to lie coiled and ready to act as a mooring line. And I made myself a paddle of a piece of weathered wood. All that remained was the launching. It was a tense moment as I pushed the craft carefully into the water, holding to the rope and praying that it would be right. The day was waning, and we had no idea what we would do if our handiwork failed us.

With hardly a tremble, the scalloped boat took to the lake, riding softly at the rope's end. A green and white fairy ship on a silver mirror, I thought, and was filled with delight. Exi broke the spell by asking bluntly, "But will it hold us?"

It was a relevant but disagreeable question. So I said (somewhat too loudly) that it had *better* hold us, and added that I'd try it and find out. I pulled the boat close and, barefoot, stepped cautiously in and sat in the central disk. It was remarkably buoyant; the saucer-shaped blossoms allowed no water over the sides even when I rocked the boat back and forth. It would work. I splashed back to shore, drawing the boat in as near as possible.

"Ready?" I said, after they were all aboard but me.

"I think we are." Exi looked over the company. "Yes. Yes, we are ready. Let us go."

I gave a gentle push, climbed into my place, and with my hands paddled our boat out into the slow current moving down the lake. Our vessel wobbled and pitched a bit at first, but then I felt the current steady it and begin to draw it toward the river.

Late afternoon light gave a velvet quality to land and water as our boat with its five passengers slid soundlessly from the lake into the river to begin, as the river here began, a southerly journey. The waterway was wide, deep-flowing, and smooth, apparently carrying the waters from many streams. On our right the banks were gentle sandy slopes lapped by ripples. On our left the water almost undercut the land, which rose vertically to dark forests. For a while we were too absorbed in our new experience to talk, each of us gazing at the water beneath us or at the sights beyond us.

"Maris," said Exi, when the twilight began to deepen to night, "Maris, I do not think we should go on all night."

"No, you're right. I wish we could, but it would be foolish."

"How shall we spend the night, then?"

I realized how uncertain about water travel Exi was by the fact that he asked me rather than told me. "What do you think of tying up to a sturdy-looking tree and not going ashore but just floating in one spot until morning?" I suggested. He assented.

Carabus and Mr. Green agreed on the solution. Red had fallen asleep. So before darkness was complete, we had moored our boat to a tree and it swung back and forth very gently at the end of its rope, a cradle whose weary occupants slept peacefully through the quiet night.

The next day, for hour after hour, we drifted with the current, watching the slow procession of forest and woods, beaches and banks. A mark of everyone's relaxation was the fact that when Mr. Green got started on an I-remember-when statement, no one seemed either bored or annoyed, and when he finished, Carabus commented, "Most interesting."

Red began to blossom before our eyes. He developed an enormous appetite and, between naps, showed delight in the unrolling landscapes and riverscapes. It was Red, too, who raised the question of a name for our boat. "Truly I think it's lonesome. Not being called anything, I mean."

We amused ourselves for a while by suggesting such names as *Saucy Six, Tea Time, Cups 'n Saucers*. Then finally we decided Red was right, and named her *Starflower*. It was a bit romantic, but somehow it was fitting.

Late that afternoon we beached the *Starflower* on a particularly inviting spit of sand and walked about, stretching and enjoying the exercise after the long laziness. When night reached down into the forests *Starflower* was once more tied up securely, this time to an old stump sticking out of the water, and we slipped easily into our second river night of sleep.

By the next morning everyone, including Red, was ready to consider what had happened and to poke at the mysterious future.

"I wish we knew more about what we are needed for by Them, and about the Beasts that got Locus and Isia," I said.

"They were awfully big!" Red shook his head as though he were remembering that instant when the world caved in on him. "But I couldn't see them well. I heard, and fought back."

"Oh, we *all* heard those *dreadful* unbearable screams night after night! We heard—"

Red interrupted Mr. Green gently. "I didn't mean that sort of sound, Somy." (Somy was a lovely nickname for Mr. Green, and I wondered if I dared call him that but decided not.) "It was different. Just before the house fell. Like a—a ripping and a tearing, I guess."

"Like claws ripping at something?" I put in.

"Y-e-s, yes. Like claws."

I hadn't mentioned even to Exi the great paw with extended claws that I was sure I'd seen the night of destruction and disappearance. Now I described it as best I could, shivering slightly at the memory. Silence followed my telling, as if it was too awful to absorb. I went on to give them a vivid picture of my vision (which Exi had recounted only briefly). They seemed stunned and depressed by the picture I drew. The day seemed darker.

"How can we *possibly* confront such monsters and *live?*" Mr. Green was in a flurry of distress. "How *can* we? Certainly *I* am as desirous as *anyone* of rescuing our friends, but you *must* see it seems rather *hopeless!* Does it not?"

"And," said Carabus, "we don't even know if we are on the right road."

Exi replied soberly to our fears and doubts. "It is not," he said, "a question of whether we can. We must. Nor is it only rescuing our friends. Never forget that obviously there is something we must do for Them that They cannot do. And I feel very certain it has to do with the monsters, as you call them, Mr. Green." When we would have interrupted, he silenced us with a raised wing, and continued. "We came together in the room of rising waters. Did not each one feel he was led there?" We nodded. "And Grandmother and her helpers served us food there?" Again we nodded. "Also Grandmother came to Maris and to me before we all met." Everyone registered surprise at that, including me, because I hadn't realized how important it was. "Finally, Maris was given the Mantid's Mirror, and I trust its vision. Now, are there any further questions?"

Of course there were none. But for the remainder of the day and during the third night, although the river was as gentle as ever, time had a thin edge of restlessness. In the morning both Exi and I were of the opinion that we must take stock and prepare, even if we didn't know for what. Whatever it was, we must be ready. There was no disagreement on this.

So, at a particularly lovely beach of golden sand, where the river made a wide bend, I urged the boat ashore with the aid of my paddle and we went about the business of preparing for the unknown. Red and I stayed with the beached *Starflower*, going over every inch of the craft carefully, tightening ropes, examining seams, and finding her wonderfully intact. Meanwhile the other three went off to forage for food. What they brought back—an assortment of legumes and greens not too different from our usual fare—I sorted and stored away in the *Starflower*. After a couple of hours, the mound of supplies had reached its limit. Any more would make the *Starflower* unwieldy. When finally we pushed off from the sheltered shore, each of us sensed that this was a final stage of the river journey.

Sitting in my compartment, my paddle resting on my knees, my bare feet stretched out, I contemplated the passing landscape with part of myself while another self was concerned with other matters. Engrossed in my thoughts which twisted as the river twisted, I was startled to hear Red speak.

"Has anyone else noticed?" he was saying.

"Noticed what, Red?" Carabus asked.

"That it's changing. Out there, I mean." Red motioned towards the farther shore.

"Yes," said Exi, "I too have been watching. There are differences."

"And *I* have been aware, and have been *testing* my awareness" —Mr. Green sounded portentous—"and I have *learned* that the river is slower, wider, and yellower."

"Yellower?" Exi asked.

"Yes. *Much* yellower."

I brought my attention to focus on the immediate surroundings. The *Starflower* was certainly moving more slowly, and on a waterway that had spread out and had become not so much yellow as sand-colored. There was no doubt, too, that the landscape had altered and was altering. Trees were larger and more lush in foliage. Many more heavy-leafed vines festooned the trees. The earth floor of the forest was increasingly crowded with giant ferns and tall grass.

"But it isn't a forest! It's a jungle!" I burst out.

"Does it resemble what you—saw in the vision?" asked Mr. Green.

I considered carefully before answering. "Well—not quite. But it's awfully close, I'm afraid."

For a while longer we watched intently, letting our craft creep ahead with the sluggish current, seeing the river grow wide enough to contain an occasional small island. After I had seen a few enormous plants, too much like those in my vision to be ignored, I said that I thought we had better stop soon.

The whole company knew this was the same as saying, "I think we are nearing the danger. We had better get prepared." Tension and vigilance increased, and Exi spoke for all when he suggested that maybe, if the right-sized island were to come into view soon, we could stop there. The next one we passed was rejected because it was too big, but the second one appealed to Exi and, with me wielding my paddle, the *Starflower* circled the island warily. It was almost circular, with a steep bank on the side nearer the shore and a sloping beach on the midstream side. It was wooded, but not so thickly as the mainland. It seemed sheltered but not suffocating. In our short trip around it, there was no sign of any inhabitant. Reassured but unwilling to take chances at this point, I moved the *Starflower* beachward very slowly, and even when it was in shallow water I asked that we stay still for at least fifteen minutes. Nothing stirred on the island. Finally we decided it was safe to go ashore.

After the *Starflower* was unloaded, we pulled her across the beach and into the woods. We turned her upside down to dry, covering her with leaves and grasses to hide her whiteness. Supplies were concealed in a grass-lined hole that we dug. Then we set about exploring the island. It was quite a presentable island, we discovered. A stand of large trees, broad-leaved and broad-based, almost completely ringed the perimeter and covered much of the interior. There was, however, one good-sized clearing nearer the steep side, filled with tall ferns, flowers, and grasses, but with no trees. It was in this place we decided to settle for the night.

When Exi suggested that, rather than having one large shelter, it might be wise for each one to have a separate sleeping place, we all agreed. Before long, five odd and very individual tents were arranged around the clearing. Exi, Carabus, and Mr. Green each dug a shallow depression fitted to his own size, and pulled long grasses down into roofs above the depressions. Exi's roof was meticulously measured and carefully woven, Mr. Green's ornate, Carabus's very plain and sparse. Red made his shelter by tying together the tops of about a dozen flowers, so that when he crawled into it to test it he became a gnome under an arch of yellow daisies. It took me longer to make my shelter because there was more of me to cover, but I found a cluster of ferns sturdier and taller than the grasses or flowers and was able to bend them toward one another sufficiently to fasten them together with grass into an envelope of fronds. Inside this envelope I laid a bed of leaves. Our food we decided to leave where it was concealed, only removing what was needed.

When all was prepared, I said that I felt I had to go to the river and look. I had no rational reason for it. But there it was, a demand from my innermost being.

"I know," replied Exi, "I know. But please, Maris, do not stay long and worry us. It will be dark soon."

I went quickly through the undergrowth and on into the great trees, slowing my footsteps only when I could hear the river's slosh and hiss against the steep side of the island. Very cautiously I proceeded to where, concealed behind a leafy screen of branches, I could peer across the water and see the land beyond. I didn't expect much to be revealed. Perhaps I needed just this chance to turn the mystery over in my mind, as one would hold some unknown plant or stone, turning it over and over in the hope that it might make itself known. One fact was verified at least. There were many of the huge archaic plant fronds growing among the other trees; and these plants were certainly the plants of my vision.

So somewhere over there, across the ugly water and far into the monstrous forest, were Locus and Isia. And the boy. And the fearsome Beasts. Somehow I, with four small unimpressive companions and no weapons, must find the way to those who waited.

As I was turning away from the river to go back to camp, I saw that a mist was rising from the river. Even as I watched, it obscured the farther shore. Hastily I started back. Fog closed around me, deepening the twilight and damping the usual noises of my footsteps. It was a fearful period of fighting to hold off panic. I kept telling myself that the island was not big, that I couldn't be utterly lost, that I mustn't hurry. But when at last I heard familiar voices and saw my friends, I could hardly keep from crying.

Without a word, I slid into my tent to warm myself and to eat a belated meal. The others stood around quietly waiting. I knew they wanted information, and finally I was able to tell them what little I could. "So you see," I concluded, "I didn't really see anything. Not that would help us, I mean. And I haven't the slightest notion of what we should do next."

On this note of indecision we climbed into, or under, our tents. If it hadn't been such a not-knowing time, I could have been amused at the picture we made. Sleep, however, although I was very weary and warm and my stomach was filled, had never been further away.

What to do? To have come this far—and it *was* far!—and to be at an impasse. How did you learn how to get to a place you had never been when there were neither maps nor guides to help? Whom could you ask? Shortly before daybreak I drifted into a restless, anxious half-sleep in which irascible crabs scuttled about in murky water among black rocks, and one particularly angry crab kept poking his head out, snapping his pincers, and growling, "Why not? Why not? Why not?"

I was awakened by Red standing near my shelter and saying softly, "Why not what?"

"What?" I said, feeling confused.

"That's what I asked, Maris. Why not what? You've been muttering 'Why not? Why not?' And I just wanted to know why not what."

I wanted to laugh because it all sounded so absurd. "I don't really know, Red. I guess I was dreaming. I'm sorry I disturbed you."

"Oh, you didn't at all, Maris. And anyway, it's morning."

"So it is!" I realized light was flooding the clearing, and I asked where the fog had gone.

"It just sort of—went off, I guess you could say—awhile back. Just sort of went off."

Then I did laugh aloud, seeing what my dream was meaning. "Why not!" I said. "Oh, Red, why not just go off! I mean that we don't have to wait to be told or advised. We never have before, really. We've been helped *after* we've acted. Every time! After we've gone ahead. Not before."

The others had gathered around, listening to my excitement in evident perplexity. "It seems to me," said Mr. Green, speaking more or less for everyone, "that would be a *most* foolish, not to say *foolhardy*, manner of proceeding! There are times, Maris, when I do *not* understand you!"

"I know. I know what you mean. And I don't blame you at all, because I don't understand myself! It just popped out, what I said. And it doesn't make sense. And couldn't possibly be right. We can't just go, not without knowing more than we do. And yet we can't know more than we do without going!"

Both statements seemed so incontrovertible that no one could think of any more words. For a considerable time we were silent, while I brought food and we all munched thoughtfully.

"Well," I said at last, "I'm willing to compromise. I can row myself and one of you across to the other side and we can look closer. I'm not sure it will prove anything. We can try, though."

11

IT WAS A SPARKLING RIVER THAT GREETED US AS WE HAULED THE empty *Starflower* to the beach—a lovely, golden river. Together we had decided, after a long discussion, that Red should accompany me. He, of course, was eager to be chosen, and I was eager to have his perceptive, agile companionship. I told him so. I had to admit to some worry about his health; yet he assured me that he was quite recovered.

With Red sitting on one side and me opposite him, I paddled the *Starflower* into the current and let it drift slowly downstream from our island, all the while guiding it in an oblique line toward the mainland. This maneuver gave us time to watch carefully and yet, if enemies were watching us, to make our approach so devious as to be almost unnoticeable. The nearer we came the more awesome the land appeared. Towering giants of trees made the forest where we had been before seem small and unimpressive. Everything was unbelievably magnified. Enormous ferns, palmlike plants, sword-bladed grasses, crowded in under the tree shadows, jostling for space. Vines and roots twisted through every opening until the forest-jungle seemed a vast and unmoving octopus of vegetation.

"It's awful, isn't it, Red!" I exclaimed, unable to keep my anxiety to myself.

"Yes, Maris, there's a lot of it sure enough. I don't see how anyone lives there. If they do."

I wanted to say I knew the Beasts lived there, but it seemed so impossible that I kept silent. We moved ever closer to the shore, inching through the yellow water, which lost its sparkle and grew thicker, heavier, as we approached the land. The whole venture took on an aura of utter hopelessness, and I was about to suggest turning back, when we simultaneously exclaimed, "There's an opening!" We had seen a fairly wide swath into the jungle, twisting away into the tangled growth. I headed the *Starflower* toward this place. Later on we wondered what impelled us to such a risky action, but at the time neither of us considered any other possibility.

No living creature was visible except ourselves. Very cautiously I paddled into shallow water, then, barefoot, stood looking along the trail—if it was a trail—to where it twisted leftward into the jungle. I suggested that we should explore.

"No," replied Red, more authoritative than I'd ever heard him. "I'm sorry, but one of us has to stay here, with the boat. That's only sensible, don't you see, Maris? And as you are the—the motor, I guess you could say—and I'm smaller, and faster, you'd best stay here and I'll look around a bit."

I wanted to argue but I saw how right he was. Watching him go from me lightfooted, quick, I wanted to rush after him and walk with him. He looked so small, with even the grass towering above him. I also had to admit that my own lonely fear was hard to endure and that it, too, made me want to run to Red's side.

Red was considerate, however, never going out of my sight. When he came to the turn that would have taken him beyond, he stopped. He stood for a long time peering into the distant jungle. Then he climbed one of the giant ferns and, balancing lightly on its curled tip some fifteen feet or more above ground, again peered for a long time into the dark tangle beyond. On the way back to me and the *Starflower* he paused often, examining the earth of the path and the plants bordering it.

Because I had been unable to guess whether he had seen anything much on his tour, I was trembling with impatience when at last he came back. "Did you see anything? Or anybody? Will it be possible for us to go? How big is it? Red, *do* tell me what you've seen! Please!"

"Oh, Maris, you shouldn't be so hurried. It never gets to where it wants. First I'd enjoy a bit of food. Then I'll tell you what I can. And show you some things."

I got food from the boat and we ate in silence.

"Well," he said, after swallowing his last bite, "there wasn't a lot, to tell the truth. Nobody along the way. From the top of that big plant I could see quite a stretch, and away off, quite far, I almost thought I saw a sort of tree house. I'm not sure. But I wanted to tell you everything." I asked how far off he thought the tree house might be. "I should guess at least half a day's walk. Looks to be some higher ground that way, too." I asked what else he knew.

"Only two other things. I found a lot of these caught in grasses along the path." He held out to me a long yellow hair, and I knew, as I took it, that it would prove to be a hair of one of the terrible Beasts. And, for the final information, Red led me to the beach where the path ended, and pointed out, in a patch of sand back from the water's edge, the print of an enormous paw.

"Oh, Red, it all seems sort of hopeless, doesn't it!" I said.

"Maybe not hopeless—but it will take a lot of doing, you might say."

The return was harder and slower than the coming had been, for the *Starflower* had to be pushed against the current. I was glad because it didn't give me much time to mess about in my mind. I beached the *Starflower* just as the mists began to come, and by the time Red and I and our friends had hidden the boat and reached camp, the fog had enclosed us once more.

Red immediately climbed into his nest for a nap under his flowers. I told Exi, Carabus, and Mr. Green of Red's explorations, and also shared my discouragement. After much talk, we decided that we should probably do our traveling overland only by day. Also we decided that we'd better practice doing it quietly.

The next day was one of hard work. For hour after hour we practiced ways of going through the forest so as not to be seen or heard. Finding an especially dense part of the island, we took turns trying to cover a prescribed course without being detected. Four would act as enemy, and one would attempt the task. In the beginning Red was far superior, sneaking his delicate self so silently and invisibly through the tangle that he was upon us before we were ready. I was the worst, being the largest. At the end of my first few trials I was bruised, scratched, dirty, and almost at the point of tears. It was Mr. Green saying, after two very poor show-ings of his own and a third wherein he improved markedly, "It's the sideways going! That makes a difference!" that gave me a new approach. On the next attempt I tried to be as still as possible inside me and to let each new piece of snarled woodland show me its unique pattern. From then on I squirmed under logs, wiggled through tall grasses, went slim and sideways between close trees. It became exciting to discover all these variations and to vary my reactions to them. I began to increase my skill.

Baths or foot soakings in the river and the smell and taste of food combined eventually to diminish the day's frustrations. When we drew closer together in our small circle we felt more equal to what lay ahead.

We would leave with the earliest light, paddling the *Starflower* to the beach with all our remaining stores aboard. Red and Mr. Green felt the boat should be anchored offshore, while the other three saw more advantages in beaching and hiding it. Both ideas had flaws, so we decided to choose whichever seemed better when the moment came. The problem of how we could make our way through the jungle singly and silently, yet keeping in touch with each other as we went, was most perplexing. The final decision was that Red and I were to take the left side of the trail we had discovered, and the others the right side, keeping off it but near enough to see it from the jungle cover, and going separately but close enough to call if necessary.

I was awakened next morning by Exi after what seemed only a few minutes of sleep. I began to protest, then saw that the first very thin light was searching into the fog.

We went deliberately about our various tasks, very serious and with few words. By the time the mist had gone, we had eaten, gotten our cache of food, carried the *Starflower* to the shore, tested her, and loaded her.

"It was a nice island," Red said wistfully as we pulled away. "Is," muttered Carabus. "Is! Not was! May be back, you know."

The voyage across the river was uneventful, much the same as when Red and I had crossed. The land of the Beasts, as the boat drew nearer, appeared ominous and colossal. Living trees and fallen trees, ferns, vines, roots, grasses, were everywhere.

"There's the opening," said Red, pointing.

"Yes," I replied. "And I guess you and Mr. Green had the right plan. We'd best anchor the *Starflower* out in the stream. Even if we managed to hide it in that jungle, we'd never be able to get it fast. This way I can take all of you and the food ashore, paddle out again just out of sight, anchor it, then swim ashore."

"But you'll get wet," protested Carabus.

"I'd rather be wet and feel the *Starflower* was safer from them!"

"I agree," said Exi, "and I took an opposite position to start with. So—do you see anything, Red?"

"No, sir. Not a stir."

"Very well then. We had better get on with our work."

The beaching and unloading was done quickly. I paddled out into the river again, and when I could no longer see the trail's opening, I anchored the *Starflower* offshore. I put the gift of the Mantid between my teeth and lowered myself into the water. The swim back to the beach was not difficult in the slow, almost tepid river. And there we were, eager to be off.

"Shall we start?" Exi said.

I stepped quickly off the trail to my left, into the jungle labyrinth. Suddenly I was alone, completely alone in the dark tangle.

It was worse by far than the invisible nothingness Exi and I had experienced in the marble chamber. Nothingness seemed preferable to this snarl. Here in the shadowed interior of the jungle, droplets of wet stood on every vertical surface, dripped from unseen levels overhead, oozed down trunks and blades and stalks. Enormous trunks were brown basaltic columns around which coiled unmoving serpents of slimy green vines and aerial roots. The giant ferns were fearsome creatures from another world. Underfoot was moss, cold, green, and so thick that at every step I felt water seep into my shoes.

There were, however, certain advantages in the wetness. Leaves, vines, branches, being less brittle, did not rustle if by accident I brushed one too hard as I worked my way forward, and my feet made no noise except an occasional squish. At any rate I kept going along, twisting, turning sideways, over and under, trying to remember what I had learned. From time to time I moved to the right a few yards to be certain I was paralleling the trail. Once I was panicked at losing it, but some distance on found it again.

The hours inched forward. I began to feel numb, hardly aware of coldness, fatigue, hunger. I might have gone on endlessly except that I was brought to a halt by the sound of my name being whispered, and then I saw Red's gnome face peeking cautiously from around a tree.

"Sorry, Maris," he whispered, "but I guess sometimes you have to go against orders. Leastways I've done it! My idea is that you need to eat and rest and get warm. You look done in. Now I've found a fine hollow tree, and you just come along."

Following him without question, I was soon bending double to crawl into a dark, pungent cave at the base of one of the largest trees I'd yet seen. I sank down onto the earth and found it soft and dry. Gratefully I rested. Red stood at the entrance, saying nothing. He waited until I had eaten some of my packet of food and until he saw I was drying out a bit and getting drowsy.

"No, Maris," he said. "You mustn't sleep, you know. We must go on soon. But I'll stay in view, if you don't mind."

Rest and food had helped. And the going on was much less of a strain now that Red was my guide. All of my effort could go into the creeping, crawling, climbing, slithering and dodging in which we were engaged, while I let Red carry the burden of keeping us on the right way. He was always there, just ahead, almost out of sight but never entirely so. Occasionally he stopped as if listening, his antennae moving back and forth deliberately, then went on. For a long time we continued in this fashion, until again I felt myself succumbing to the hypnotic spell of the jungle.

Suddenly I realized that Red had stopped and was standing very still. So I stopped. Neither movement nor sound was there, and yet— At Red's gesture I went forward to where he was. The jungle floor ahead was markedly steep, and at the end of a rise of about a hundred yards or so it looked as if it either terminated or fell away. With exceeding caution we crept forward, tree by tree, using all our skill not to make a sound. We finally reached the top and, when we peered from a thick fern cluster, I knew that here was the goal.

The land did fall away sharply. Below us lay a dry valley. Around its perimeter the trees and ferns were few and well spaced, obviously with intent, while in the valley's center there was no

growth at all. Or rather, there remained only four gigantic trees, at
the four corners of a quadrangle. Between these living supports,
high fences of sharp jungle trunks had been built, while in one
tree, thirty to forty feet above ground, was a house of some sort,
entirely enclosed. To the right of where Red and I were hidden we
could see the trail sweeping around and downward to the quadrangle, to end in front of what appeared to be a double portal,
now shut.

"This is it, Red!" Unable to contain entirely my excitement, I
had to whisper to Red, who nodded but did not reply. He began
to work his way, in silence, sideways along the crest, motioning
me to come. Soon we were at the edge of the trail where it slid
over the lip of the hill into the valley. I was overjoyed to see, across
the trail, three beetle heads poking from the jungle, and one by
one they scuttled over the space to join us.

No one seemed to know what to do next. We had to get into
the valley, into the quadrangle and back again with three more
persons. It was utterly impossible! Between where we now stood
and the gates there were very few hiding places. Near the quadrangle there were none at all. And even if we did reach the gates, what
then? I was shaken with a wild urge to run headlong down the trail
and pound at the portals, to shatter the ominous silence, waken
the Beasts, demand entrance.

As I struggled against this impulse, there was a sudden scarlet
flash, and a familiar voice piped softly, "Don't." It was Hatch,
perched on my shoulder. "Don't, Maris. Plenty to do! Plenty! But
not that! Only foolish, that wish! Rushing feels better, but no help
at all!" He fluffed and settled his feathers.

"How did you know where we were?" I asked.

"Didn't, for sure. Guessed a bit. Found your places. Asked a
few trees. And the Mantid gave a clue."

Exi spoke. "It looks rather difficult, does it not? I am not at
all confident."

"Needn't worry. Maris's job alone, this one. Easy, hard, who
knows? Courage counts. Courage and staying."

"Why me?" I said, my stomach flopping over at Hatch's words.
"Why me alone? We're all in this together, aren't we? Aren't we?"

Hatch left my shoulder for a nearby branch, from which perch he could see all of us.

"Not much time—but listen. Bad things are splitting the country, jungle against forest, mountain against valley. You've seen. You know. They want it changed, but must not do it alone. Our job and Theirs. Each must do what he can. Most need is for some one of the people to pitch in."

"I still don't get it!" I was feeling more and more afraid and about to be abandoned.

"Be still!" Hatch ordered. "It's because you're different from us. And you had the vision. It must be neither Them nor Beasts, if healing is to come."

I still didn't understand, but Hatch was flitting ahead, leading us leftward along the ridge. We worked carefully and silently along the crest, always keeping inside the surrounding jungle, until we reached a spot well away from where we'd started. We were now looking down at one of the side walls of the quadrangle, which was unbroken by any opening. From here the place assumed more than ever the proportions of a medieval fortress, huge, unconquerable.

"Come!" Hatch urged, and darted back into the dense growth. In a few moments we arrived at a circle of smaller trees, unusual in their darker green and their slender pointed leaves.

"Why, they're laurel trees!" I cried. "What are they doing here?"

"Belong to Them," said Hatch. "Very old times. Safe in here. Sacred. Come!"

Entering the grove, I was immediately touched by a softer air, sweet and in some strange way healing. I could tell from the expressions and reactions of my companions that they too were touched by it.

Mr. Green stretched and expanded. "Upon my *word*," he said, "what a *splendid* location! I am reminded of the warm and prodigal woods of my *home country!* How *very* splendid!" Exi gazed at each tree in his methodical way, as if he had never seen a tree before. "Here is peace, I think," he said.

Carabus nodded. Red wiggled about, and I laughed at the absurd happiness on his funny face. We ate and the food seemed new, a banquet of rare dishes. The earth in the sacred grove was a thick carpet of velvet under our tired feet, the sky over us a ceiling of powdery and benign blue. Soon everyone slept, except Hatch and me.

"Now it is yours alone," Hatch said.

"Well, what do I do now?"

"Go."

"Where do I go?"

"Into the valley of the Beasts."

"To the gates?"

"No! Never! The side!"

"But there's no way in."

"Who knows?"

"All right. Maybe there are other ways. I don't want to be stubborn. Or afraid. But how can I tell what way?"

"Go down with courage. Listen! Always listen!"

"Do *you* know the way?"

"No."

"How can I find it then?"

"It's your way, not mine."

"Yes. Yes, I suppose so." I sighed. "And what about the others?"

"Safe here. They'll wait."

"What if they try to come after me?"

"Can't. Come along, now!"

12

I STOOD ALONE AT THE CREST OF THE SLOPE LEADING DOWN TOWARD the side of the enclosure of the Beasts. Hatch had gone. I didn't have any choice except to choose to go. And I had a feeling of being abandoned and abandoning almost to the point of indifference. I started down the hillside.

Once clear of jungle, I walked on a hard, dry ground where nothing grew. A different sky arched over me, a colorless and empty sky. It was cold, brittle, stale air through which I went as I came closer and closer to the wall of spiked grasses which, as I approached it, showed itself to be higher, thicker, more impenetrable than I had imagined. The colorless light and arid earth drained me of feelings, and I moved dispassionately forward until I stood only a few feet from the wall and stared at its blankness. Because I couldn't go any farther, I stopped. I couldn't remember why I was there. For a long time I remained unmoving in the silence. There was some reason for something, but what was it? A hurt? A loss? I turned my head back and forth slowly, trying to remember. Happiness—that was a clue—the sound of happiness—yes, the sound of happiness, small, essential—*Locus!* Of course! With this I was flooded by memories of what I was about. And most important, I was warm again. I shook my fist defiantly at the cold sky, and because my knees were weak, sat down with my back against the fence, considering what to do.

To climb the wall was impossible. To go along the wall would bring me eventually to the front gates. Hatch had warned against this. I could neither fly nor burrow. I had no skill at invisibility.

What must I do, before I was discovered and captured or extermi-
nated? Hatch had said it was my way to find, alone. What else had
he said? To listen. "Always listen!" he had said. I composed myself
as best I could under the circumstances, trying to hush my questions and to open my ears as wide as possible. Silence was absolute.
Had I not earlier seen the signs of Beasts, I would have believed I
was the sole living being in a dead world.

To pass the time, I began inspecting the ground around me. It
was even more barren and arid than it had appeared to be when
I'd been standing up. Every grain of dry dirt, each fragment of
gravel, every minute hollow or bulge, became a unique piece of
dead matter, individually shaped and textured. I hadn't ever realized how many hundreds of thousands of shapes there could be,
nor how all these differences could be spread out, one against another, endlessly, to merge into a desert of sameness. Wherever I
looked, this earth never changed. Or did it, right there, to my left?
Yes, there *was* a faint circular ridge, very narrow, marking out an
area of ground about three inches in diameter. How strange, I
thought, leaning nearer to see it. It looked like something deliberately made. I bent forward for an even closer inspection, and as
I did so I was aware of a delicate humming sound.

Not knowing why I did it, I reached out and tapped with one
finger, very gently, on the middle of the circle. The humming
ceased. I held my breath and waited. The humming began again.
I tapped and the humming stopped. A hair-width crack appeared
at the ridged edge of the circle and slowly grew wider; and finally
I saw a small circular door, hinged on one side, swing back to reveal a dark hole into the earth.

"Well," came a no-nonsense feminine voice, "you might better
enter than to let all this cold in. Come quickly, please!"

"But the hole is much too small!" I said in exasperation.

"Do stop fussing and come in!" The sharp little voice sounded
as if its owner might at any moment slam the door in my face.
Desperately I put my hand down into the hole, and after a sudden
flash of dizziness, I found myself no longer by the Beasts' walled
enclosure but in an utterly other place.

It was a delicate and, yes, gentle was the word—a delicate and
gentle room where I stood. A flight of small steps ascended behind

me into darkness, presumably to the door through which in some mysterious manner I must have come. And all around me yards and yards of silken cloth were festooned in graceful curves over every inch of walls and ceiling, cloth of a fineness such as I'd never before seen, not in the ant kingdom, nor even in my grandmother's cashmere shawl I had so loved as a child.

If this had been all, I could have spent hours enjoying its loveliness. It was not all, however. The focal point of the room was its center where, seated beside a spinning wheel of gleaming white, a befurred, plump black spider, about the size of Exi, stared at me.

"How do you do," I said politely. Although the phrase struck me as being quite meaningless, I couldn't come up with a better one at the moment. The spinner said nothing, so I tried again.

"I am Maris. I don't quite know how I got here, except Hatch said to listen and I did and I heard you—and I'm sorry if I am in your way, and—"

"My goodness," snapped the spider, "you do go on a lot!" She studied me reflectively. "You got here by listening and knocking. And reaching. And because I asked you in. Which of course means that you are not in my way, or I would not have invited you. Time enough to ask other questions at a later hour." She did something to the spinning wheel and it began to hum and turn. "I must finish what I am doing. Do sit down and rest and eat or something! But be quiet!" With that, the spider gave all her attention to the wheel, and the room was filled with the sound of its merry whir and of the spider singing softly to herself.

I sat down and leaned against one gossamer-hung wall and began to munch food pulled from my pocket. The touch of the weightless silk on my neck and cheek was soothing, almost voluptuous. I sat quietly watching the spinner until I fell into a half-doze. When I came fully awake again, the sounds had ceased and the spider was putting away a new spindle of the creamy-rose thread. "Very well, that is done," she said. "Now, then, young woman, we can talk. Come and sit nearer."

I did as I was told, seating myself close to the wheel and the spinner, looking into the spider's face and holding my questions back.

"So you are Maris." The huge, many-faceted eyes were full

upon me and I sensed that they held a bit of drollery mixed with the dignity. "I am Arachne the Spinner. I am also a weaver. When necessary, I am a guardian, too." I opened my mouth to ask what Arachne guarded but caught myself before I said it. "And what are you?" asked Arachne. "Why, I—I'm a girl and—well, I really don't know!" I always seemed to be utterly disconcerted by the strange questions I was asked on the journey.

"You mean you have no tasks?"

"Oh I have *those* all right! Right now I'm trying to find a way to get my friends out of the prison of the Beasts, and, I guess, to do something They need me to do. And I've found paths and made boats and cooked food and invented oars and—"

"Why did you not say you were a journeyer, then?"

"I didn't know it had a name, I guess—"

"My goodness, for such a big girl you are rather muddled!" Arachne shook her head doubtfully. "Now you know, at least. You are a journeyer."

Arachne watched me with unblinking and thoughtful eyes. I jumped when she said, in a matter-of-fact voice, "I believe you may have a chance. You are solider than you appear to be. If you do not make it, at least you will give the Beasts a difficult time!"

"Then you don't like the Beasts?" I asked.

"Like those creatures? I hate them! Cruel, impersonal, cold, they are, caring for nothing but their own comfort, using anyone who comes to satisfy their needs! No softness! No mercy! No vision! Splitting the land!"

"Do they—do they kill everyone?" I asked, while Arachne regained her plump poise after the outburst.

"No, not everyone. They keep a few creatures around to serve them or to amuse them."

With a sense of increasing despair I wanted to ask how the spider knew so much, but Arachne anticipated the question. "You see," she said, "I go into their kingdom sometimes, partly because I bother the creatures by putting my used and imperfect thread in their corners, partly because I keep hoping I will find a way to undo them. That is really why I stay here." She sighed. "Obviously I have not found a way yet, or else they would not still be thundering about above my head."

"What will I be able to do against them?" I asked. "I'm afraid it's no use! It's hopeless!"

"You may be right," Arachne replied calmly. "On the other hand, you may not be right. You may be the one who is needed to do it. At any rate," she went on, beginning to lift things from a storage box nearby, "we are going to try."

"We? I thought I had to do it alone."

"You do. But I, and possibly my friend, Botta, can assist." She was pulling more and more items from her box. "He always listens in when I have guests. If he is at home." She raised her voice and called, "Botta! Do come in if you are there!"

Whereupon there was a flurry of wall hangings, and a large but compact brown figure tumbled out, regained its balance, and grinned at me with an ugly, bucktoothed, friendly face. I took the outsized paw, shook it, and exclaimed, "Why, you're a gopher!"

"I am? You're way off! I'm Botta." He chuckled.

"Stop it, Botta!" Arachne ordered. "This is no time for foolishness!"

"Yes ma'am," he said, folding his forepaws on his chest ostentatiously.

"Were you listening?"

"Of course."

"What do you want to do, then?"

"I'll join up. Sure."

"I thought you would." By now Arachne had a large heap beside the box, but seemed unsatisfied. Once again she reached in, lifting a small packet triumphantly. "I knew it must be in here!"

"The net?" Botta asked.

"What else could I mean?"

"You've waited a long time to try it out."

"Yes."

I was beginning to be rather edgy at being treated as an expendable piece in a checker game. "And where do I come in?" I said. "I've got to do the work! I ought to be consulted!"

"Do be quiet, and eat some more! You will come in, and we are *all* going to work, but since you have no idea of what is necessary and we do, please for goodness sake let us make plans!" In a less abrupt tone, she went on, "You see, my dear young woman, we want to help you if we can, Botta and I. We have been preparing to help some one—and it seems to be you—for a great length of time now. You must have gathered that already. This"—and she held up the tiny package—"is a net I have made of the finest, strongest silk I have, with my best skill. It will hold the heaviest weights and will prove useful in several ways, I hope. Botta, although he may look a dunce, and often acts one, is a serious digger, and conscientious too. He has done remarkable things to his residence, which adjoins mine, and because of his hard work you can get into the Beasts' Kingdom. Whether you can get out again remains to be seen. Now—can you trust us enough to let us plan?"

I said I could, and that I was sorry for sounding impatient, and then I asked if they knew who the prisoners were. I held my breath. Arachne looked at Botta. Botta looked at Arachne.

"Answer her, Botta! You were there last!"

"Yup. I was. There's five or six, maybe—I don't know. Very odd lot they are, for sure. A sad little mousy thing with big eyes, kept in a cage with a bird who won't sing. A woolly fellow, brownish, curls up sometimes near the cage when they aren't using him for a cushion. I think they've got Toad, too—can't see what they'd want him for. Maybe to toady to them." Botta chuckled to himself. "Then a young boy. Good to look at, he was. Does all the rough chores. Gets thinner every day. Maybe more. I don't know."

At least Isia and Locus were alive. And the boy with the pleading face, he was there. I found my fear grew less as the awareness of need for my courage increased. I *had* to save them! I had to!

It seemed to me an unbearable wait before the others finished their conferring. I didn't even try to listen; I was impatient and willing to do whatever they suggested, the sooner the better. When Arachne said they were ready, I jumped to my feet. "Take this," Arachne commanded. She handed me a slender stick with an egg-shaped container hanging from its tip.

Botta lifted up the draped silken coverings on one wall, pushed open a door, bowed roguishly, and waved us through. At first the darkness stopped me, but very soon my eyes accommodated to the new surroundings. I found that the tiny container on my stick was a lantern holding a fat glowworm, giving more light than one would have thought. We were in a tunnel, not wide, but high enough so I hardly had to bend. The farther we went the more thankful I was for the work Botta had done in making this passage. I followed his waddling figure with great respect, holding the lantern to give as much light as I could to both these remarkable helpers—Botta ahead of me and Arachne behind, carrying the precious net. Spaced irregularly along the tunnel ceiling were vertical shafts leading to the surface. When I paused and peered up the first one, startled to see a slice of sky, Botta said, "Air, light. Come on, time's short."

At a sudden turn in the otherwise quite straight passage, he turned to me. "You won't like what comes next," he announced bluntly. "Can't help it! I've never got used to it myself." With no further explanation he disappeared around the bend.

Arachne prodded me from behind; so I followed Botta, trying to anticipate what lay ahead. I was totally unprepared, however, for the horrid sight confronting me. We stood before an enormous refuse pit. A ragged hole, obviously where refuse was dumped in, gaped open to the sky over a conical heap. The smell of the place was sickening. Botta immediately started to pick his way along the extreme edge of the stinking pile, staying as close as he could to the wall out of sight of the open hole. He motioned for us to do the same.

I held my breath, trying not to look any farther than my feet while I hurried after the gopher. Even so I couldn't avoid taking in some of the foul air, nor could I avoid seeing, embedded in the mess, bones and skulls of large and small creatures in addition to broken implements of unknown kinds.

"Nasty, isn't it?" Botta said, scratching his feet in the ground to clean them.

We went on. After a distance of level going, the slope of the tunnel began to rise very gradually. At last we reached a spot where the passage widened into a small room and ended abruptly.

"Here we are." Botta peered up a shaft. "Get ready," he said.

"For what?" I asked.

"You'll see."

At that instant a familiar screaming roar shattered the silent tunnel room. While it still echoed down the passage, another came, and another, and others, until all space was filled with the demonic sound. The ground above the tunnel shook, and bits of dirt fell as if dislodged by the weight of heavy bodies. There was no mistaking the voices. They belonged to the Beasts. A last flurry of dirt fell as the roars died away.

"Now, quickly!" Botta ordered. "Not much time!"

Everything happened at once. Arachne was up the wall, had unfurled and lowered an almost invisible silken net, Botta had climbed it and, with his hind legs holding on to this ingenious ladder, had begun to dig furiously, widening the slender shaft. I hugged the wall and covered my face from the rain of dirt spewing from his powerful forepaws. He was so skillful and fast that I was unprepared when he said sharply, "Now you, girl! Hurry!" And I was up the ladder and through the hole and standing in the enclosure of the Beasts before I knew what had happened. There was no time to look around, for Botta had started ahead at a trot while Arachne closed in behind. Between them they rushed me, stumbling and clutching the lantern, across a wide darkness until we stood beside a massive column thrust upward into the night sky. Panting, disheveled, trying to collect my senses, I nonetheless recognized that the column was in fact one of the great trees I'd seen from outside the enclosure. Arachne disappeared up the trunk into the dark. Soon I felt the brush of something against my face, and Botta had snatched the lantern and was saying, "Up you go! Quick!"

As I began climbing the net ladder, I heard Botta call, "See you later. I hope." On that note of questionable encouragement, I ascended into the unknown. I knew I had reached the top when Arachne's voice sounded beside me. "Take care. Just above you is the way in. All you have to do is push it up and enter."

"Why," I asked, clinging to the frail net, "why can't the prisoners leave, then, if I can get in so easily? Why can't we get them right this very minute down our ladder and escape!"

"It is not possible. You have to get all of the prisoners ready, and there is no time! Already they are returning from the river. Listen!"

It was true. I could hear in the distance, and moving nearer, assorted growls, roars, throaty noises, and could feel rather than hear the weight of many feet on the ground. The vocalizing increased in intensity and volume.

"What do I do?"

"Pay attention, now." Arachne spoke rapidly, urgently. "I must be gone at once. You go in. Hide yourself wherever and however you can, and soon; although the Beasts are not usually concerned with their captives until day. Do not think they are stupid, however, for they are not! Try to work out a plan after you know more. I will send a small relative of mine soon, and she can bring messages to me. Botta and I will come whenever you are ready." The noise had swelled to a peak of cacophony. Arachne's final words were shouted. "Quickly! Inside you go! Courage! That's what's needed."

I felt overhead with trembling hands, encountered a flat surface, pushed, and lifted myself through a trap door which closed with an ominous snap behind me. Well, here I am, I thought, at the end of my journeying. At least this part of it. I wondered if it would be the end of me as well.

13

It was black as the interior of a box. As a matter of fact, it *was* the interior of a box, an oversized box for prisoners—of which I was now one, I thought grimly, standing very still until I could see something, or otherwise get oriented. I wished Botta hadn't taken the glowworm lantern back in those final frantic moments. But he had.

Soft rustles began to be audible. Gradually I could make out a square of lighter darkness somewhat higher than my eyes, and in it a star twinkled impersonally. A window! This gave me a disproportionate sense of freedom and relief. The rustling continued. Still I couldn't see anything definite, although I began to imagine shapes, vague blobs emerging here and there; and I wanted desperately to speak out, but this impulse I restrained, fearful lest I make a wrong move. I waited, heart pounding so loud I was sure the room was pulsing with it.

"Who is it?" A flat whisper shattered the silence with an unexpectedness which made me jump. "Who is it?"

"A friend." This sounded stilted and foolish to me, and I added, "Maris. I've come to help, if I can."

"Then it wasn't just a stupid dream!" The voice was very near and, though still a half-whisper, had in it a surprised sort of gladness. Now I could just make out a figure standing in front of me, a slender shadowy figure somewhat taller than I. "It wasn't a dream! It was a truth!" Strong fingers gripped my shoulder briefly, as if to welcome and reassure me. The voice continued, no longer in a whisper but softly, low-pitched, definitely a boy's

voice. "They'll check on us soon. Somehow we've got to hide
you until then. Later we'll have time. In the middle of the night
while they're—well, busy." I could hear his quiet breathing.
Then he began talking to himself rather than to me. "Such a
bare room. I don't know—yes—maybe it might work."

His hand on my arm, he guided me a few paces forward,
then to the left. Several forms were distinguishable, but I didn't
ask about them then or try to recognize them. Obviously the
situation was too urgent.

"See if you can get in this," the voice said. Hands guided my
hands down until they touched what felt to be a large wicker
receptacle. "The basket they lower us in. I don't think they'll
look in it. They never have. So if you fit . . ."

Getting myself into the basket would have been hard enough
by day. In this blackness, with only touch to help me, I was about
to give up in despair when I remembered Isia's favorite position,
and managed somehow to curl myself into an awkward circle.
A cover closed over me, leaving me miserably uncomfortable.

Actually it wasn't long—though it was a tortured forever to me
—before noises from below and outside increased, penetrating
even into the stuffy hole where I lay. There were roars, shrieks,
snarling laughter, rude growls, a babble of hideousness from many
throats.

"Quiet!" roared a bullying and harsh voice which rose above
the rest. "Fools! Swine! You, dunce of a guard, up the tree! Up,
I say! Or I'll rip you apart myself! With pleasure!" Something
crashed against the prison room. "Hurry, stupid fool! I am
hungry!"

The room shook, as a suspension bridge shakes when someone crosses it. I heard the trap door open. A new voice, less
commanding but equally harsh, snarled, "Slaves, are you enjoying life?" Loud humorless laughter. "You! On your knees!"

"Yes, sir," came the boy's voice wearily.

"All the refuse present?"

"Yes, sir. Locus in the cage, Isia chained to it, Toad in his
cage, Parula in the corner, and I. All here."

"So you are! A stupid lot!" Again the chilling laughter. "Well,
get some rest! Lots of work tomorrow. Corpses and feasts, corpses

and feasts! Maybe that yellow rag for dessert, if it doesn't sing!"
The trap door banged shut, the room trembled, and the renewed
roaring from below gradually faded into the distance.

I lay in cramped, horrified paralysis. When the basket lid
was lifted, I couldn't move until strong hands helped me. Stag-
gering to my feet, I was weak and shaking and altogether unnerved. Coming at the end of a long, long day, this last trial was
almost too much.

"Sit down," said the voice. "It hits everyone this way at
first. You get used to it. A little bit, anyway." Gratefully I sank
to the floor and stretched out my aching legs. "I'm going to make
a light. This is a special occasion!" He sounded cheerful again.
A rasp of metal against stone, a spark, a minute spurt of fire,
and suddenly the flame from a stubby candle startled the gloom,
wavered uncertainly, caught hold in a steady ivory-yellow glow.
And there we all were, watched by our own gigantic shadows.

It was, as the boy had said, a bare room. No chairs. No beds.
No floor coverings. Neither table nor cupboard. Only gradually
did I permit my gaze to go from the barren walls downward.
Against one wall were two ugly rusted cages, each about three
feet square. In one of them was Locus, huddled forlornly in the
corner.

"Oh, Locus!" I cried, going to the cage and taking the tiny
paw which was pushed between the bars as soon as Locus spied
me. "We'll get you free! We must!"

"Me, too?" queried a solemn voice. I turned to the second
cage and looked into the face of a large toad. Ribs showed
through his gray-green knobbled sides. His protruding eyes were
sad. "Yes, you too," I replied. Then, in the gloom of the corner
behind Locus's cage, I saw a rounded woolly pillow. "Isia!" The
pillow slowly straightened out, with a metallic clanking of a
chain fastening it to the cage. "Isia! You poor dear!"

"Well, Maris," he said weakly but with a bit of his old whim-
sicality, "I have missed you. Even in these luxurious surroundings.
Rather like the last place we were together, don't you think?
Tree tops, rock-a-bye, Beasts below, and all that sort of thing.
At least now I stay awake better. And I'm an accomplished foot-
stool. My fierce faces amuse them, so they let me stay near Locus.

And Maris," he added seriously, "I *have* watched over her as best I could."

"Isia," I said, stroking his head, "you were braver than brave! I know you've watched over her. And we will get away! We can't have come this far and not be able to free ourselves!" In my heart I knew this wasn't necessarily true. It was a comfort to say it, though.

I stood and faced the boy, this stranger I'd known since the Mantid's vision. I could not have said then what he was like, although later I realized I had absorbed his physical appearance quite fully, from his dark head with its ragged hair and its well-shaped and ever-so-slightly pointed ears, to his unshod and dirty feet. I saw, without knowing, his unkempt tattered clothes, his pallor, and his strong-boned but gaunt body. At first, in this strangeness, all I was really aware of was his face. In his face were wonderful dark luminous eyes, and a mouth strong and unsmiling but capable of much feeling.

It was he who broke the silence when he remembered that his upturned, cupped hands were not empty. He stepped nearer, holding his hands for me to see. In the bowl of his curved fingers lay a bird, a small yellow bird, feathers bedraggled, eyes closed. "This," he said, "is Parula. I'm sure she's ill but I'm not sure what to do. Can you help?"

I put out my hands and the almost weightless little bird was transferred to my care. Not that I knew what to do, either. Such a pitiful bit of bird! What did it need? Warmth—warmth can heal! Of course it can, I said to myself, folding the fragile body within one hand, loosely and gently, and then tucking hand and bird inside my jacket.

"I'd better blow out the candle," said the boy. "It's growing short. Then we can talk."

We sat on the bare floor, near each other but not touching, while his low voice told me of many things. I put questions occasionally, but for the most part was contented to listen, and to fondle Parula when I felt the tiny bird stir in my hand. He began not with himself but with a brief account of an ordinary day in the kingdom of the Beasts. Usually, he said, the prisoners were left alone during the night hours, after the routine check.

The guards remained below. The Beasts always went to the river in early evening, to drink and to watch for prey; that was the only time all the Beasts were gone. Sometimes many of them spent all night roaming, searching, roaring. Sometimes, as tonight, they returned and then most of them took off on what was evidently a major hunting expedition, from which they always returned bloody, laden with food, and particularly demanding. The days from dawn to dusk were endless labor, varied according to the size of the prisoner and according to what the Beasts, in their greed, wanted.

"Don't they ever sleep?" I wanted to know.

Yes, they slept, but only intermittently. And not all of them at once. So there was always work to do for someone. Often several Beasts would shout at the same moment, an impossible and horrible situation. Poor Toad, some of whose family had been killed by the Beasts, was used for exercise; and with five or six of the great things shrieking at him to jump so they could catch him—"Higher! Higher, idiot!" they would roar—he was failing rapidly. Probably could not last too long now, unless . . .

"What do they do when—when a prisoner—"

"Destroy," he said. I remembered the refuse pit and shuddered.

Their continual harassing of Parula to get her to sing— which she couldn't do unless she was happy—had driven her to collapse, he told me. As for Isia, thus far he had managed to keep going primarily because the king used him as a royal footstool.

"And Locus?"

Well, Locus appeared to be rather special. He could not be more definite. But they treated her far less roughly, made no demands, except that the king seemed to like her near him, was quieter when she was, in fact. They even offered her their choicest dishes (if anything they ate could be called choice). He suspected that they first took her from us because they had hoped she would give them something, though it was most unclear what.

Then I told him briefly about Them, and the others, and me. When I asked him about himself, he fell into sudden shyness, and only by prodding him was I able to get a few facts. If he had to have a name, he guessed it was Jetsam. He couldn't say why it was Jetsam, for he had almost no memories of his child-hood—that is, his early childhood. As a little boy he had roamed the forests—oh, quite a great distance from here—living as a free wanderer, learning the streams, plants, trees, animals. He remembered vaguely somewhere a tall dark man who had carried him. He had been with the Beasts for a very long time—several years, he guessed—having been captured in a sudden attack one night when he had gone exploring far from his usual haunts. Since then he had been their servant, guarded fiercely every moment he was not in this room. What did he do? Oh, built and rebuilt fences, swept the enclosure daily, disposed of refuse, and whatever else they ordered. Yes, he had seen many other prisoners come and go. None had ever escaped. Not that he knew of. There never seemed to be much reason to hope for escape.

Listening to his matter-of-fact answers, I visualized the lines of anguish in his thin face and asked about how he knew that I would come. "Well," he replied, "you see, I found this stub of candle one day when I was—emptying things, you might say, into the pit. I felt suddenly I couldn't stand it any more; I'd set fire to the whole place and maybe we could escape! Probably not. But I'd try. Then that night before I could begin, I dozed off and dreamed that an old woman said, 'Wait. You are needed.' And I saw a girl's face. So I waited, not really believing." He paused and sighed. "It was true!"

I was moved by the simple trust of his final words, and I reached out in the darkness and touched his hand. And at the same instant Parula's little feet gripped one of my fingers.

"Parula is stronger," I said.

"I am, too," said Jetsam. "Now we must plan."

The first problem, we agreed, was how to account for me. Because we couldn't expect to escape yet. Several ideas were ad-vanced, each one discarded as more absurd than the last. We grew tense and frustrated. I asked why I couldn't just appear and say, "Here I am!" and let them take it or leave it.

"They wouldn't," Jetsam replied. "Take it or leave it, I mean. I know them! They'd take *you!* And worry you and torture you and shriek at you until you gave a reason! One thing they can't stand is no reason!"

"We're sunk, then. It's no use." I'd had no rest for ages. I just wasn't strong enough, hadn't the courage Arachne had thought I had, couldn't possibly—

"I've got it, I think!" Jetsam's suppressed excitement pushed despair aside. "I've got it! And they'd believe it, too!"

"What is it? Tell me!"

"You be Parula!"

"What! Oh, that's the worst of all! It isn't fair for you to try to be funny right now!"

"Maris!" he said sharply. "Listen to me! I'm serious about this. Look here—they believe in magic. They don't have any. But they believe in it. For them it's a reason. We'll tell them—no, I'll tell them—that during the night Parula disappeared—or rather, that she was changed into you. Can you sing?"

"Not really. I can carry a tune. I know some songs, I guess."

"That'll do. They won't know the difference." After a pause, he said, "Yes, you be Parula. You're not to talk, only to sing. When I tell you to."

I was beginning to see possibilities. "But what will we do with Parula?"

"I've been thinking about that. First I thought we could let her fly away, but she can't. Yet. They took some of her wing feathers, which haven't grown back enough. Till they do—which won't be long because I've been watching them—you keep her hidden, somewhere."

"In my pocket. I could keep her in my pocket, couldn't I?"

"Good. Let's tell her, though, before we go on."

Drawing my hand from inside my jacket, I could feel the little bird holding on to a finger with a firm grasp. And as Jetsam recounted the plan, Parula gave quick chirps of response.

"She agrees," Jetsam announced. "She's a plucky one. Put her in the pocket so she can get adjusted to it."

I lowered Parula carefully into the pocket where the gift of the Mantid was, hoping it would safeguard the bird, or at least keep her company. After a few almost imperceptible movements, Parula settled down.

"All right, Jetsam. Now what?"

"I'm not sure. I think we've got to just take each thing as it comes now. Watch for any chance. Be ready for any help from anywhere. Sounds kind of vague, doesn't it? And it is kind of vague too. I don't know what else to suggest. It has happened so all-of-a-sudden that I'm not quite collected, you know. I need some rest." And with that he curled up on the floor and was asleep as quickly as a tired child.

Much too keyed up to do likewise, I sat quietly and tried not to think, which I wasn't good at. For a while I listened to the sounds of my companions. The occasional faint "glub" must be Toad. And that silly snore—of course, it was Isia, who doubtless had kept up as well as he had because he could sleep under almost all circumstances. Nothing from Locus. But then Locus never made any noise except when she purred. And she was most unlikely to do that here.

When I wearied of listening, I began watching the small square of window above me. I didn't know how much time passed until the black opening showed a faint paleness. It went from utter black to washed-out black to blue-black to gray-blue, and slowly took on the thin color of dawn. With increased daylight, the prison room showed itself shabbier and smaller than it had appeared in candlelight. The mute longing in the eyes of Locus and Toad, in their rusted and confining cages, the loyal solidity of Isia enchained, the relaxed face of Jetsam sleeping on the hard floor, his dark head on his arms—these sights were painful and saddening. Yet somehow—almost in the air—there was a feeling of hope I hadn't noticed when I came. I was glad, and I could only trust it would be fulfilled.

My ears caught the distant roars almost at the instant Locus and Toad did. The pupils of their eyes widened with terror. An uncontrollable shudder went over me as I realized the Beasts had seen me when they took Locus and Isia! They would know me. The wild and hideous sounds rapidly came nearer. Neither Isia nor Jetsam seemed to stir from their sleep, although Jetsam did move one hand as if in a gesture of protest. Not until the loud voice of the night before shouted, "Get them, imbecile! There's work to do! Move!" did Jetsam awaken. He was on his feet immediately. "Get ready," he ordered me, his face unsmiling but his eyes aglow. "Back into the corner where Parula was! Let me talk."

Utmost courage and self-control were required, I well knew. I hadn't time to tell Jetsam my fear that our plan couldn't work. I tried hard to be ready to face whatever came. The trap door burst upward to reveal a creature even worse than I had imagined. He—I assumed he—was huge and filthy. This was my first impression. I forced myself to look at him boldly. His body was covered with yellowish hair, matted, mangy, soiled. It hung over his wicked eyes and made a ragged fringe under his snout, which was rather pointed. The four huge feet had long cruel claws. The body was grotesque, out of balance, reminding me of an animal I'd seen once at a zoo. What was it called? Hyena, that was it—a huge hyena with cat's feet and hair, and the head, except for the eyes, of a—of a—a *pig*, a wild pig.

"On your knees, fool!" he roared.

"Yes, sir." Jetsam said, obeying slowly.

"Everyone here and ready! At once!"

"Yes, sir."

The Beast only then spied me in the corner—as if his vision was poor, in spite of those huge evil eyes—and when he saw me he bellowed like a creature in a frenzy.

"What's that thing? You miserable liar! Cheat! How did it get here? Help, some of you stupid guards!" Two more Beasts crowded through the trap door. "Take that"—and he indicated me—"and destroy it! And then we'll take him," meaning Jetsam, "to the king!"

Before the two guards could reach me, Jetsam was on his feet facing them. "The king," he said in a loud voice, "will be angry with you if you destroy the bird. She is ready to sing now."

The guards stopped. Apparently they couldn't see well and didn't recognize me. The leader glared at them and bellowed, "Get rid of it!"

"You will regret it if you do," said Jetsam firmly.

"You tell me what to do! Why you—" and the Beast moved viciously forward.

Jetsam stood solidly. "Wait!" His voice rose. "The king demanded a song! He wants a song! The bird used her magic and became larger so she could give the king what he desires! He will kill you if you take it away!"

Apparently the leader was impressed. His tail continued to lash about angrily, but he went no nearer to Jetsam. "We'll see, you wormy morsel! We'll see!" he snarled. Then to the other Beasts, "Come on, fools! Get them all down! Hurry! There's work to do!"

Silently and with remarkable agility considering their size and shape, the Beasts took the basket in which I had hidden the night before, dumped into it Isia and Locus and Toad in their cages, and lowered it through the trap door on a rope.

And then it was my turn. At a sign from Jetsam, and with trembling knees and an emptiness in my stomach, I got into the basket and gripped the sides with tense fingers. Through the trap door. Into space and down. I'd never been afraid of heights nor was I now. Anyway, it wasn't very high—not more than thirty feet—and my conveyance dropped slowly and with few jerks. It was what I saw as I looked down that made me afraid, regardless of what I told myself about courage.

The enclosure within the walls was much larger than I had thought. It seemed, seen from above, to be literally crawling with Beasts and gruesome activity. On the farther side a low-roofed building leaned against the wall, ugly and misshapen as the Beasts, but apparently the hub of the kingdom. A crowd of the Beasts milled around in front of it, tearing and clawing at bloody corpses. A disorderly pile of flayed skins was just beyond. Scattered everywhere were entrails, hunks of flesh, partially cleaned bones. Other clusters of Beasts were carrying on incomprehensible work with the same lack of order.

The nearer I came to the ground, the more I had to fight not to be overcome both by the volume of noise and, even worse, the hideous stench filling the air. Not until the basket clumped down and I stepped out, did I realize that I, Locus and Toad in their cages, and Isia were surrounded by a ring of the Beasts, the more terrifying in that they stood soundlessly with fangs bared. I couldn't hold back from reaching into the cages to pat both Locus and Toad, and from touching Isia. No one tried to stop me, although one of the circle took a step forward, only to be pulled back by a companion. Soon Jetsam was delivered into the group. There was neither sound nor movement from captors or captives while the lift basket was pulled upward again so that the leader Beast could leave the prison room. His assistants left by way of a wooden pole placed against the supporting tree. (That was what made the crash against the prison, probably.) They were agile in climbing down it, too, despite their awkward appearance and their size.

"To the king with these idiots and liars!" bellowed the leader as he pushed through the ring of guards. "Won't take long to see who's right and who's a fool!"

We were herded across the enclosure toward the building, which I had previously decided was the place of the king. The leader stalked ahead officiously, shoving with his massive shoulders and growling when other Beasts got in the way. I tried not to see the mess through which we passed. I wasn't always success-ful. And I couldn't escape the smell. It was everywhere. It was ob-viously as much a part of the kingdom as the inhabitants them-selves. I had noticed it before, but here, ringed about and pressed in by the Beasts, I felt it as a virtual presence.

"In with you, stupid fools!"

We had reached our destination. The circle of guards had separated, and we stood before a half-opened door. Obviously the leader intended us to enter, for he roared again, "In!" The two Beasts carrying Locus's and Toad's cages in their mouths went first, then came one yanking Isia's chain with Isia on the other end, and finally Jetsam and I walked in. The place grew ominously still. Surely now I'd be recognized. I faced, across a fair-sized, bar-ren room, a Beast half again as large as the others, every feature ex-aggerated in a negative direction. He was semi-recumbent on a raised platform, extending and retracting his claws while he stared at the prisoners. On either side of and below his platform were guards standing at rigid attention. Locus in her cage was placed near the king on his dais, and despite her obvious shrinking from him, his expression softened momentarily as he looked at her. Isia climbed to a spot near the huge forepaws and made himself into a careful cushion. A disconsolate gray-green lump, Toad sat in his cage where it had been dropped. Jetsam was on his knees before the dais, apparently knowing from experience that this would be demanded.

When the king finally spoke, it was in a deceptively soft voice—deceptive because I could hear under the softness the arrogance of a power never questioned. His cold eyes fixed on me. "Where is the yellow thing? And what is this?"

"Oh Mighty One!" The leader Beast stepped forward, making an obsequious bow, nose touching the floor. "O Mighty One, this stupid slave"—and he glared sideways at the kneeling and impassive Jetsam—"says the yellow thing changed overnight— overnight he says!—into this other creature! We bring him before you, Mighty One, for judgment."

"Judgment? For what?" Sarcasm was heavy.

"For lying! For being a liar and a fool!"

"You, then, make the judgment? You, then, have the knowledge and the proof?" The king's voice grew less soft. His eyes glistened with harsh light.

"Oh, no, Mighty One! Never! Yours is judgment and wisdom, only yours! But to expect you to believe such stupid tales! Why, it's clear—surely—this could not be! There's no reason! Obviously he—"

"You are the greatest fool! The most stupid!" The voice rose, snapping whiplike in the room. "I will decide about reasons! I alone! Let the slave himself tell me."

I held my breath when Jetsam raised his head and began to speak. Briefly and with remarkable self-possession and courage, he told the king what he had already told the leader Beast. He spoke slowly, choosing his words with care and making the story so reasonable that even I felt it could be true.

"And thus, O Mighty One, your desire for song can be fulfilled at last," Jetsam concluded. "Only command, and you shall be obeyed."

The room grew heavy with tension and Beast smell. No one moved. At last the king lifted a massive paw and placed it with careless heaviness upon Isia. He stared at me until I felt as though

his icy disbelief was paring away my very substance and I doubted
my ability even to move, much less to sing.

"Prove it!" The king's roar struck me without warning, and
with a reflex born of fear I began to sing, through a dry throat:

> *"There once was a weaver,*
> *He lived all alone,*
> *He worked at the weaver's trade . . ."*

What prompted me to choose this tune I never knew. At the
time the song just came and I gave it.

"A poor song," growled the king when I finished. "A poor
singer. Hardly better than nothing. But something. Now get out!"
he roared. "All you fools with work to be done, get out! At once!"

I stood still, warned by a glance from Jetsam. In snarling
haste the leader pushed his subordinates and Jetsam out the door.
And I and my three smaller comrades were alone with the king.
His eyes glittered in his gross pig face. He extended his claws
on the foot resting upon Isia, digging the claws into the furry
body and pressing down deliberately, all the while watching me
with a malicious expression.

"So this is my singer," he growled contemptuously. "What a
thing!" He cuffed Isia aside. "What things you all are! Not a
single adequate creature anywhere except myself! Look at you!
Scrawny, snivelling, weak, stupid, untalented! No one cares about
perfection except myself! And I am surrounded by helpers equal
to their prisoners in stupidity." He sighed and groaned. "All right!
Don't waste time standing there! Sing!"

Swallowing hard, touching the warm ball of feathers in my
pocket to remind myself of what I had to do, I began again. I
forced thoughts out of my mind as much as I could, knowing I
wouldn't be able to keep up the grim game if thinking interfered.
Just open your mouth and sing, I told myself—anything you can
remember. At least they don't remember you.

The day moved painfully from hour to hour. It wouldn't have
seemed to move a single second had it not been for the room's
several high windows that permitted me to see a corner of sky

and a bit of wall against which I could detect the passage of changing light. The variety of music I dragged up from forgotten corners astonished me: nursery rhymes, melancholy ballads, musical comedy songs, folk songs, occasional pieces that I invented on the spot. Sometimes the king listened. Sometimes he roared commands at lesser Beasts who came and went, and once in a while he dozed off. Whenever he was giving orders or sleeping I stopped and sat down, jumping quickly to my feet at the first sign of his awareness of me. Always he dozed with one or both heavy forepaws resting on poor Isia, whom I didn't dare to comfort by so much as a glance. Toad in his cage was taken away by a particularly odious Beast, and was returned, much later, scratched and inert.

Outweighing all other horrors of the endless day was the fact that nothing was right for the king. Even while he listened to my songs, he growled to himself. Every song was a source of displeasure, expressed either in sarcasm or in hostility. That was a song? Could I not do better than that? No one ever did anything well! What a fool I was! And stupid! Not only was it I who was a fool! Everyone was! Isia never made a proper footrest, and when he tried to amuse he was impossible. Not a single Beast of the many who came and went on business was acceptable to the king. He harassed, he found fault, he condemned, he threatened, until I began to feel more and more depressed. Had he just complained in a self-pitying way I could have fought him off more easily. But his intolerance was aggressive. Self-respect was beaten down. It was late afternoon when I finally realized what the most terrible thing was in this place. Under the king's all-encompassing dissatisfaction, vitality was wounded and crippled. Self-rejection and doubt, a sense of worthlessness—these permeated the entire kingdom. And all who lived here, Beasts and captives, lost every hope.

Strangely enough this idea, dreadful though it was, helped me to endure the criticisms and the taunts, and to keep on singing regardless. Partly it helped because knowing what it was separated me from it. More than that, my anger at myself and my friends for almost being overcome by it was so fiery, I felt

I not only could but would withstand it. I was so angry that I began to sing, just as loud as I could, something I suddenly recalled. I had reached the words about "trampling out the vintage where the grapes of wrath are stored," when suddenly the king gave a shout.

"Take them away!" he bellowed. "At once!"

Night had come at last.

14

It took but this one day for me to be convinced that escape must come soon. As courage and trust were slowly destroyed inside the captives, the possibility of freedom grew less. I said this to Jetsam as we sat on the floor of our dark prison and ate such scraps and fragments of decent food as Jetsam had been able to salvage during his labors.

"Don't you see, Jetsam," I said, after telling him my feelings, "that even you have gotten used to it? You take it for granted. And that's a terrible thing! You're losing courage. I don't think you believe much in yourself, and you've got to! If no one believes in himself, They are helpless!"

"I never thought of this, you know." His voice had a ring of genuine surprise in it. "Sounds impossible. It really does. And I'm ashamed to say so. Maybe I've been so dense because I haven't had anyone to try my thoughts with. Like you. But now that you say it I see it. We've got to get away! I see that. How to do it—well, that's another matter."

"My dears, if you would join us over here, we could all talk about escape. It does concern us too, remember." Isia spoke from the other side of the darkness, sounding wide awake—a remarkable fact—and even a bit irritated.

Jetsam and I felt our way to the cages. "All right," said Jetsam, "does anyone have any ideas?"

"No." Toad sounded weaker than before. "I'd as lief die as take another day."

"Now Toad," Isia said sharply, "you mustn't talk that way.

You're tired and sore, but we'll get out yet! You'll see! Hang on!"

"What we need," Jetsam reflected, almost to himself, "is the key for the cages first, and then some way to climb down from here when the Beasts are away."

"You don't want much!" Isia sounded increasingly distressed. "And I suppose I go about chained for the rest of my life!"

During this exchange, I suddenly realized that I hadn't told much about Arachne or Botta. So I proceeded to give the story of how I had come to the Beast's kingdom and up to the prison. When I finished, Jetsam, Isia, and Toad began to talk all at once, while Parula, perched atop Locus's cage, chirped excitedly. Jetsam's voice won out.

"But this is wonderful! We do have a chance! We've got to get word to them somehow. And find ways to get keys and break chains. There is a chance! There is!"

"I know where the key is." Strength had come even into Toad's croak. "I've seen it, every time they take me out . . . hangs on a cord thing, outside *his* place . . . that horror of a king . . . same key for cages, gates, chains, I'd say . . . only seen one, anyhow . . ."

Jetsam chuckled at Toad's response, and I realized I hadn't heard him laugh before. I felt like laughing too. On that note, unable to produce further ideas, we ended our talking. Rest and sleep, we decided, might improve our condition more than words.

Morning found us still devoid of workable plans, so we couldn't do anything but let the usual Beast day seize us. Held up by absurd and unreasoning hope, I found that the preceding day had taught me my job rather thoroughly, and less energy was needed to keep singing. Also it became quite clear that the king either did not actually listen or was more perverse than I had assumed, because songs he had criticized for one reason yesterday he now dismissed for totally different reasons. I saw no sense therefore in trying to do anything special. I let the tunes and verses come and go in whatever haphazard way they would, and tried to ignore the king's comments by looking at various spots of wall or ceiling, counting cracks, or imagining what this or that stain resembled.

At one such time I was examining the bottom sill of the high window in the left wall, with the words of some childhood nursery song coming forth quite automatically, when I thought something moved along the window. I must be getting tired and jumpy, I decided. But I kept my gaze on the sill nonetheless. There it was again. Maybe it wasn't an illusion after all. Yes—no —yes, it did move! Something about as big as the ball of my thumb, something that crawled and apparently knew what it was about. It stopped moving whenever the king glanced in its general direction, and then it crawled rapidly when he looked away. In these erratic stops and starts it managed to cross the window sill, proceed upward to the ceiling, and make its way across the ceiling to a spot directly above my head. I didn't dare look upward continually, so I snatched only quick oblique glances that allowed me to be sure something was there but left its identity a mystery.

Then the king fell asleep. Hardly had I taken this in when suddenly, before I could decide if it was safe to look up, a dark gray spider appeared only a few inches from my eyes. Hanging from its virtually invisible thread, it peered at me with a pert little face, and I could see its mouth move but could hear nothing. It gestured for me to come nearer. I leaned my head forward until my ear could feel the tickle of spider feet. A thin cracked whisper came. "From Arachne. She will come tonight if I can get the key."

The king stretched and yawned. The spider whisked itself aloft faster than the king could open his eyes. The whole astounding scene had occured with such speed that I would not have believed it had I not seen the spot crawl back across the window sill and disappear.

From then on, the day was both more endurable because of a renewed hope and less endurable because I wanted the others to know. My preoccupation with escape made my singing less planned and less musical, if that was possible. The king criticized more viciously than ever, and with some reason, probably. But I hardly heard him. And I wouldn't have minded at all except that he mistreated Isia when I made too bad a job of my work. Somehow we managed to endure through the long afternoon.

By the time we were at last dumped indifferently in our prison room, I could hardly contain myself any longer. As the trap door slammed on the departing Beasts, I grabbed Jetsam, pulled him to the cages, and blurted out the story of the spider in a rush of words. "It may be tonight! Tonight!" I ended.

No one replied. No one could find anything to say until Jetsam spoke. "Why hasn't this happened before now, I wonder? It doesn't seem possible. After so long. Really it doesn't."

"Maybe it isn't." Toad sounded as if he was trying not to believe in such a remote possibility, although wanting to cling to it.

"Yes, maybe it isn't," Jetsam said, "but also maybe it is. At least we'd best be ready, *if* it is. Someone's taken a lot of risk to watch out for us, and get word to us, don't you think?"

"I think—" said Isia, "and I can think, even if you wouldn't guess it from watching me—I think it hasn't come before because we had to have a link to Arachne. We didn't even know about her. Also I think you two active ones should find each lock, in case the key does arrive, so we won't be slowed up in doing whatever we will have to do when whoever it is comes. If someone does."

For the second time in twenty-four hours I heard Jetsam's warm chuckle. "Isia," he cried, "you're a wonder and a joy! All right, Maris, let's be at it!" Almost gaily, we fumbled about in the darkness until we had located all of the locks and could touch them quickly and accurately.

After a silence, Jetsam said, "If we have to go down the web thing—if your friend brings it—put Parula in one pocket and carry Toad, will you? I don't have any pockets left. Anyway, I need to be free to—well, to do whatever I might have to."

We heard the growling, snarling exodus of the Beasts on their usual trip to the river. The silence deepened. Every sound there was seemed loud in our small room—breath, rustle, heartbeat. I was twisting my hands together almost unconsciously when a different sound alerted my ears and arrested my breathing. I could tell Jetsam, too, had caught it. It was a tiny chink of metal against wood, coming from an obscure direction, irregularly. It came again, nearer. Again. It was above the floor, and moving upward. "Jetsam! I'll bet it's the spider with the key! Dragging it up all this height."

I went straight to the window and put my hand up to the square of faint starlight, resting my fingers on the window's edge.

There was the tickle of spider feet on my palm, then a final chink, and I felt a small metal object resting in my hand. The thin whisper of the afternoon was in my ear. "Give the key to him, quickly!"

I handed it to Jetsam, who had moved to my side. He went away from me at once, sensing the need for action.

"Arachne is coming. Use key to pry open trap door. Let her lead. I must go." And the whisper was gone. I had wanted to say Thank you. Now I couldn't. Anyway, there wasn't time. I called to Jetsam and told him the message.

"Good," he said. "I've got things unlocked. Better get your passengers ready while I try the trap door."

Groping my way to the cages, I picked up Toad and put Parula in my pocket. Patting Isia, who seemed speechless at losing his chain, I permitted myself the brief luxury of taking Locus in my arms and hugging her before putting her on the floor. Meanwhile Jetsam was struggling with the trap door, as I could tell from the grunting and scratching and muttering.

"Can I help?" I ventured.

"No! I'll do it! Just can't seem to get the key into the crack! Blast! That's not it!" More muttering and scratching. "There, now! That's done it, I think! Yes!" And there was the plunk of a door flipped back.

"It took you long enough." It was Arachne's welcome voice. "Now be sensible and not sentimental, please. Do just as I say. We have little time. You go first, Maris. Either carry the smaller ones or let them come behind you. Then you go, young man. When you are all down I will gather my net and follow. Botta is waiting. Go at once!"

Swinging out and down into the night, hands and feet clinging to the meshes of net I couldn't see, I climbed toward the ground below. The net trembled only slightly above me when first Locus and then Isia took hold for the descent. A stronger shake marked Jetsam's coming. We were fearfully exposed, with only darkness as a cover, and a spider and a gopher to aid us against the power of the Beasts. Even time was an enemy. As foothold followed handhold, handhold followed foothold, minutes seemed to race past. When would the distant voices of the king and his hosts be heard? How soon?

Unbelieving, I felt ground under my feet. And heard the voice of Botta out of the night saying, "Steady, my girl. Hold it!" And Locus and Isia, then Jetsam, also on the ground, pressing close together, all of them. And still the silence held.

"Come on!" Botta's words prodded us. "Quick! I've got the hole open!"

We stumbled awkwardly after him, not knowing the contours of the ground by night. "Hurry!" he kept saying, as if we weren't going as fast as we could.

"Almost there! Keep it up!" Simultaneous with this cry of Botta, excited, imperative, came the snarling chorus of the Beasts returning.

"Here it is! Down you go!" And Botta was literally fierce as he pushed us one by one into the hole, where we landed helter-skelter on top of each other, a tangle of arms, legs, feet, fur, and dirt. I got up as soon as I could, afraid for Toad and Parula. But Toad croaked that he was all right, although he had dirt in his eyes. And Parula's chirp announced that she was in one piece. By this time the others had gotten themselves unsnarled, and Botta handed me once again the glowworm lantern, produced from somewhere. "Let's go!" he snapped.

"Where's Arachne?" I wanted to know.

"Capable of taking care of herself! Hurry!"

Off we went along the tunnel, the lantern giving just enough light for us to follow the squat little figure of the gopher scurrying ahead. When he stopped, I guessed from the smell that we were at the refuse pit.

"Listen!" he said. "This is hardest. Stay close to me, and to the edges. No noise. Out with light." And the glowworm faded into darkness. "Now!"

We had reached the halfway point of the pit's edge and were proceeding in orderly silence when I saw that Locus had broken ranks and was scampering soundlessly straight across the exposed center of the pit. In the faint wash of starlight she was virtually bouncing in an ecstasy of free movement. I lost my head. "Locus!" I cried. "Locus, come back!"

Following my outburst a rage of roaring sounded above us. A

roving Beast appeared silhouetted against the night sky. He gave the alarm and then leaped into the pit, snarling and furious. Botta saw the peril immediately. He hurried to the mouth of the tunnel beyond the pit and began calling us. Over and over he called, "Maris! Locus! Isia! Jetsam! Here!" The confusion of Beasts who had come at the alarm, not knowing quite what they were pursuing, helped us in our rush to escape. Locus, I, Jetsam, we all were in the tunnel. Isia, always the slowest, was almost there when a great paw reached out and pinned his rear part to the ground. At the same moment Jetsam grabbed Isia, pulling him into the tunnel. Isia groaned softly. Suddenly Arachne was there, flung her net over the tunnel's mouth, and the Beasts roared in impotent rage outside. We were free, at least for the time being. Very shaken, we followed Botta around a bend out of sight of the Beasts.

"Let's have some light," said Botta, when we paused to catch our breath. I lifted the lantern, which was glowing again, and saw to my horror that Jetsam stood holding Isia in his arms, while Isia's blood dripped slowly onto the tunnel floor.

"He's badly hurt." Jetsam was almost in tears. "He's badly hurt! His very back legs—his poor legs—they're gone."

I couldn't speak. I just stood, beginning to see what I had done. It was Arachne who came forward at once. Ordering Jetsam to sit on the ground and hold the limp and injured Isia, she went to work. She drew out of herself endless yards of fine silken thread until it lay in a soft heap beside her. Some she used to sponge away the blood from the wound and then, deft as a long-time nurse, she used the rest to bind up Isia's injury until his tail stump was swathed in snowy white gossamer gauze. Finally she stepped back, her plump black figure very maternal, her voice brisk and business-like as she said, "It is, I think, not so bad as it looks."

"Yes," Isia said weakly, "I do think you are right. Got quite a few legs to spare, you know. Might even be able to go faster, being shortened a bit, you might say. But very sleepy . . ." And his voice trailed off. Jetsam got up slowly, lifting Isia so as not to jar him. I could tell that he was angry with me.

"There is no time to waste." Arachne took charge coolly. "We must get out from under their land before they begin to dig."

She started off. "And they will," she added over her shoulder.

We heard the roaring and clawing already louder behind us as we set out down the dim tunnel. I was so totally unnerved that the lantern bobbed up and down crazily and our huge shadows pursued us like drunken ghosts. Once I turned to look back at Jetsam, but turned away in silence at the reproof on his face. The tunnel appeared much the same, although it seemed years since I had gone down it in the opposite direction. This time my heart should have been lighter because my two lost companions were with me. Yet I was sorrowful. Would I never learn? Was I forever doomed to do the wrong thing?

From time to time we halted while Arachne spun a steely web across the tunnel behind us, aided by Botta who dug furiously at the walls until each web was partially dirt filled. I was scarcely aware of reaching Arachne's spider-silk room with its white spinning wheel and its lovely walls. Not until I heard a sigh did I rouse from my unhappiness.

Jetsam had laid Isia down on a bed of gossamer, and was now standing in the middle of the room, the black look gone from his face, his eyes aglow. He sighed again, "I have never seen such a thing! It's so beautiful! And free!" And in his happy sound I was forgiven.

PART III

A New Way

15

IN THAT GENTLE HALF-LIGHT, LULLED BY THE SOUND OF THE SPIN-
ning wheel, for two days and nights we slept and ate and slept
and ate and slept. Botta kept popping in with food of assorted
kinds, which we consumed greedily before we dozed off again.
Periodically Arachne dressed Isia's wounds with fresh-spun gossamer, and her nods and hums to herself were quite heartening.
Somehow, although we knew the Beasts must be searching in
a fury, we were at peace.

On the third morning, before Arachne or Botta had come,
Jetsam rolled over on his soft mattress of spider silk, stretched,
yawned hugely, stood up, rubbed his eyes, and said, "What a
great feeling it is to be full, and not tired! And free!" As Arachne
entered he bowed and said, "Madam, how can we ever thank
you! Or Mr. Botta!"

Jetsam's voice, more resonant than I'd ever heard it, roused
the others. Locus bounded awake, while Toad, looking more
rounded than a few days ago, said "Yes!" in a bass voice. Even
Isia opened one eye and nodded his head. At that moment Botta
came through his door, as absurd as always, and Jetsam and I
began to laugh. Botta didn't mind. He only said he was glad to
be such a success.

After breakfast, Jetsam said again to Arachne that we were
deeply grateful and then that he thought we'd better talk about
what came next. "From what Maris has told me," he said, "this
rescue is only one part of a larger task, which must have something
to do with Them and Beasts."

"You are right, young man. Go on." Arachne watched him intently.

"Well—it's hard when you don't know—but I think we'd better try to get away from the Beasts' kingdom for now. So we can have time to figure out what to do, or what we are needed for. I've had a hunch for a long time—way before Locus and Isia came—that something had to happen, that—oh, I can't say it."

Arachne almost smiled. "You have said quite a lot, even so. And generally correct. It may surprise you, Jetsam, that I know very little more than you have guessed. When the Beasts first came—a long time it has been—matters were not so bad. Once even, before you were captured, Jetsam, She arrived."

I interrupted. "You mean—the old woman—the—you mean—Grandmother?"

"Yes, Maris, I mean Grandmother." Arachne looked reproving, but went on. "But the Beasts would not listen. Not even to Her. They grew worse and worse, and Botta and I often discussed moving. After you came, Jetsam, we knew we had to stay until something happened."

"And do you have any notion about what should happen?" Jetsam asked.

"Not really. I feel in myself that the Beasts have to be brought to the Place of Them, or They to the Beasts. Peace must be made, and healing must come."

"Why do They need us, though? Aren't They powerful?"

"Very powerful, Jetsam. As are the Beasts. That, I am convinced, is the problem. Power and power must be united by the small."

I began to have a dim sense of direction. "You mean," I asked, "like a boat that joins two continents?"

"Yes, Maris, like that."

"And we might be the boat? Maybe?"

"Maybe. Or maybe pilot and crew." She refused to say more. She did warn us that the Beasts were very angry, that Botta had been busy filling in all his old tunnels, and that we'd best get ready to find our friends in the grove and get far away from the Beasts' kingdom as soon as we could. Isia, she said, wouldn't go with us, because "his life in its present state is going into another. His injuries only speeded up the process."

Getting ready to go physically wasn't hard, because we had nothing to take except ourselves and some food packets Botta fixed for us. Saying good-bye to Isia was hard. As I looked into his funny face, I didn't think I could bear it. "Woolly bear, we'll miss you," I said, patting him.

"Tell Exi and Red about everything," he whispered, "including me." And he went back to sleep.

Just before we left, Arachne gave us each a suit made of spider thread so fine it was invisible when put on—which she made us do. She said the suits would guard against dangers, make us harder to see, and protect us in extremes of weather. We were leaving at a carefully chosen time. The Beasts were all out on a rare daytime expedition, looking for us no doubt. They would not be there to see us go. As when I first entered the house, the stairs and doorway seemed much too small to let us pass, and yet we did, suddenly finding ourselves on the earth under a colorless and empty sky.

I had never imagined that the towering, dark jungle would appear other than fearful, but as we made our way up the bare slope at a slow pace, hoping to be less visible so, I thought nothing could possibly be better than to reach the dark wetness. We kept watching for signs of Beast life on the tilted sides of the valley. Nothing moved. If one of the Beasts were to appear from anywhere, we would be helpless because there was no possible escape. The absence of sound, too, heightened our anxiety. No sighing of wind in trees or grasses. No gurgle of water. No chirping or croaking. Locus was silent. Only the soft clump of feet, and occasionally the hollow tick of a foot against some small pebble.

Despite the feeling of being on a treadmill where one walked and walked and stayed in the same place, we were approaching the trees. Finally we broke from our measured walk and ran the last twenty yards to the slope's crest and into the great wet masses of trees and shadows. For a few moments we stood, hearts pounding and breath laboring from our uphill sprint. By contrast to the stench of the Beasts' kingdom and the deadness of the valley through which we'd come, the jungle seemed as wet and clean as morning.

We responded to this with a great burst of good spirits and poor planning; soon we were hopelessly lost in the jungle's aisles. However, by slowing down and going carefully and watchfully, I eventually located the darker green of the laurels. I pushed back the pungent branches and we entered.

The grove was sweet with the air of a summer afternoon, the green velvet turf dotted with tiny flowers sun-warmed and fragrant. In the center of the grove my friends still slept where I had left them, relaxed as children. Though it was difficult to be sure, I was convinced that all of them had improved in health during their enchanted slumbers. As always after a separation from them, I was conscious of great love for these odd creatures into whose company I had come, and whose lives were now an inseparable part of my own.

I gazed at the four sleepers, wondering how best to waken them. Jetsam, Locus, Parula, and Toad remained motionless before the wonders of the grove and its occupants. Then Parula solved the problem by beginning to sing a high and joyful song, which filled the grove.

It was Exi who first awakened, with the other three following quickly. I had to restrain myself and Locus's eagerness, while I watched their bewildered attempts to come into the present. They were like four boats that had been becalmed, and now the wind had come again, and they were finding it difficult to get sails hoisted and rudders set. When finally they were oriented, they turned as a unit toward me.

"I thought you had already gone," Exi said. "What are you waiting for? We had only just gotten to sleep."

"It would seem to me that you could have asked for whatever you need *before* we started to rest rather than *after*, Maris." Mr. Green was being insufferably patronizing. "I have *always* said that women—"

"Oh, shut up!" Taken off guard by this most deflating reception, I was angry. "You're so pompous! You don't even know what's gone on, or why—or—or anything!"

I started to walk off but Jetsam blocked my path; he put his hand on my arm. I pulled away. He only smiled and said calmly, "I don't think they really know you've been away. And they're still half asleep and don't know what they're saying. Wait a minute."

Red proved Jetsam's point by suddenly coming fully awake, rushing toward me and crying, "Please, Maris, don't leave! Don't you see that everything's all mixed up?"

With this, everyone began talking at once, introducing everyone to everyone. Exi was presented to Red at least twice, and Jetsam was introduced to Mr. Green by three different people. We told of our terrible adventures. Even Toad, with some coaxing, joined the telling and received such sympathy for his treatment from the Beasts that he ended with his bulbous eyes tear-filled and with Red patting him on the back comfortingly.

Supper was relaxed because we knew we were safe for the moment in the grove. Afterwards we talked of the next step in our journey. We had to escape the kingdom of the Beasts and hunt for some way to help Them, but nothing was clear-cut.

We left it there until morning. When I awakened in the magical grove I wanted to stay just where I was until I couldn't take in any more of this world of velvet grass, soft wind, sun smells, and new light. And I was not alone.

Suddenly Jetsam grabbed my hand and pulled me to my feet, shouting, "Come and join us in dance and song!"

"Kind silly sir, of course!" I replied, with a curtsy, and together we skipped and whirled into a company infected with joy. The entire grove appeared to be moving with life. Locus raced around and around in a frenzy of excitement, while her purring filled the air. Music for the merriment came mostly from Parula. She perched on a branch and sang as if she had never sung before. The funniest sight of all—the sight which eventually brought Jetsam and me to a halt because we were undone with laughter—was the awkwardly wonderful dance of the beetles and Red and Toad. Exi, Carabus, Mr. Green, and Red hopped and skipped forward and then backward in a sort of a circular square dance, while Toad was the erratic center, bouncing up and down spasmodically and uttering unmelodic croaks whose unintentional syncopation gave him obvious pleasure. It was all so absurd and so marvelous that finally I

just sank to the ground near the dancers, laughing until tears ran
and I had to cover my face with my hands.

Jetsam watched until he too could stand it no longer. At last
he called something to Parula. She left her branch and flew to his
shoulder, changing her wild and intoxicating song to a soft tune
and then to a series of single low notes. As the music slowed and
finally ended, the dancers did likewise. The beetles appeared a bit
self-conscious, caught off their usual dignity.

When we left the magic grove, tension and fear settled over
us again, and our wild interlude was soon almost forgotten. We
decided we'd best travel by day because the Beasts would most
likely be hunting for us by night. We planned to go as straight
north as we could, hoping this would lead us sooner away from
the Beasts. I tried to tell Jetsam how we had practiced moving
when we started our jungle rescue trip. Being lithe and well
muscled, he learned well. Locus and Parula were naturals.

Not so poor Toad. All three beetles tried to show him, and he
really wanted to learn, but creeping was not for him. Fortunately
for everyone, the jungle floor was damp, so Toad's ups and downs
weren't noisy. But they were dreadfully visible. And while the rest
of us managed to do quite a good job of whisking from cover to
cover and keeping generally out of sight, Toad was forever flying
into the air like an erratic missile and landing in some odd place
where he could be seen at once if anyone was watching.

By sundown we were snapping at each other, and very tired and
hungry and rather desperate. Exi suggested we climb into trees
before darkness came and stay there until morning. Jetsam and I
had a time doing it because the jungle trees were thick and hard
to get up, but we managed somehow to reach a branch where we
could put Locus between us. We ate some of our remaining food,
said very little, and spent a miserable night. Only once did we hear
Beasts in the distance, but that was enough to freeze us to our
branches. As a matter of fact, my hands were so stiff from holding
on that it was at least an hour, after Exi called us to come
down the next morning, before I could flex my fingers easily.

Although it was something to see day come and to know we
were still all in one piece and in one company, the day did not
promise well. Our food gave out with breakfast. The jungle-forest

seemed sinister. We crept and slithered through it, while Toad plopped. By midafternoon, when we suddenly emerged from the jungle and found ourselves at the edge of a marshy lake, we were too tired to notice him. Until he leaped joyfully into the marsh and disappeared.

"Are you leaving us?" I cried, rushing to the marsh edge.

Toad's nobbly face emerged. "I don't want to, Maris. It's only that—well, you see—oh dear, it was so long in that awful place with no wetness and no swimming, and I need it."

Jetsam understood best and helped Toad to leave without feeling uncomfortable. We all reassured Toad, and said we loved him and we'd miss him, and told him to enjoy himself, and waved good-bye as his bumpy head disappeared below the marsh surface.

Because we couldn't go forward in the direction we'd been going, Exi suggested we spend the night there. Red, the beetles, and Parula, were soon on nearby branches taking Exi's advice. I spotted a tiny island about ten feet offshore. Picking up Locus, I waded out to it, shoes and all. Jetsam followed. We sat down.

"Jetsam," I said. "I'm worried about a lot of things, going way back to the beginning, when Scuro was lost—" Suddenly I began to cry, overcome by the memory of Scuro, which I had resolutely turned away from whenever it had pushed at me. I told Jetsam about the small black dog, and how he had started the whole journey, and how I missed him and hadn't dared think of him. My story wasn't coherent, but Jetsam seemed to follow all I said, and to make sense of it as well.

"Maris," he asked, when I was quiet again, "Maris, do you know where Scuro is?"

"No. Only that Exi said that he wouldn't be hurt. And that They would teach him. I guess that's another reason why we've got to find Them."

"You know," Jetsam said unexpectedly, "I think we'd better decide before long what to do next. I wonder and worry, too. What Arachne said about the work to be done was for all of us."

Which was what I'd hoped he would say but hadn't believed he would.

16

THE NEXT MORNING JETSAM AND I TOLD THE OTHERS WHAT WE WERE feeling about the urgency of a next step. All of them responded wholeheartedly. No one at first had any clear idea of how to proceed, but even Locus and Parula stayed to ponder. And, as had happened often before, it was Red who gave the answer.

"Excuse me," he said, when Exi and Jetsam were trying to decide which direction to take, "but couldn't we—I mean, why wouldn't it be a good idea now that we're farther—well, does anyone know where the *Starflower* is?"

"Red, dear friend," Mr. Green shouted, "you are undeniably *the most* intelligent of us all!" He looked around aggressively, but no denials were forthcoming. "Why did no one think of it! Of course we must find the *Starflower!*"

They began talking all at one time. Nobody was hearing anybody until Exi interrupted the noise. "I feel confident that we can work out possible ways to find our boat if we agree that is best. But let us not forget that it does not take us farther from the Beasts."

"Exi, sir," said Jetsam, "I think we're fairly safe if we keep to water. Wide water like a river, I mean. I have more reason than most of you not to want to see the Beasts again. But we may have to. And they hate water, I know that."

"Very well." Exi paused. "We seem to be of one mind now to go and find the *Starflower*. Only two questions must be answered first. Where is she? How do we get there?"

We agreed that our island should be somewhat south and west

of where we were. As for the second question, Jetsam said calmly that he would build a raft and we could try to go by water.

Jetsam went into the woods, found five reasonable-sized and recently fallen trees, and together we tugged, shoved, and rolled them out to the clearing near the water. With sharp rocks he and I began to knock off the branches and any loose bark. Red and Mr. Green set to work collecting marsh grasses and making rope to bind the logs together. The rest gathered what food they could. By late afternoon two large piles of food bundles were ready, and we had finished our log scraping. With three beetles, an ant, and two humans swarming over the five logs, it was not long before they were lashed securely together and were ready for the water. At this point Jetsam announced that he was too tired to do more, that it was almost sunset, that he wanted to eat and sleep. This seemed sensible—although I wished Jetsam could be less grumpy when he was tired—so we ate and slept, Jetsam, Locus, and I on the island, the rest in trees. No Beast sounds woke us.

The next morning the clearing shone in the early sun. Everyone was fresh and restored and the world looked beautiful. Compared to the *Starflower*, the raft seemed ugly and awkward, but even it was acceptable in this new day; and after all food was piled aboard, Jetsam and I shoved the raft into the water. I held its mooring rope while Jetsam carried the others to it. Eventually I climbed on. And at last Jetsam, carrying a pole and a makeshift paddle, waded out, pulled himself aboard, handed me the paddle, stood up, and thrust his pole into the water.

"We're off!" he cried happily, as his first push sent us moving slowly away from shore.

The first half hour or more was spent maneuvering the raft around among grasses, reeds, and along obscure channels. Finally we floated into the middle of the shallow lake. Behind us lay the jungle shore from which we had come. Ahead of us—who could tell?

Jetsam stopped poling. "There should be an exit to the South or West, at least I hope there is. But I can't tell where."

Parula suddenly flashed overhead, then in a series of dips and glides circled the lake and disappeared into the trees at the far left. Before we could be upset, she returned, to flutter above the raft for a moment, and once again go toward the place at which she had entered the trees. This time she glided to a branch and perched there like a golden blossom.

"She wants us to come to where she is." Jetsam pushed his pole down and the raft began to move. I kept my eyes on Parula, trying to use the paddle to hold the raft on a straight course. We were virtually opposite Parula's tree before it was clear that the lake did not end. Or rather, that some part of the water went on around a southerly bend.

"There is a river!" Jetsam shouted, giving his pole a great shove, which took us gliding into a neck of the lake and on into an obvious waterway. I sighed with relief as I felt the raft being drawn into a slight but definite current.

"Jetsam, why don't you rest for a while? You can, now, can't you?" Nodding, he got carefully to his feet and went to Exi.

I stayed where I was, at the front, both because I felt someone needed to steer from time to time, and because I liked to see Jetsam making friends with Exi and the others. I sat peacefully, my paddle trailing in the water. I was filled with a sense of freedom from the Beasts for a while and with the sights and sounds of a river, almost as I had been that first day of the *Starflower's* voyage. Time passed almost unnoticed.

"I think we're coming to a bigger river," Jetsam exclaimed finally. "Look up ahead!"

Certainly something new was at hand. Our river, so lazy, so calm, seemed to be suddenly buckling ahead, like a damp floor. And beyond it we could see an expanse of water that stretched away to a distant shoreline. Jetsam shoved his pole ahead of the raft, forcing it to a halt, and before it could swing around to continue downstream, he began shoving sideways. Seeing what he was up to, I used my paddle to help and, after some strenuous work, we got the raft to where Jetsam could wade ashore and tie it to a tree.

I was surprised to see that the sun was getting low, in fact, had almost reached the treetops of the far forest on the other side of the large river. "I didn't know we'd been on the way so long!" I said.

"I did," said Mr. Green peevishly. "I most *certainly* did! I have known it for a *considerable* period of time!"

"Somy," said Red, "you mean your stomach has."

"Very well. So I *am* hungry. I will confidently say that *others* are hungry too!"

"I think," said Exi, stepping forward until he could see everyone at once, "that Mr. Green is right. I would judge that we should stop and consider, and perhaps we might also stop and eat."

The bank proved to be a reasonably adequate camp site.

"Jetsam," said Exi, "I have an idea that you are eager to know what is beyond. Why not take Parula and Red and look around before it gets dark? The rest of us can prepare food and other things here."

"Thank you, Exi, sir. I will." Jetsam whistled Parula to his shoulder, and he and Red started into the forest in the general direction of the new river.

They returned after we had gathered food and prepared a meal. Not until after we had all eaten did they tell us what they had seen. Red began.

"Well, I climbed a big tree. And there is a river. And I think—though maybe I'm wrong—that it is our river—I mean the one we went on before. I think it's ours because of the forest down the way. It's dark and gloomy, and twisty, like the one we left—" Red stopped, his face solemn and filled with worry.

"You mean like the forest of the Beasts?" I asked.

"Yes, Maris. Like that."

"Then we must've come in a sort of half-circle around the Beasts' kingdom. And can't be too far upstream from the *Starflower*. But I hate to think of going again so near those terrible things!" I found that I drew back violently from the idea.

Exi's calm voice came in. "I should imagine none of us wants to, Maris. Surely you and Jetsam, Locus, and Parula must feel strongly about it. Yet if our earlier decision is still right, we have to go down the river to find our other boat, don't we? And perhaps beyond that."

"If I may speak, Exi, sir," said Jetsam, "I'd still say our chances of avoiding the Beasts are better if we keep traveling by day. And if we stay in the middle of a river as long as possible."

The sun was on the verge of setting, as Jetsam and I wandered together down the sloping bank to the stream. Jetsam wanted to be sure the raft was safely moored. By common consent, both of us wanted time alone to talk. The raft was secure. I sat on the grassy earth, watching Jetsam toss bits of this and that out into the water.

"Do you really feel we're as safe as you said?"

Jetsam didn't reply at once. Thoughtfully, he broke a twig into tiny pieces and tossed each piece into the stream. Then he said, "Probably not quite. But remember, they don't like water; in fact as I said before, they hate it. They only crossed a stream to get Locus and Isia. And you went down the river before and didn't see them."

"They weren't so mad then."

"That's true. That makes us less safe."

We sat for a while longer, watching the sky change from a luminous afterglow of sunset to a muted pearl gray to a dark where stars began to emerge. But I couldn't remember when I'd last seen the moon, and I spoke of this to Jetsam.

"What is the moon?" asked Jetsam. "I can't remember it."

I was filled with a momentary desolation. No moon! Why not? I shivered a little, and drew nearer Jetsam.

"Oh," I said, "I can't describe it. You'll maybe see it some day and remember." Jetsam had to be content with that.

Nevertheless I lay awake a long time that night, disturbed by the moonlessness of the world I traveled in. I looked toward the almost invisible trees and tried to imagine the moon rising behind them. I tried to visualize the shadows of things in full moonlight. Why did the moon matter so much? I did not know.

When I was awakened by Jetsam next morning, I had forgotten the night's preoccupation. It was apparent that Jetsam had been working, for all food supplies except breakfast were on the raft, while beside Jetsam lay one newly peeled, tapering branch and he was doing the final rubbing on a second one.

"We'll need longer paddles in the deeper water," he said, as if conversation had never stopped.

"Has everyone else eaten?" I asked.

"We've waited for you, miss," said Red politely.

17

THE SLIGHTLY CORRUGATED WATER WE HAD NOTICED YESTERDAY SOON
gave way to increased bumpiness as the stream met and merged
with the faster, wider, deeper river. With me on one side of the
raft and Jetsam on the other, we succeeded in riding the waves
quite successfully, however. Almost before we were prepared, our
raft slid between two wooded islands, dipped through the last
wavelets, and was pulled into the river's stronger current.

"I think it's our river!" I exclaimed, seeing the jungle of primeval plants and trees. "And we didn't see this branch when we came
by here because of the island."

"It looks as if you are right," said Exi. "And unless my memory
is totally untrustworthy, I would guess that we are not too far
from the island and the *Starflower*."

Carabus, Mr. Green, and Red agreed.

It was not yet midday when Exi said, with an excitement he
rarely showed, "There is the large island we rejected. Ours should
not be too much farther on."

A few more slow curves of the river and there was our island,
with its wooded roundness and its gentle slope of beach on the
side from which we were approaching.

"Oh, Jetsam, hurry!" I urged, beginning to paddle shoreward.

"No." Exi commanded firmly. "Not yet, please. We must be
sure nothing is there." And he asked that Parula be sent to survey
the island from above.

When Parula returned to Jetsam, he said, "All clear. Nothing
there."

With both of us paddling away, soon the raft was grounded on the beach and all the company and all the food were ashore. I helped Jetsam drag the raft well out of the water.

"I don't see why we should cover it," I said. "Don't you think it looks more like a log jam than a raft?"

"I do," Exi replied. "Therefore no one would think anything about it. Yes. Quite so."

"Now we can show Jetsam the *Starflower*, can't we? Please let's hurry!" I could hardly contain my eagerness.

Red spoke. "But that isn't so easy, you know. We left it on the other side. Remember?"

A shocked silence followed Red's words. From the expressions on the various faces I knew that they were feeling, as I was, chagrin and frustration at having forgotten. Seeing the puzzled look in Jetsam's eyes, I explained the situation.

"Oh, I don't see that it's as bad as you make it," he said calmly. "There'll be ways to get the boat. If it's still where you left it."

"Which it probably isn't!" I cried angrily.

"Which it probably is." Jetsam remained calm.

It didn't take us long to find our old home ground in the flower-filled clearing among the great broad-leaved trees. Our various tents had returned to the wilderness, but the grasses, ferns and flowers were readily available. I couldn't resist an uprush of pleasure on seeing this place.

"Well anyway," I said, "we're here. Together."

"That's the spirit!" Jetsam said confidently. "Let's get busy."

And we did. Once again shelters were constructed and food stored nearby. Then I suggested that Jetsam and I walk to the steep side of the island so I could show him the farther shore.

Soon we stood and peered through the protective trees. On the other side, beyond the wide, slow river, the land of the Beasts still lay dark and monstrous and fearsome.

"Where did you leave the boat?" Jetsam asked at last.

"Over there," I replied, pointing in the direction we had gone to find the prisoners. "I anchored it downstream from the Beasts' trail and swam ashore."

"How far away is it, do you think?"

"Well, in the *Starflower* and going with the current—let's see—

it must have taken us fifteen or twenty minutes, I guess."

"Straight across?"

"We angled. Why?"

"I could swim straight across in five minutes, I'm sure, then work my way along the edge until I found the boat."

"No! You can't! You mustn't! Please!"

"It wouldn't be so dangerous, Maris, really it wouldn't."

"But it would!"

"Look," Jetsam interrupted. "If I swim quietly—no splashing—and stop sometimes, I'll seem like a floating piece of something. If anyone sees me, I mean."

"Fine. Then I can go too. We'll look like two pieces of floating something."

We swam straight across, slowly, splashless. Then we let the current carry us downstream, not too far from the Beasts' shore. Every minute, we were on edge, watching the jungle. Nothing moved. The sluggish yellow water carried us past the path that Red and I had first explored so long ago. I wanted to show it to Jetsam but didn't dare risk a sound. Finally we came around a slight bend and there was the *Starflower* riding gently at her anchor.

She lay comfortably on the river like an enormous blossom, rising and falling in almost imperceptible rhythm. The makeshift paddle was in the central section where I had left it. A few leaves had blown into the boat. There was one small broken place on the outer rim as though a floating log had bumped against it. Otherwise the boat was exactly as it had been when I slipped over its side.

I resolved not to say anything to Jetsam, not to ask a single question, but to let him respond as he wished. We clung to the *Starflower* in silence, our arms and heads inside, the rest of us floating languidly in the water. Suddenly his hand gripped my arm.

"Listen!" His whisper was a command.

"I don't hear anything."

"Just listen."

I held my breath. At first nothing broke the quiet lapping sound of water. Then I caught, very faintly, noises I knew I would never forget.

"It's them! The Beasts!"

"Yes, they're coming."

"I'm scared, Jetsam."

"We're all right at the moment. They hate water, except for a bit to drink. But they're really upset, to come at this hour! Just let's stay out of sight, even if we are around the bend."

We hung on to the boat, our heads almost under the water. At long last, the sounds faded into the jungle. Another frightened few minutes, and then Jetsam helped me into the boat, climbed in after me, and we both got to work, I with the paddle, he with his hands.

We reached the island after a fast trip, hid the *Starflower*, and were back at camp well before fog or darkness. The others heard our story with serious faces, except Locus and Parula who seemed always preoccupied with little joys of one kind or another.

"Well, at least now we know that the Beasts are close around to be reckoned with," Exi said, when we finished.

"And our beautiful *Starflower*?" Mr. Green said in a loud challenging voice to Jetsam. "You have said nothing at all about our *Starflower*. How did you like her?"

Everyone, including me, looked at Jetsam.

Jetsam smiled and spread his hands. "There I go taking things for granted again. I think the *Starflower* is great. Well-built, light, easy to handle, good to look at."

"Good," said Mr. Green. "I just thought we should know."

"Of course," Jetsam said. "There's only one thing—"

"And that is?" Exi asked.

"That is, it isn't large enough for all of us."

"Well," I said, "can't we just add onto it?"

"That will make it harder to handle, won't it?" Red inquired.

"I suppose so, Red." Jetsam was serious as he continued. "But if we're to go on, we've got to travel with as many supplies as we can. And as protected as possible. Isn't that right, Exi?"

"It sounds right, Jetsam."

"Well then, we've got to have more space. Before, you didn't have Locus, Parula, or me."

All this seemed very reasonable, and the simple answer was to take both boats even·if they were absurdly unrelated.

"We have looked odder," I said to Jetsam when we were

launched next morning, "but I'm not sure when!"

The raft was first with Jetsam and me paddling and steering. Our supplies were on the back part of the raft. Trailing behind at the end of a grass rope was the *Starflower*, like a child being taken for a walk by a solemn parent. Each of its cupped white compartments was occupied by one of the company. We had decided to make our way on down the river; it seemed the most likely way for us to go.

For a while we paddled along in silence, dipping our makeshift oars into the water as nearly in unison as possible. Not much paddling was needed; the current was slow but strong. We just steered, while the morning flowed with the river, until Exi called, "Have you noticed the changes that are taking place?"

We lifted our paddles and inspected the river ahead. "Where?" Jetsam asked. "I don't see—"

"Not the river," Exi said sharply. "Look at the two sides of the river!"

Putting our paddles sideways to stop the boats, we stared at one side, then the other.

"Why, sir!" Jetsam said at last, "they're totally different! The left side—their side, the Beasts, I mean—their side is—is—"

"Yes. Precisely how would you describe it?" Exi was deeply concerned.

"Well, it's darker than ever I remember it. The trees look all blackish, and ugly wet, like crawling things underground—but so giantlike, almost as though they were reaching for something—us, maybe."

"And our side—it's like a desert—no trees or grass or anything! Just bare rocks, or sand."

"Also it doesn't look as if we could climb it. Banks are too steep." Jetsam considered a moment. "But why are we so upset? We aren't stopping, are we?"

"No," replied Exi. "No, we are not stopping yet. However, we must stop sometime, must we not?"

Red spoke suddenly. "But aren't we doing what we were going to do anyway, trying to get nearer to some answers? Going until we find a reason to stop? I think we just keep on."

Jetsam laughed. "Red, sometimes you go straight to the point better than anyone."

"Thank you, Jetsam. All I would add is that wherever we are, don't we need to be as clear as we can be about what that where involves?"

When the sun was high and pouring down, glinting from the water in thousands of moving jewels, we dropped anchors midstream. After a brief lunch and a time of stretching, the boats moved on.

"I've been thinking," said Jetsam after a while, "that we can't just go on and on down this river, avoiding both sides and pretending they don't exist. Somehow I've an idea that trying to do the work we have to do, whatever that is, means that we've got to go ashore to do it."

I listened to him in silence, watching the glassy water ahead, as he put this to the others. What a difficult thing it was always to have to get on with it, to be pushed into finding out what came next! All of which, and more, I said to Jetsam, who answered calmly that he guessed that was the best way of it all right.

Thus the day wandered into the evening with no change for the better on either bank as far as we could see. Even if we'd wanted to, we couldn't have altered our course. Frustrated and tired, none of us seemed to feel like talking.

Jetsam went back finally to ask Exi if we should stop. It was quite dark, and from where I was sitting, the *Starflower* was only a light blob behind me. I watched him until suddenly the sound of rushing water penetrated my mind. Before I could move to discover the source, raft and *Starflower* were swept into rapids and went spinning and tossing about out of control. It would have been fearful enough by day; but in the night, my terror was enlarged by crashes and outcries and loud boiling of water over rocks. Jetsam had the presence of mind, almost at the instant the boats were being pulled into the rapids, to shout, "Try to hold on!" The only thing I had was the raft. I fell down on its pitching surface and worked my fingers between the logs to get as tight a grip as possible. For what seemed an eternity I and the raft were flung up and down, banged into, washed over. I had no idea whether the others were alive or not. I could only endure until I was numb and spent.

When it was finished, it took me a long time to know that it was over. My mind was not functioning, but my ears sent Jetsam's call to my brain.

"Maris! Exi! Anyone! Where are you?" His voice was loud and sharp with fear. "Maris! Exi!"

"Jetsam!" To me my own voice sounded very weak and far away. "Jetsam!"

I could hear him sloshing through water, then I felt his arms lifting me and carrying me some place, and then I was set down on dry, sandy ground. Locus landed in my lap abruptly, wet and shivering. One by one, I heard the voices of Red, Exi, Carabus, Mr. Green, as each was set down nearby.

Jetsam spoke our names and we each replied. It was more than good to hear each voice speak out. "Now what do we do? Is there any food?" Exi asked.

"No, sir," Jetsam said. "Not as far as I can tell. The *Starflower* turned upside down finally, I guess, because you three were hanging on to one part of it when I found you."

"And we dare not make a fire."

"I'm afraid not, Exi, sir. From the stumbling about I've done, I've felt nothing but rocks and sand."

"Well then, I think we had better get as close together as we can and try to rest until day comes."

18

DAY DID COME AT LAST TO AN ODD CLUMP OF CREATURES CURLED around each other like a nest of mice.

"Good morning," Mr. Green greeted everyone. "A very, *very* good morning! Because we have been *saved* from a dreadful fate! Only my great-uncle—the one I am sure I have mentioned before —has had *any* experiences even touching *this one* for dangerousness!"

"Certainly didn't enjoy it," was Carabus's comment.

Upstream the white water of the rapids was glistening in the morning sun. It was apparent now that the river narrowed at that point and rushed through an abrupt gorge. Then it settled into a shallow, cresent bay. This bay had been our salvation, for here the river had desposited us and our two battered boats. Bits and pieces of the *Starflower* still circled lazily like old leaves in autumn in the river's eddy. The raft, broken into two parts, lay aground on the beach. The jungle of the opposite shore was dark and ominous, and seemed to loom more gigantic than ever. But the beach upon which we stood was more overwhelming to us at the moment. It was a vast expanse of beige sand with a few outcroppings of gray rock scattered about. No plant or tree grew on it. No breeze stirred. Far inland this same beige wasteland stretched away, slowly rising until it merged into darker slopes. These eventually lifted up to a mountain range of incredible height. Jagged granitic peaks stood straight against the sky, remote and unconquerable.

Red, always practical, said, "You know, if I may say so, there just might be—that is, couldn't it be that some of our food packages are floating around out there?"

"Why not? At least we can find out." Jetsam rolled up his pants and waded into the shallow water. I followed him. When we reached the spot where the remains of the *Starflower* drifted, we peered and poked into the water until we found three sodden bundles of food.

The meal that followed should have been miserable. It wasn't. The nutlike seeds and fruits and the leaves had not been altered much by the night's immersion. Hunger and gratefulness for survival gave the food added flavor. No one missed having a fire, because we hadn't had one for so long anyway. Exi portioned the food, saving some for another time because we had no idea when or where we could get more.

"My word," said Mr. Green, wiping his antennae with his forefeet, "that was one of the *finest* meals I have ever had! *Now* what do we do? Build more boats?"

"I don't think so." I looked at Exi.

"No, no more boats. As I think we agreed late yesterday, we need to get on our feet and move in a new direction. Our major question then was how to do it. I rather think this question has been answered, although not quite as we might have expected." He paused.

"Not quite! Not at all!" Carabus was emphatic for once, and the others nodded agreement.

"Very well. Not at all as we expected," Exi continued, "but we are here, boatless and almost foodless, and we have to move on. Since there is no real choice of direction, should we not get started soon?"

"I think we should." Jetsam's face was eager. "It's a long way to those mountains and that's where we've got to go."

"How do you know?" I asked.

"We can't just poke along the river, or we might as well be on it. Anyway, there isn't any food here. If we're going to find someone who can help us learn how to bring healing we've got to get moving! And the mountains are the only place to move to."

His enthusiasm for the new venture swept all of us into action. Exi, the other beetles, and Red went first, then I came along, with Locus wandering beside me; while Jetsam, Parula on his shoulder, was last. I felt sad to leave the river behind, for it had carried us on a remarkable journey and had been kind to us for the most part. It was sadder to leave the *Starflower*—or its poor shattered pieces. I turned around several times to see the river and the bits of white floating there, until I could no longer be sure what I was seeing. At last I gave a wave and turned forward.

We were quiet as we moved ahead, a silent, solemn group searching for a new way. And each of us seemed to be searching in himself for some new meaning, as well.

"Look," said Jetsam suddenly, excitement in his voice. "Look beyond us there!" He pointed toward the mountains. "Isn't that a clump of bushes or something?"

We had come farther than I had been aware of. The river was out of sight, the jungle beyond it only a blurred purple-green, while ahead of us, although the peaks of the mountains appeared no nearer, the barren land began to slope upward gradually. There was, most surely, a hillock, and on it a patch of grayish olive trees.

"Let's get there!" Jetsam grabbed me by the hand and started off. Locus and Parula were already on the way. Unresisting, I ran by his side, hardly aware of the increased heat. As we came nearer, the little hill was seen as round and compact, covered with six or eight dwarfed trees. When finally we reached the place, we found a minute spring of clear water and dropped beside it in the shade, splashing our faces happily and cupping our hands to drink. Jetsam went out and urged the others to hurry—which they did not do, but only marched resolutely onward until they too rested in the scant but welcome shadows.

"This is good," said Exi, stretching his legs one by one, with a special care for the lame one. "I should think this was an excellent time and place to eat what food remains."

When once again we started off for the forbidding mountains, even Jetsam, I suspected, was hesitant to leave the cool little grove, although his explorer's instinct was aroused by what lay ahead.

For at least two hours, maybe more, we walked toward the mountains, over the same kind of rocky ground much of the time. However, there was a slow rise that was evident whenever we looked back. Also we did pass several other clumps of trees, none so appealing as our first one but each one encouraging us. The heat grew. Jetsam and I were damp and sticky with perspiration, and I noticed Exi beginning to limp more than usual. I mentioned my concern to Jetsam.

"Yes," he said, "we're all tired, I guess." He gestured ahead. "But you know, I wonder if there isn't some shelter and some chance of food not too far off."

I looked where he was pointing. There did seem to be a cleft in the nearest mountain—or rather, foothill of the mountains— and a soft misty green that could mean a small canyon or valley. "Why don't we let the others rest?" I said. "We can go and find out what's there."

"All right," he said, After diplomatically maneuvering Exi and the others into taking a rest period under a few sparse bushes, Jetsam asked me, "Can you go fast?" I said I could and away we went, jogging over the uneven ground. I felt as if I had to push myself with every bit of strength I had left, but I kept going. Sweat was running into my eyes and down my legs, and I was just about to say I couldn't go further when Jetsam halted.

"It is a canyon, a real canyon with trees and a stream and probably food! Just look at it!" he shouted.

"I'm looking," I replied, breathless.

Our jaunt had brought us rather more quickly than we had anticipated into the true foothills, with the mountains very close beyond rising sharply and suddenly to incredible heights, one laid over another into the violet distance. The foothills themselves were not small but were gentler and covered with trees and bushes and grasses in a variety of greens. Directly before us was the cleft we had seen from a distance. It proved to be, as Jetsam had said, a real canyon, all sweet-smelling coolness. There were trees like willows, trees full-bodied like chestnuts, staunch ones like beeches, lovely ones like young maples. (I say like, because none were ex-actly the trees I knew.) Jetsam waded right into the shallow stream and sat down, splashing water over himself like a baby in a tub. I did the same. We laughed and splashed each other and got thoroughly wet. Then we sat on a rock in the sun and dried out, not saying much but letting ourselves get rested.

"I'd better go back for the others," Jetsam announced after a while, and left.

The canyon was very silent. I continued to sit on the rock and absorb my surroundings. After the sandy waste and the barren earth over which we had plodded since morning this was a spot to soothe the eyes and comfort weary feet. In addition to the trees, there were low, drooping bushes and mossy turf, like a velvet throw rug. Some bushes had purple berries; this meant food of a kind at least.

I had risen from the rock, deciding to go back out into the sunlight, when the rest arrived. For a while there was a flutter of bathings and soakings, coolings and groomings. Exi obviously was improved by his rest, and the others seemed not to have suffered from their coming. When we were settled down, Exi took command again.

"You must forgive me," he said, "if I slowed down somewhat out there. I am not as strong, or as young, as I once was." He made one of his grave and courtly bows. "Even so, I have not, I believe, lost my wisdom."

When Exi said this he wasn't being proud, just honest. And he was right. He was the wisest, and the leader, and we all knew it and nodded accordingly. "It is clear," he continued, "that there is food around here. And there is water available. I suggest that we make a camp and settle for the night, because I think we have nothing to fear for the time being."

I could tell Jetsam didn't like this from the way he tossed his head. Exi caught it too, and before Jetsam could protest, Exi turned to him and said, "I am sure you would rather go on, Jetsam, and would tell me, if I let you, that we still have several hours of day left to us. Please remember, however, that we are eight, not one, and that some are older and less vigorous than you and Maris."

Jetsam had closed his mouth when Exi turned to him, and now he appeared chagrined and uncomfortable.

Exi went on, "Now I count on you to take charge of building and organizing our camp. Why don't you take Maris and Red and explore for the right place? The rest of us will gather edibles."

"Yes, sir!" Jetsam was all eagerness again. "We'll get right to it!"

Under his direction we began hunting for a suitable night

shelter. Several ideas were suggested but discarded, because they did not seem right.

"Well, what's left?" I asked finally.

Jetsam rubbed his head with the familiar gesture. "There's one place where the canyon side comes closer. Let's look there." There was a lobe of the mountain that protruded outward nearer the stream, so that the canyon narrowed and had at that point a steep side of stone. The three of us poked our way through trees and bushes to this stone outcrop. There in the face of the cliff, where the smooth granite came down to meet a slight uprise of open green turf, was a semi-cave. This indentation, or overhang, was polished smooth inside, and the arched roof made it a true shelter.

Yet our discovery brought a confusion of feelings, for next to the rear wall was a fire pit, ringed with stones. Ashes in the pit and soot on stones and wall were ample evidence of considerable use. Others had been here before us. But who? Or what? Enemies? Friends? Jetsam's face was grim and tense; Red drew his sword. We moved closer together. Red turned over the ashes carefully with his sword point. "My opinion is that this has not been used for quite a spell. Ashes old, caked from damp—and a bit of green growing there."

So we went back to the others and told our story. They were dubious, but eventually we all agreed to make a shelter out of the half-cave. We gathered up our bundles and went to the shelter. It didn't take long for us to settle in and eat. And by the time we finished, it was growing dark. Before night came completely, Jetsam and I managed to enclose our hollow with a veritable bramble patch of old, twisted branches.

Exi and Red took first watch, each of the rest of us trying to get comfortable enough to sleep. I was sure I wouldn't. I kept remembering that terrible night when the Beasts came, and I kept Locus very close to me. But before I could worry too much, it was morning.

19

Awakening in our cave, I was filled with that kind of anticipation usually associated with Sunday outings in early childhood, which was odd, considering the uneasiness of the night before. Somehow the scents of musky dampness from cool stone, of resinous cut branches, and of sunlight—for sunlight does have a particular odor—combined to stir even Carabus into more than usual vitality. As I sat watching the beetles and Red busy around the cave, my gaze caught something none of us had seen last night.

"Jetsam!" I called. I pointed to the uphill side of the cave, where the edge folded into the granite cliff and the interior became the exterior. "Do you see what I see? It's a path! Right along the base of the cliff, going up the canyon!"

After a minute or so of looking, "Yes," he said. "Sure I see it! Wonder why we didn't notice it yesterday."

By this time the others had joined us. "I should suppose," Exi said, "that the shadows were too deep yesterday and this path was hidden. It most definitely seems to be going to some particular place."

We moved nearer to where the path led out of the cave. Red walked onto it, examining it carefully. "I do think—well, a lot of feet have been here—it's hard to say how long since—" His voice stopped as he continued to peer at this unexpected trail.

We ate breakfast quietly. Then Exi called us together.

"Am I correct in saying that there is no question but that we follow this path to its destination?" He waited to see whether there

154

would be disagreement. There wasn't, so he went on. "We have no idea where it will lead us. We do know, I think, that by following our noses, so to speak, we arrived here. Whatever work is awaiting us, I feel sure this path leads to it."

"And I say," put in Mr. Green, with a resonant enthusiasm, "I say, let's *enjoy* it, let's *live* it fully, let's not just be *bowed down* by the *weight* of it!" There was a burst of yeses, and we went forward rather less formally than usual but well enough organized so that Red and Exi went first and Jetsam and I were the rear guard, with the others in between.

It was a gorgeous morning, different from any we had previously had together. Autumn was surely in the air. There were colored leaves as we climbed, at first just an occasional small patch but then larger and larger clusters. There is a heady flavor to such days, and it actually tasted on my tongue.

The mysterious and well-worn path kept close to the base of the mountain at first, curving as the mountain curved. Its rise was slow but definite, making us aware in our legs that we climbed. Little by little the stream fell below us. Diminutive cataracts from time to time rolled from above across the trail, and their cold water was irresistible. Odd little pear-shaped fruits hung from low trees above one or two of the brooks, and we nibbled on them and found them firm and not too sour. What with these and the omnipresent berries, we had no need to stop for lunch.

Sometime in midafternoon Exi and Red, who had been walking some distance ahead, suddenly turned around and came to meet us. "What's wrong, sir?" Jetsam asked.

"I am not sure anything is wrong," Exi said. "But if you will notice, we are approaching a pass, and Red and I wondered if perhaps one of us should look ahead a bit before we all blunder into—well, into some danger."

The trail had taken us slowly up the mountainside, until without noticing, we were nearing its summit. Or rather, we were nearing a narrow saddle made by "our" mountain and the one that had all along been on the opposite side of the canyon. We followed Exi a few yards forward, around a bend, and saw what he and Red had seen. The trail went through the saddle and disappeared.

"Yes, now I see," said Jetsam. "Shall we go ahead and explore?"

"I think not," Exi replied. "I think Red should do it."

"You see I'm slender and—well, I can climb high and see far. It isn't that you aren't—well, you do understand, don't you?"

"You're just the one," Jetsam said.

So Red went on his six silent and delicate feet to where the trail seemed to end. Instead of going through the pass, he left the path and made his way carefully up the trunk of a large tree and was hidden from sight. After a few minutes he emerged again, took the trail forward and was gone. I held my breath—and I suspect others did too. But very soon he reappeared, calm and unhurried, and returned to us.

"What did you see?" Exi asked.

"It's quite all right—that is, it's lovely, and I didn't see any enemy or such, and—oh dear, you must all come at once."

We all tumbled over each other—not really, but we weren't any of us very polite. We crowded into the pass and stared beyond and down. Jetsam, standing behind me, grabbed my shoulder in amazement. Even Locus and Parula were still.

Below us lay a most exquisite jewel of a valley. I was certain as I gazed that I had never before seen so lovely a sight, nor ever would again. Surrounded by the great raw rocky peaks we had glimpsed already but which now were closer and more awesome than ever, the valley itself was a nest of the softest green, embroidered with swatches of autumn brocade. It was perfectly round. In the very center of it was a lake, as round as round, and like an opal flashing back the sun. Warm afternoon light laid a rosy patina over shafts of trees and exposed meadows so that the entire valley seemed to glow in a way that to me meant only one thing—welcome. And before I had time to consider, I was through the pass and running down the trail toward the valley.

Jetsam was right behind me. Locus flung her little self helter-skelter ahead of us, and Parula soared away into the trees and was lost to view. We could not, of course, run all the way down the narrow, twisting path, much as we wanted to. At last our breath gave out, mine and Jetsam's, and we pulled up at a wide level place where there was grass and a miniature waterfall.

"Where do you suppose Locus went?" I asked.

"Where Parula did, no doubt."

"Where is that?"

"Haven't any idea. Down there, I should think."

"Do you think we ought to worry?"

"No. There's something sort of safe and secure about this place. Don't you feel it?"

"Yes. Oh, yes!"

Once we had caught our breath, we were off again. We didn't wait for the others, knowing they would be slower and quite safe. We jogged along at a more sensible pace this time, so we could look about us. This slope of the mountain seemed even gentler than the one we had come up. The path was wider and friendlier, with frequent openings in the tree cover, appealing spots of warm sunlight, and scatterings of small, short-stemmed, blue lilies.

Everything important is always around a corner, I was thinking to myself as we turned one. I couldn't have been more accurate if I had been trying to, because there, in the midst of a clearing surrounded by russet-leaved bushes, sat Locus in evident delight before a winged creature almost as large as I. It was raising and lowering its wings slowly and rhythmically while it gazed upon her with enormous eyes. I stopped in astonishment, and Jetsam almost fell over me.

"What—" he started, but I held up my hand for him to be quiet.

Locus and the other one did not see us at first. Then tears came into the great eyes of the winged being, tears as large and round as the eyes. The wings closed above the creature's back—wonderful dove-gray velvet wings they were—and the eyes turned toward me.

"Maris! Dear Maris!" said a familiar voice. "And Jetsam! I rather thought maybe you'd be coming along soon. Locus doesn't say anything, but she knew me right off, bless her! I've changed a lot, but I still have my feelings all over the place."

I almost knew, but for a moment my mind fumbled. Jetsam had a remembering expression on his face. Locus ran from us to the newcomer and back in enthusiastic abandon, as if she were sure we were all long lost friends.

"My face is different, I guess, isn't it? I guess I was—"

Suddenly I knew. "Isia!" I shouted. "Woolly bear!" I rushed to him and tried to hug him, but with such wings I couldn't. So I patted his soft head and stroked his body and his velvety wings, and I kissed the top of his head, and I cried over him. Until Jetsam, in masculine annoyance, said, "Oh, stop it! You're getting him all wet!"

"I don't mind at all, really I don't," Isia said. "I know just how she feels. It's wonderful to be together again!"

We admired Isia's new body and told him how handsome he was, which was true, and he did a soar or two for us. As he fluttered about us, now here, now there, we could see what we had not seen before. Toward the tip of each wing, on the inside, was a large patch of electric blue bordered with purple. Isia was proud of these lustrous "eyes," which shone whenever the sunlight caught them. I would have been proud of them too, and I told him so.

"Yes. I am certainly different than I was. I must have been a sad sight in my other life—fat and fuzzy and slow, making faces to be more important, and all that sort of thing."

"It wasn't like that at all! You were nice." I could tell he didn't like that too much. "And brave. You stayed with Locus and tried to protect her."

"And," added Jetsam, "you had a lot of courage in front of the Beasts."

"Ugh!" Isia shuddered. "Don't remind me of all that!"

"What happened after I—after I—"

"After you almost got him killed," said Jetsam, bluntly.

"Well—" Isia began. But just then the rest of the company arrived. They halted in surprise and question just as Jetsam and I had, but much sooner recognized Isia; in no time everyone was talking at once.

Eventually we let him tell his story. For quite a while, he said, he stayed with Arachne in her home, being fed and nursed. Yes, Botta had been in and out, exceedingly busy. No, they had not seen the Beasts, although they had heard them often enough. Then one night Arachne had wrapped him in yards and yards of the softest silk until he was so enfolded he couldn't move and only his head was free. She had carried him out in the darkness to some place unseen and unknown, had told him not to fear, that all would be well, had swathed even his head in silken folds. Then he felt himself lifted, and the last he remembered was a sensation of swinging gently in the dark, as if he were a leaf on a tree. He said he had no idea how long he was in this condition. Then there was dim light, a hard struggle against suffocation, and at last a breaking free. He had found himself, very weak and lightheaded, clutching an unfamiliar plant, surrounded by torn shreds of gossamer, and looking, he supposed, as he did now.

Didn't it take caterpillars longer to become butterflies than the time we'd been away from him? I asked. He guessed he had heard Arachne say something about speeding things up.

Where had he been? Well, he wasn't at all clear, although it couldn't have been far from the Beasts. And how did he get here? He had been escorted. More than that he would not say.

"Do you live around here, then?" Exi asked, at the end of Isia's story.

"Oh, no! Dear me, no! I forgot! I'm supposed to be a welcoming person, and to let my friends know so we can all escort you! Wait here!"

Before we could ask why, or how long, or what friends, he had disappeared over the treetops.

"We had best follow his instructions," said Exi calmly. "It is a good time to rest and prepare ourselves."

With that, Exi began to groom himself carefully—antennae, legs, shell, under wings. Mr. Green and Carabus did the same. Red went over his body first and then began polishing his beloved sword. Parula was still missing, but none of us seemed to have any worry on her account.

"Jetsam," I said, feeling more uncouth by the moment, "I think we'd better do something about how we look. You are a mess!"

"So are you!" he retorted. "Let's get clean, anyway. There's a stream over there. You go first."

I found the water—another of the small clear mountain creeks such as we had drunk from—hidden behind trees. Taking off my clothes, I shook the dust from them and laid them in the sun, then washed myself in the cold water. It was a shock, but good. When I had dried myself and put on my clothes again and combed my wet hair with my fingers, I felt considerably fresher, and only hoped I looked it. Certainly Jetsam did when he returned from his bath.

When we were all standing together in the clearing, Exi scrutinized us and said, with one of his rare demonstrations of sly humor, "My word, are we not a splendid company! Dressed for a royal reception, I should say!"

He had only just said the words when over the treetops came a crowd of huge and glorious butterflies, led by a flaming orange monarch. Our group of seven drew close, Exi a step in front, while the butterflies settled one by one on the ground before us. Their slow-pulsing wings were a sea of amazing color. No two were exactly alike. There were sulphur yellows with brown edges, powder blues with tiny russet circles, black ones with elegant tails, snowy whites edged with gold—so very many combinations and variations that my eyes were bewildered. I spotted Isia among them, and had a notion that he smiled at us. But he said nothing. It was clear that this was a high moment, and that the monarch alone would speak.

The monarch moved directly in front of us, settled his brilliant wings together over his back, and spoke.

"May we welcome you to our country." His voice was low and gentle, but commanding—a friendly voice, to be trusted. "We have been expecting you. Therefore we are twice happy to give you welcome."

Exi bowed. "I suppose," he said carefully, "we should not ask how you knew we were coming."

"You should not ask." The monarch seemed in no way offended by the question. "You will learn when it is time."

"Thank you," Exi responded. "I had no wish to intrude. I wanted only to know what to anticipate. However, I am willing to forego that wish." He paused. The monarch remained silent. Exi continued. "And now may I express, for myself and all my companions, the joy we feel in being so received. Whatever you wish us to do, wherever you wish us to go, I am sure we will happily agree." He bowed again.

Once more the monarch spoke, this time to all of us. "We will be your escort down into the Valley of the Opal. That is to say, some of us will. I and my aides will precede you." His voice had a hint of laughter in it as he added, "I am sure your entrance will be more relaxed this way."

Slowly he lifted himself on his graceful wings, quiet as an enormous leaf borne on the wind; he was followed by eight of the larger butterflies. They went like a rainbow over the trees.

After the royal retinue departed, Isia apparently saw our hesitation in the face of such overwhelming beauty, and sensed that we didn't know quite what to do next. So he made his way through the confusion of wings and colors and joined us.

"You all look too solemn for words!" Soon the sunlit clearing was filled with voices. We found that all of these beings, although they were different from each other in many ways, spoke in the same low, quiet, self-contained way.

After introductions and a period of getting acquainted, Isia turned to Exi. "I think we'd best start down now. You go along the path and we'll go along above the path."

And that was exactly how it was. Jetsam and I were so excited at nearing the Valley of the Opal that we had to work to keep our pace slow enough to include the others. Except Locus, of course, who had to be held back.

The path down into the Valley of the Opal grew more and more beautiful as we went. We walked on soft green turf rather than pebbles. In fact, every bit of earth was covered either with lush grass or with plants of all sizes, from short-stemmed lilies to asters and hollyhocks, from berry bushes to fruit trees to birches and maples and evergreen trees. Blossoms, fruits, and autumn leaves were all mixed up together, yet nothing seemed out of place. From time to time Isia, with a long glide, came near to us to be sure we were seeing everything, and to pass the time of day with Exi or Red or some one of us.

As we came nearer the valley's floor, the path leveled and became much wider, until at last we were going along a broad avenue of turf. On either side was a row of trees, alternating rust or gold autumn colors, with pink or white spring blossoms. Never having seen such a wonder, I stopped in amazement, only to have Isia hover near my face and say not to stop now. There would be plenty of time later. So we moved forward.

Then the lake, the jewel-like lake, was visible ahead down the grassy aisle. And silently from between the trees left and right came more and more butterflies, until at last we approached the shore surrounded by a cloud of colorful pulsating wings. Thus we emerged from the trees. The butterfly cloud folded back as a wave might do, and there we were, standing in a meadow beside the water, facing a flower-covered mound upon which rested the monarch.

20

THE OFFICIAL RECEPTION WASN'T LONG. I SOON CAME TO UNDERSTAND that the butterflies thoroughly enjoyed ritual and drama, so they kept their affairs short and filled each day with as many as possible.

We were taken to our "residences," which turned out to be spacious bowers in trees, one for each of us (except for Locus and I who were together). Each held grassy couches, tables with food, and the filmiest robes I ever saw, marked like butterfly wings. Whether these robes were to make us or our hosts more at ease I wasn't sure, but as we wore them we fitted more gently into the landscape. It soon became apparent that we were to stay awhile. The days passed quickly.

Along toward evening of the fourth day, Jetsam and I were lolling in the grass at the lake's edge, stuffed with warm sunlight, soft turf, clear water, rest, and food. He looked fine and I felt the same. Isia came sailing down to alight near us, raising and lowering his gorgeous wings. "Hello," he said, as if he was trying to sound casual.

"What's up?" I asked.

"Nothing much, really. We *are* having a special kind of banquet and ceremony tonight of course. I just thought I'd tell you so you could—well—dress up a little, maybe."

"Isia, old friend," said Jetsam. "You're trying to say a change is coming. And this is the beginning, isn't it?"

Isia nodded.

When we finally gathered together at sunset in the wide space between the trees, we were very impressive. Each of us wore a rich new ceremonial cloak that had been left for us in our rooms. When we approached the place of the ceremonies, the sun was just setting and its last light put an extra warmth on everything.

The monarch was seated, or stood before (it's difficult to say how such beings as butterflies and beetles do it) a table on a raised mound. Around him in concentric circles were other tables, dozens of them, at which were all the butterflies of the kingdom. As we came nearer, I could see that there were empty places at the monarch's table. I feared we were to sit with him, which was correct. Slowly we proceeded, winding our way through the other tables, until at last we came and were seated. I would have preferred a less conspicuous place. Not until I saw the monarch's face across from me and the merriment in his eyes, did I feel at home.

"Welcome," said the monarch, as he always did at the start of every ritual. But then he went on, in a tone I had not heard him use—more solemn, more dramatic. "This is a highly joyful and a deeply serious occasion. There are joyful matters to be brought to conclusions. There is a serious endeavor to be undertaken. We shall celebrate them all, one at a time."

In some mysterious fashion he must have given a signal, for all at once there was a rustle of raised wings as everyone looked up toward the treetops. And over the trees and down into the midst of us came four of the blue butterflies of the monarch's guard. Between them they carried a small evergreen branch. Seated side by side on the branch were Parula and Hatch.

"May I propose a toast?" said the monarch, raising a frail translucent goblet.

I saw that I had one too. Everyone had a goblet. We all raised ours.

"With the coming of a new messenger, unexpected wealth is added to our land, and to all other lands except one. The old messenger, Hatch, is the scarlet thread of Their wisdom woven into our lives. The Golden One, Parula, a newcomer, has now been taught by Them and entrusted with grave tasks as a messenger. Two messengers can perhaps bring a new order, if we here present can alter certain things of which we will speak later. For this time, however, let us drink to messengers old and new."

I drank from the little goblet. Parula and Hatch perched quietly on the green branch, as solemn as owls. Then there must have been another of those signals, for there was a hush over the assembly again.

I looked around to see what was happening and ended up looking at the monarch. To my embarrassment, I saw he was peering at me, only at me, with an expression in his many-faceted eyes that I couldn't understand.

"Maris," he said.

"Yes, sir," I replied, not knowing for sure how to address him. I got up and did one of my awkward curtsys.

He smiled. "Maris, I have a surprise for you. Do you have an idea about it?"

I shook my head, utterly puzzled.

"Let him be brought," said the monarch.

Beyond us, down a side aisle of the trees, I could see a procession of lanterns bobbing in the darkness. As they came nearer, the lanterns became fireflies walking slowly along in two columns. Something was between them, but in the night it was hard to see. Then the procession came into the pool of light which shimmered over the banquet area, and I saw. I completely forgot dignity and silence and the monarch. I jumped to my feet and ran among the tables and the smiling and tolerant butterflies. I rushed into the heart of the firefly columns, causing them to break ranks.

"Scuro!" I shouted. "Scuro! Scuro! You're alive! You're all right! I thought you were gone for always, so I didn't ask! Oh Scuro!" And I really cried, huge wet tears of mixed-up happiness and excitement and disbelief.

"Maris," said a strange voice, "I'm really here, you know." And a rough tongue was licking my face, and my hands were twined in curly hair on a solid body.

"You can talk," I said stupidly.

"Of course." He backed away a bit and gazed at me with his head-cocked whimsy, which I had forgotten. "Doesn't everybody?"

Speechless, I started back to our table, while Scuro and the fireflies, proceeded as gravely as if there had been no disruption. I slipped into my place. Scuro was presented formally to the monarch, bowed his head, and took his position at our table. So we were eleven.

Moods changed fast in this kingdom. With a lift of wings and a laugh, the monarch moved ritual into feast. Hordes of fireflies twinkled in and out among the tables, serving a banquet I couldn't begin to describe. Gaiety, chatter, food and drink, toasts, trying to tell each other everything all at once—this was what our table was like.

Scuro said he had been in a land he could not yet talk about. I would learn in my way, he said. It had to do with Them, yes. He had been taught a great lot and had gone from childhood to adulthood, he told me. No, he could not and he would not say more about Them. Wait, he said. Be patient.

I tried to give him an account of my journeyings since that long past day in the hills above the sea. It was good to do it. It gave me a chance once more to see everything lined up together. In some way I began to see the world before Exi and the world after Exi as both belonging to me.

So I was ready when the monarch said, "Let us now consider the work that lies ahead."

Exi and Isia knew what it was, I was sure, or at least they knew a lot about it. Perhaps Scuro did. Maybe Hatch knew, too. And Parula. The rest of us waited, half afraid, half excited, to learn what was to come.

"For a very long time," said the monarch, "the land of the Beasts and the Place of Them have been divided from one another."

"Why?" Jetsam asked.

"Because some of the Beasts grew impatient with council meetings, considering them much too slow, and broke away in order to have a kingdom more to their liking. This has not worked, for two reasons. First and most important is the fact that nothing that has genuine life in it will grow if it is hurried and bullied and ordered to grow, and so everything the Beasts have taken over has either died or withdrawn from living. The second reason is that the separation hampers growth even in the Place of Them because too much energy is being used in keeping the

Beasts from expanding their kingdom."

"I don't understand, sir," said Jetsam, "why the Beasts can't be conquered. Aren't They stronger than the Beasts?"

"Yes and no. If They wanted to use the Beasts' methods, They would be stronger. But this They will not do—indeed, this They cannot do, else everything would be ruled in the Beasts' way, by power alone, and would eventually die. So you see, Jetsam, it is not simple."

"I see, sir. And is this where we come in?"

"Yes. The job can be done satisfactorily only by those who are not of our world. When you arrived, we hoped you could help, but the Beasts got you first. Then Maris and Scuro came. They took Scuro, but left Maris to find her strength and her way, with Exi's support. She is doing that." He looked at me and smiled. "And now you three are together, and on you rests the burden of solution."

"What do we have to solve?" Jetsam asked.

"Your task is to try to find a way to bring the Beasts and Them together without one completely destroying the other."

"But that's impossible!" I exclaimed.

"Maybe it is," the monarch answered calmly. "Maybe it isn't. At any rate, They have asked me to put it in your hands, for we of our world are too close to it. We cannot solve it."

My mind wandered during the entertainment that followed. Isia told me later, somewhat hurt that I had not paid attention, that there were ancient dances, songs, and tales from early times. But I had other matters to occupy me.

After the evening had ended with the usual ritual processions and all the butterflies had retired, our company gathered near the residences. We drew as close together as we could, not for the sake of secrecy but because we seemed to need each other. After a long wait, Jetsam cleared his throat.

"Do you have any advice, Exi, sir?"

"No," Exi replied in a gentle voice.

"Then may I say what I've been thinking?"

"Please do, Jetsam."

"I haven't gotten very far, because I don't really know yet where to go. But I've been thinking that this job, however it's to be, is mine and Maris's and Scuro's. That's how it was given. And that—well, it isn't going to be a picnic. And the rest of you aren't really involved. You needn't come along, you know."

Jetsam's speech stirred up a crackling burst of protests, none of which could be heard above the others until Mr. Green raised his loudest and finest theatrical voice.

"I *must* confess—and I am *sure* I speak for everyone—I must confess that I am *deeply* disappointed in you, my boy! *Deeply!* After the *terrible* things we have gone through together—after what we have *endured* as comrades—that you should *question* our loyalty, should *doubt* us—I find myself quite unable to believe this of you!"

I started to reply, but Red cut me off. "Now Somy," he said, "I don't think he meant that. It's just that nobody wants anybody to get into a lot of trouble and danger unless he wants to. I mean, I think he and Maris just want us to choose to go ourselves—don't want to feel we feel he feels we ought to—oh, dear, does anyone see what I mean?"

"Yes." It was Carabus. "For myself, I go with my friends unless they don't want me to go."

"We want to go with you," said Exi. "And each has spoken for himself."

"Yes, sir. And thank you, Exi, Mr. Green, Red, Carabus. I don't know what we'd have done if you hadn't wanted to. And now, sir, what do we do?"

"I can only say what I said before. I have no advice to give. It is not my wisdom that will serve this time. This is for you three to work out. We will follow and help."

"Then," said Jetsam, sounding very young, "I guess we'd better go to bed. I can't come up with anything at all. Can you, Maris?"

I couldn't either. So we went to bed.

My sleep that night was sporadic and unsatisfying. I turned over and over on the grassy bed, pulled between a round of useless thoughts and fragments of dream. One such bit—about a bloodstained Beast and a full moon—brought me totally awake. The light was just beginning to come, Locus was eyeing me hopefully, so I decided to get up and out. When I reached the lake I found Jetsam and Scuro already there.

"Good morning," I said. "I guess you couldn't sleep any better than I could."

"That's right," Scuro said, shaking himself thoroughly. "He thrashed about so that I finally woke him up."

Jetsam laughed. "Yes. It was a good thing too, because I was having a terrible dream about Beasts."

I told him about mine. He couldn't remember his, but we decided we'd better sit down and talk about what to do.

"Scuro," asked Jetsam, after we were settled by the water's edge, "Where do They live? You've been there. You must know something."

Scuro scratched behind his right ear, pondering. "Thing was, you see, They brought me to this place at night with my eyes covered." He scratched behind his left ear. "Not much help. It's a long way. It's beyond those far mountains somewhere, on a very high place. Cold getting there, splendid when you arrive. That's all I have."

"So They are in the opposite direction from the Beasts, then. And somewhere in those mountains we saw from the river," I said.

We sat for a long time. When we started talking again we agreed, rather dismally, that all any of us could see to do was to go back into the Beasts' kingdom and lure them away, "unbunch them," as Jetsam said, and capture them. It was impossible, we agreed. But it had to be done. Scuro suggested we go overland rather than by the waterways. It meant going up and down mountains. I also meant—maybe—a better chance of surprising the Beasts, by coming at them from an unexpected direction. It sounded absolutely awful.

When I returned to my room, I laid my few precious possessions out on my bed. I hadn't opened my bundle since our boat wreck. But the spider-thread suits were there, all five of them, and the gift of the Mantid, and a few wheat grains from the ant kingdom. I looked at them all thoughtfully. Why not try the Mantid's gift? I asked myself.

Alone in my room, I found myself trembling and upset, wondering if it was right. Should I do it? Was this a time? I took the delicate thing in my hands and sat on my couch, trying to put everything out of my mind and to be still. I remembered the other time, and how I couldn't force it but had to sink into a deep darkness and aloneness and to let go. It seemed forever that I waited. Slowly, slowly I lost myself, drifting out of where I was to a place of night and mist. Then the gift began to flutter in my hands as it had before, and I put my hands to my closed eyes as I had before, but this time a purple wave rushed toward me and over me, and as I emerged I could see a terrible scene on a far shore. Scuro dashed across a bare field, leaped a pit, and fled onward before a great monster with teeth like knives. The monster leaped too, but the scene changed before I could tell whether he made it across the pit. Another purple wave, and then I saw Jetsam, with blood running down his arm, saying something to me that I couldn't hear. He was shouting, and tall shadows moved behind him. And it was finished. Whatever the gift had meant to say had been said; I sat alone with it in my hands. When at last I gathered myself and went to Jetsam, I felt rather cheated because this experience seemed so obscure and so short compared to my first one.

He kept very silent for quite a period after I'd described my experience. I thought maybe he didn't believe me. Or maybe he did and was as fearful as I. It was neither.

"Maris," he said at last, "I've got some brand new ideas from your Mantid wing!"

"Tell me what!"

"No," he said flatly. "I've got to find out where the new ideas fit in before I talk about them. But I really believe we have a chance!"

Somehow we actually enjoyed our last day in the Valley of the Opal. In the evening we donned our colorful cloaks again and gathered for a final banquet. The monarch was exceptionally welcoming and merry, and we had a good evening.

Finally the fireflies brought the beautiful translucent goblets to each place. The monarch raised his wings for silence.

"May I propose a toast?" He raised his goblet. "To these eight! May their task be fulfilled and their journey bring peace!"

In a vast flutter of raised wings the entire company drank to us.

After a whisper to Jetsam, Exi proposed a toast to the monarch, his host of butterflies, and the Valley of the Opal. He thanked them for their kindnesses, and said we would do everything to bring about the desired end. We drank to that.

"Now," said the monarch, "let our gift be brought."

The blue butterflies who acted as the monarch's special guard of honor moved regally forward then, to place on our table before Jetsam a small silver box. Jetsam, after a moment's hesitation, opened it. We all gasped. In the box lay a single opal from which all the colors of the rainbow seemed to glow forth.

"This," said the monarch, before any of us could speak, "is from our central treasure, and of what we have, we considered it to be the most valuable gift we could give to help you in your work. What it will do, what it can do, we are not sure because it has never been used. In the beginning our opals came from Them. This we know. They have strange powers. This also we know. And we know that we are their guardians, so eventually and if possible this is to return to us. You must care for it and see what it has for you. More than this I cannot tell you."

Jetsam's eyes had been staring at the stone all the time the monarch had been talking, as if he had never seen anything so wonderful. He lifted his face, which seemed to glow from the opal's glow, and looked around at his companions and then at the monarch.

"Thank you, sir!" His voice almost failed him. "Thank you for all of us! We'll do our very best. And I promise to get it back to you. Unless everything is lost, you will get it back. Thank you!"

A restless night followed, and before sunup we were well on our way up the first long rise beyond the Valley of the Opal. The monarch and his host went with us until we were quite far above the valley and the lake.

"We can go no further," said the monarch. "This is the edge of our land—where these mountains begin. They are, I fear, wild and pathless mountains and you must go carefully. Beyond them lies the great river, and beyond that the land of the Beasts." He paused, his face very grave, his huge eyes not the least bit merry this morning. "Please take care," he said.

We said good-bye to Isia, which was hard, and then we were

alone, facing the huge rocky peaks. They reared above us in gray sawtooths of granite, barren and cold. Where we stood there were some trees, but the ground was already less turf than gravel, and plant life was obviously sparser. Even the nearest mountain appeared treeless.

"Well," said Scuro, after a nod from Jetsam, "guess it's for me to find a path." And he started up the hill with us all trailing behind.

21

It's hard to climb steadily where there's a trail, but when there is none, climbing is doubly difficult. For Jetsam and me the climbing was hardest, because we were heavier and also because we were the only ones who didn't go on four or six feet. Scuro was a marvelous guide, zigging and zagging to find us the best route up a ravine, over a slide, around an overhang. He would go ahead and stop, go ahead and stop, at each stop looking back head cocked and tongue lolling, to be sure we were following. Locus, of course, covered more ground than anyone, although even she slowed up as the morning wore on.

By the time the sun was at zenith, the chance to rest and eat seemed a magnificent gift. Jetsam carried a large packet of edibles slung over his shoulder. We had come to a shallow depression between two upslopes of mountain when we decided to halt. It was a pleasant meal, but a short stop. We were soon on our way once more.

The afternoon was much harder than the morning. The farther we went the steeper the way became, the more rocky the places over which we clambered, the more forbidding the peaks around us. Plant life dwindled to a few scattered bunches of poor grass. It was harder to breathe as we went higher, and a cold wind began to blow. We stopped oftener as the afternoon progressed, not just because Exi seemed to be losing strength and limping badly but because everyone, including Locus and Scuro, seemed to be dragging. At one such stop Jetsam said, "We've got to have shelter soon. It'll be awfully cold up here when the sun goes, I'm afraid."

As he spoke, I saw him shiver a little although he tried to hide it. I was shivering and not hiding it. "Scuro," he continued, "can you look about and see what you can see?"

"Can and will," Scuro replied, trotting off slowly. He wasn't away for long, and returned looking not only tired but unhappy. "Not a thing."

"Not even some small bit of protection from this wind?"

Scuro closed his eyes. "Maybe. A small bit only. Just over this hill. Don't think much of it, really."

We followed him. It was almost nothing, as Scuro had said. A pile of jumbled rocks on a flat place. A very slight windbreak, with the chance that if we huddled close together we might keep each other warm. Actually there was no choice but to try it, for it was nearly dark.

"Jetsam," I said, "we can't last here all night! We'll freeze or catch pneumonia or something! What can we do?"

"I know. It's awful. But we can't go blundering off into darkness. And, anyway, there's nowhere to go. I don't see what we can do."

"If I may say so, what about those suits you have? If you follow me." Red spoke softly.

At once I took the spider-thread suits out, and Locus, Jetsam, and I put on ours. Immediately we were more comfortable. There were Parula's suit and Toad's suit still on hand, and the question was, who among the five others needed them most. Scuro assured us he was all right, that his coat was thick and made to withstand weather. That left four.

It was Carabus who decided. "Mr. Green and I have thick shells and are in good health. The worst that could happen is you might have to get us unparalyzed tomorrow. Exi needs warmth because of his leg, Red because he has no thick outer covering. They should have the suits."

After some protest from Red and none from Exi—a sign of how uncomfortable he was—they donned the remaining suits, which seemed to adapt to any size creature. We drew as close as we could, ate some of the food we had carried, and, pressing one against another, tried to sleep.

It must have been several hours later that I was aroused from a

weary stupor, cramped and cold despite Arachne's suit, to hear
Jetsam muttering to himself. First I thought he was talking in his
sleep. Then I could tell he wasn't. I could hear him fumbling about
with something. Suddenly a glow lighted the darkness, and I wondered how he could make a fire without wood. I knew at the same
moment what I saw. It was the opal! He had set it on the ground
in the midst of us, and it was a many-hued, gleaming fire. Eight
sets of eyes stared at it, eight bodies relaxed in its warmth. We
slept soundly at last.

We awoke when the sun had climbed high enough to get to us
in our rock pile. After we rubbed our legs and arms into life, we
crowded around the opal's warmth, ate our breakfast, and talked
about our situation. The wind, which had died down during the
night, gave signs of starting up anew. From the looks of the mountains ahead of us, in the direction Jetsam and Scuro said we must
travel, this day would be harder going than the day before.

"It seems to me," Jetsam said, "that we have to go down
through those twisty ravines and then up again to that highest
peak. Do you think that, Scuro?"

Scuro turned his head toward the mountains, and his nose
went through the gyrations it always did when he was testing the
world. "Don't see any other way," he said finally.

"That's what I was afraid of," Jetsam said.

"Not too bad for a while," Scuro said. "Mostly down for a
while. Rough, but down."

Red, who had been wandering around and over the rock pile
and peering with his sharp eyes in all directions, was of the opinion
that we might even get into some trees again. Before we started
out, I took the spider-silk suits and packed them carefully away,
except the one Exi was wearing.

It was easier going down. Still it was midafternoon before we
got within tumbling distance of any trees. It was late afternoon,
with shadows lengthening fast, when finally we came to a wooded
canyon with a stream. The trees were sparse and scrubby, the
stream thin, but we discovered a tiny nut which grew thickly on a
species of shrub. And there were dozens of these shrubs. So Red,
Carabus, and Mr. Green gathered nuts by the hundreds, while
Jetsam and I brought leaves and branches for our beds.

That night we slept well and warm and at once.

The next morning after a meager bath and a monotonous menu, we set forth feeling remarkably fit. Exi was better. The sun shone brightly. Jetsam whistled to himself. The blow came when Scuro, after one of his frequent exploratory thrusts, returned to us slowly, grimly, as if he didn't want to come at all.

"What's wrong?" asked Jetsam, his face tight.

"Well, it's almost straight up now. And mountain top lost in clouds. Bad going, I'm afraid."

"Better now when we're fresh, I guess, than later." Jetsam straightened his shoulders and tried to look encouraging. "Let's get going."

After a short, steep climb we emerged from the trees. Scuro had not exaggerated. Ahead of us rose the highest mountain we had seen. Its base was a jumble of spilled rocks rising in sharp cones to its jagged flanks. Crevices in its sides were deep and shadowed, and fearsome. Its head was entirely covered by clouds. And there was no way around it, either, because it stood surrounded by perpendicular granite upthrusts that were obviously unscalable.

I am sure we would have stayed indefinitely stunned before this awful sight had not Jetsam and Scuro had the courage to plunge forward and make us follow. Before we had much time to collect our fears, we were on the rock piles at the mountain's base, clawing our way upward. Luckily this part was hardest for Jetsam and me because of our weight. When we reached the steep and threatening flanks of the mountain, Jetsam and I had to sit down and get our breath back.

"I said bad going," announced Scuro. No one could argue this.

"Fasten everything you're carrying to your backs, all of you, so hands and feet will be free," Jetsam said. He helped and I helped until each bundle was secured. "Scuro and I will lead. Exi, Carabus, Mr. Green next. Then Locus and Maris. Red last, because he is lightest on his feet. If anyone seems to be bad off, call out to me, Red."

"Now," he went on, pointing toward the nearest cleft in the mountain, "Scuro believes we'll do best by taking these slanting crevices as much as possible. Not so exposed, and something to hold on to. Here we go."

It was slow and bruising work to make our way upward through the endless series of crevices. It was like trying to climb tilted, tumbled chimneys filled with jagged bricks. And it was cold, forever cold. Probably this was good, because our struggles might have been even more dreadful if it had been hot. Yet I missed the comfort of sunlight. We went up the mountain in switchbacks, moving from one crevice to another as each one angled higher. Jetsam and Scuro were right about the clefts being less exposed. Whenever we had to make our way between clefts, we were hit by freezing gusts of wind and had all we could do to hang on.

The first day and the second day up were much the same. Struggle, climb, weariness, food, climb, fitful sleep beside the opal. The morning of the third day, on one of these terrible open slopes, we met a most awful crisis—and learned, incidentally, how much we cared for each other. Up to this point Red (our "sheep dog," Scuro called him) had not needed to voice any warnings from his rear guard position because not one of us had done more than plod along.

Suddenly Red shouted from behind me, "Watch out!"

I dug in with my heels and looked up, to see a confusion of beetle legs and bodies tumbling at an angle toward the sharp drop-off of the chimney just below us. We couldn't move fast on these steep slides between crevices, but we all tried to do something. Jetsam started down, Red up, while Scuro and Locus went in the direction of the falling bodies. None of us could get there in time, and if it hadn't been for Carabus, all three of them would have plunged to disaster. But somehow Carabus managed to brace himself long enough to stop Exi and Mr. Green and to give them a chance to get their feet under them and hold on. But in doing this he was forced to the edge, and before Red could reach him, over he went.

"Wait! Red, don't do it!" Jetsam called.

Red, however, had already started down, going around the sharp drop-off to the left. When I got near to the place where Carabus had gone over, Jetsam was already there lying on his stomach and looking down.

"Don't come any closer!" he snapped. "We can't lose anyone else! Don't let the others move!"

I could tell from his voice that he was having all he could do to hold on to himself. So I obeyed, getting into as secure a sitting position as I could and ordering the others to stay where they were. Scuro and Locus were uphill from me and ten feet or so from each other. Exi and Mr. Green had frozen in the spot where Carabus had stopped them. We were like six strange statues carved on the edge of an abyss. I was not aware of the biting, fierce wind. I wasn't afraid. I only felt shock and a terrible emptiness. It seemed as if we stayed so for hours and hours. Actually it wasn't long—not more than fifteen minutes, I suppose—until we heard Red's voice from down below.

"All right! He's all right! Caught himself on a rock! He's all right!"

Jetsam dropped his head onto his arm for a brief moment. Then in a controlled voice he called back. "Can we help, Red? Do you need help?"

"Don't think so—think we can make it. Give us time—"

So for another eternity we waited. Knowing that they were alive and struggling. Knowing we could do nothing. Now I could feel the wind, and felt it for them too. As it pushed at me I knew it pushed at them, and as it chilled me I knew it chilled them.

"I can see them coming," Jetsam said. "Diagonal across the lower slope and up they come! They're making it!"

When at last Carabus and Red emerged, the sight of the solid brown beetle and the slim-waisted ant marching toward us as if nothing very important had occurred was almost too much.

Gradually and very carefully we gathered together. Jetsam joined Carabus and Red, and they collected me, and we shepherded Mr. Green and Exi to where Locus and Scuro were. Then all of us picked our way up the dangerous slope of shale to the next crevice—which we had been trying to reach when all this had happened. Once out of the wind, we all collapsed in wordless relief; rocky ground seemed velvet, the angular cleft a warm house. And then we all began to talk at the same time.

We never were clear about the how of our near tragedy. Exi blamed it all on his lame leg and his inability to keep up. Mr. Green said *he* had stumbled, and Carabus said nobody was at fault, that it was just loose rock and weary climbers. Whatever caused the mishap, Carabus, we all agreed, had been splendid and had saved Exi and Mr. Green from possible death by taking their weight on himself.

Try as we did, though, we couldn't make Carabus a hero. He remained as matter-of-fact and quiet as ever.

Red was equally reluctant to accept praise. "You just do things, you know," he said. To which Carabus nodded emphatically.

After we had quieted down, huddled together in the cleft, we ate and rested. It was growing colder by the minute, and above us clouds were heavier and darker. Scuro, after conferring with us, made his way upward and disappeared from sight in another of his explorations. Meanwhile those of us who had worn the spider-silk suits before put them on again, and Jetsam got out the opal so we could get warmed a bit.

The news Scuro brought back would, at any other time, have depressed us very much. However, under the circumstances when he scrambled down to us, his coat powdered with wet snow, we showed only a minimum of upset. "Cold up there," he announced, shaking himself and sending snow in all directions. "Shouldn't wonder if we can get over the top, though, before dark. Better do it."

"What's it like beyond? Could you tell?" Jetsam asked.

"Couldn't see too well. But couldn't be worse, could it?" He cocked his head roguishly. "Have a hunch it'll have more shelter. Trees and such. If we get over the top."

"Well, shall we make a push to get over, then?" Jetsam waited for a reply, but no one spoke. "I guess we'd best try it. Same order as before. And *please* go carefully!"

There was no need to tell us that. As soon as we had climbed around the turn in this crevice, we were hit by the icy wind again, but this time its gusts carried fine stinging snow into our faces, half blinding us. The spider suits kept the wet snow from soaking through to our skins, and did protect us somewhat from the cold. Scuro and Locus shook snow from their coats. Mr. Green and Carabus dusted each other off from time to time.

I was not aware when we passed the crest. I don't think anyone was, except Scuro. We were all too tired, too cumbered by cold, too blinded by the driving snow to be aware of anything. I first noticed a change when I had to pause for breath and realized that it came easier. I looked up from the ground and saw that the snowfall had decreased. Also, large flakes were drifting straight down from the gray sky, not being driven by wind. The others had stopped too. Scuro turned and viewed his battered flock. "We're over the top," he said cheerfully. "Stay with it. Gets better now."

Then we were going down a slope and before long had entered a forest of evergreen trees. The ground leveled off and there were only scattered patches of snow in places where the trees were not so close together. There was no need now for caution, so we bunched together as we went along. Jetsam and I were side by side.

"What happens now, do you think?" I asked.

"I don't know any more than you do, Maris. I can only guess that we are dropping down toward the river—at least I hope we are. If our idea of direction is right, we should be."

"Can't we stop soon?"

"Not here. Not yet. It's too unprotected. We need to find a more sheltered place before dark if we can."

I suggested that Scuro go on ahead and see what he could find. What he found, as we soon discovered for ourselves, was that our forest aisles ended rather abruptly at the edge of a mesa or plateau on which we stood looking down on a series of similar plateaus, each lower than the one before. It was rather like being at the top of a flight of giant stairs. The height of each stairstep was at least eighty to a hundred feet, but this was a sloping rather than a sheer drop, and appeared quite negotiable. At the bottom of the stairs, was a plain and beyond it an irregular line.

Jetsam drew the line with his forefinger. "That," he said triumphantly, "will be our river! So we've been going right!" He grabbed Scuro and they did a silly dance of delight. "Now then," he said, "let's get down to the next level and see if we can find some shelter. It'll be getting dark soon and the rain's wet."

Without further ado Scuro and Locus flung themselves down the slope, followed by Jetsam and me. We sat down and slid after them, finding that the short, strong grass covering the slope was a splendid slide. The other four came after, more sedate on their insect legs. By the time I had reached the bottom and gotten to my feet, Scuro and Locus had discovered a sort of half-cave and were enthusiastically making it bigger. Dirt was flying in all directions, and Jetsam was laughing. Eventually we all joined in, and the final result was as cozy a scene as anyone could desire.

Tucked into the excavation like fledglings into a nest, our stomachs filled with nuts we had picked, our bodies warmed by the opal's fire, we slept.

PART IV

Triumph and Disaster

22

SNATCHED FROM SLEEP BY SOMETHING THAT AT FIRST I COULDN'T identify, I opened my eyes. I knew from the breath-holding silence, that others were also awake. I breathed as lightly as I could and waited for some clue. Then it came—far off but absolutely unmistakable.

It was the screaming of the Beasts.

Locus trembled against me, and I couldn't hold back a shudder. Scuro growled, and I remembered that he was the only one present who had never heard the Beasts. In a whisper Jetsam explained the sound to him, ending up with, "so we're getting close, and they're still prowling, and maybe we can catch them after all."

The distant shrieking faded into silence. No one spoke. I continued to have the sense that everyone was awake and on edge. Mr. Green verified this at last by saying irritably and aggressively that he didn't see *why*, "for goodness sake," we didn't get up and *do* something. Anything! He, for one, *could not stand* that sound!

"Even so," Red said quietly, "let's rest. At least I'd guess we'll need it." Mr. Green muttered, and Red whispered back, and finally Exi said, *"Please!"* in his leadership voice. And there was silence once more.

When morning came, we were once more faced with the question of what to do next. Foremost in our minds, and hardest to accept, was our own decision to try to find a way to bring the Beasts to Them. The most natural thing now was to turn around and go in the opposite direction. But we had learned that the natural thing was not always the right thing.

We had five or six of the great plateau steps to descend, with long areas of forested level ground between each step. It was hard to guess how long this would take, so we didn't even try to estimate. We just started.

It took much longer than I had thought it might. Only one of the remaining steps permitted sliding. The others were either rocky or covered with thorny thickets, or had close-growing trees.

It must have been near to midday when we stood at the edge of the last plateau and looked down toward the river valley. This plateau was a sort of promontory thrust out farther than the rest of the mountain mass and, because it didn't have too many trees, we could see in all directions. Below and ahead of us lay the river; it emerged from trees and ran through a barren plain, where it gleamed like silver. The same bare land came all the way to the foot of our plateau and on around to our right, apparently following the base of the mountains in that direction. As we talked about what we saw, we realized that we were approaching the river at a point somewhere between where our island was and where the boats had been wrecked (which was more or less what we had planned), that the bare plain was an extension of that wasteland we had crossed after the boat wreck, and that the forests to our left held the places of our early journeyings.

I went to Exi and put my hand lightly on his back.

"It's funny, isn't it," I said, "to be looking at all this. Sort of like going over your own life."

"So it is, my dear Maris, so it is. And that, I rather believe, is at various times a most necessary thing to do."

"Exi, do you think I've done the right things so far?"

He came as near to a smile as he ever did. "How can I know that? And what are right things?" He paused thoughtfully. "Do you feel you have chosen life, or been pushed into it?"

I let this question stay in my mouth for quite a long time of chewing. Then I said, "Both, I'm afraid. But I think I've done more and more choosing as I've gone along."

"You have answered your own question," he said.

We had learned from experience that one of the best methods

we had for making decisions was for us all to sit around and say whatever came into our heads regarding the matter at hand. So we found a relatively comfortable spot back from the edge of the plateau and began to talk. We started as we always did, with ideas we knew wouldn't work. This got us loosened up.

Finally Exi said, "Now that we have cleared out our heads, perhaps we can settle into our major problem. If we are to do what we must—lure the Beasts to the Place of Them in such a way as to render the Beasts powerless—and if the Place where They are is on this side of the river back in these mountains somewhere, then the Beasts have to be gotten across the river. Isn't that so?"

We all agreed that it was.

"Well then," Exi continued, "how can it be done?"

"Build a bridge," said Mr. Green.

"What makes you think they'd cross it?" Jetsam asked. "And anyway it's too wide."

"Not further upstream it isn't. We could *do* it. My *uncle* used to work on beaver dams and—"

"Forget your uncle," said Red. "What about why? I mean, Jetsam's question—why would they cross?"

"Bait," Mr. Green said sharply. "Bait!"

"Who? You?" Carabus put in.

"Well, now," spluttered Mr. Green, "I didn't *mean*—really—"

"Nice juicy beetle. Might work, at that."

Jetsam laughed. "Come on, Carabus, don't tease. As a matter of fact, maybe Mr. Green is on the right track. The Beasts don't like water, we know that, and yet—"

"They did get Isia and Locus on this side!" Suddenly I began to see possibilities.

"Yes. Therefore," Jetsam went on, "we can get them across again. I don't think we need to go so far upstream as that, though. Just about where you built the *Starflower*—wasn't the river fairly narrow?"

Those of us who knew said it was.

"All right. We could build a bridge there, maybe."

Scuro cleared his throat. "About this bait business," he said. "Should think we'd need it."

Locus moved close to me, her eyes frightened.

"You shan't use her," I burst out. "Not if we never get the Beasts!"

"Didn't have that in mind," replied Scuro calmly. "Me. I'm fast."

Once more I was ashamed for not seeing ahead of my own nose. I lapsed into a silence, which everyone ignored.

"But," Jetsam went on, as if he sacrificed his friends every day, "just to have a bridge and bait isn't enough, is it, sir?"

"No." Exi pondered the question. "No. I see what you mean. We must not only get the Beasts across the river, but we must get them much farther than that, and there must be motivation to pull them on, and ways to separate them from each other as we lure them. It is a big task."

For a while words failed as we brooded over this "big task." It seemed utterly impossible.

At the same moment Red and Jetsam spoke. "Pits," said Jetsam. "Fire," said Red.

Then I remembered the terrible vision I had had when I tried the Mantid's gift, back there in the Valley of the Opal. I could tell from his face that Jetsam, too, remembered it. Our eyes met. He nodded, but didn't explain to the others. "What do you mean, Red? Fire?"

"Well, you see—well, I thought, from what you said—that is, if they notice a bit of smoke—I mean several bits of smoke here and there—won't they maybe be curious, if they're hungry, that is—"

"Are you saying, Red," asked Exi, "that perhaps one way to lure them is by building a series of small smoky fires, each one farther away from their kingdom, in the hope that they might keep on hunting for whatever creatures built the fires?"

"Yes, Exi," Red answered.

"That is all very *well*," Mr. Green put in, "but may I ask how we break them *up?* It seems to *me* that *if* they came at all there would be a big pack of ravening Beasts after us and *much* too much for us!"

"That's where my idea comes in!" Jetsam was getting excited; his eyes were sparkling, his hands gesturing. "I think it really might work! Look here!" He drew river and mountains in the dirt. "We make a series of deep holes, spaced several miles apart. Start just across the river. Work in the direction we want the Beasts to go. Cover the holes so they can't see them. Build smoky fires by each hole. We lure them on; confuse them. When they come at us, several fall into the hole. We go to the next place. Get several more. And so on! It's a great plan, don't you think so, Exi?"

Exi didn't reply at once. "I am afraid," he said finally, "that I would not call it a great plan yet. I do think it has excellent possibilities, but much detail needs to be worked out. The Beasts, after all, are not stupid and we must know exactly what we are doing. It is a place to begin, however. Shall we proceed down to the river valley and make a camp?"

"Let's go!" Jetsam jumped to his feet eagerly.

"Hold it," Scuro said. "Can't just go rolling down into that bareness! Too exposed. Follow me."

Scuro, whose authority as guide no one questioned, turned away from the river and led us back toward the mountain. Very soon we saw what he was doing. He had noticed that there was a narrow, rocky, hidden canyon leading down to the plain well back from the tip of the promontory, hidden from view of the river.

Compared to what we had been through already, this descent was simple, even though we were dusty and ready to rest when we reached the bottom. There the plain stretched away, barren and rocky. To our left was the flank of the promontory where we had been, and ahead of us the river was marked by masses of green where the forest ended.

"What an excellent place for a camp!" Mr. Green said.

"Except," Carabus stated, "for no trees, no food, no water."

"I know it," Mr. Green replied. "I only meant if there *were*, it *would* be."

We couldn't help laughing, and Mr. Green joined in. Exi suggested we'd better work our way in the general direction of upstream and forest. By the time we had gone a mile or so farther along the mountain base, we had reached the edge of a forest of enormous oaks of various kinds, their branches making a canopy which filtered the light, their trunks sturdy and comfortable. It was here, with the mountain slope at our backs and stalwart trees around us, that we made what a mountain-climbing party would call a base camp. For it was from here that our other plans would have to be carried out.

It sounds strange to say it, but we actually enjoyed making our home—or I.H. as we named it after Red said it was our "impermanent home." We began with a cluster of five big oaks, two of which had holes in them from ancient fires. These hollows became two rooms, one for Locus and Red, one for the three beetles. Scuro and Locus dug a ditch from a nearby spring to us, making a little pool at our end. Red who always seemed to know about such matters, hunted until he found a tough vine, and this he made into rope. Jetsam and I tied it around the five trees and then interlaced fallen branches between strands of the rope. When we finished we had an untidy but strong fence around us, leaving only the smallest space between two of the trees for a gate. Locus gathered rocks for the base of the fence. Exi, Carabus, and Mr. Green made endless excursions for wood and food. After several days of work, I.H. was finished. It was the nicest place we'd ever had.

That night we sat together after supper and felt quite at peace. We talked of this day, of bits of beauty we'd noticed, of our earlier lives. We even listened to two of Mr. Green's long stories about his relatives and almost liked them. (The stories, I mean. We never got very attached to the relatives.) We avoided discussing the future, as if we could not bear to spoil the joy of the evening.

Jetsam, though, was a realist. After the others had retired, Jetsam said, "You want to know what I think?"

"No. I don't. You'll ruin things. What?"

"I think we need help."

"And what," I said sarcastically, "makes you think that?"

He refused to be baited. "No, seriously. I mean it."

"Fine. And how do we get it? Just whistle?"

"Please, Maris. Don't be like that. We *do* need help."

I relented. "All right. I agree. What's your idea?"

"Well—" He hesitated, as if half afraid to say it. "Well, there's Botta. And Arachne. And Toad."

"But Jetsam! Someone would have to go clear into the Beasts' jungle!"

"I know it."

We sat silently, side by side. I don't know what he was pondering. My mind and my imagination were flooded with scenes of the jungle, the Beasts, Arachne's house, our harrowing flight down the tunnel, Isia's wound, the prison.

"I'll go," I said, swallowing hard. "I'll go for help."

"No, Maris. It would be foolish for either of us to go. It seems to me there's only one of this group equipped to go alone. Keen eyes, slender and very quick, can climb anything, spunky, sensible, daring—"

"Red!" I interrupted. "We couldn't send him!"

"We're not sending anybody! He'd have to choose to go! You'll have to admit he has the ability."

I knew, of course, that Jetsam was right, although I lay awake for hours arguing with myself. And I knew Red would be eager to go.

And he was. In the morning Jetsam told the group his idea about needing help, and they agreed, as reluctant as I had been. At once Red spoke, announcing in his shy way that he was the one who should try. We all protested, but we all knew he would go. Very soon after breakfast he was off. He refused to take food with him, saying he wanted to travel light. I did persuade him to wear one of the spider-thread suits, and he promised me he wouldn't take it off. He headed toward the river and disappeared among the oaks.

"He'll make it," Jetsam snapped. "Come on, now. We've got work to do."

Exi spoke up at once. "Whatever our next moves are to be, surely they will require that we know all we can about the surrounding land. Why don't you, Jetsam, Maris, and Scuro, go and investigate? The rest of us will stay here."

It sounded simple enough. And I grabbed on to doing something as the only escape from the awful fears lurking just below the surface of me. Jetsam, I was certain, shared in my anxious need to be occupied.

Before we could go, however, Exi and Jetsam decided it was necessary to have a discussion about geography. I was restive, and protested, but they were firm about it and we settled down to a painstaking session of maps. Jetsam smoothed a big spot of ground and with a stick began to draw. It wasn't long before everyone —me included—was crowded around helping, with various remembered facts and quite a bit of speculation, to fill in details. Judged from the sun's direction, the river, we guessed, ran roughly from northwest to southeast. The Beasts' kingdom was therefore east, possibly a bit south, of where we now were, the Valley of the Opal somewhere in the maze of mountains to the west. This mysterious country also held the Place of Them, we knew; but this was one of the blank spaces on our map. The river, from our first cave shelter after Locus and Isia were carried off, to the rapids, and including the tributary leading from the marshes, was not too hard to map. We also filled in the area including the Beasts, Arachne, and the laurel grove with a fair amount of certainty. When we had put in all we could, we realized that it was the country to the west —maybe slightly south, we weren't sure—that we had to find out about. Otherwise we could never lead the Beasts towards Them.

So, with a map sharp in our minds, or at least sharp in Jetsam's mind, the three of us started off. The rest of that day, and all of the day following, we went until we were exhausted, marking trees, noting outstanding features of the landscape, finding places for hiding should we need them in the future, observing where available supplies of food and water were, and where fires could be built or pits dug. We found that we were in a long valley running east and west, with mountains on either side. The south range, by far the higher and more forbidding of the two, held the Valley of the Opal and the Place of Them, we guessed. The north range, composed of smaller and more separate mountains, must be where the Ants lived and where the floods had forced us upward in that faraway time.

We tried very hard, during these two days, not to talk about Red except to say we were sure he was getting along all right. We weren't sure, of course; and the second night, back at I.H., I couldn't stay away from the subject of Red and my worries.

"He's so frail to be out there alone," I said.

"That's what I say!" Mr. Green, with his devotion to Red, had until now demonstrated remarkable restraint. "That's just what I say! I haven't slept a *wink* since he's been gone! I keep thinking what he has *done* for us, so brave and all—" Mr. Green's voice broke so he couldn't go on.

Silence fell upon us. I don't know what others were thinking. I know that I was flooded by visions of Red pursued by Beasts and being unable to find a proper tree, or trembling on a high branch while Beasts howled below him, or lost in a hostile jungle without food. Others must have been haunted too, because when a sudden sharp scratching sounded in the quiet night, there was a concert of exclamations, and Locus landed in my lap.

"What was *that?*" Mr. Green whispered.

"Quiet!" cautioned Exi. "Listen!"

For a few seconds we heard nothing more. Then the sound came again. It was as if someone was prowling about outside our camp.

"It's *them!*" Mr. Green's whisper was agitated. "The Beasts! They've got *Red* and they're coming for *us!* Let's get into our trees!"

Jetsam had been creeping silently toward the gate. He shook his head and held up his hand for us to be still. As he seemed more curious than alarmed, no one moved. The noise stopped, then began again—a strangely muffled, continuous, scratching noise. Jetsam crept soundlessly to a place near the gate. The scratching paused, continued, paused, continued. My palms were wet. Suddenly Jetsam pointed at the ground just inside the gate. Slowly a small mound rose up, then soft soil fell away from its center and a pushed in, bucktoothed, dirty, furry face poked through.

"Anybody home?" said a cheerful voice. "Any vacancies?"

Jetsam, being closest, pulled Botta into our camp and clapped him on the back joyfully. Locus and I rushed to him.

"Case of mistaken identity," he said. "I'm not who you think I am. I'm Botta, nobody but Botta!"

"The most important fellow I can think of at the moment," said Jetsam. "Come meet the others; give us the news!"

Botta told us that Red had found Arachne's house, had introduced himself and explained his mission. No, Red hadn't any real trouble. No, he hadn't run into the Beasts. Although the Beasts had stormed around a lot overhead soon after Red had arrived at Arachne's. No, Botta didn't think this was because the Beasts knew

Red was there. They had been generally restless and unpredictable lately. Yes, Arachne would be coming, but she had had to collect certain necessary supplies first. Botta didn't know what they were. Red? Well, when he, Botta, had started our way, he, Red, had headed north to look for Toad.

When we asked Botta why he hadn't knocked or called out or something instead of frightening us out of our wits, he replied, "Never go in a gate when you can go under it." Then he yawned, said he was tired, curled up, and promptly fell asleep.

23

"I WANT TO GET OUR FIRST PIT READY AND TRY IT OUT," JETSAM SAID the next morning. That ruled out further exploration for a while, and I, for one, was glad.

Once Exi and Jetsam had settled on a location—outside the fence on the opposite side from the entrance—the work began. Botta's powerful forefeet tore into the earth as he sank a shaft a good eight feet downward. He backed out and made a second shaft close to the first. Then a third. And a fourth. He put Locus and Scuro to work joining the shafts by digging away the dirt between each pair. They were nowhere near the excavator that Botta was, but slowly the hole grew in size and depth. The rest of us, except Exi whose crippled leg prevented it, were involved in the task of removing the soil thrown up by the digging. My jacket, already frayed, became a carrying sack for dirt. Jetsam made a sort of sled out of fallen branches onto which Mr. Green and Carabus pushed dirt. We took all this earth out into the forest and scattered it about and tossed leaves over it so it wouldn't show.

By late afternoon we had a pit about eight feet in diameter and eight feet deep, a fine yawning pit that I knew Jetsam and Botta would have to try out before they would be satisfied. I was right.

"Botta," said Jetsam, as soon as the last load of dirt had been disposed of, "let's see if it works."

The apparently tireless Botta was on his feet immediately. "Fine," he said. "I'll be it!" He hurried into I.H. through the gate, leaving it open behind him. He called from inside, "I'm a Beast! Here I come!"

We heard scurrying feet. Then the fence shook under a crash. Nothing happened. Jetsam and I, followed by the others, ran into the camp in alarm. Botta was sitting against the fence rubbing his head, a bewildered expression on his ugly face. Jetsam began to laugh, and I couldn't resist doing the same—because, as he sat there he became everyone who has ever gotten all prepared, announced proudly what he was going to do, and then didn't.

Botta grinned at us. "Not as much of a Beast as I thought," he announced. "Or the fence has stretched. A proper Beast would jump it fiercely! Lower it a bit, Jetsam, my boy, and we'll try it again."

We loosened the ropes, letting a section of fence sag down until it was only half as high. We returned outside to the pit. Once more Botta shouted his Beasthood. Once more we heard scurrying feet, but this time followed by a whish and then a plop down in the pit.

"It works," came Botta's voice from the hole. "A bit hard on the inside, but it works!"

It took some doing to get him out. Jetsam had to jump in and hoist Botta up, and then I had to lie flat and give Jetsam my hand to help him clamber out. This proved to us that the pits could trap something, especially if we could keep the beasts who didn't get caught from helping the ones who did. Jetsam suggested that we make a pit cover before ending our day's work.

"I wouldn't, if I were you," Botta said, brushing dirt and leaves from his fur. "I'm sure Arachne will have ideas when she comes." He marched ahead of us through the gate, found a patch of warm sunlight and curled up in it, falling asleep at once.

Jetsam and I repaired the fence while the beetles prepared supper. We were just about to eat when a tapping sounded at the gate. Jetsam went quickly, but before he opened it, he asked who it was. "For goodness sake, young man," snapped a familiar voice, "do stop asking foolish questions and open that gate! I cannot carry these much farther!"

Hastily Jetsam flung the gate wide. There stood Arachne, her solid no-nonsense black-furred body weighted down by a snow-white spinning wheel and several boxes that were fastened to her back. Before we said a word we removed her burdens. She stretched in relief, brushed her black coat, straightened the exquisite shawl over her shoulders, and walked with great dignity into I.H.

"Well," she said, surveying the place, "it isn't too dreadful. Young man, you may put my equipment in there." She indicated the larger of the two hollow trees. Arachne had the faculty of making Jetsam seem younger than he was; he seemed about ten years old as he obediently placed the wheel and the boxes inside the tree and returned. Arachne's huge eyes held a hint of humor as she said, "Oh, don't be so cowed, young man! I won't eat you! But my equipment is essential for all of us."

"Arachne," I said, "I am so happy you have come to help us! May I introduce my other friends?"

The beetles and Scuro stepped forward solemnly to be presented, one by one. It was evident from the very first that Arachne liked them, and that she was particularly taken with Exi.

We knew from Botta that Red had gone on northward, Arachne had no further information about him. He had tried to tell her our tentative plans, but had not succeeded too well. "A fine young man," Arachne said, "and brave. Not too clear, however. And he did not eat enough."

Exi then told her in precise detail everything that had happened since we left the sacred grove. Fortunately Exi was a good storyteller. When he finished, I gathered courage to relate my vision from the gift of the Mantid, about Scuro leaping pits and Jetsam all bloody. This interested everyone. Exi eyed me as if he wondered why he hadn't been informed before, but he made no comment. Then Jetsam outlined what we had done by way of plans, even drawing a rough map for Arachne.

When we had finished, we waited for her to respond. She said nothing for a while, her great eyes shining in the firelight. It seemed very important that she approve of our activities, and we were relieved when she began to speak.

"You have done well," she said. "You made your journey to here, you planned, and then you called. As a helper for Them, now I can respond. We can go on together to see whether we can bring about a peace."

"Even you," Exi said quietly, "are not sure that it can be done."

"Even I am not at all sure. Much is unknown, much unpredictable. Each step taken is vital, each creature involved is essential.

No, I am not sure."

Somehow these words were helpful rather than depressing. Even if we failed, I thought, even if we were destroyed, it would be with dignity, because she was with us.

There were no stragglers when Exi suggested it was bedtime. We were very weary. Arachne settled into the lower part of the hollow tree where the beetles slept, her spinning wheel beside her. Locus went into her own hollow, with Scuro staying at the foot— which he had decided to do while Red was away. Botta, Jetsam, and I stretched out near each other.

I awakened from a real sleep, realizing that the sun was almost there, and hearing the sounds of the humming spinning wheel and Arachne's singing. I hurried my breakfast, for the others had finished. Jetsam said that it was time we decided where to build our other pits, and then to go and do it, which seemed sensible.

Arachne called from where she sat spinning. "It would be best if Exi, Locus, and I stayed here. We have work to do. We will be here when Red returns."

"But," Jetsam protested, "we can't leave you alone like that! We'll be gone at least a day and a half, maybe more, and—"

"Young man! I have taken care of myself for much longer than you have. I am sure Exi has, also. We are quite capable of caring for the small one. Now get your food bundles and be off!"

Jetsam didn't know what to say, so he said nothing. He began at once to get things ready. I helped. I also said in a whisper that he mustn't be upset by Arachne's abruptness. He tossed his head and muttered, "I'm not a child!" But he went ahead with our preparations and soon we were off into the oak forest.

With Botta and Scuro leading us, it was impossible to be anything but cheerful. They teased each other endlessly. They made jokes out of even the toughest job.

By the time we started back for I.H. on the second afternoon, we had accomplished much more than I had thought we could. We had gone all the distance we had explored previously, and well beyond. We had blazed more trees and memorized new landmarks until I felt we knew the country thoroughly. We had gone along our near mountains—the southerly range—until the valley between the ranges had narrowed, and just before the narrow part began we had built a second pit. Proceeding on through, we found that the valley widened slightly and appeared to bend around a southern peak. We knew we couldn't go farther, but we built another pit in the middle of the oak forest where the valley seemed to flare out. Our one night away we spent in a small cave in the base of a southern cliff in the narrow stretch of valley.

It was well after dark the second night when we neared I.H. Paces quickened. For myself, I wanted to run and would have if I could have forced my legs faster. I knew Red would have arrived, and I had never wanted to see someone more intensely. We crowded through the gate into I.H. "Red!" I cried. "Red! Where are you!"

Only Arachne and Exi and Locus were there.

"Where's Red?" Jetsam asked.

"He has not come." Exi sounded as if he was trying to be matter-of-fact. He wasn't quite successful. His slow voice had an edge in it. "He will come soon, we are certain."

"You've had no word?" My legs were shaky with fear.

"No, Maris. No word," said Arachne. "For goodness sake, now, do sit down and eat! It is good you are back, all of you!"

"But Red! He is *lost*! I *feel* it!" Mr. Green was anxious beyond control. "I *must* go and find him! I must!"

"You'll do no such thing!" Arachne snapped. "Be sensible and eat dinner, which we have kept for you hoping you would come."

Eating was Arachne's solution for everything; I remembered that from my first encounter. And of course it was futile to go searching for Red now, late at night. So we tried to eat. To the questions from Arachne and Exi about our adventures and accomplishments we gave brief answers. Finally we just sat in silence. The night grew deeper and longer.

Suddenly Mr. Green turned excitedly. "Listen!" he commanded, as if we had been doing anything else for the past hours. "Listen! Something is coming!"

A distant crackling came from the darkness. It grew increasingly loud. Scuro awoke and growled, sniffing the night. I had to admit the sound was ominous, as if giant feet were coming in a measured march through the leaves. Red couldn't make that noise!

We crowded inside the two trees, holding our collective breath while the sound came nearer and nearer. Could it be the Beasts? Or some unknown enemy? What could we do? The noise stopped.

"Here we are—I think—I mean I hope they're in."

It was Red's voice. I had never seen Mr. Green move so fast. He literally fell over us and over his own feet getting to the gate, flinging it wide and shouting, "My dear, *dear* Red! I thought you were *lost* or *devoured* or had met some *dreadful* fate! My dear, *dear* Red!"

"Please," said Red, when he could break in, "please be still—I mean, there's someone—oh, dear, it's so good to be here that I'm all muddled. Please wait a minute."

We stopped milling about, seeing his evident distress. He turned toward the open gate and spoke to the shadows. "It's all right, Bront—do come in."

Through the gate, like a creature from primeval jungles, came a huge horned toad. He was at least two feet high at the shoulders, and, when he got all of himself inside the gate, at least four feet long. Great spines ran along his back and stood out from his head, and his feet had elongated and clawed toes. He seemed to be covered with plated armor. Instinctively I backed away from him, terrified by his fierce appearance, until I looked into his face. It was as lovable a piece of ugliness as Toad's face had been.

"Red," said Exi, "may we meet your friend?"

"Dear me, of course! I'm so mixed up. This is Toad's cousin— I mean he is called Brontosaurus, and Toad thought he'd do bet-ter—faster, I guess—doesn't need water—scares people too—not really, he's nice, and—"

Exi interrupted gently. "We will get acquainted as quickly as we can, Red. May I present us to you, Mr. Brontosaurus."

"Call him Bront," muttered Red. "He likes that."

"Very well. May I present us to you, Bront." And Exi named each of us and pointed us out.

Bront looked increasingly embarrassed as Exi went from one to another. Finally he said, in a low husky voice, "I'll never get it."

"Yes, you will, Bront," Red said.

"Not for quite a while. I run fast—no one believes that of course—but other things take time." He cocked his awesome head, peering at us cornerwise. "I'm pleased to meet you, all the same."

The following morning we went over everything once more. Red listened carefully to our descriptions of the country we had explored thus far, and was impressed that we had been able to build three pits. He, in turn, told us more of his travels.

After he left Botta and Arachne, he had prowled around the edges of the Beasts' kingdom and had learned several important things. They were very restless, as Botta had already said. He had heard them both night and day growling and rumbling about and quarreling, but he hadn't seen them leave their kingdom. Then he found his way north to Toad's marshes, where he met Toad and some of his relatives. He learned that the Beasts had come there twice, but had been outwitted by the water both times, and had gone away in a tail-lashing rage. Toad had the opinion that the Beasts were finding it harder now to get food or slaves and were, as a result, "getting ripe to pick." (Toad's words, not Red's.) Toad was eager to help, but because he was so slow and unwieldy on land, he had suggested that he and his water friends would work at home and let Bront help us. Bront had lost members of his family to the Beasts, and Toad knew he would willingly join us.

To reach Bront, Red had had to go farther north, crossing the stream near where we had made the *Starflower*. And it was very easy to cross at that point. (Only when he told this did it occur to us to ask how he got across the river in the first place. Well, he said calmly, he just swam—left on his spider-thread suit and swam. Just like that.) Wandering and hunting for Bront led upstream, past our old cave and past our ruined tree house—now almost absorbed back into the forest—and on to a warm canyon where he found Bront. And here they were.

Our work now, we agreed, would have to be first of all the completion of our chain of pits all the way to the great mountain of Them—if we could find it. When the pits were finished, not before, we could begin to polish plans for getting the Beasts into the pits.

All right, we said. Very well. Let's get to it. We set out almost buoyantly. With Bront, we were eleven. Nobody was to stay be-

hind, although we wouldn't go all together. Scuro went ahead with
Red and Bront, to show them the terrain and perhaps to explore
further. Arachne, Locus, and Exi would come last. Arachne revealed now that she had been making hundreds of yards of sticky
webbing with which to cover the pits and further ensnare whoever
tumbled in. Locus and Exi would help Arachne place her nets.
Red, once having learned the route from Scuro, would return
and be the guide for the webbing party. Jetsam and I, Carabus, Mr.
Green, and Botta would go straight on until we found a place for
our next pit.

We left the webbers busily at work, and the scouts were soon
out of sight in the quiet forest. We were beginning to know the
way, to recognize certain trees and clearings and marks we had left
on previous trips. By noon the next day we had passed our third
pit, stopping just long enough for lunch, and were proceeding up
the valley farther than we had ever gone before. Scuro and Bront
had come back to report that the valley curved westward and then
shrank to a very narrow pass leading into a wide desert. When we
reached the westerly curve, we agreed that it was a good place
for our fourth pit. We spent the afternoon digging and carrying
dirt.

That evening the webbers caught up to us. They had covered
the three pits and, as Red reported, "You can't see them—I mean,
they sort of reflect the trees back, or something—very confusing—
they're marvelous traps."

Bront located a ledge just above the valley floor quite near to
our freshest pit, and we all settled there for the night, not too comfortable but exceptionally safe.

24

As we clambered down from the ledge next morning, I said, "I think we should go through that pass Scuro said was at the end of the valley."

"To be sure," Exi said. "Shall we get started? Rather, I should say, the rest of you get started as soon as you wish. I shall stay and help with the cover for the fourth pit."

It was exciting, I had to admit, to be approaching another pass. You never know what lies beyond. The cliffs were drawing nearer together on either side of us, and the forest was thinning out. Finally we paused beside a solitary spindly oak and looked ahead into a very narrow defile banked by vertical rock walls. The northern and southern mountains seemed to lean toward each other to touch, although they couldn't quite do it. We stopped talking. I'd suggested we go through this pass. I took the privilege of leading.

It was strange in the pass. No trees or bushes grew there; not even grass grew. We walked on bare ground, our footsteps sounding back and forth from wall to wall as if we were an army rather than eight half-fearful, half-expectant, cautious souls. The pass was not long—perhaps a quarter of a mile or so. As I emerged from the defile, I stopped in my tracks. A vast desert stretched beyond us, flat, barren, desolate. Our small group seemed smaller than ever, facing this expanse. To the north, the mountains receded and diminished in size. Ahead of us, the desert went on and on to merge into a misty horizon. On the south side of the desert was the most extraordinary sight of all. Rising from the barren plain was a great and beautiful mountain unlike any I had ever seen before. It lifted up, terrace upon terrace, a gigantic pyramid of violet-green thrust into a cloudless sky. It seemed to shimmer and quiver as a thing seen through waves of heat (although the day wasn't hot), and its details were blurred.

"That must be it," Jetsam breathed softly, after we had stood in silent astonishment for a while.

"You mean where They are?" I asked. "The Place of Them?"

"Yes. It couldn't be anything else."

We probably would have stood endlessly staring had not Botta announced, "Best place in the world for another pit," and hurled himself at a spot just beyond where the pass ended, and began to send dirt flying.

He was right, of course. It was the best laid out natural trap I had ever seen, for no one rushing through the pass could fail to fall into it. Bront went back to tell the webbers what was going on. The rest of us gave ourselves to pit making. This was the hardest digging job we had, for the gravelly sides of the pit kept crumbling away into slopes, and we just couldn't get vertical sides. We tried and tried, and got mad at it and at each other, and had to excavate Botta twice when the sides fell on him. The pit grew larger and deeper, but kept its slopes. We were in despair and about to give up when Bront and the webbers emerged from the pass. They stopped as we had done before the sight of the mountain.

"It is so," Arachne said to Exi, her voice resonant with feeling. He nodded. As I looked at their faces, all wisdom and all compassion seemed to glow from them and surround them with light; and I thought in wonder, these two belong to Them. That is their home, and they know it and long for it. Among other things, we must try to get them there.

The moment ended, and Arachne descended into the pit with her bundle of webbing. Aided by Exi and Locus, she fastened nets at each corner, drawing them upward, attaching them together, tightening them, while Botta maneuvered dirt behind them. The result was an extra deep, extra large, and very straight-sided pit— by far the best of the five. After the others climbed out, Arachne proceeded to line the inside with a layer of sticky webbing, finishing it as she backed out. Then she placed the webbing across the top, and I could see why Red had been so excited about these tops. They did have some unexplained quality that made them not transparent, as I would have expected, but opaque so that I couldn't see the pit at all.

"Exi," Jetsam said, "Don't you think we need to find a place to spend the night? We can't go home, and it's too far back to the other places."

The sun *was* about to drop below the horizon, and the purple shadow of the great mountain had almost reached our side of the desert basin. Exi agreed, but said he couldn't see much promise in the desert. Then Scuro announced that he and Bront had found a place earlier. Within less than half an hour they had led us south along the base of the cliffs to a small canyon which proved to be a true box, an entrance on one side and sheer walls on the other three sides. It had a tiny spring, a cluster of trees, and a few bushes.

Exi surveyed this natural enclosure. "Do you think you could?" he asked Arachne.

"I think I could. Yes."

"Could what?" My curiosity won over my politeness.

"For goodness sake!" Arachne snapped, as I thought she would. "Make a door for it, of course!"

"You mean to trap Beasts?" I said.

"Yes, to trap Beasts! It would hold a great number." Exi replied.

In the morning Exi said that he and Arachne needed two helpers to assist them in attaching nets to the sides of the canyon entrance in such a way as to make them instantly available when the time came—if it came. He didn't say how they would do it. But he did say that Bront and Red, because they were both agile climbers, would be the best helpers. It was decided that the rest of us would start back, stopping at each of the five pits to gather firewood and lay a fire. The four who stayed behind would catch up with us later.

The next days were much busier than we had anticipated. There were five woodpiles to stock, five fires to lay in just the right spots and in such a way as to make them as easy and sure to light as possible. Firewood was not easy to come by, and a great deal of time was spent hunting and gathering.

We all returned to I.H. at midday of the second day. We spent the afternoon discussing possible plans for the next steps. The burden of our chosen task was on our backs. And the momentum we had gathered we didn't dare lose.

Once I'd asked Jetsam how many Beasts he thought there were. Not more than forty, he had said. Now he repeated this.

Arachne spoke. "I believe that's correct. Botta and I used to try to count them—only as sounds, mind you—as they went over our heads."

"Good," said Exi. "I think the netted canyon could hold at least twenty-five of them. If we can get fifteen into our pits."

"We can't," Jetsam answered. "They're big. If we manage to get them to the pits at all, we'll get maybe twelve or thirteen, if it works, and the rest in the canyon, if we get that far." It was evident that Jetsam didn't intend to get caught in overconfidence.

Exi went on with his questioning. "What would you say, Jetsam, was the thing most likely to pull the Beasts into pursuit?"

"Two things, sir, and it would be hard to know which would do it most, food and sport. When they're hungry they're wild, and they roar out to hunt in a wild sort of way. But when their stomachs are full, they get bored and restless unless they have something to hurt or pick on or laugh at."

"So if our bait, as Mr. Green so aptly put it, were either possible food or possible diversion, it might lure them. Is that it?"

"Yes, I would guess so."

Scuro, who had been listening intently, said, "And what if the bait was both?"

"It would be even better!"

"Well, then, I'm it, as I said before," stated Scuro. "Should think I'd look like good eating. And I'll give 'em sport all right!"

I began to argue with Scuro, but Exi stopped me. "Scuro has a real point, I believe. We must have some means to lure them, and it must be as compelling a lure as we can make it so they will pursue it a long distance. Scuro is fast, intelligent, and can find his way in difficult country. He is brave. He is also good looking and would, I suppose, if you were a Beast, be very tempting."

When Exi had finished, Scuro shook himself and said, "That's settled then." And he returned to his listening.

At last, after hours of words and ideas, we had a tentative notion of how to proceed. Jetsam, Scuro, Locus, and I would return to the spot where the *Starflower* had been built. Here, after Jetsam and I had built a pit at the crossing point, we'd light a fire and hope the Beasts with Scuro as bait would respond. If they did, we'd take turns trying to lend them to I.H. and onward to the other pits. We'd take Locus with us because her keen nose and animal sense might help in times of flight. Someone would be stationed at each of the pits: Bront at I.H., Carabus at the next, then Botta, Mr. Green, and Red. Exi and Arachne would wait at the canyon trap.

It was just barely getting light when I wakened. I poked Jetsam and we got up heavily. The others were already awaiting us with breakfast. No one talked much. I checked our provisions and my few precious possessions in my pocket. Jetsam said he had the opal.

Finally Exi spoke. "There are some important things to remember always, no matter how hard life presses at you. One of these things is that wherever you are, and no matter for how long, there must be a home to hold you. You cannot know who you are unless you are contained in some way that gives you shape. Otherwise you are like a small wind, or like water losing itself in sand." He paused thoughtfully, looking at us, who had all stopped to listen. "You see," he continued, "at any place or time we have no way of knowing if we will be there a day or a week. We must let our destiny come to us. In one sense this is always true. Therefore it is needful for each of us to be defined—to live, not just wait to live. Do you understand?"

We nodded, and said our good-byes all around, trying to behave as if it were any other day. But it was a sad parting for us. There was no way of knowing whether we would all be together again or not.

Quietly we walked through our gate, turned away from our friends, and started off through the trees. It seemed strange to be deliberately going toward the things we most feared, to be going through the hushed forest as if we were off on a picnic, when actually we were headed into conflict, fear, even into disaster.

Remembering that we had been four days on the river in the

Starflower before we reached our island, Jetsam and I hoped that
three days on foot would get us back to the place where we had
built our boat. It took three and a half days.

Before noon on the fourth day we saw the river widening
slightly, and in only a few more minutes we stood by the small,
placid lake where we had launched the *Starflower*. It seemed such
a short time before that I had found this lake, such a short time
since I had set the injured Red down and I and the beetles had
made our boat. But also it seemed as if a hundred years had
passed since the day when I first glimpsed Jetsam and the others
in the vision from the Mantid's Mirror. It was both, I guess.
Things are, somehow, both yesterday and a century old.

Locus and Scuro began leaping back and forth across the
stream a few yards beyond where it came into the river pool.
"Here's where the first pit belongs," Scuro called, after a return
leap. "Here's where they'll cross, I'll bet. Need to break them up
early."

This put an end to my reminiscing. Jetsam and I joined Scuro
for a discussion, and decided that Scuro was right.

"It's awfully far from any of the others," I said.

"I know," Jetsam replied. "But it's here we have to pull the
Beasts across, and we've got to throw them off balance from the
beginning."

"Yes, I guess that's a good trick. To trap one or two here, and
then let them think it was just an accident and won't happen
again."

"Well then, let's get on with it."

Then I remembered Exi's last words to us all before we left.
"I think first we need to make a home. Even if we're not staying
long. Then the pit."

Jetsam didn't answer. He remembered too. So we began to
work, to make a place to live, rather than a shelter to flee from.
And while we were working I thought to myself, how funny it is
that you keep finding yourself where you don't expect to, doing
things you didn't expect to, and yet finding everything quite
familiar and friendly if you let go to it.

We found a spot where the bank sloped upward from the
stream and then settled into a gentle concavity before going up-

ward again. In this shallow cup was a single oak tree, old and tall, with a few berry bushes, a thorny shrub, grasses, and flowers clustered in its shade. We cleared away much of the grass in a circle around the tree, using the grass for matting to make beds. We managed to break off a great many thin branches from the thorn bush, getting well scratched and stuck in the process, and these we made into a low barricade between the hollow and the stream. Just inside this barrier we made a fine fire pit. Then we gathered firewood and dug for roots to add to our food supply.

The sun warmed the hollow and dappled it with light and leaf shadows. The grass shed a sweet odor in the air, and the stream purled pleasantly along its pebbled bed. As I think about it now, I doubt that we could have faced what we had to face or done what we did if we hadn't had those hours, fostered by Exi's ancient wisdom.

When there was nothing left to do, with what we had available, to improve our home, I suggested that we make our pit. We built it between the fire pit and the oak tree. As Scuro put it, the Beasts would come "over the thorns—plop—and over the fire and into the pit—plop—and away we go—" It was deep and wide, lined with some of Arachne's sticky net we'd brought along, and covered with the amazing webbing. We had to mark its corners with large rocks so that we could remember its location and not stumble in.

I had looked forward to having a fire that night. We'd not had one for an eternity. Jetsam, however, suggested that maybe we'd better get a good sleep before tempting the Beasts. So we sat around awhile in the darkness after supper, not saying much but basking in the soft night. Before long Scuro and Locus had curled into their earthy nests, and Jetsam and I decided to do the same.

25

After we'd eaten breakfast, Jetsam sighed deeply. "I wish it was all done with!" He sounded almost angry. "Done and finished!" He kicked the ground, threw a rock at the stream, and sighed again.

"I know how you feel."

"Well, wishing won't make it." He straightened his shoulders and ran his fingers through his hair. "Scuro, my friend, I'll race you around the pool!"

And they were off, followed by Locus, leaping the stream and tearing wildly along the other side of the lake, along the still water as far as where the river began to be a river and then back again, and leaping the stream to wind up breathless and hot beside me. Scuro and Locus had completely outrun Jetsam, but they had all enjoyed it.

I said finally that I'd been wondering what more we could do to get ready for the Beasts. Jetsam suggested making weapons. "We've got some natural things, like sharp rocks and pieces of wood and thorns. Why don't we gather a pile of things and just see what comes out." This sounded something like a puzzle. So I agreed.

Before we could begin, Scuro got up from where he had been lying in the sun to dry out and said, "Been wondering. Maybe Locus needs some training. She'd do better later, be safer too, if she learned a bit. I could teach her."

It had come to my mind recently that if Locus had some discipline I wouldn't worry about her as much as I did. Certainly, she too had been called by Them to try. Jetsam and I responded at once to Scuro's plan. Scuro spoke to Locus then, and obediently she trotted after him away from the stream, up the slope and into the forest.

Jetsam and I set about collecting in earnest. In half an hour or so we were sitting on the ground in our home enclosure with a pile of wood and rocks and other things spread out before us. We lifted and examined and experimented, and by evening we had the following: one club made from a length of wood and and egg-shaped, smooth stone tied securely in a natch with reed-grass woven rope; one hammer very similar except for a shorter but thicker handle and a slightly larger stone; one knife, consisting of a sharp rock made sharper by chipping away at it with a second rock; two half-finished spears—long pieces of wood peeled, tapered slightly at one end but needing to be burned in a fire to sharpen their points; and quite a few yards of grass rope. We weren't sure we'd need all this, but we felt better both for having it and for having made it.

That night all four of us were weary, needing rest before we ate and got ready for flight. Locus tucked herself into a ball beside me and fell instantly into a whisker-twitching sleep. Scuro lay near us, his head resting on his outstretched paws, his eyes open and shining.

"How did she get on?" I pointed to Locus. "Did she really learn anything?"

"She's a wonderful pupil, smart as anything, gets ideas fast, doesn't get mad if I tell her what's wrong! Afraid I wasn't as good when I was taught." Scuro sighed, although I didn't detect any great repentance. However, the suggestion that followed did credit to his having been trained by Them. "Everyone's tired," he said. "Mostly from fret. Won't do, you know. Trouble comes when it's ready, but getting scared and tight won't help us be ready when it comes. Let's have a feast with a fire, not just fear!"

Jetsam and I both got the idea and grabbed it enthusiastically.

"Scuro, you're a real gem!" Jetsam exclaimed. "Why didn't we think of that. Of course! We'll get the fire all ready, and as soon as it gets dark we'll cook a banquet! We can eat until we hear the Beasts."

"Yes," I said. "And couldn't we maybe finish our spears, too?"

Jetsam agreed and began twirling the fire stick. A wisp of smoke, a tiny flame, and our first real fire for a long time flickered in the darkness. While the flames burned high in their first rush, we put our spear tips in, turning them fast and then pulling them out and drawing them back and forth across a grooved rock to sharpen them. They began to look very professional and vicious. As soon as the fire died down into coals, we laid in it roots and nuts wrapped in wet grasses. We drew nearer to one another, watching the coals shift and settle, smelling the roasting food, trying to get quiet.

"I do wonder about the moon."

"What?" Jetsam sounded as if he thought I was crazy.

"Remember way back, when we were on our raft after leaving Toad? And I said that the moon was missing? Well, it still is. And it seems very strange. It might seem less terrible—what we've got to try—if the moon came."

"If I could remember what it was, I suppose I'd think so too." Jetsam poked the fire, making a flurry of fireworks. "But I don't."

"Big, round, shiny plate of a thing, sometimes," Scuro said. "Thin slice of a thing, mostly eaten, sometimes. I remember it, from before. I've missed it, too. Matter of fact, I asked Them once. They knew what it was but just said to wait, that when things were wrong it wouldn't come until someone tried hard enough."

I looked up at the black arch of sky. The stars were in place—the Dipper, Polaris, the Milky Way, and all the rest—and that was reassuring. Still, it was strange about the moon. What were we to wait for? No one seemed to know, at least none of our company. What had to be put right before the moon would rise once more? What kind of trying was necessary?

"Let's eat," Jetsam said, fishing food from the coals. "I'm hungry."

I was too, so I stopped thinking about the moon, and we ate with gusto even though we were waiting for doom to descend.

We continued to wait all through that night. I half slept, and roused often to see Jetsam adding fuel to the fire, to listen for the sounds of Beasts and to hear only the stream. Locus and Scuro rested in the way of their kind—eyes closed and bodies relaxed but ears ready in an instant to alert them and send them into action. No action was required. When the sun came, it shone upon a scene as quiet as the day before.

By midmorning Jetsam and I were restless and tense. Scuro watched us pacing about purposelessly, and I thought there was some amusement in his eyes. Finally he went and worked with Locus at the water's edge, adding to her training and leaving us to our worries.

"We've got to do something!" Jetsam burst out. "I can't stand this much longer! I'll have to stir them up or bust! Let's make our fire smoke now, not wait for night." So we built up a roaring fire. We gathered heaps of leaves, soaked them thoroughly and piled them on the burning wood. Soon there were clouds of billowing smoke not only rising upward but flowing outward to fill our camp and make us watery-eyed. Jetsam and I stayed stubbornly there beside the smoky, choking fire, while Locus and Scuro kept their distance, viewing our actions with tolerance if not with approval. The morning became afternoon and nothing had happened. We let the fire die and the smoke disperse, and finally just sat and looked at each other in utter frustration.

"Now what?" I asked. "The others will begin to worry and wonder. How can we get things started?"

With the smoke gone, Scuro and Locus had rejoined us. Now Scuro spoke. "Barking might get 'em," he stated. "Build up a proper fire; then I'll give it a try."

We built a "proper fire," blazing and crackling. We armed ourselves, Jetsam and I, with club and spear; Jetsam put the knife in his belt and I coiled the long rope and hung it over one shoulder. Then Scuro leaped the stream and was gone into the forest in the direction of the Beasts.

There had been so many hours of anxiety lately that I seemed to be getting used to them. I took Scuro's departure as one more of the unavoidable series; and Jetsam and I stayed by the fire, waiting as if nothing was about to come except maybe a guest for dinner. Before long we heard Scuro begin to bark from the distance. He kept at it monotonously, over and over, as a dog does when he's trying to get someone's attention. We could tell from the direction of his barks that he was moving about, then that he was slowly returning to us, back and forth but always nearer. Sunset had left the sky, and night was very close when Scuro gave a final defiant bark, leaped across the stream, and trotted into camp.

"Well," he said, "let's see what that does."

Jetsam and I had prepared food. While we waited we filled ourselves full, feeling we needed all the strength we could accumulate if anything did happen.

Then just as the night was reaching that point where you want to go to bed and sleep, and just as Scuro had stretched, yawned, and said maybe he'd better make some more noise and Jetsam had said he guessed that was right and he'd put more fuel on the fire—the first scream sounded. We were on our feet, every one of us, in the instant. It was obvious that the Beasts were far off yet. The screams came out of the darkness faint, unresonant, and directionless. But we could no longer doubt that our plan was getting somewhere.

"It did it!" Scuro exclaimed. "Really worked!" As if he hadn't expected it to.

"Look here," Jetsam put in sharply. "Let's not get so pleased with this that we forget what's next! Everything's next, and all at once, if they keep coming."

"How long do you think it'll be, Jetsam?" I asked. "Before they come, I mean?"

"Oh, I guess maybe—oh—an hour or less, depending on what the forest is like, what they run into."

"Well then," I said, "let's build our fire good and high, so it'll die down some before they come. Then Locus and I will go downstream a way, on the path home, and get into a tree."

"Right—you wait there until you hear me say 'Off!' Then you and Locus start running. Let Locus lead. From what Scuro tells me, she is a fine guide now and you can trust her. Keep well into the forest, back from the stream. Make noises like animals if you can, from time to time. We'll be doing barks and things from our side; we want to get them as confused and irritated as we can. This may make 'em easier to outwit. I hope."

Each of us carried food bundles on our backs. Also Jetsam and I each had club and spear, and Jetsam the knife. Each of us had a length of rope. At the last moment we decided that we should wear our spider-silk suits, which caused a considerable amount of unloading and reloading. Meanwhile, now and again we heard the Beasts, and it was evident they were coming closer through the black jungle. Then Jetsam spoke, his face serious and his eyes flashing in the fire flames.

"I think it's time, Maris. Go and find a place to wait. Scuro!"

Scuro went quietly around the fire, skirted our concealed pit, and went upslope beyond the fire and toward the beasts. He merged into the darkness. Now the plan was under way and there was nothing any of us could do to stop it. Jetsam removed our markers from the pit corners. (I had even forgotten they were there, and realized what an unsafe leader I'd be.)

I listened. They were getting closer. Their horrible voices resounded in the night, raising in pitch when Scuro barked. Hurriedly I fastened one end of my rope to Locus and the other around my waist, balanced my weapons, said good-bye to Jetsam, and left.

Locus trotted off as confidently as if she'd been leading all her life. I followed, drawn by the invisible thread of rope like a large cart being pulled along by a small pony. Out of the firelit circle we went, then downriver, past where the *Starflower* had been launched, then up a slight incline. I could sense trees all about me. The rope slackened. I slowed down. I could hear Locus sniffing about, and guessed she was hunting a hiding place. A special kind of tug let me know she'd found something. It was a fair-sized tree, judging from its girth as I felt it. My hand explored and found a lateral branch beginning quite near the ground. Locus waited for me to climb up first. Burdened as I was with her food, club, and spear, I found the climb very awkward.

Eventually we were up, side by side, in a crotch where the branch forked. It wasn't comfortable, but it seemed secure. I could see a distant glow through the trees, which couldn't be anything except our fire. Now that my eyes were adjusted, I could see stars above me. And I could hear. During the next hour

there were several times when I almost wished I couldn't. As the
Beasts came nearer and nearer, their voices grew louder, more
rasping, more menacing, more fearful. The cries went back and
forth, as they tried to follow Scuro's trail. He let them do this,
I guessed, as part of the campaign of tiring them, because he
only gave an occasional single bark and that he sort of swallowed.

I tried to think about other things—Grandmother, the Mantid, Grandan (who hadn't been in my mind for a very long
time), the monarch and his valley. This helped only a little. I
had just wandered back to the fear when I heard a concerted
roaring of Beasts, Scuro barking, and then Jetsam calling my
name.

"Maris!" he called. "Maris! Off! Off!"

After a stunned instant, I was scrambling down the tree with
Locus and was going in a rush through the forest with the rope
taut and urgent, stumbling over uneven pieces of ground and
grass tufts, bumping into bushes, scraping against trees—not due
to Locus's guiding but to the fact that I was larger than she
and she couldn't judge the space I needed with precision.

Behind us to our left I could hear the terrible confusions of
flight and pursuit. Scuro was barking and baying, now here, now
there, and the Beasts' cries were consequently erratic and confused.
They didn't know what they were doing, whereas Scuro did.
Their voices sounded increasingly angry—which might, I hoped,
spoil their judgment and sap their strength. I knew that I was
to help by making animal sounds once in a while. So I did,
when I could muster breath enough. Not very good ones, I'm
sure. But they weren't human, at least, and I hoped they might
help Scuro and Jetsam.

When dawn came (or rather, when I saw Locus trotting
along, pulling me down unfamiliar forest aisles, and realized day
was at hand), I could hear Beast noises changing. Instead of the
loud and terrifying pursuit cries there were growls, rumbles,
snarls. And they didn't seem to be moving. Scuro had stopped
barking. Locus and I halted. To be still in a quiet forest was
hardly believable.

I sat down heavily. Locus stretched beside me. Part of me
knew we shouldn't stay right there, but another part of me

wanted just to sit. Before I had a chance to see which part was stronger, Jetsam suddenly appeared out of the trees, his finger on his lips to keep me from calling his name in excitement.

As soon as he reached me, I flooded him with wanting to know everything. He shook his head, whispering that we must get farther away first. We went five or ten minutes farther, found a lovely all-embracing oak tree, climbed to a very comfortable seat on one of the lower branches, and settled down. Locus fell asleep at once.

"Let her sleep," said Jetsam, when I wanted her to eat first. "Let her sleep. She'll eat more then."

"Jetsam," I said, keeping my control as well as I could. "Jetsam, unless you tell me how you are, how and where Scuro is, what those creatures are doing and have done, I can't stand it."

Jetsam grinned at me, but he told me what had gone on. He and Scuro had waited, he near the fire, Scuro beyond it. Suddenly the Beasts were on the far side of the stream, king, his leader, and all. Jetsam shook his spear. The Beasts hesitated, milling about angrily. Then Scuro came forward, stood where they could see him in the firelight, and taunted them. He leaped away. They followed pell-mell across the stream, while Jetsam fled into the darkness.

"Did you get him—in the pit? The king?"

Jetsam wasn't sure, because he had had to run as fast as he could to catch up to Scuro, but he didn't think so. Seeing my dismay, he assured me that from the sound of things two or three Beasts had been caught.

Where was Scuro? He was keeping watch, from a safe hollow in a tree stump, over the resting Beasts. They had settled haphazardly in a clearing not too far away, having pursued until their weak eyes were no longer good guides.

"What about their noses?" I asked.

"I wondered about that myself. They do use them some, but they don't seem to be very secure about it. You know what I think? It sounds silly, but I think they smell so bad it covers up everything else!"

26

WE SLEPT FITFULLY, ON AND OFF THROUGH THE DAY. CONSIDERING the amount of energy we had put out the night before, our rest seemed quite unsatisfactory. But considering what we were trying to do, we were lucky to have as much sleep as we did have.

When Scuro trotted toward us that afternoon, I at any rate felt better than I had when I had reached the tree in the morning. Jetsam dropped to the ground lightly, greeted Scuro, then helped Locus and me down.

"Well, how is it?" Jetsam asked Scuro.

"They're fussing about. Restless I guess, but can't see quite enough to chase. Want me to begin getting them worked up?"

"Not a bad idea. Maybe it'll make them less accurate if they're excited. We'd better have a head start, though."

"Jetsam," I said, "Jetsam, they *can* see in the daytime! After all, we were pushed around during the day!"

"True enough. But did they leave their enclosure by day while we were there? Did they really see us well? Did they do much except eat or make demands? And did they hunt you by day, way back in the beginning?"

I shook my head.

"I learned when I was with them that their day vision was pretty poor. That was how I could steal candles and things from the dump."

"All right," I said, "so let's get on with our work."

"Scuro," Jetsam said, "give us about ten or fifteen minutes to get ahead. Then bait them into coming after us before they can see clearly. Maybe that will muddle them and weaken them."

Scuro watched us out of sight. And I kept looking over my shoulder, to Jetsam's annoyance, until I couldn't see Scuro any longer. I couldn't help it. Every parting seemed permanent. After Scuro disappeared, we jogged along through the trees with the river just out of view on our left. We knew it must be kept that way until we turned sharply away from it toward the West and toward our series of pits and waiting comrades. And we were sure that we couldn't reach the turn before the next night, because we had been more than three days coming. No matter how much faster we went on this hectic return trip, we couldn't do it in less than two nights.

When we judged that enough time had elapsed we stopped, got our weapons in hand, and prepared to start our flight as soon as we heard the roaring pursuit begin. We heard Scuro's barks echoing through the forest, and after a time we heard snarls and shrieks increasing in volume until it seemed certain the Beasts were on the move.

We plunged forward into the deepening twilight.

Our second night was much like the first, except that it was longer because we started before dark. There were the same trees multiplied by thousands. The bumps and hollows of ground were all there too, and I fell over or into every one of them. Locus was again a fine guide, lightfooted and careful; before it got completely dark, while I could still see her, we seemed to fly through the forest. It was almost exhilarating to play the role of decoy. But as night increased, our progress was a nightmare of dim shapes and blacker shadows and stumbling and being slapped by unseen branches and making animal sounds and being surrounded by noises—snarls, howls, grunts, screams, barks, calls—seeming to come from everywhere and nowhere. From time to time, I could distinguish Scuro's barks and Jetsam's howls and snarls off to our left, nearer the river.

Somewhere in the middle of the night, when I had almost reached the point of wondering if I could go on or if it would be easier just to let myself be captured, Jetsam grabbed me.

"Maris," he whispered, "we're going to swim a bit. That should really mix them up for a while."

Hearing only quite distant growls, I asked, "Where are they?"

"We slowed 'em! Went round some bushes and into the water three times! They're not untangled yet! You and Locus can rest."

"We will."

Locus and I didn't even bother to go to a safer place. I sank down beside a tree, and Locus curled up beside me, and there we stayed. I knew I must stay awake and alert until I was needed, so I forced myself to follow as much as I could the movements of the others, and to describe what I heard to Locus regardless of whether she listened or understood or slept.

"Well, this helps, doesn't it? I feel maybe I can go on now. When we have to, that is. Not one second before! Listen! The Beasts are really snarling and mad! Getting louder! There they are, coming nearer! Should we go? Not yet, not yet, I guess. Now they're at the river! Can't find anyone, and no scent to follow! It's scary, they're so angry! Let's get going, Locus!"

I jerked the rope, adjusted my bundle of food and weapons, and away we went once more. From somewhere between us and the Beasts, Scuro's challenging bark sounded. A roar of rage, and the Beasts took up the pursuit. Again we became the pursued in the weary, endless effort for peace.

The rest of the night passed somehow. In some blurred and remote hour the sky began to lighten and the Beast sounds diminished and at last ceased. I ached in every inch of me. Despite my attempts to prevent them, tears of fatigue and physical weakness ran down my face. I just collapsed, right where I was, put my head on my arms, and that was that.

I awoke after what must have been several hours of sleep to find myself curled around Locus inside a roomy hollow tree. At first I was startled and sat up in alarm, only to look into the hollow-eyed, dirty, smiling face of Jetsam.

"You're awake," he said. "Good. You've had quite a rest since I pulled you here from the heap I found you in."

I emerged from the hollow into warm and wonderful sunlight. I hugged Scuro, who wiggled and walked over to greet Locus; I hugged Jetsam, who let me but appeared very embarrassed. Then we all looked at each other gratefully.

"Guess we're glad to be here," Jetsam said. "But you know, Maris, the worst is still ahead and we've got to figure out ways to deal with it or we'll never succeed."

"How do you mean—the worst?" I asked.

"Well, we've got five pits, the canyon trap, and thirty or thirty-five Beasts still to go. It will take at least three more nights. The farther we go, the tireder we'll get, and the farther the Beasts go—and the more they lose, if we're lucky—the angrier they'll be and the more dangerous."

"All right. It's the worst that lies ahead."

He rubbed his head as if to make it think better. "The Beasts are sleeping in a half-cave about fifteen minutes away. They are almost as tired as we are and no doubt hungrier. I'm sure they won't wake up before sundown, and probably won't start after us until dark unless we stir them up. Which we don't plan to do this time."

After some discussion, we decided that Scuro would go on ahead to I.H., tell Bront we were coming, hurry on to tell Carabus at the next pit, and come right back. Scuro got up from where he had been resting near Locus. He shook himself, stretched, and stood before us eager and lively. "Can do it easily. But need to get started."

"Off you go then. Tell Bront and Carabus what to do. Hurry back. And take care."

His black body was soon lost to sight.

We agreed we couldn't keep up the pace of the last two nights. We had to rest sometime, which was why I suggested that Locus and I start for I.H. We could help Bront tackle the Beasts at the I.H. pit, see how many we trapped, and then be the decoys that pulled the rest toward the next pit. Scuro and Jetsam were to get them to I.H.

"Then we'll go a different way to Carabus's pit," Jetsam said, "rest awhile, and be ready there when the pack arrives. After we catch what we can there and force the rest on beyond, we should be able to get some more rest. I hope we can get them chasing two baits—Scuro and me, you and Bront."

"What if we can't—if they don't—?"

"Do what we can, what seems best when we come to it.

Now you and Locus better get moving. See you later." He patted my shoulder and gave me a little push. I knew he hated sentimentality, so I resolutely moved away in Locus's wake, forcing myself to walk rapidly into the woods in the direction of I.H.

Almost at once I began to recognize where we were by signs we had learned and marks we had put here and there. My spirits lifted at the sight of the known. Locus was affected in the same way, and soon we were half running among the trees, through shadow pools and dusty sunlight in the wonderful beauty of silence. We must have shortened the time between the river and I.H. by at least an hour, and it was about midafternoon when we arrived. I.H. was lovely and sad to behold, its gate wide, its enclosure as welcoming as ever but no one there to welcome. Our friends were elsewhere, except Bront, waiting the coming of terror. Locus and I stood inside I.H. and looked around, wondering what to do.

A monstrous sneeze announced the presence of Bront, whose ugly head rose up from behind the woodpile.

"I was practicing hiding," he said apologetically. "But I guess I'm better at running. Which is what Scuro says I'm supposed to do when the time comes."

"When was Scuro here?"

"Oh, quite a long while past. I'm very glad to see you again, by the way. The food is inside the old tree room, there near you. I'll call you when it's time." His armored head sank out of sight behind the woodpile.

I set about getting food for Locus and me. We ate all we could. Then we curled up inside the familiar room and slept. When I next became conscious, it was dark inside our room and Locus was tugging at me. Quickly I was on my feet; I fastened the rope to both of us again, took club and spear in hand, and stepped outside.

I could barely see our fence and the silhouettes of trees. I listened. In the far distance I heard—was it?—yes, I was sure I heard a bark.

"Bront," I called into the shadows beyond the fence, "don't you think the fire should be started?"

"Scuro said not until he gave us six barks fast in a row."

"Oh. Well, I leave it to you." Of course Scuro and Bront would have planned! "What can I do to help, Bront? What do you want of me?"

"I think that you two better get out of the inside there and come beyond the fire and the pit and go a way toward the next pit. Soon as you see me, or hear me—start out."

This sounded fine but somewhat vague, and I said so.

"Best I can do," Bront responded calmly. "Scuro said that from here on we'd each have to figure it out as we went, and that so long as we cared about each other it would probably come out as best it could, considering the hardness of it."

My ears caught a rising and swelling of sounds, still far off but obviously moving in our direction. I followed Locus through the gate, and made a cautious half-circle around the pit to where Bront was. I reached in the darkness and laid my hand on Bront's rough back.

"I'm glad you came to us, Bront," I told him. "I'm proud you're our friend."

"Why, thank you! I'll try to be a good one. And now you'd better go on a way, I think."

Both of us were aware that the noises of the chase were growing nearer. Locus and I made our way into the trees until we seemed well separated from I.H. We stopped and stood listening. We could begin to distinguish barks and growls from the snarls and subdued roars of the Beasts. A grim excitement made my heart beat harder and made my hands wet. I gripped club and spear tighter. The rope was taut between me and Locus, so I knew she was ready to go. The sounds came nearer and nearer.

Bront had lighted the woodpile, and flames leaped into the blackness to cast a demonic glow into the surrounding trees. I didn't want to leave until I saw Jetsam and Scuro, but I knew we must. Locus was pulling at me. I held back until I saw Bront rising like a terrible fury from beside the fire, and saw him standing in huge courage ready to be pursued. Roaring, snarling growling, barking echoed and re-echoed and clashed in dissonances that seemed enough to break trees and shatter rocks.

Then, above all other sounds, rose a screaming voice, hysterical and authoritarian, "I want him! That one with spikes! Him!"

Locus was pulling me through the darkness faster than she ever had before, and I was going at a stumbling run, my thoughts back there in that inferno of fire and rage and confusion, my feet trying to flee.

"Him! Him! The voice was a frenzy of demand. "Him! Hi—" It was snapped off in the middle of the work as if someone had thrown a switch. Momentarily all voices ceased. When they started again, there was a new note of fear mixed in with the wild hostility. At least so it seemed to me. There was no time to stop and think about it, but I sensed that whatever had happened was somehow good.

Bront, Locus, and I were now the pursued. I was personally responsible for diverting the Beasts from Scuro and Jetsam so they could go straight to Carabus and the next pit. Fear rushed through me but only briefly.

In a mysterious fashion, partly because of Scuro's teaching, Locus and I merged into a single unit of decision and action. We ran, we turned, we doubled back, we made animal noises to be sure our pursuers never quite lost us. From the confusion of sounds behind us, it seemed that the Beast pack had probably been split, and that some were after Locus and me, some following other quarry—Bront, I hoped. It was hard labor, the business of being a decoy. If I had to explain why, despite the superhuman efforts required, I was able to keep going on that night with less awareness of exhaustion than on the two previous nights, I guess I'd have to say that total responsibility gives more strength.

I felt as if we were being endlessly hunted in the maze of an endless and invisible forest, and was beginning to wonder how many more years we would, or could, keep on, when I heard the wonderful sound of Jetsam's voice shouting in the darkness.

"Keep coming! Then let Scuro take it! Keep coming!"

Gratefully I rushed toward the call, side by side with Locus. Suddenly Carabus's fire blazed forth. Its brightness made us falter a brief moment. Then as we plunged onward I caught a glimpse of Carabus piling on more wood, and I thought I saw Jetsam's head. Scuro barked. The crashing of Beasts behind us grew in magnitude, the snarling and screaming grew in ferocity, and I realized in terror that they were almost on top of us. Without thought, gripped by the instincts of a cornered animal, I turned around and faced them. The fire was not near enough to give much light. I got between Locus and the Beasts, and grabbed club and spear, ready to fight them until they overwhelmed me. I didn't have time to think that this was probably the end of our efforts—at least of mine—when they were upon me and I was beating at them with my weapons, trying to keep my feet, trying to cover Locus. Then I went down, and the world became a fierce chaos of pain. Beasts screaming, the awful smell of them, the weight of them! And Locus and I were left behind in the darkness as the Beasts rushed over us and past us.

At first I couldn't believe it, as I lay there half stunned. But as soon as I heard Scuro's urgent barking and Jetsam's shouts, I realized that Scuro must have shown himself to divert them from us. So the stupid, dangerous creatures had plunged on, finding us less desirable. I picked myself up, scratched and bruised but without major injuries. Locus was unharmed, I could tell. My spear was broken—I hoped it had done something before breaking—but my club was intact. Where Carabus or Jetsam or Bront were, I had no idea. Nor did I have any clear notion of what Locus and I should do, except go in the general direction of the next pit. I was too tired and aching, and too shocked by our near finish, to do more than plod ahead.

We marched right ahead into the area of Carabus's pit. The fire was dying down, but it still shed a considerable glow around, and as we came into its light I was aware of odd sounds and smells. I stopped. Almost without interest I thought, Yes, of course, there are Beasts in the pit. I went over to look. No sight could have been more rewarding, although I hardly took it in at the time. For thrashing about in the pit, completely entangled in Arachne's sticky webbing and utterly unable to free themselves or even to open their mouths wide enough to scream, were four Beasts. I could not feel sorry for them. I couldn't feel glad for us. I couldn't feel anything. I looked, nodded to myself, felt Locus tug at the rope, and went dazedly on.

I don't remember much of the rest of the night. There wasn't a lot of it left. Jetsam found us at daybreak and took us to the cave where he, Carabus, and Bront were resting. It was the same cave in the south cliffs we had used when we were pit building. I didn't care at the moment, though. I just wanted to be let alone and to sleep.

27

"How are you feeling?" Carabus peered at me inquiringly.

If I had to be dragged from sleep, Carabus was a good one to do it, because he was so matter-of-fact. It took a few seconds for me to find myself. When I stretched, it felt as if a large extent of me ached. Cautiously testing out my arms and legs as I unfolded, I found out that everything was working. So I looked up at Carabus.

"I can move, at least. Let me get up and see how it is."

With a few groans and grunts I got to my feet and stumbled into the clearing outside the cave.

Carabus said quietly that there was a spring nearby. There was no doubt I needed it, I thought as I knelt beside the little spring and gazed at myself in its mirror. My face was dirty, my hair snarled and twiggy, and a ragged scratch marred my already conspicuous nose. What a sight I was! After assuring myself that my precious bundle was secure in my pocket, I set about grooming myself as well as I could. When I returned to my friends, I was more nearly presentable.

It seemed almost miraculous to be able to sit with friends, to eat fresh food gathered by Locus and Carabus, and to make an accounting of our progress. After we pooled what information each of us had, we found that we probably had a total of ten or twelve Beasts. We thought we had the leader in Bront's pit, mostly because his uncontrollable greed for Bront had dulled his wits.

Jetsam asked Scuro how the uncaptured Beasts seemed to be.

Scuro lifted his head from his paws. "Mad and hungry. The two bunches got together just before day came, across the canyon near the north slopes."

"Could you tell how many?" asked Jetsam.

"Nope. Too close together. Too humpy. Didn't want to stay around, either. Quite a lot, though."

"Well, anyway," Jetsam said, as if to reassure himself and us, "they're tired, too."

Jetsam asked me if I thought Locus and I could go on to the next pit where Botta was. I said I thought we could. Then he said maybe, after I had told Botta what to expect, Locus and I could go on to where Mr. Green was, alert him, and climb up to the ledge nearby and wait. I said I wanted to do my full share of the work, and he told me not to worry, that I would.

Locus and I soon were making our way along the route close to the base of the cliffs. It was hard to realize, as I caught an occasional view of the massive mountains above the cliffs, that somewhere in those reaches was the Valley of the Opal. Somewhere up there was snow. Somewhere was Isia.

Unlike Bront, Botta did not arise like an avenging angel from his woodpile as we came. In fact, I couldn't find him when we first came into the camp. I called once, then again, and getting no response I began to wonder if he had left or been hurt or something. I stood by the fire pit and gazed around with concern; and then I saw him, sound asleep in a patch of sunlight at the base of a tree. I couldn't help being amused at his peaceful repose in the face of impending invasion.

"Hello," was what he said when I wakened him. "My goodness! Is it as late as that?" He unrolled himself, scratched, yawned, and was on his feet, bouncy as a new rubber ball.

"As late as what?" I replied.

"As late as someone like you telling me the Beasts are on the way, of course. That's it, isn't it?"

I told him that was it. I told him what had been going on, how everyone was, how many Beasts we thought we had, what the plans were. He listened carefully. When I finished, he gave me a bucktoothed grin and clapped his forepaws together.

"Off you go, then!" he cried. "Off you go to Mr. Green! Guess

I can take care of my share all right! Don't worry!"

As Locus and I departed, waving, he waved back and then went into a flurry of shadowboxing. Certainly there was no need to fret about him!

It was a longer trip from Botta to Mr. Green than it had been from Carabus to Botta. Locus and I pushed forward at a faster pace. We headed as straight as we could along the narrowing valley, permitting ourselves only one short halt on the way. The sun had just gone, leaving sky and trees bathed in silver-blue when I heard a familiar voice.

"So at *last* someone has arrived! I cannot really *believe* my eyes! At *last*! My dear Maris, it is so very *gratifying* to see you and Locus. I had begun to wonder if something *dreadful* had happened to *everyone*!" As he orated—for Mr. Green never just talked—he marched toward us, impressive in his beetle armor. "I was *watching* for someone, and as soon as I saw you, I came *at once* to meet you. Welcome! *Welcome*!"

I was quite overjoyed to see him and couldn't help recalling with surprise what a trial he had been to me in the beginning. He wasn't lovable like Red, but he had his own kind of charm and integrity. I let him know how glad I was to see him. Then, because darkness would soon be coming, I gave him as brief a picture as I could of how matters stood and what to expect. Locus and I would get ourselves onto the ledge where we could rest and be prepared to help when and where we might be needed. I didn't think the chase would reach us much before dawn. Therefore the Beasts wouldn't go far beyond this pit. If they did I could let them chase me. All of the pursued would need rest. Mr. Green agreed, insofar as he understood what I was trying to say.

Locus and I made our way to the ledge hurriedly, managing to clamber up the final stretch while a last faint tinge of silver remained in the sky. I roped myself to Locus, just in case we might have to move fast, put my club beside me, and lay flat on my stomach, near the edge where I could look down into the forest below.

Some waits are exciting. Some are dreary. Some are terrible because you know what is coming. But some waits, like this one, are almost unbearable because you look and look and all you see is nothing—darkness.

It is hard to tell what this night was. I wasn't really a part of it, and yet I was with every one of my friends. Scuro's barking very far off at first, was the thread on which all events were strung. It made a complicated pattern in the invisibility. I knew from changes in its pitch when the Beasts were nearing Botta's pit, saw faintly the glow of the fire, and I could tell when they arrived because Scuro's voice stopped for a while, to be replaced by the screaming of enraged pursuers, some of whom must have been trapped.

Scuro began again, and the pattern moved back and forth in the night, rising, falling, louder, softer, but always coming nearer. I wanted to rush down to it all, but didn't. Soon I began to hear other voices—a shout from Jetsam, Bront's baritone call, and a higher pitched phrase from Botta. And then Mr. Green's fire was a bright, pulsating beacon drawing all sounds and creatures toward itself. A din beat against the rocks of the cliff. It sounded as if dozens of frenzied devils were loose, roaring, screaming, raging. Interspersed with this incoherence were snatches of words I could recognize. "No! Over here! I said—" "Scuro! Where are—" "There's Carabus!" "Get him!" "Watch out for—"

What I heard was enough to make me know that a terrible battle was in progress. I was utterly beside myself with anxiety. I took my club in hand and was ready to start down, when I heard Carabus.

"Don't go down." His head came over the side, and then he stood close. "Jetsam's hurt—only a little, but Botta's helping him—and it'll be dawn soon and you're needed here." He disappeared over the side.

I got to work as soon as the faintest light came. I scooped out a sort of bed in a hollow place back from the edge, removing rocks, smoothing the ground with my hands. Then, because I couldn't recall any nearby trees or bushes, I took off my spider suit and then my frayed jacket, which had served so well for so long, and rolled it up for a pillow should Jetsam need one. I had no idea what Carabus meant by "only a little."

As the sky began to brighten further, voices came to me from below the ledge. I was aware that the world had fallen silent, as if the Beasts had had enough for the time being.

Carabus spoke first. "There now, Jetsam, don't try to go fast! Please do let us help."

"Yes," Mr. Green broke in, "that's what *I* say. I said lean on *me*. I am strong. My back is *very* strong."

"Oh, fuss!" Botta was as matter-of-fact as Mr. Green was not. "Get the job done. Now then, all together. Mr. Green and Carabus on one side, Bront on the other. I'll push. Up we go!"

The battered company came in sight over the edge of the slope onto the ledge. The other four were half supporting and half pushing a sagging Jetsam. His already tattered shirt was torn completely off his left side. Across his left shoulder and down his upper arm were long, bloody gashes, and blood dripped from his left hand.

"Jetsam!" I cried, running to meet them. "What have they done?" I put his right arm around my shoulders and helped to get him to the depression I had scooped out for a bed. He sank down into it, put his head on my jacket, and closed his eyes. "We've got to stop the bleeding."

"We couldn't," said Carabus. "Our feet weren't right."

"Of course," I said, and knelt beside Jetsam. I examined his wounds, which were ragged and raw. As I wondered how to stop this slow draining of blood, there leaped to my mind the sight of Arachne swathing Isia's wounds in yards of spider silk.

"Wasn't he wearing his spider suit?" I asked them.

"Nope," replied Botta. "Said it was too hot, when he got to me. Took it off."

"Where is it?"

"Lost, I guess."

"Well, who else has one? Please take it off. We'll need it!" Carabus handed me Locus's. Using it as a bandage, I managed to get it pressed against the wounds, and with relief saw the bleeding cease. I used mine for a bandage. Jetsam was so still though, so drained of vitality, I felt an awful despair.

"Don't look so anxious. I don't believe it's as bad as that," said Carabus.

"No," Botta stated, "he's young. Got knocked down once, but not too bad. He'll heal. Let him rest, and quit worrying."

I made myself listen to them. They cared as much as I, and they would want to do more if they thought more was needed. Anyway, there were other things to be done, and we had to get at them before we all rested.

I asked about Scuro and was told he had stayed to see that the Beasts were bunched together for the day. Then he would go on to Red at the final pit, and to Arachne and Exi. He would return to us as soon as he could. I didn't see how he could keep it up much longer.

We needed food. By pooling what remained in all our bundles, we got only a couple of handfuls of nuts and a few dried berries. Locus, Carabus, and Botta went exploring, and did find, a short way up the mountain, some rather tasteless but filling roots, and a few berries.

Our last problem was a shelter for Jetsam. For a while after the sun rose, he lay in its full warmth, breathing quietly. Then he began to toss and turn, and little glistens of sweat came on his face. He needed something over him. Bront and Mr. Green found four crooked sticks; I dug four shallow holes; and we managed to prop these sticks upright with the help of dirt and rocks. The remnant of Jetsam's shirt, which I had removed, was hung from the posts and became a weird canopy over his head and shoulders. We all breathed easier when his restlessness subsided soon after the shade fell across him.

Bront, who loved sun, stayed close beside Jetsam, assuring me that he would watch over him. Locus, Mr. Green, Carabus, Botta, and I moved back into the shade of a clump of low bushes. Throughout most of the rest of the day we were silent and stretched out, not always sleeping but at least resting. Much later Scuro arrived and dropped down beside us. He too was spent, his coat disheveled, his paws obviously sore, because he licked at them for a long time.

When the shadows were lengthening and the day's warmth was going downhill, Jetsam woke up. I heard him speak to Bront, and went to him. He stretched himself, felt his bad arm and shoulder with his right hand, wiggled the fingers of his left hand, sat up, and said in a full voice, "I'm hungry!"

"How do you feel, Jetsam?" I asked. "Are you able to get up? Do you feel sick? Should't you lie still?"

He laughed. "Don't be a worrier, Maris. I'm really fine— stiff, and sore, yes, but all right. The Beast was off balance when he clawed, so I don't think he clawed me too deep. After I eat, we'll look. But I'm hungry!"

The portions of roots and berries we had laid aside for Jetsam, if he should want them, were brought. If appetite was any measure, he was certainly all right, for in no time he devoured every morsel we had saved for him. When he finally got to his feet, he seemed steady. He did wince as he removed the makeshift bandage and as he flexed the muscles of his left arm. Even so, he could use it, and the long clawcuts didn't look inflamed.

"Guess I'll live," he announced happily.

I helped him into what was left of his shirt. The bloody spider suits we rolled up to carry until water was available to wash them. All eight of us gathered around Scuro, now that Jetsam was active, and heard his report. Six or maybe seven more Beasts had been trapped during the night in the two pits. The rest were getting panicky, Scuro felt. Jetsam was hurt when some of the Beasts had tried to bolt back through the woods. Scuro had headed them off, and Jetsam had come to his aid when the Beasts attacked. Though they were bunched together in the narrow part of the valley for the day, Scuro seemed convinced that we'd have to "push as well as pull," or some Beasts would get away.

As night began to close down, we went from our ledge to the forest below. I was tuned to a high pitch of readiness. Probably Mr. Green was in the same state. The others, I guessed, would be less tight but equally ready. It was decided that Mr. Green, Locus, and I would proceed to the pass, go nearly through it, and place ourselves on each side of it to lure the Beasts there and try to keep any of them from turning back. We three soon went off into the darkness. Scuro headed directly for the Beasts. He would lure them on. Jetsam, Bront, Carabus, and Botta, were to close in behind and roar, shout, beat on trees, do everything possible to make the Beasts afraid to retreat.

It was black as a cave when we entered the pass. I let Locus lead us entirely. My feet were loud, and I could hear Mr. Green clicking along behind me. I remembered how close to the end of the pass, where it opened out into the desert, we had built our last pit; and I wondered aloud to Mr. Green just where we would put ourselves. I trusted Locus to let us know when we reached the end, and she did, by halting her slow progress and then going very slowly forward, almost creeping.

It was as surprising as it had been the first time—to emerge suddenly from the narrow pass into the vast desert. Even at night it was awesome. The shadowless, barren plain reflected back the starlight until it seemed to hold an unearthly glow. Far away, farther than by day, loomed the great mountain, its gray bulk gleaming above the desert floor. Quite unconsciously I drew back for a moment, finding the impressiveness too much. I looked away from the large scene to an indistinct darker small blotch fairly nearby.

"Red?" My word was swallowed in space. "Red?"

"Here, Maris," replied a faint but familiar voice. "Come forward slowly—around the pit, be sure—watch your step."

We weren't long in reaching him, and Mr. Green boomed out greetings.

It was a strange and lovely half hour or so we had there, the four of us; strange because we were an especially odd assortment of personalities, and because this was a time out of time, set down at the edge of an unknown wasteland and an unknown future. It was lovely because we stood quietly around a bright-burning fire warm in the presence of each other, reminiscing about things we had done together. We kept piling wood on the fire in a fine prodigality. There was lots of it, and we all seemed to want a great blaze.

When at long last we heard Scuro's bark, faint and far off, we uttered a collective sigh. I took up my club. Mr. Green came to my side. Without knowing quite why, I ordered Locus to go on to Arachne and Exi. She left, reluctantly but obediently.

"I should *guess*," said Mr. Green, "that we would be *most* helpful if we took positions on either side of the pass."

"I should guess so," I replied. "And Red, what a fine time this has been. I'll remember it. And do please be careful."

"I'll do what I must," he said softly. "Don't worry. And it has been a nice evening—I know what you mean—"

Mr. Green and I turned away, paused until our eyes grew accustomed to the darkness, then went back toward the pass.

28

Mr. Green and I got ourselves as close as possible to the steep edges of cliff at the exit of the pass. What we would do when the Beasts came we didn't know.

Slowly at first, with long silences between, came the sounds of the chase. They grew in intensity. As soon as the grim and fierce pursuit entered the pass, every bark of Scuro, every snarl and roar of Beasts, every shout of anyone, echoed and re-echoed against the rocky sides and poured an incredible dissonance into the night. There were moments when I wanted to bolt, to cover my ears and run away, it was so awful. Ahead, Red's fire was a beacon of light. Then Scuro shot out of the pass at full gallop, barking furiously and looking neither to right nor left but going directly toward the fire. I shouted at him, but I knew he couldn't hear me.

The Beasts came—a foul-smelling horde of pushing and disorganized Beasts. They crowded one upon another, snarling, biting at each other sometimes. Most of them, that is. Some tried to turn back into the pass. I beat at them violently with my club out of the darkness and yelled with a voice louder than I knew I had. They must have thought some invisible monster was at them, for they wheeled in obvious terror and followed the pack again. Mr. Green, I learned later, had gotten the tails of several Beasts in his sharp pincers and startled them away from flight.

After the whole company of pursuers had spewed from the pass, the others of our group came—Botta, Bront, Carabus, and

Jetsam, in that order. Jetsam paused long enough to tell us to go on.

"We've got 'em on the run!" he shouted. "Come on!" His voice was strong and urgent with a sort of joy of the chase. His upper body was naked now (the frayed remnant of shirt evidently having given up) and gleamed with sweat. He brandished his club in his right hand, and in his weakened left hand he held his spear. "Come on!"

The scene we rushed into was terrifying. Red had made the fire enormous, and everything around was fiery movement and black shifting shadows. Scuro was beyond the pit, dancing about in a frenzy of barking. Beasts seemed to be everywhere, churning and roaring. Some started for Scuro and Red. Others followed. I called to lead still others on, and so did Mr. Green. Botta, Carabus, and Bront closed in behind the confused remainder, all roaring at them.

We all stumbled on, leading, following, and pursuing. It was hard going for me, for I didn't have Locus as a guide. I blundered about for a while, and finally oriented myself by the black mass of mountains on my left, went toward them, and then worked my way along their base. I hoped I was going in the right direction to reach the final place of this long and harrowing flight—the box canyon where Arachne and Exi waited.

The rest of was happened was a nightmare.

As I neared the canyon, suddenly the darkness was illumined by two small fires. Exi and Arachne had evidently placed them on each side of the big trap, and the Beasts were to be lured, or driven, between them. I heard Scuro ahead, barking from higher up. He had climbed above the canyon and was trying to bark them in. I darted into a protected shadow of rock near the entrance and waited. It all worked out as planned—except for one thing. A group of four or five of the Beasts panicked just as the pack was rushing into the canyon. They broke from the rest, turned suddenly in a fierce retreat. It looked for a second as if all the others might follow, for the whole horde seemed to hesitate. It can't happen, I thought to myself, it just can't! It mustn't! I started for them.

Then Bront gave a mighty roar and the main body of the pack surged into the trap.

"Drop the nets! Drop them quick!" Jetsam shouted. "Get what we can!"

And the huge nets came unrolling down the air, Arachne and Exi coming with them and fixing them at once to the ground.

Jetsam shouted again. "Botta! Come! We'll go after the ones that got away!"

So some had escaped. But at least we had most of them, I was sure. When I reached the nearest fire, I could see a tangled mass of Beasts inside the net, hopelessly caught. It should have made me happy, but it didn't. Nor did the sight of Arachne and Exi standing in the firelight with Locus, Mr. Green, Carabus, and Bront crowding around them. I greeted them by saying, "Where're Jetsam, Red, Botta, Scuro?"

"Gone to capture the others, of course!" Mr. Green sounded confident.

"How can they? I am afraid!"

"Yes, Maris." Exi was serious. "I, too, am afraid. They should not have gone. Nothing can ever be accomplished with perfection, and to think it can is to invite disaster."

We were silent then, the quiet broken only by the low protests of the captive Beasts and occasional cracklings from the fire. If Exi felt this way and said as much, there was nothing we could add.

We just sat until the first faint smudges of dawn crept up the East. The canyon was against the west face of a mountain, so that when the sun did come it sent a shaft down upon the mountain of Them, far across the wasteland, but left us in the depth of a pyramid of shadow stretching out away from us. As light came, we all turned silently northward, facing the pass.

Out onto the barren plain, moving slowly toward us, came only two lonely figures. None of us moved to meet them. There seemed no need. As they came nearer, we could see Jetsam carrying something; Scuro walked behind him. When they were within hailing distance, the tragic picture was clear. In Jetsam's arms was Botta, limp and still. Fastened to Scuro's back was a platform of oak branches and leaves, and on this lay Red. They came slowly up to us.

"Botta, I hope, will live," Jetsam said, his face old and sad.

"And Red?" Exi asked gently.

"He is dead."

It did not matter then how these things had come to pass. Later we learned that Red had tried to keep the escaping Beasts from getting into the pass, and that Botta had fought to save Red but couldn't. At this dark moment none of it mattered.

As I looked down on the rust-red, lifeless body, resting like a carved image on Scuro's back, I felt loss, and grief, and that most awful wonder that what was once is no more. I couldn't believe it. I wanted to go to Red and touch him to waken him. I wanted to speak his name. And I knew I could do nothing.

Actually it was a brief moment only that we all stared, bereft and paralyzed, but it seemed hours and hours.

It was Arachne who finally said, "Botta must be cared for." So I learned that in the face of shock and grief simple necessary acts are the first helpers.

Like sleepwalkers we moved under Arachne's guidance, hollowing out a bed in the ground, getting branches to make a shelter, lining the bed inside the shelter with soft leaves. Jetsam had been holding Botta all this time, and after he had laid Botta in the bed and Arachne began her ministrations, Jetsam just stood there, his hands clenched at his sides.

I went to him, putting my hand on his arm tentatively. "Jetsam," I said. "I'm sorry."

He put his hands over his face.

"It wasn't your fault," I said, not knowing what to say.

"It was! It was! Why didn't we let them go? Only a few of them—we could have followed them later—but no, I had to—" His voice, muffled by his hiding hands, broke off.

"Jetsam, please don't—"

"Oh, leave me alone!" He turned and walked away from us.

"Let him go," Exi said, as I half put out a hand to stop him. "I am sure he needs to be by himself with his feelings. They are partly right, you see; and whether right or wrong he has to struggle with them. No one else can do it for him. It is a sad time."

So I watched Jetsam's disconsolate figure until it disappeared around the flank of the mountain to my left. Then I turned to face my friends. Scuro stood unmoving, still bearing on his back Red's body in its leafy bed. Arachne was being assisted by Carabus and

Mr. Green; Exi and Bront waited nearby. Poor little Locus had been forgotten; she stood there, trembling, her eyes fear-filled. I held out my arms and she ran to me. As I held her, a new sort of strength came into me, a recognition that our work wasn't finished yet and that, if it was to be finished, I had to give everything I could to the common cause. This included the tasks at hand.

"Exi," I asked, "shouldn't we take Red down—I mean, shouldn't we make some sort of—of—funeral pyre, or coffin, or something?"

"You are quite right. Of course we should."

No one but I could remove the burden from Scuro's back. I unfastened the grassy thongs with which Jetsam had tied the body in place, and I lifted it gently from Scuro and laid it on the earth. Red—for it had been Red—seemed smaller in his stillness, and yet larger in the light of his heroic death. He had never been imposing, as Exi was, or flashy and handsome like Mr. Green. Just ordinary. Yet how often he had carried more than his share of the job to be done. Now I could cry, looking down at him, and it was good to cry and to release the locked-up love and the paralysis of shock.

When Exi and Bront returned with some gatherings, I was calmer, ready to do what was to be done. Together we made a sort of dais of short branches lashed together with tough grass. We covered this with a mat woven from the shiny leaves of a shrub. On this dais I laid Red, and on his body placed his proud sword and a handful of flowers that Locus had brought. This was all we could do. Eventually he had to have a proper funeral, but not here in this impersonal desert.

Carabus came then and said Arachne needed water for washing Botta's wounds. I asked Scuro where to go, since he usually had a nose for where things were. It didn't take long for him to lead us to a small spring seeping out of the rocks a bit above and to the right of the canyon trap. The main problem was how to get the water down to Arachne. Finally I soaked the bundle of spider-thread suits until they were completely filled with water, and then I hurried down so she could squeeze as much as she could from them. Meanwhile Scuro tried to dig at least a makeshift ditch to channel the water as near to us as possible. The result was not too bad. A pool formed only about thirty feet from camp, so that the saturated suits began to bring good amounts of water.

When I had time to look at Botta, I was horrified. His furry body, wet now from Arachne's continual washing, was torn in many places by deep jagged wounds, one especially bad across his round face. His eyes were closed, so I couldn't tell for sure if the left one had been blinded. He was as limp as he had been when Jetsam had first brought him in. When I asked Arachne if he would recover, she made no reply, only kept at her washing. This was, I began to realize, a substitute for the continual tongue-washing that a wounded wild creature gives itself if it is able. So I doubled my number of trips to the pool, keeping Arachne continuously supplied. She was anxious, I could tell. After all, she had known Botta much longer than she had known us; they had been close neighbors and had worked together.

The long day went on. Very few words were said; no one wanted to talk. We worked together doing what was necessary— making a camp and sleeping places and a fire pit, gathering wood, finding and preparing food. The site of the camp was slightly north and around the bend from the trap, so we didn't have to look at the Beasts. And for the most part they were silent too, although occasionally a groan or growl was heard.

The sun had gone when Jetsam returned. He came to us quietly, his face drawn, his eyes haunted. His body, however, no longer sagged in despair, and he met Exi and me, who chanced to be standing together, with a straight look.

"Jetsam," Exi said, as if he had been there all the time, "would you be good enough to build a fire for us?"

My impulse had been to greet Jetsam rather more intensely. Exi's matter-of-fact approach was better. Jetsam uttered a relieved sigh as he set to work. Carabus joined him, saying nothing, and soon they had a truly splendid fire blazing away.

As long as any light remained in the sky, Jetsam kept at work, gathering more wood—which they didn't need. From time to time he paused to stare at Arachne and Botta or to stand motionless before the body of Red on its leafy resting place. When night came, we gathered close together beside the fire, and near to Arachne and Botta. The smell of roasting nuts and roots was sweet. There were no Beasts to fear, and no grim hare-and-hound game to play. This night should have been one of celebration.

Food, I thought, was the last thing any of us wanted, but with sticks I lifted our bundles of food from the coals and passed them around. To my surprise, we ate with considerable appetite, even if not with enjoyment. But we ate quietly.

It was Mr. Green, of all creatures, who broke the brooding silence. "I have been *thinking*," he said, "and I think our beloved friend Red would *want* us to go forward. He would *want* us to keep trying to *fulfill* our purposes and achieve our *goals*. He gave his *life* for that!"

As always, Mr. Green's words were dramatic, but under the circumstances they seemed to fit very well. Not only to fit but to help. Each of us nodded, or murmured agreement, and Exi said, "I agree completely. We must and we will keep going, I am sure. Whatever that may involve."

I gazed out across the great dark desert that stretched between us and the Place of Them and pondered on what lay ahead. Suddenly, as I gazed, I saw a strange light touch the summit of the distant mountain of Them. The light grew in strength. Slowly more of the mountain was bathed in it. And from some place inside me came the knowledge of what was happening. I swung around to look behind me. It was a moon, an enormous platter of a moon, rising above the jagged cliffs of the canyon, pouring its rich illumination down onto the plain.

"Look!" I cried. "Jetsam! Exi! Everyone! Look behind you!"

"It's not true!" Jetsam's voice was filled with awe.

I realized then that perhaps no one, except Scuro and me, had ever seen the moon. "It is true," I said. "It's the moon."

"Where has it been before, I *ask* you, *where*?" Mr. Green was almost angry in his surprise.

"I only know its coming is related to Red, and somehow I think it's related to the Beasts. Scuro told us that it wouldn't come until someone had tried. Do you remember?"

"I see what you mean," said Jetsam. His face was transformed as the moonlight bathed it.

Arachne pulled us back with a jolt when she called, "Come at once. Something is happening to Botta!"

We were beside Botta's bed in a rush. In the combined firelight and moonglow, Botta's round body was clearly visible under its wrappings of spider silk. He lay inert. The left side of his head, including the eye, was covered with bandages. The other eye was closed. I looked at Arachne, trying to read her expression. Was it good or bad? I peered again into Botta's ugly face, to see if I might read the answer there. And the good right eye opened and peered back at me.

"Oh, Botta!" I cried. "Botta! Botta!"

He nodded his head like a goblin in half a nightcap. "Don't know . . . what . . . that is," he whispered—and I knew he meant the moon—"But it's done it, done it . . ." And he closed his eye again and quite obviously was sound asleep.

This broke our tension as nothing else could have done. Once we knew Botta slept a healing sleep, we felt we could do the same. So we all relaxed.

I sat for a long time with my back to the fire, watching the great moon afloat in the night. It was more wonderful than I would ever have dreamed, to have it there. What Scuro said They had told him was true. Red had given his life trying.

Finally I stretched out on my back, letting the moon fill my eyes and my mind. And the vision came to me that those familiar shadows on the moon's face were no longer what I had always believed them to be—rabbit, or woman with streaming hair, or man. What was in the moon was an ant, the contours of a wonderful red ant who tried.

I never told anyone this. But it is so.

PART V

Final Things

29

Silence was a being in this desert land, and as I paced the moon across the sky and watched her sinking slowly westward, I felt as if dark-clad silence sat beside our fire with us and brooded over us. The great mountain, which was the Place of Them, changed as the moon changed—from a mass of gleaming metal when the moon was overhead, to an imposing silhouette of cosmic size as the moon moved down the sky and at last slid out of sight. The body of Red changed too, as the moonlight moved over it, taking on a strange life of its own as first this surface and then that caught the gleams.

With the earliest light of dawn, I went to Arachne. Botta was asleep, but Arachne's nod sent me off to our pool to bring the wet cloths for Botta's treatment. Jetsam was already up and moving about restlessly, fire tending, food gathering, "making things neat," in his words. I doubt that he had slept much, but I didn't ask. Once we met in front of Red, and we both stopped and looked full at our dead friend. I felt that for Jetsam this was the first time he could let himself do it. He reached for my hand and held it very tight as we stood there. He started to put out his other hand toward Red, then drew it back in a helpless gesture. His eyes filled with tears.

"It wouldn't help," he whispered. "It wouldn't help."

"No," I said. "It wouldn't."

He started to turn away.

"Wait," I said. "Did you see him in the moon's light? And how fine he was, and big, and sort of . . . forever?"

247

"Yes. Yes, he was like that."

"Well, I wondered if maybe you could make something so we could honor him somehow. I mean—well, his last words—almost —were 'I'll do what I must.' "

It was a better idea than I had thought, and Jetsam grabbed it and clung to it as if it were all he had. So while the rest of us did the chores to be done, Jetsam worked at his monument. With Scuro's help he found a smallish tree some distance up the cliffs behind us and he felled it by chopping away at its base with a sharp stone. It was a giant's task, but he did it. Then he and Scuro somehow dragged it down into our camp, and Jetsam began to work on it with his stone knife. We stayed for almost a week because of Botta, and every day, from first light to darkness, Jetsam worked. His hands bled and then grew calloused. He talked very little, mostly to ask about Botta. What he had achieved at the end of the time was unbelievable. And it was his healing. I could tell from the way his face changed and how his eyes lost their terrible guilt.

Botta's healing was more of a problem. His body wounds were deep, and as the torn fur fell away they looked raw and feverish. The slash across his face was the worst, and his left eye was swollen shut and obviously infected. We were all worried about him. What finally helped him turn the corner was something Mr. Green con-tributed. One day he came rushing into camp, an unheard of event in itself, and said, "I *found* it! I really *found* it! I *never* thought I *could!* Here it is, Arachne, take it *at once!* Use it!"

When we had calmed him enough to find out what it was, we learned that for days he had been searching the woods above the canyon for a special root he had remembered his grandfather using to heal wounds. And at last he had found it. Arachne did take it, and she did use it on Botta's wounds. From then on the feverishness began to decrease and the swelling in the eye to diminish.

At last one bright day, after a good breakfast, with Botta sitting in the morning shade looking more nearly himself than he had for a long time, Exi called us together. We gathered in a ragged circle around our cook fire, which had sunk to a bed of warm coals, and waited. Exi and Arachne were side by side, and our attention was on them. Exi spoke first.

"We have come a hard and painful way together," he said. "Some of us have been comrades longer, but all of us are bound with ties of joy and danger and suffering. Each, I believe, has a sense of a work to be completed."

"And we are not sure how we must do it," Arachne put in quietly.

"No," Exi continued, "we are not sure. We only know it is to be accomplished. Does anyone have ideas?"

There was a period of silence. No one seemed willing to say what we all knew. Finally Mr. Green, who was but slowly coming out of the shock of Red's death, said that he supposed we had to cross the desert and climb the mountain.

"Yes," Exi agreed. "That is not exactly what I meant. Of course we must go forward to the Place of Them. What I was really asking was *how* do we proceed? With Botta. And with Red."

Unexpectedly Jetsam spoke, his voice low but intense. "I will carry Botta, as soon as he can travel. And Scuro will carry Red. I have asked him. Red must go with us all the way. Or I shall stay here with him." His voice broke.

Arachne's huge eyes, filled with pity, turned toward Jetsam, and her voice was as soft and gentle as I had ever heard it as she said, "Jetsam, don't be troubled. I am sure we all feel as you feel. I have spun a sort of carrying basket for Botta."

"Very good." Exi looked at each of us in turn. "I think we know where we must go, then. And how we start. Is there any further thing?"

"Yes. I have made a Remembering Tree, to put here so that always and always Red will be known by travelers." Jetsam's face came alive as he spoke. "If Scuro will help me, we can put it in place. And please everyone stay here."

So we stayed until Jetsam called us. We arose and walked in an unplanned procession, I carrying Botta, to where Red lay so still on his funeral dais. Directly behind him rose Jetsam's monument. He had made the small tree into a vertical column. The upper half was a marvelously carved ant, with drawn sword, climbing upward, while the lower part, the base, bore the words, cut deep into the wood, "I'll do what I must." Jetsam and Scuro had dug a deep hole, sunk the carved column into it, and buttressed it securely with dirt and rocks. It looked as if it could stand forever.

No one spoke, and the silence was a presence around us. Then Arachne moved forward, and laid over Red a gossamer robe of shimmering color, like a waterfall's mist with sun shining in it to make rainbows. The whole scene was indescribably beautiful and moving.

Without words, in the same formal way, we returned to our circle.

"I believe we can begin to prepare for our next step," Exi said at last.

That afternoon was filled with activity. The usual things had to be done, such as food packaging. Scuro had gone off earlier to check on captive Beasts, and he reported that all those he visited —in the canyon and the last two pits—were alive, very ensnared, very quiet. Weak and hungry, he was sure. He almost felt sorry for them, he said, but not quite. We assumed that all the other captives were in the same condition. He had seen no signs of the few who escaped, and we decided there was nothing we could do about them.

By nightfall everything was ready for departure, and we came together for our final evening in a sad place. There wasn't a great deal to say. We remembered parts of our travels, as people will who have shared much. One of the happiest aspects of the evening was Botta's participation. Although he was still heavily swathed in Arachne's bandages, and although his left eye was still covered, his voice was strong and his face, or what was visible of it, expressed the old Botta.

Jetsam and I were unwilling to sleep away the night. Long after all the others were at rest in their various ways, I sat by the fire, arms wrapped around my knees, and waited. Jetsam was near me, stretched out on his back, his eyes wide open looking up at the sky.

After a long time he whispered softly, "It's coming, Maris. Look."

I knew what he meant. I turned my head toward the east to see again the wonder of moonrise. It had been coming later each night since its first appearance, and was on the wane now, behaving exactly as a proper moon should. This subtracted nothing from its glory, and I, who had seen it so often in my life, felt the same excitement as I sensed in Jetsam.

We set out across the wasteland well before dawn, in an attempt to avoid as much of the blazing heat as we could. I carried food and my few possessions. Jetsam had the opal, a stone knife, and Botta. What Arachne had called "a sort of carrying basket" proved to be an ingenious knapsack-cradle arangement to be slung over the shoulders, in which Botta rocked gently along, safe and comfortable. On his back Scuro carried the funeral dais bearing Red under his regal robe. Somewhere Locus had found more flowers, and these we placed on the robe.

Exi and Arachne went first, followed by Scuro and the bier, then Jetsam with Botta. The rest of us more or less bunched together, with Carabus acting as rear guard even though we were not expecting any enemy.

Distances in such a place are impossible to estimate. By the time the sun was well up and hot on our backs, we could no longer see our camp or the rocky pass; all the mountains behind merged into one massive jagged barrier. Yet we seemed scarcely to have moved toward the Place of Them. To our right was a wasteland with distant small mountains, while to our left nearer mountains threatened to close in. Both were unpromising.

Midmorning found some of us really suffering from heat. We transferred the bier from Scuro to Bront, for whom heat was a happy thing. Poor Scuro was panting heavily and looking miserable. Jetsam had swung Botta's basket in front of him to protect Botta from the sun, but even so, the gopher was very obviously having a difficult time. Locus was just able to keep going. And nowhere was there tree or shrub or small grass or anything.

I could tell that Exi and Arachne were worried. When the sun reached its noon peak, it was clear we could go no further. We stopped heavily, encompassed in the unbearable and inescapable waves of heat.

"I just can't do it," I gasped, sinking onto the hot bare ground. "I'm finished. And look at Locus. And Botta. And you, too, Jetsam. We can't!"

"We've got to," Jetsam answered. "But I don't see how."

"Why not try the opal?" Arachne asked.

"But it's for heat," Jetsam said. "That's not what we need."

"How do you know what it's for? Did those who gave it to you say it was for heat? Did they?"

"No, they didn't!" I burst out. "They said—the monarch said —you remember, Jetsam—that they didn't know what it would do, that it had strange powers. Remember?"

"Yes," Jetsam replied. "All right. Let's try." And he extracted the little silver box from his pocket. He knelt on the ground beside me, scooped out a hollow, opened the box, took out the precious opal and laid it in the hollow.

Breathlessly we gazed at it and waited. Then we felt a cool, fresh air move invisibly around us and knew the opal's power was at work. In the same way as it had brought comfort in the midst of a scorching day. All colors moved in its depths, from ice blue to fire gold, and it gave of its opposites according to our differing needs—desert's warmth in a snowstorm, a mountain's coolness under desert sun.

"Now I guess we can go on," Jetsam said eagerly, after we had regained some of our vitality.

I noticed that Exi looked at Jetsam with some question, but I didn't know why. We all ate hungrily and, strangely, did not feel thirsty any longer. Soon we were ready to go. Jetsam swung Botta onto his back, took the opal in his hand, and started out. It took only a few minutes of traveling, however, for us to realize that the opal wasn't functioning. The heat was as terrible as before, and now the sun was directly in our faces.

Jetsam halted. We all halted. He stared at the opal in his hand as if he didn't believe it.

"What's wrong?" he said. "It doesn't work."

"I could have told you, Jetsam, but you would not have believed." Exi's voice was almost stern. He continued, "You have forgotten that this opal belongs to Them. You expect that such beneficient powers will just acompany you and serve you as you desire. It is not so. They will only help you if you treat them with dignity and humbleness."

Jetsam knelt down once again, made another hollow in the

ground and smoothed it with great care. With both hands, as if he were making an offering, he placed the opal in the circular cup of sand. "I am sorry," he said, to no one in particular and to everyone.

We spent several hours resting beside the opal, until the sun began to lose its force and we could move safely into the sunset. Carabus and Mr. Green went on ahead to explore.

The rest of us set out together and traveled throughout the night. It was cool and lovely, and we wondered why we hadn't thought of night travel before we left camp. It was not difficult to see the thin tracks of our friends even by starlight. When the moon came, late and small, the desert shone, and we walked easily and at a good pace. Finally there was no doubt that we were nearing the mountain. It loomed at last before us, an enormous, gleaming height, more imposing and mysterious than anything I had ever known.

Carabus came to meet us just as the stars were growing pale. He and Mr. Green had made a camp at the mountain's base beside a pool. There were berries and nuts for picking. Only a little way, he assured us. The only trouble, he said apologetically, was that, so far, they could see absolutely no way up the mountain. As far as they had gone in either direction, it was a sheer cliff of polished marble, quite unscalable.

At the moment we were not concerned with this fact. We were eager only to get to the promised oasis. Dawn found us there, welcomed by Mr. Green and by the sight of food and a small, limpid pool.

30

THE SUN'S RAYS REACHED US IN EARLY AFTERNOON. AS I AWOKE, I could see Jetsam, curled up at the foot of a massive oak, still fast asleep. Arachne and Exi were talking quietly. Botta, rocking gently in his basket on the branch, was bright-eyed and smiling as he watched Scuro and Locus playing a roll-me-over game on the grass. Carabus, Mr. Green, and Bront were nowhere in sight.

After I washed my face and ate, I joined Arachne and Exi.

The three missing ones I discovered were off trying to see where, if anywhere, we could start up the mountain.

"It seems thus far," Exi told me, "that the entire base of the mountain is sheer, smooth, overhanging marble on which not even we beetles can get a foothold. Arachne and I have been considering possibilities, but there really are none until we know more."

Just after sundown, which came soon because we had slept away so much of the day, Carabus, Mr. Green, and Bront returned to camp.

"You just think you're *getting* some place," Mr. Green exploded as soon as they arrived, "you put *all* your strength into *forging ahead*, and what happens? I *ask* you, what *always* happens? There you are, *bang*, right up against *another* barrier! It gets *very* tiresome, I *must* say! If *I* were arranging things, I—"

"But you aren't, you know," Carabus interrupted. "And They expect us to try. We have. And we will."

"You mean that you have been all the distance around the mountain and it is all like this?" Exi pointed to the steep cliff above us.

254

"Not *exactly*," replied Mr. Green. "We went as far as we could go in each direction. Bront and I explored *way* around *that* way." He motioned to the right. "And we finally came to a *frightfully deep* canyon which *no one* could cross. Except somebody like Hatch or Parula. Or Red. And we don't *have* anyone like that." He looked at us sorrowfully and cleared his throat several times before he went on. "*Furthermore*, everywhere beyond this very *obstinate* mountain there is *nothing* but the same *awful* desert we have suffered through."

Bront had nothing to add. But Carabus, in his succinct way, described a hole he'd found in the cliff face and said he'd followed it way back into the mountain, with it getting smaller and darker all the time. He'd stopped, he said, when he thought he'd been gone long enough. But the hole hadn't ended. Exi, after talking with Arachne, said we'd better try the hole in the morning.

Early the next day we made our way along the mountain's base to the place Carabus had described. He led us along a winding route through woods and across green glades, but always with the polished impregnable cliffs rising above us. Unfamiliar mountains on the east side soon made a wide valley which was just beginning to close in as we reached the hole. It was quite dramatic as we came upon it, for the trees nearby were few and the gleaming marble sides of the mountain seemed almost to flow inward toward darkness and the tunnel's mouth.

With one accord we stopped and closed ranks, Bront and the bier in the midst of us. We stared at the opening in the rock as if we expected it to speak to us. But there was only a great silence. Exi motioned to Arachne, and they separated themselves from us and together walked up to the marble cliff and into the hole. I caught my breath as they seemed to vanish, but they emerged almost at once.

"Come!" Exi said matter-of-factly. "We can all go in together, to start with at least."

The nearer we came to the opening the larger we saw that it was. When we entered, it was under a high vaulted arch of striated rosy stone. Inside, we found ourselves standing in a rounded cavern, dimly sunlit in the entrance area but more and more shadowed until its back curves receded into nothingness. The cavern was cool, not cold, and it echoed even slight footfalls.

Exi said, "Carabus and I will try the tunnel. It is my place to do so, and Carabus has already been part way. You will all please wait here."

We wanted to talk while we waited, and we tried to, but the echoes created such confusion that we couldn't tell who was talking; so finally we just quit. Every move any of us made, shuffle of feet, sneeze, change of position, made the cavern resound as if it were talking to itself in a strange tongue. (I have wondered since if maybe it was, in fact.) It was a great relief when we heard insect footsteps approaching from the darkness.

We had a bad moment when Carabus appeared alone. But he quickly silenced our questions by stating that Exi was awaiting us "up on top." When we asked on top of what, he only said we'd learn soon enough.

Sizing up Scuro and Bront, Carabus decided they might have to do "just a little squeezing, not much." He made it quite clear, however, that neither Botta nor the funeral bier could be carried through in the regular way. So we took our remaining pieces of rope and made two pulls, one fastened to the dais bearing Red, one to Botta's basket. Scuro would pull the bier, with Jetsam behind him. Arachne would pull Botta, and I would follow. Locus would come after me, then Bront, Mr. Green, and Carabus bringing up the rear—"just in case," he said. He seemed to be trying to fill Red's place, in his own taciturn fashion.

It wasn't at all a pleasant episode, for me, at least. To have to crawl on hands and knees, sometimes even to inch along on my stomach, in total darkness, feeling closed in and suffocated, is not my idea of pleasure. I know Jetsam shared my feelings, and I don't believe Scuro liked it. The others not only didn't mind, but rather enjoyed it. Perhaps it reminded them of ancient ancestral tunnels deep under the earth, where safety and comfort prevailed. It was a relief to me when I crawled up a rather sharp incline in the tunnel and all at once it widened and grew lighter and then I burst out into daylight again.

The view across the wasteland was breathtaking. We could see the fateful pass; and I even fancied I could see the Remembering Tree, but Mr. Green felt I was wrong.

We had emerged from the tunnel onto a level shelf of the mountain, a shelf that obviously slanted very slightly upward to our left and which, to our right, came to an abrupt end in a sheer downward drop. There appeared to be vegetation above us, on further heights, but none where we stood. Even so, there was a strange beauty about the bare rock; it was not forbidding, only quietly impersonal.

"So," said Exi, "we have come this far. Shall we go on?" We turned to the left and started up the slowly rising mountain shelf.

It is very difficult to describe the mountain. Only twice was I able to see all of it, once from the great wasteland when we viewed its shimmering and shifting terraces in sunlight and in moonlight, and then again when I saw it for the last time. And even in those wide views it never quite let itself be clear and solidly definable. Always it seemed surrounded by an invisible veil, and you could never be quite sure how it was.

When we set out from the end of the tunnel we walked on bare rock. Locus was bouncing along beside me, when suddenly she stopped, holding one paw up in an attitude of utter unbelief. I stopped too, at first to see what had confounded her and then because I saw, beneath our feet, exquisite tiny blossoms literally pushing through the rock. With all of us it was the same.

"My word," Mr. Green said, amazement on his face. "I never knew such things could *happen! Look* at them! Just *look* at them! Every color of the *rainbow!*"

They were every color, from the deepest blue-black purples to golds and pinks so pale they were almost white. Locus, who had a passion for picking flowers, tried to take a light blue one in her forepaw. It disappeared into the rock, only to push up again when she backed away in surprise. She tried a deep rose flower. The same thing happened. A lemon yellow. It disappeared and reappeared. I had to try picking one myself so I could see it be reabsorbed into the rock.

"It happens when you step on them, too," said Jetsam, demonstrating.

He was right. As his foot went down, those blossoms under it sank away before his foot touched the rock and came up as soon as his foot was lifted. So as we went forward, it was on a

carpet of thousands of flowers so close to each other that the
rock became invisible, and yet no flower was ever touched by
us in any way. For a long time I kept my eyes on the ground
as I walked, fascinated by the unbelievable number and variety
of flowers. Even Arachne for once had a bemused expression in
her eyes, and I wondered if she was memorizing hues for future
spinnings.

Then I grew tired, my senses could no longer take in the
infinite array, and I went off "woolgathering"—an expression
my mother often used about me when I didn't hear what she was
telling me. When I came out of my woolly state, the situation had
totally changed. The flowers were gone.

We had apparently rounded a bend and on our right, folded
into the mountainside, was a clump of small trees, fluffy with
velvety moss-green leaves. The trees grew so close together and
the leaves were so thick that it was impossible to see what was
inside the grove. Naturally our first impulse was to find out, so
Exi walked over and pushed his head between the branches.
When he pulled his head out and returned to us, he said, "I
should think everything on this mountain has its reason. The
flowers have said what they intended. Now I believe we are to
bathe. Arachne, will you go first?"

Arachne disappeared into the grove. When she emerged Exi
said for me to go in. Stepping into this grove was like going
into April all at once. In the middle of the small grove was a
fountain pouring crystal-clear water into a grassy pool. Where the
water went was a mystery, for the pool never overflowed and
yet no stream led away from it. Here and there on the green
turf surrounding the pool were a few jonquils and crocuses. That
was all. But the air had April in it. I stripped off my worn
clothes and stepped into the fountain. On second thought, I
removed my few possessions from the pockets and took my
clothes in too, washing them out and spreading them on the
grass, and then going back in myself. And I came out feeling
ready to proceed, with a vitality I had not hoped for. Even my
clothes looked better, despite their rips and holes.

The same was true for each of my friends. And at the end,
Arachne took Botta in, much to his disgust. They reminded me

of a mother and a rebellious child. But when Botta came out, he came on his own feet for the first time since he was hurt. And he had an enormous smile on his ugly face.

"Shows what a good bath'll do," he said pertly. "Feel better than I have in a long time." He limped slowly toward us, his left eye still partly closed but showing a roguish glint nonetheless.

So, despite Jetsam's and my tattered clothes, and Botta still having to be carried on Jetsam's back, and the robe-draped body of Red on its bier, our company moved ahead with new vigor.

For a while our way passed through stands of small hardwood and evergreen trees, with grassy earth underfoot and occasional flowers. Then we walked into a cool fern glade and beyond it into an incredibly brilliant meadow. The mountain's slowly rising shelf here widened suddenly, flared out into a large open place literally flowing with light. Everywhere the sun poured itself down, but despite the full sunlight the air was balmy rather than hot.

Botta wandered slowly about, watching Locus play and trying from time to time a little motion of his own. After Jetsam and I had removed the funeral dais from his back, Scuro joined Locus in a frolic. Jetsam stood on his head, bounced upright, and then stretched out full length on the earth. Bront looked almost cherubic as he took in the rich warmth, his eyes closed. Carabus and Mr. Green were rubbing and polishing themselves, while Arachne and Exi remained somewhat apart, talking quietly. I stretched out beside Jetsam.

We fell silent, eyes closed. I began thinking to myself that I couldn't recall such a day since those we spent in the Valley of the Opal. And I began wondering why Exi wasn't prodding more, when really we should be doing something. I had just begun to start to wonder if I should say something, when a shadow fell across my face. Startled, because the sky had been so cloudless, I opened my eyes.

"Isia!" I shouted.

I leaped to my feet. The sky was filled with butterflies floating down upon us, their great wings outspread as they rocked earthward on the air currents. They were every bit as exciting as when I'd last seen them. In the midst of them was the orange and black monarch who moved toward us. And although I called Isia's name, his eyes greeted me in return. Just in time to keep me from rushing to him, I remembered the rituals of the Valley of the Opal and I held myself back.

"Our greetings to you," the monarch was saying, as the butterfly host moved back, leaving him, Exi, and Arachne, in a separate cleared space.

"And our greetings to you," Exi replied. "We find your presence most auspicious, although we do not know what lies ahead. You and your people are surely a gift from Them."

"We received a message to come to you. We bring you something and we shall take something; then we shall rejoin you later." The monarch bowed. Exi bowed. The monarch continued. "Will you be good enough to bring your company together?"

"Of course," said Exi graciously. "You came upon us most unexpectedly, you see."

Without any request from Exi, we threaded our way through the myriad pulsing wings until we stood together beside Arachne and Exi. Jetsam, with unconscious dignity, had borne the bier of Red and set it down in the midst of us.

After we arranged ourselves in a group, the monarch spoke, this time to us all. "We bring two more members for your party, two who seem to feel they belong with you." His voice had a smile in it. "I am in full agreement."

At a sign from him the ranks of butterflies parted to make an aisle, down which came Isia and a strangely familiar figure I couldn't at first recognize. Then I knew, almost at the same instant that Exi spoke.

"May we welcome you, Grandan, and you, Isia, to our group. You will add much to our journey."

31

EXCITED AS I WAS TO SEE ISIA AGAIN, I MUST CONFESS THAT I concentrated on Grandan at first. His aged ant body with its missing leg, his dark brown quietness, sent me back in time to my last sight of him as he limped away down the dim corridor.

The monarch opened and closed his wings three times. He looked at us seriously. "And now," he said, "I must tell you what we are to take from you. They have asked that we bring Red to Them, to await your coming. You see, every journey up Their mountain is unique, and what it holds depends on the journeyers. Therefore They prefer to have each of you as free as possible to concentrate on what lies ahead."

A deep and thoughtful silence followed.

The monarch bowed. At one of his silent commands six of the larger butterflies moved toward the bier and everyone else stepped back. With silent grace the six unfolded a shimmering irridescent material, spread it on the grass like a graceful rug, and lifted Red and his funeral dais onto it. At a second unspoken order, the butterflies surrounded the rug. A single motion only, it seemed, and the funeral cortege was airborne, floating above us until it was out of our sight. When it was gone, we looked once again at the monarch.

"And so, my dear friends, farewell for the time being." The monarch bowed to Arachne and Exi, then to the rest of us. "You must, very literally, make your way. We will meet later, I am sure. Farewell!" He unfolded his wings and rose, followed by all his company (except Isia, of course).

An enormous sadness came over me. There was such beauty and it lasted such a little time! And quiet courage, and it led to death! Why were we here? Where were we going? Up a strange mountain, preceded by a dead comrade, all because of stupid and ugly Beasts who couldn't live except by violence and destruction! And we had no idea of what the outcome would be! As I fell deeper into my despair, I didn't notice what was happening until I heard Jetsam's voice.

"Maris?" he called. "Maris? Where are you?"

And suddenly I became aware that I was utterly shrouded in a thick gray fog. The sunlit day was snuffed out. Everywhere was a dark, wet, swirling cloud. I could see no one. I could hardly make out the ground under my feet. Voices of the others came from here and there out of the fog, calling to each other in varying degrees of consternation.

"Everybody stop moving," ordered Exi's voice sharply, from some indeterminate direction. "We don't know where the edge is and we must not lose anyone!"

I hadn't thought of that. I froze where I was. Exi called our names and each one answered, execpt Locus who couldn't talk. This sent me into a panic. I said so, and Exi said for me to stay where I was and then asked Scuro if he could do anything.

"Already have," Scuro replied calmly. "She's right beside me."

"Excellent," said Exi. "Now please all of you do not move. This a very difficult situation."

I could hear him talking to Grandan in the strange words of the ancient people.

"Someone," came Exi's voice again, "Someone, Grandan suggests, is seeing our journey through blackness. If the monarch was correct, and I am certain he was, then the mountain is being what we are—or at least what some of us are."

I was overcome with my own guilt. Here I was, depressed, discouraged, almost hating the journey, blaming the mountain, filled with self-pity. It was my fault we were in this horrible plight. Before I could speak, Mr. Green's voice was heard.

"I am quite *certain*," he said firmly, "that this is *my* fault! *Entirely!* I never thought one person could have such *power!* I *was* feeling upset after the butterflies took *Red*, our dear friend.

I am *very* sorry. I shall *combat* this feeling at once!"

"It's not you at all," said Jetsam. "It's me, because I was thinking about Botta's hurts, and then about Red and how I had caused it, and everything seemed so hard all at once, and—"

"No, Jetsam." I was determined to have my say. "It was my bad mood that did it. I was feeling sad and only seeing the dark things. I'm to blame."

"Perhaps it is a combination of all of us," Exi said. "In any event, the situation seems to be changing."

Slowly the thick heavy clouds were growing less impenetrable. It didn't happen suddenly, probably because none of us could change suddenly. The fog kept swirling about, but now and again I got a glimpse of one of the others. I worked hard trying to look at the journey in a new way and to see Red's death as meaningful in the reconciliation of the Beasts. Slowly the darkness grew lighter; then once or twice a spot of sunlight broke through, and finally the grass was bathed by a pale sun.

"Well," said Jetsam, blinking his eyes and rubbing his head, "I guess we learned a thing or two that time!"

I had, but nonetheless I felt a great loss with Red gone. I guess several of us were in the same state of mind, because, although the clouds of fog dispersed, an almost invisible mist stayed in the air. The day lost its brilliance. The wide meadow, which had been so rich in color, was grayed and somber; it even seemed to have grown considerably smaller.

Without discussion we started off. Exi, Arachne, and Grandan went first, but otherwise no order was kept. I walked along beside Isia.

"Isn't it hard to walk instead of fly?" I asked, for he seemed to be having difficulty making his great wings behave.

"Yes, it is," he replied, pausing to open and close himself.

"Then why do it?"

"I must. You see, each one of us in this group has to go step by step to Them. And that means step by step and not flutter by flutter."

"All right." I smiled at him. "It's good to have you along no matter how you go."

He stopped again, moving his velvet wings. "Maris, I haven't said—I am so sad about Red—he was a good friend—"

"Yes. I miss him."

"Dear me," said Isia in a distressed voice. "Now we've done it."

A large drop of water splashed on my forehead. It was raining suddenly—a slow insistent rain, very wet—and I realized that this was not at all the best sort of weather for a butterfly.

"Go ahead, quickly," I said. "Let me be sad here by myself for a while. Please go!"

He went, reluctantly. I didn't stay long, but I let my sadness run its course. When it stopped raining, I wrung the water from my clothes, and found that I was absolutely alone!

Not only alone, but going through an extremely narrow defile of sand-colored rock higher than my head. Between the two constricting walls there was just room enough to walk. No greenness was anywhere, and no other living creature. I called out, but my voice echoed against the walls and died. Ahead of me the sandstone corridor went on and on. There was no way to climb out, for the sides were smooth and very vertical. I tried reaching up and trying to pull myself out, but my groping fingers found no hand-hold.

All right, I told myself, don't panic now! If the rain was yours this stone corridor is also yours! So I kept going, thinking very hard about why I was where I was and trying not to be afraid. My thoughts kept pulling toward earlier childhood, and as soon as I let go to them, pictures began to form on the sandstone walls—scenes of myself and my parents, of my first fearful school days, of one particular party when I was seven from which I ran away and hid because I felt so awkward. On and on the scenes went, tumbling over each other in a kind of urgency, it seemed to me, an urgency for me to read them right. Slowly I began to understand. I was shut into this constricting corridor so that I might see my life. How limited my days had been! I could see it as never before, perhaps because I had learned love and grief, and how we need each other—and also because I had to see myself as straight on as possible before I could see Them.

The pictures faded rather quickly then. And soon the floor of the corridor began to rise and the walls to grow lower and lower until I walked out into a pleasant grove. All my companions were there together, resting or eating or talking.

"*Greetings!*" shouted Mr. Green. "We *really* began to think you were *lost!* Jetsam said *he* was, for a while, although I *cannot* see how anyone could get *lost* on this wide *clear path!* But do come and *eat.*"

So I did, trying to act as if nothing much had happened. I sat down beside Jetsam, who was leaning on one elbow as he reclined on the ground beside a pine tree. He was idly rubbing Scuro stretched out beside him.

"So you got lost too," I said.

He nodded, a distant expression on his face.

"In a rocky corridor?" I asked.

He turned startled eyes to me. "A corridor? Of course not! In a huge plain with no landmarks in it. I was sort of scared."

"Me too," I replied. I decided there was no use in trying to enter each other's lostness, at least not now.

Scuro lifted his head long enough to mutter, "Got lost a few minutes myself." Then he dropped his head and went back to resting.

I couldn't stop puzzling and worrying around the obvious fact that only Jetsam and I, and Scuro a little bit, had gotten lost. It was very odd. What made the difference? Jetsam and I were people—that was one thing. But Jetsam hadn't come from my world. Or had he? In some earlier time of his life before he could remember? Maybe that was why he had been in a "huge plain with no landmarks." And Scuro? He wasn't people—though he had been in a people world since his first puppy days, and had shared a lot of my troubles. Maybe the difference was that the others had never really thought about themselves, as people did all the time, and wondered and worried and had questions.

After a pleasant hour or so through quite ordinary mountain terrain, with usual trees and shrubs, and a trail with usual rocks and grasses, we came around an unusually sharp turn and found ourselves confronted by a blank wall. Literally. There we stood on a place of flat earth facing a vertical rock barrier covering the entire width of the area. There were no trees nor shrubs nor grasses. Only barren and level ground with a sharp drop to our left and an equally sharp rise to our right, and the impassive naked wall in front.

"*Well—*" said Mr. Green, in perhaps the shortest sentence he had ever spoken.

We all agreed that this was a time for another rest. Each of us settled down. I lay on my back, arms under my head. Sleep seemed as remote as the top of the mountain, but after a while my eyes grew weary of staring at the wall or at the pale sky and I closed them. Countless images began walking across my eyelids, some of them unknown and ghostly figures seeming to beckon to me. They were maddeningly elusive, refusing to stay in one place long enough for me to understand their gestures.

I don't know at what point the notion came to me that they were behind the wall, but when it came it was very definite and I couldn't argue with it. Finally one figure emerged, more solid than the rest. It was raising an arm over and over in the well-known gesture of "Come!" The whole thing was absurd, but there it was. I couldn't deny it.

Probably it was because the entire upward way had been so irrational that I could let myself do what I did. I opened my eyes, arose, walked directly to the wall, and began knocking on it. Of course everyone was startled, and those who had been asleep wakened.

"For *goodness sake*, Maris," snapped Mr. Green. "Have you taken leave of your *senses*! What *are* you doing?"

"Knocking," I replied. "Just knocking."

"Why?" asked Exi.

"Because something inside there wants us to come, that's why!" I began to feel foolish, but I kept knocking.

"How do you know?" Exi persisted.

"I saw them. Inside my head, I mean. But I'm sure they're there."

Unexpectedly Jetsam came to me. "I saw them too," he said quietly. And he began knocking.

With varying degrees of reluctance and disbelief, one by one the others came and joined in. Locus was last, not quite getting the point until Scuro barked at her and she came to his side and lifted her paw and struck the wall.

Suddenly and in utter silence the wall began to move. It opened itself in the middle and became two enormous stone doors swinging wide, to left and to right, under a huge stone lintel bearing strange reliefs of sun, moon, and stars intertwined with what looked to be letters of an unknown alphabet. Beyond the gates was a rose-gray landscape. Everything we could see was of the same color—grasses, trees, shrubs, flowers.

"So it took all of us," said Exi.

And after the last one came through the great portals, they swung closed as silently as they had swung open. At our backs was the impenetrable wall. We stood in a new land.

The vaguely present sky imparted a sunset glow to all things. Jetsam looked like an Indian in this strange light, his shirtless, coppery body crowned by his dark shaggy hair. Soon I was aware that the dusk was deepening, the rose-gray color fading from trees and shrubs. We drew nearer to each other as the darkness enclosed us; yet we were separate, and thoughtful.

Gazing into the velvety night, I knew I had a different meaning to myself than ever before. The long journey that had brought me here had done this. I would have been hard pressed had I been asked to define me. Yet I knew that Maris *was*, as distinct from Maris's mother and father or what they wanted her to be or thought she was, or what she thought they thought she was, or any of those things. So I sat there just letting myself be, until I saw a dim white glow through the trees, quite distant. It became a line of light, then two lines of light, until the light resolved itself into two lines of fireflies coming toward us and finally stopping when they were on either side of us.

We couldn't make out particular fireflies; the pulsating and erratic light of their little bodies was more like a string of pearls with fire inside than like a row of individual creatures. The first one in the right-hand row, however, separated its glow from the rest and landed directly in front of Isia.

"He says," Isia reported, "that we are to come with them."

In a series of strangenesses, those of the next hour or so were not, I suppose, the most. Even so, it was odd enough. We went forward into an apparently dense, pathless forest that con-

tinually parted before us and closed behind us, moving inside
two wavering lines of light that kept exactly abreast of us—
never ahead, never behind. After fifteen or twenty minutes of
this I got used to it, more or less, and I guess the others did
also because we stopped flinching before the wall of forest we
kept walking through.

When I realized that it was no longer a half-seen forest parting itself before my eyes, but something else, I glanced at Jetsam
walking beside me.

"Where are we, do you think?" I asked. "It's blacker than
night now."

"I know it. In a tunnel, I guess. Sometimes I get a glimpse
of walls or something. And it feels as if we're climbing, too."

We continued at the same even pace. But soon I saw what
Jetsam meant. Occasionally, sometimes to the right, sometimes
to the left, beyond the line of fireflies I too saw light reflect for
a brief second on what seemed to be smooth stone or earth.
Certainly we were not in a forest. Also I detected a faintly hollow sound from our footfalls, and we did seem to be climbing.

I nodded to Jetsam that I agreed. He nodded back. We
seemed reluctant to speak. It was almost as if we were afraid,
although there was nothing to fear in the diminutive living
lanterns guiding us. Or was there? They were utterly impersonal,
that was the trouble. And despite their fragility, they flowed
onward as if nothing could stop them or turn them from their
course.

When they did stop, we were caught unawares and almost
fell over each other as we backed up to stay within their light.
Ahead of us lay absolute darkness. Once again the single firefly
detached itself from the right-hand line and came before Isia.

"He says we must go alone now—each of us alone—one at a
time, he says—forward. He can't, or won't, say into what." Isia
translated slowly. "Yes. I understand." There was a long pause.
"He says one of them will take each of us a little way, then
leave, and we mustn't go until we're taken—and then it's up to
us—" Another long pause. "That's all. Exi's to go first."

The firefly who had been addressing Isia flew to a spot directly in front of and above Exi, and then began to move slowly

forward. Exi followed. The solitary light was so dim we could barely see Exi as he went from us. Very soon we could see only the tiny pulsing firefly, and then he too disappeared. After a long interval a second firefly escorted Arachne away from us and they were drowned in blackness. Then Grandan was taken.

32

My firefly came for me after Grandan had gone, and I was afraid. My whole being wanted to hold back, to stay beside my friends.

As I walked forward following the firefly, I found its light to be even less than I would have imagined. I put my feet down carefully, not being able to see what lay under them. And then before I was prepared at all, the firefly was no longer there. A terrifying nothingness surrounded me. I stood as still as the dark. I was trembling. The only sound I could hear was the huge drumming of my own heart. What should I do? The obvious answer was to go forward, but I wasn't sure where forward was. With painful caution and slowness I slid one foot ahead, then the other, in an awkward shuffle, meanwhile extending my arms wide and moving them from front to side to front. If anyone could have seen me, I know I would have looked like a simpleton playing blindman's bluff by myself.

Eventually, after I had decided I must be going in a futile circle, I felt my left foot slide into a shallow depression and grow cold. Dropping to my knees, I felt with my hands what seemed to be a small stream flowing from somewhere beyond me. It was one definite item in a vast indefiniteness, so I decided to stay with it. I took my shoes off and placed them, tied together, over my shoulder. Then I got both feet into the stream and shuffled wetly along its bed. Things went splendidly for quite a distance, despite the fact that my feet soon got so cold they almost lost feeling.

I didn't trust entirely to the stream's course, however, and kept my arms outstretched just in case I bumped into something. Which suddenly I did. Very hard. As far as I could tell with my hands, I was up against a wall, a solid, smooth wall. For a moment I was totally paralyzed at the idea of being alone in complete blackness with my one guide gone. But was it gone? No, it still flowed over my feet. I explored the wall downward and found a hole through which the stream came. I knelt and learned by trying that I could go in. It was big enough. But should I? Where did it go? Would I be trapped inside? Every choice possible at that moment was dreadful. I chose to keep on following the stream until I was forced to go back.

After only a few yards of crawling along, I was wet clear through. The water must have been running four to five inches deep, and when you are on your knees that is enough. Also the walls of the tunnel were dank and dripping.

I was dismally cold and frightened to the edge of panic, when I saw a faint glow ahead. Where a glow is, there must be something other than this fearful dark, I told myself. I couldn't imagine that anything could be worse.

But when finally I crawled out of the tunnel and looked at the source of the light, I wasn't sure. I stood at the side of a large, more or less round, cave. In the center was a raised mound of black rock, and on this was seated a woman beside a fiercely burning fire. Around her and the fire was a circle of alternating skulls and lilies, and outside them a circle of lighted candles. The entire floor of the cave below the black, raised rock was covered with a brownish slime or ooze, and the water from this drained away into the stream I had been following. I shrank back against the side of the cave in terror at the awfulness of the scene.

The woman either did not see me or it did not matter to her that I was present. She sat cross-legged, a dark veil over her head and shoulders. She did not move. The fire cast a redness over everything. The slime on the cave's floor seemed to bubble and stir as if it were molten lava, although it wasn't hot on my feet, only sticky and thick as the bottom of an ancient swamp might be. And I imagined a faintly evil odor rose from it.

The fire burned hot and unwavering, as if it came from a source inside the black rock. The red walls of the cave, the ooze, the black impersonal rock, the ring of ghostly skulls and lilies, the silent veiled woman—all these could have been here since the beginning of time. Nothing human existed except me. The woman was not human.

The foul odor grew stronger. Every inch of my physical self wanted to back down into the black tunnel again and get away. Its terrors at the moment seemed preferable to the thing before me. Yet I had learned in the course of this long journey that to everything there must be a response. If this veiled creature was going to ignore me, then I had to respond to her.

Pushing myself away from the wall, with great effort I began to move. Slowly, very slowly, I went, hands clenched. As I came nearer the circle of candles, skulls, and lilies, I realized I was unable to turn back. I was drawn to the scene ahead. Suddenly the woman's face lifted, the veil fell aside, and eyes as empty of personal response as a reptile's gazed at me briefly, a half-smile appearing and disappearing until her face dropped once more.

I am ceasing to exist, I thought to myself.

Even as I thought this, was virtually overcome by it, a dim memory knocked. What was it? It was like a solitary fly buzzing in a darkened house. I wanted it to go away, to leave me to merge into the fascination ahead. It wouldn't. I closed my eyes to concentrate on its going away. But this only gave it a chance to make itself heard, and there it was, urgent and sharp, telling me I did know who I was; I had known there in the dark before the fireflies came. I was Maris! Yes, I was Maris. A person. Not slime. Not flame. Maris.

When I opened my eyes I knew I must go forward, but that I could also resist the nothingness there. As I came closer to the terrible center, sometimes I felt I would give in; but I had only to close my eyes and let the memory enter, and I was myself. At last I stood directly before the great, rounded black rock and its evil. (I kept sensing it as evil, although now I am not so sure.) The blazing fire did roar upward from inside the rock, as I had guessed it did. I felt as if I would melt. I wondered why the ring of candles didn't. And as I examined these more careful-

ly I saw that, unlike the skulls and the lilies, each candle was
different from each other candle. Not strikingly so. But subtle
variations in length, tilt of wick, direction of flame—these made
every candle unique. This recognition gave me a monumental
joy. I and the candles had identity!

I focused my attention on the candle directly in front of me,
in that arc of the circle nearest my reach. It seemed to have a
particularly golden flame. I stretched my hand toward it, and on
its waxen sides, dim but unmistakable, came the letters of my
own name.

So this was why I had come then. Without any further question or hesitation I wrapped my hand around my candle, lifted
it from its place in the circle, and, after a brief glance at the
woman, turned around and went as fast as I could to the small
tunnel by which I had entered the cave. I had a feeling of pursuit as I hurried to squeeze myself into the narrow opening. One
final look was all I allowed myself. The head was lifted again,
but I have never known if I actually saw an expression on the
woman's face at that moment, or, if I did, whether it was anger
or pity.

The return through the tunnel was in several ways harder
than the first trip. I was determined that my candle should not
go out, which meant I had to proceed on two knees and one
hand. I was shaken and spent from my encounter. At the same
time, however, I had found my candle at the edge of annihila-
tion, and this gave me strength.

At last I emerged into that absolute darkness from which I
had first entered the tunnel, and stood upright again. In the
small circle of illumination from my candle, I could only see the
enormous wall of rock with the opening at its base, the stream
glistening in its channel, and, spreading out from the channel
on either side as far as light reached, a smooth, empty plain.

It was good to stand for a while, wet and still, breathing the
clean air and gazing at nothing. I waited until the terror of the
cave began to diminish somewhat in my mind and my clothes
changed from soggy to damp. Then I sat down, massaged my
feet into life, and put on my battered shoes. The only thing I
knew to do was to follow the small stream back in the direction

from which I had come, and now I could walk beside it rather than in it, for I had my own light.

No matter what I did to my candle, it didn't go out. It felt like beeswax to my hand, but it neither dripped nor grew shorter. I even knocked it over getting into my shoes. My instant panic was quite unnecessary; it burned just as brightly on its side as it did upright. So I made my way slowly back by its light.

One by one we came together, arriving in the order of our departure—Exi, Arachne, Grandan, me, Isia, Mr. Green, Locus, Jetsam, Scuro, Botta, Bront, and Carabus. Each came bearing a light in hand, teeth, or pincers—Jetsam and I, candles; the others, lanterns of varying shapes and sizes, each having on it its owner's name. We came from individual paths, that moved in like spokes of a wheel, converging at a common hub. We came wordlessly, and with a deep solemnity. I guess we all knew—except maybe Locus—that behind this time of assembling lay twelve strange experiences, and yet neither then nor later did we ever discuss them.

When at last we stood in a group, Locus best expressed our feelings by her rapturous, wriggled greetings to each one, right around the circle. Not even Mr. Green, however, broke the silence, and when Exi and Arachne lifted their lanterns and moved purposefully off to the left, away from the stream, we took up our lights and followed without a question.

When I began to notice suggestions of walls in the flickering light, I had no notion of how long we had been walking. Soon after, I saw a ceiling, and then it was only a short interval until we stood in a large vaulted hall of earth and stone. An enormous closed door was visible in the far wall.

"Please wait," Exi said softly. He walked to the door and knocked a gentle beetle knock.

The massive door slowly swung open. What was inside we could not see, except that it was filled with warm color. Almost immediately through the door came two unbelievable beings, each carrying a flaming torch. They were tall, much taller than Jetsam, taller by far than my father, who was over six feet. They were draped and enfolded in robes of a black iridescent material which shimmered and faded as they moved. Their heads were

covered by masks exactly alike—a terra-cotta face with moss-
green circles around the eyeholes, a bulbous white nose, wide
scarlet mouth, and bristled pine-needle hair. They were awesome
but not frightening. When they reached us they bowed, then
turned around and held their giant torches high, motioning us
to come. We did, passing through the door, two by two, into
the room beyond. After we had entered, the door swung shut.

The room was the largest I had ever seen. It looked as if it
had been carved out of the mother rock by careful and loving
workmen, so satin-smooth were its walls and its lofty ceiling,
which arched upward to a center opening. This evidently served
as a chimney, for directly below it in the middle of the room
a warm, comfortable log fire burned. Naturally there were no
windows, but at irregular intervals around the room the walls
were ornamented with hanging fabrics of all the colors of
nature, from spring's green-gold to autumn's russet.

When the tall masked torchbearers had brought us to a spot
about ten or twelve feet from the fire, they lowered their
torches. We halted, which seemed right because they bowed
and withdrew, to place their torches on either side of the huge
portal. It was then that I became aware of many other torches
burning in other such holders all around the room.

There was a movement across the room beyond the fire. What
I saw was blurred and indefinite but startling enough even so.
There was a sudden opening in the ceiling, a flurry of motion,
and then one after another a succession of beings climbed slowly
down a swinging ladder or rope and fanned out, alternately left
and right, until they circled the room. Each one, before taking
his place, extinguished a wall torch. When the last one put out
the last torch, we stood in a silent expanse of gentle firelight,
ringed by a host of half-seen masked figures.

One figure stepped from the shadows and approached us. He
was middle-sized and roundish, covered in the same dark and
shape-shifting robes the earlier torchbearers had worn, but his
masked head delighted me. And the moment Locus saw him
she went into such an ecstasy of joy that Scuro had to growl at
her. The mask was like a huge mahogany egg, making the face
a fine oval shape. It was framed with fur, rich brown in color

and rising up into two eartufts. Enormous golden-yellow eyes dominated the face, and a curved beak completed it. Surely this is the grandfather of all the world's owls, I thought, as he stood before Arachne and Exi.

Using no words, but with the most skillful pantomime, he indicated what we were to do. Following his gestures, we drew back a few feet from the fire; then we formed a small circle, all equidistant from each other except Arachne and Exi who left extra space between them as a sort of gateway to the fire. Finally we set our individual lights on the ground before us, a circle within our circle. Owl returned to his place.

The silence grew in intensity; I felt as if it was rolling outward in waves of soundless sound. Slowly it changed into sibilant whispers, seeming to come from everywhere, and the sibilance grew into words. "It is she ... it is she .... it is she ... it is she," rose and fell and rose into a chant and ceased.

And I saw standing beyond the fire a solitary and unforgettable figure. Instinctively I bowed my head.

"Grandmother! O our Grandmother!" whispered the voices. "Grandmother ... Grandmother ... Grandmother ... " The voices soft as the sea on a pebbled shore, sighed and died away.

She came in dignity, circling the entire room once. The masked figures bowed gravely as she passed by. When she had again reached her starting point, she moved toward the fire, walked through the opening of our smaller circle, and stood as the center of us.

She was somewhat as I remembered her from the long ago time of my beginnings in her world, although she seemed taller. Her draped robes were as hard to describe as before, colors and textures shifting continuously from dark to bright, coarse to velvety, cool blue-greens to rich wine-reds—changing so subtly that you couldn't ever see it happen. But it was her face, her incredible face, that held me and would not let me go. The eyes, large and deep brown, were radiant with love and pain, sorrow, pity, joy, as if all life everywhere and forever had been born, lived, died, and been born again while she watched and waited. Furrowed and seamed with wrinkles beyond count, nonetheless her face was beautiful, as ancient as worn mountains are, and her mouth was gentle, and generous both with grief and laughter.

We stood as still as plants, while she turned slowly, letting her gaze encompass us one by one. "Children," she said, in a low-pitched, resonant voice. "Children. You have all come a long road. Even the smallest, Locus, has given with courage. I have helped where I could, and you have helped me when you could— more often than I would have supposed possible with so many beginners." There was neither judgment nor sarcasm in her words.

She paused thoughtfully. "Arachne," she said, a suggestion of a smile curving her lips, "you, Grandan, and Exi, I have known the longest of any in this company. By far the longest. Come to me."

Each of them stepped away from the circle and moved closer to her in the center. She touched each in a quiet gesture, as if in blessing, her gaze intently fixed on each large-eyed insect face.

"You have guarded these younger ones well," she said. "Their journey has been made easier by you. Not less painful but more purposeful—which is as it should be." Again she paused, seeming to be listening for something in this sea of silence in which we floated. I heard nothing. Yet suddenly she turned her head as though a voice had spoken, then held out her hands, palms upward, and said to the three who waited, "Are you willing to be part of the company of Them?"

My body trembled at the question, and my eyes filled with tears. It wasn't that I was surprised or unhappy, but that I had wanted this so much since that day when, facing the desert beyond the pass, I had seen Arachne and Exi in a new way.

The answers came, almost in unison, in a whispered, "Yes, Grandmother! Yes!" The old woman, her lined face lighted with a smile, reached forth, and touched each one of the three again. "So you shall be. So you are." She stood tall as a prophetess speaking an incantation. And for a moment my three comrades seemed to grow to heroic size as their blessedness was laid upon them. Then they were Arachne, Exi, Grandan once more, and Owl was beside Grandmother, who was saying, "You will join the others now."

As they followed Owl, I realized "the others" did not mean us but Them—that my friends were taking places in the larger circle around the walls of the great hall. I wanted to call after them, to say some good-bye, to let them know how I felt.

"And will you all now bring your lights to me?" Grandmother said.

She waited as we lifted candles and lanterns and moved toward her. Our lights shimmered and glinted on her mysterious robes, making her the more awesome the nearer we came.

"Please put them here," and she motioned to the ground before her. "Make a small circle of light."

She gazed into this circle as if to read some secret there. Then she went among us, touching each one as she had earlier touched the older ones. Her closeness made the air sing, and a mingled scent of earth, trees, flowers moved as she moved. I closed my eyes, unable to look upon her, until her hand brushed my cheek delicately, as a moth's wing might do. For a brief second I stared at her face and into her eyes; all of my existence was there, and before I was, and after I had ceased to be. All life was there, perishable, frail, imperfect, loved. As she passed by I knew the secret. But it went from my mind in the instant, and I no longer knew it but felt it coursing through my bloodstream. (Even now I can feel its presence sometimes, although I can never remember what it was.)

The central fire had burned low, leaving the room in deepened shadows except for our small circle of lights, and, behind us, a tiny triangle made by the lanterns Arachne, Exi, and Grandan had left.

A murmured chanting began, increasing in volume slowly. It came from everywhere around us—high voices, low voices, sometimes in unison and sometimes antiphonal—building up until at last the room vibrated with a fullness of sound. It wasn't a long chant, but it was repeated over and over:

> *Grandmother . . . Grandmother . . .*
> *Night and dark stars*
> *are a beating heart*

and moon the eye
of the world.
Let night be gentle
and moonlight
see with tenderness.
Grandmother . . . Grandmother . . .
Stones are fire
made firm, and rain
blood for the earth.
Let stones be warm
and rain flow
richly to heal.
Oh our Grandmother!
Give these children
night for their being,
moonlight for their seeing,
stones for their standing,
rain for their peace.

Under the hypnotic enchantment of the voices, I lost any sense of time. I only know the words were sung again and again until they were like waves breaking endlessly. It took me a few minutes to realize when they ceased, and then the old woman was gone. A slight breath of sound marked, I supposed, the disappearance of the last but two of the masked figures. These two, the ones who had ushered us in, were now coming toward us bearing their huge torches. And almost before we knew it, we were standing outside the great doors as they closed silently but with finality behind us.

33

OUR EYES WERE NOT READY FOR TOTAL DARKNESS NOR OUR SPIRITS for the absence of our three wisest comrades. We huddled together to assure ourselves we were there. Locus tugged at me and I picked her up. Somebody said something about how dark it was. Mr. Green sneezed—at least I thought it was Mr. Green because the sound was so loud—and Scuro scratched himself, which he had a habit of doing when he was doubtful about what action to take.

Jetsam cleared his throat. "Well," he said, "I guess we've got to go some place from here." No one spoke.

By this time my eyes were growing accustomed to the dark and I could make out the shapes of the others. Gradually I could see them more clearly, even could see Isia's wings raising and lowering. And this wasn't right. Just because my vision was adjusting to the absence of light didn't mean I should be able to distinguish so delicate a substance as a butterfly's wing. I said as much.

"Look up," said Botta. "Have to do that when you're burrowing, you know."

We did, and there above us was a patch of light.

The patch grew brighter and all at once it became a golden blaze. I started to speak but Botta was quicker.

"Sun. Over the hole. Better make way while the sun shines." He chuckled.

The huge hall (cave, if that sounds more crude and primitive) was roughly four-sided, the sides quite vertical for fifteen feet or so and then sloping upward and inward, like an upside-down funnel with the sky-hole at the small end. The wall nearest us contained the doors into the place of the Grandmother, and the opposite wall was less a wall than a black opening—the way we had entered originally. This much we knew. The other two sides, we were sure, must hold the clue to where we would go next. Jetsam, the rest of us close behind, marched resolutely to his right and stood before this wall.

The light was beginning to fade but there was still enough to see by. And what we saw, in the middle of this wall at floor level, was an opening about four feet square. Inside it, all we could make out were the first few treads of a stairway hewn from the rock. Presumably it continued upward into the mountain, although we could see only blackness when we leaned over and peered in.

After a half-hearted objection from Mr. Green, we decided to follow Jetsam up the stairs. Carabus said maybe he should go first, but Jetsam said as long as he had started he was going to lead. So one by one we entered the small black opening and began the climb. When I watched Jetsam bend down and go in, I wondered why he disappeared so quickly. Once I had squeezed myself through after him, I stopped wondering; I had never climbed steeper stairs. Each step felt at least a foot high, and I could only feel for them, because once more we were going in total darkness. The staircase was narrow. I learned at once how low the ceiling was by a couple of nasty bumps on my head. As usual in this sort of work, Jetsam and I had it the hardest.

Shortly after we had started, Mr. Green called out from somewhere below, "It would be *most* helpful if we *could* proceed faster. We keep *colliding* with each other." Immediately Jetsam's voice snapped back, "I'm setting the pace! And I'm going as fast as I can! Let's not have complaints!"

No more was heard from anyone except occasional grunts and puffings from Jetsam and me and assorted scratchings and scrabbling from the others. Up and up we climbed, steep step after steep step. The muscles in my legs began to protest and, to distract myself, I began counting steps, but when I had reached a hundred and thirty-nine I stopped, since I hadn't counted from the beginning and I wasn't proving a thing. I closed my eyes. I saw then what I realized I should have been concentrating on all the time—the face of the Grandmother. It came and went, but it was *there*. I could hear in my interior the words, "Night and dark stars are a beating heart," and the words, "Stones are fire made firm," and could feel the Grandmother's touch.

Eventually my groping right foot found no step but came down suddenly on a level. I almost fell forward but didn't; I ran into Jetsam instead. We found ourselves all bunched together in a narrow, lightless corridor that came to an abrupt end.

"I *said* we should have looked for another way," came Mr. Green's voice.

"No," I stated confidently. "This is right." And to my amazement no one contradicted me. But I sensed them all waiting for something more. "Let's go over the walls and find whatever we can. It must be here."

I began following my own advice. Slowly and carefully I let my hands explore the uneven surface of the wall nearest me, from floor level to as high as I could reach on tiptoe. Nothing but rough, cold stone. Moving a pace to the right, I repeated the process. The others were doing the same, with hands or feet or feelers. This went on for a long time. Until Carabus spoke.

"Here's something! I think—yes, it is. Do come here, please!"

Such excitement from Carabus was enough to draw us to his voice with whatever haste we could manage under the circumstances. We crowded around, in a complex of arms, legs, wings, hands, antennae, fur.

Jetsam spoke eagerly. "It's a rope ladder, I think. Yes, a rope ladder."

"Where's it going?" I asked stupidly.

"Up," Jetsam replied, laughing. "Where else, silly?" And that's where I'm going, too."

After a wordless interval of scuffs and rustles, Jetsam spoke from somewhere above our heads. "Fifteen rungs to the top. Feels like a door here. No handle or knob, though. I'll knock. Everybody get ready to come up—that is, if it opens." He was silent while, with grunts and exclamations and occasional advice to each other, we got ourselves lined up, I at the head of the line. "Ready?" Jetsam asked. "Ready," I replied, my hands grasping the ladder, my right foot on the bottom rung.

Jetsam rapped sharply; the sound echoed thinly against the sides of our confining chamber. The ladder moved eerily under my hands as Jetsam shifted his weight. Again he rapped, longer, more urgently. Silence. Darkness. The silence shattered as Jetsam's fist crashed and hammered on the door. The ladder swayed with his pounding and I held on hard, my heart pounding too.

"We are here!" he shouted. "We are here!"

Before his words had stopped ringing in the black corridor, a brilliant light fell upon us from above; it hit our upturned faces with an almost physical violence. My eyes hurt so that I was forced to close them for a moment.

"Come on!" Jetsam called.

One shudder and the ladder was still. I grasped the rope and started to climb, not looking up for fear I would be too dazzled to see. I put my feet carefully on each rung, counting as I went so I would be less upset by the ladder's sway. "Six, seven, eight . . . fifteen." Jetsam's hands reached for mine and pulled me out into what seemed the most blazing sunlight I had ever experienced. But before I had a chance to look around, Carabus was emerging, saying, "Scuro, Botta, Locus—rope ladders are not easy." Jetsam went down into the hole again, and among us all, pushing, pulling, lifting, somehow we managed to get the three of them out. Isia, Bront, and Mr. Green came last.

We had at last, it appeared, reached the Place of Them. At any rate we were at the top of Their mountain, for there was nothing above us but sky—incredibly blue sky containing a sun of fiery orange-gold. It was the first time since this long journey began, I thought with surprise, that there were neither hills nor mountains higher than where I was! The sunlight poured over a huge square, bounded on one side by two-storied buildings of strange geometrical shapes, and on the opposite side by a vast and dense forest of unfamiliar evergreen trees. On each of the remaining two sides, a squat windowless tower faced across the square. The earth was reddish clay, and all buildings were made of the same material.

We had come into the great square at a spot very near one of the two towers. Filling the air around us was the sound of a drum. On the flat roof of the round, low tower nearest us stood a tall fantastic figure. He was wrapped all in russet, his legs like tree trunks, his arms like strong branches, a glittering belt around his waist, and on his head a mask of gold shaped like a small sun reflecting back the blaze of the larger sun. In front of him was the drum, big as the biggest bass drum in a symphony orchestra, and his hands, holding two sticks, rose and fell in intricate movements as they beat hypnotic, space-filling sounds into the warm day. After a time, slowly, the drumming ceased.

A small hunched figure, wearing a very dark brown robe, came slowly out of the forest opposite us, and at the same moment an old man with silver hair and a white robe over his shoulders emerged from the central door of the main building. With dignity, and in a stillness so total that I could hear Locus breathing, the two men drew nearer each other. In contrast to the great masked drummer, these two seemed small. The forest man, his brown robe drawn over his head like a monk's cowl, walked with difficulty because of his twisted and humped back. The gait of the white-haired one, despite his evident age, was strong and his carriage erect. They met mid-square, bowed, turned, and proceeded side by side to the tower at the far end of the square. Climbing halfway up the outside stairs, they stopped and faced us.

The drummer came to us then. He indicated we were to precede him across the square. Trying to go with as much dignity as possible, we went forward until we stood below and before the pair of old men.

"Welcome," said the white-haired one, in a voice low, clear, and gentle. "I am the Grandfather."

34

Jetsam stepped forward. With his shaggy, dark hair and his half-naked body shining in the sun, he was quite handsome, I thought. He lifted his head to look up at the two men.

"Thank you, Grandfather," he said, bowing. "I am Jetsam. This is our company."

"Yes," replied the Grandfather. "I know."

We contemplated one another silently—Grandfather as if he wanted to search out all our secrets, we because we didn't dare turn our gaze from him. I would have liked to. It wasn't that I feared him—for his seamed old face was in no way threatening—but rather that his eyes were so penetrating I was sure he knew far more about me than I knew about myself. And this made me uncomfortable.

"Yes," he repeated, after a long interval. "I know all of you. From Hatch. From the Mantid. From Parula. From the monarch. From Grandmother, of course. Lately from Arachne, Exi, Grandan. What I have heard pleases me."

The Grandfather turned to his silent, hunched companion, whose face remained shrouded.

"This is Dark Fire, my brother. He knows you also. For all of Us, we thank you for your courageous help. Perhaps now we can begin to reconcile and re-create. Two major steps remain. Do you know what they are, Jetsam?"

Jetsam seemed calm as he considered Grandfather's question.

Finally he said forthrightly and in a clear voice, "One would be a funeral for Red, sir."

"And the other?"

"To do something about the Beasts, I suppose, sir."

At these words Grandfather smiled a smile as wide and as rich as sunrise. He shifted his glistening white robe across his shoulders. He looked down at Jetsam with approval. "Those are the two steps. In reverse order, however. We want peace, at least as much as we can secure, before we hold Red's funeral. Would you agree, Jetsam?"

"Oh, yes, sir! Red was—" but Jetsam couldn't continue.

Grandfather nodded. "He was that and more. And will be honored at the proper time. But first we must work at the problem of the Beasts. Tonight, however"—and he smiled his wonderful smile again—"tonight I think there should be joy. You have all done well."

Grandfather and Dark Fire turned away, went side by side to the tower's top, bowed ceremoniously to the sun which was low in the West, and disappeared from our sight.

We were left alone in the middle of the deserted square. After a few moments we all began to talk at once. Locus skittered sideways and poked a playful paw at Scuro, who chased her in a brief half-circle and returned to sit beside us and scratch himself.

"Well," said Jetsam, stretching expansively, "we can't stay here forever, I guess. It isn't very cozy. Let's go into the trees."

The sun had dropped behind the large buildings now, and long, geometrical shadows covered most of the square. As we followed slowly after Jetsam, I was again impressed by this landscape. How clear it seemed, and free, and lightfilled, even after the sun had gone! I had just said something like this to the others when there came a flurry of feathers and color, and Parula and Hatch alighted on Jetsam's and my shoulders.

"Made it, didn't you! Delighted!" Hatch piped up beside my left ear. "Thought you would. Now everything's ready for you!"

"But Hatch," I said, "what is?"

"Sorry. Didn't intend to confuse. You're to stay in Their home. Gaiety, food, sleep, and all that. Clear?"

"It's clear," Jetsam said.

We walked back across the square in the gentle beginnings

of night and stood before an open, lighted door. Jetsam stepped forward and with newly acquired grace said, "May we come in?" He seemed to ask the light and the space it filled—for no person was in view—and the light itself seemed to reply. A soft, many-voiced chorus of welcomes drew us in.

Such a wonder surrounded us when we entered! The first impression was one of being bathed in golden light, like the warm illumination from hosts of candles. Every space was filled with murmuring sound and the pungent scent of pine. The room itself, oblong with rounded corners, was either made from or plastered with the light rose-brown clay apparently typical of this mountain top. At the far end of the room, opposite the entrance, a fire burned in a huge fireplace raised two feet or more above floor level. The fireplace was festooned with braces, brackets, and hooks, and smoky black pots hung over the fire. Around the walls many torches blazed. Scattered over the earthen floor were at least a dozen rugs of excellent weave, muted colors combined in simple abstract designs. It was a strangely beautiful room, at once homey and impressive, filled and spacious.

Strangest of all were the beings who occupied the room, who moved about mysteriously in its warm and almost tangible light. They were as elusive as rainbows, always visible but not quite. They seemed to sense our needs and our wants before we spoke, and served us constantly; and yet I never saw a face. Sometimes their multicolored, hooded robes were as substantial as jewels, sometimes they were only smoke spirals shifting and almost disappearing.

The only other substantial occupant of the room was the small humpbacked Dark Fire. It was he who acted as our host. He limped toward us, the hood of his dark brown robe covering his face. His voice was mild and somewhat high-pitched as he greeted us.

"The evening is for your joy," he said. "We wish it to be the fullest."

And suddenly each of us was being escorted by one of the strange beings through an archway on the left of the big room, and down a corridor from which, one by one, we were taken to individual rooms. From that point on I gave over happily to the ministrations of the mysterious beings. I merely thought how a hot bath would feel, and there was one in the room. I undressed, climbed into the wooden tub, and soaked in its steamy warmth. When I decided I'd had enough and stepped out, one of the beings placed a soft blanket about me. I looked at my shabby clothes lying on a bench near the bath and wished I had something rather more presentable. Almost at once I was given a silken robe of delicate blue and a pair of sandals of darker blue. When I thought what a sight my hair must be, one of the beings brought a comb of bone, and another held up a mirror of some polished substance. Before long I was combed and robed and sandaled and feeling like royalty.

"Thank you," I said, as I was being escorted from the room. "Thank you for your kindness and help." Murmured sounds came from my mysterious and elusive guides, pleased sounds, I thought.

When I entered the main room I was met with cries of greeting and tantalizing smells of food. Everyone was there, including Arachne, Exi, and Grandan. Locus rushed to me, eyes dancing and fur ashine, so I picked her up and held her while I went about shaking hands, patting heads, giving salutations, and in general stirring the pot of fellowship.

Grandan and Exi gave me courtly bows and murmured greetings. Both looked better than I had ever seen them. They had grown stronger and more whole. Their defective legs and other scars of age were hardly noticeable. They seemed larger, full of a subtle new vitality. Arachne had had this energy always. But she, too, seemed larger, and possessed now of a quiet contentment, without sharpness. I went to her and knelt down. She put some of her arms around me, hugged me, and then held me away to look at me.

"Yes," she said. "Yes." She turned me around. "Yes," she said again, as she turned me full circle, "You will become a fine young lady some day." She made some slight adjustment in my robe's hem. "Blue is becoming. And don't forget to stand tall, inside and outside. No scrunching. You can't improve by scrunching."

A happy laugh made me turn, and there was Jetsam. "Arachne, I love you," he said brashly. "Don't ever scrunch," he said, and burst into laughter again.

Arachne was utterly unruffled. "It is nice to be loved," she said calmly. "And no scrunching is a proper caution for you, too."

"I know it. That's why I laughed. You always hit the right spot." He stood spread-legged, his head held high. By some means the people who attended him had gotten his shaggy hair shortened and brushed, and he wore a soft leather shirt. His ragged pants had been repaired and washed.

"I'm hungry," he announced.

"Jetsam, you're hopeless," I said.

"No. I'm hopeful. Don't these smells get your stomach excited?"

"Well, yes. Of course. But it's—it's childish! To be so loud about it, I mean."

Dark Fire, who had been sitting so quietly as to be almost absent, now arose and bowed to us. "Our wishes are for your delight," he said. He walked from us and settled down in a shadowed corner beyond the fire, and here he stayed during the entire evening, a silent, dark brown, benign presence.

After that we gave ourselves to what was at hand. The very air of the room was charged with energy as the tall, shimmering beings went to and fro, stirring pots, bringing dishes of food and cups of liquid, some hot, some cold. We ate sitting down. We ate standing up. We moved about from place to place. We ate while we talked —or talked while we ate—in groups of three, or four, or all together. Even our three who had been added to Them laid aside some of their dignity and wandered about with us. Later Hatch and Parula came swooping into the room, followed by a retinue of red-and-yellow birds.

"Time for the dance!" Hatch piped. "Time for the dance!"

The bird flock flew to where Dark Fire sat, perched on him as if he were a tree stump, and began their music. A large and impressive clown-faced woodpecker joined them a few minutes later, adding the beat of his beak on a piece of wood he had brought with him. Such gay tunes began pouring forth that no one could resist. All of us, including Arachne, Exi, and Grandan, danced until we were too tired and sleepy to go on. I just vaguely remember reaching my room and sinking into a soft bed smelling of pine.

35

The problem of the Beasts and the securing of peace didn't come up for several days. We slept, ate, talked, and wandered about, until Jetsam and I were finally summoned by Grandfather.

"And now," he said, as we stood before him, "I believe it is right to learn what can be done with the Beasts. Messengers have told us that a few have died and that the king is growing weak. So we must try to help them."

Apparently both Jetsam and I registered surprise, for Grandfather looked at us sternly as he went on. "Yes, *help* is what I said and what I mean. Because they have been cruel and blind, must we be also? Revenge is no way to make Red's death meaningful."

We must have shown our shame, for he went on in a more kindly voice, telling us we were to return to the pit prisons and bring back all the Beasts, living, dying, or dead. He assured us we wouldn't be walking all that way, nor would we be alone and unaided. Eagles, he said, would carry us. And between Hatch's friends and Isia's, the Beasts would be transported. Arachne had made a great amount of her finest rope. How we used it would be up to us. We were to prepare the Beasts for the journey, and were to be ready early the next morning.

"Have you ever ridden an eagle?" I asked, when we were alone.

Jetsam didn't bother to answer.

Pale dawn light was just flushing the sky when we came into the square the next morning. I lifted my head and took in a full breath of the fresh morning. A sense of excitement replaced whatever fears had been in me, so that the arrival of Grandfather and, immediately thereafter, of two enormous eagles, seemed good.

Not much was said. Grandfather gave each of us a ball of Arachne's fine spun rope, introduced us to the giant eagles—Prince Feathers and King Feathers—wished us well, and calmly disappeared. Jetsam and I and the eagles stood looking at each other.

"What do we do now, Jetsam?"

"Get on, I should think."

"And what about Hatch and Isia and—"

"They'll be there when we need them."

That seemed to be the situation. So I let Jetsam help me straddle Prince Feathers. With his bright burning eyes and his fierce curved beak, I should have been afraid of him but I wasn't. Jetsam climbed onto King Feathers. Their great wings stroked the air, and we were aloft.

We soared in wide circles far above the land, far above tops of mountains even. All the country through which we had traveled, in which we had struggled, fled, fought, and rejoiced—all was there. I couldn't recognize much, but I did pick out the Valley of the Opal, and I caught glimpses of the river. The forests and jungles beyond the river were endless stretches of darker or lighter green. The Place of Them, I suddenly realized during one slow wide arc, was surrounded on three sides by desert. But on the fourth side, to the West, was the sea!

Before I could try to wave to Jetsam and point to this wonder, the eagles began to drop earthward in diminishing circles. Soon they came to rest quietly in a spot so familiar that I wanted to cry. I didn't, but I stood mute and shaky beside the stream where the *Starflower* had been built, where the farthest pit was, and from which our terrible flight had begun.

The tiny lake shone silver in the morning sun. The same soft grasses grew along its edges. The same peace seemed to be present. While our eagles waited, Jetsam and I went to the end of the lake and upstream to the pit. First we stood under the oak tree that had been our home for those days before the Beasts came.

"We've got to look in the pit," said Jetsam.

Reluctantly we went toward it. No sound came from it. Were these Beasts dead? I hoped they were and I hoped they weren't.

They weren't—quite. There were three of them, lying there in a tangled heap of sticky webbing. They didn't move, except for the slight motions of breathing. One of them opened his eyes and looked up at us with an expression of such pain and defeat and fear that I couldn't bear it.

"Oh, the poor things! Jetsam, what can we do?"

"They do look kind of awful, don't they? I guess Grandfather will do what's to be done, though."

Suddenly the day darkened as if a cloud were over the sun. I looked up, startled, and saw a host of birds and butterflies coming to rest everywhere on trees and bushes and at the stream's edge.

Now we had to get down to business, decide how to get the captives to the Place of Them. Jetsam and I finally hit upon a method, and with a few suggestions from Hatch and Isia, it soon became a practical procedure. Jetsam climbed into the pit, with great hesitancy the first time, and walked around the captives to check the condition of the webbing that held them. I passed him some rope which he fastened through the webbing in such a way that four long rope streamers extended from the bundle of Beasts. He lifted each streamer end to me, and I held it until it was taken up by a bird or a butterfly. When each streamer was thus suspended, hordes of birds and butterflies, directed by Hatch and Isia, took hold of the ropes and lifted the Beasts into the air and away. It was hard to believe that such frail creatures could carry such solid ones, but with seventy-five to eighty pairs of wings going at once, the energy generated did the job.

As the captives emerged from the pits, they reminded me of cargo being raised from the hold of a freighter—all packaged and ready for delivery. After the pit's contents disappeared into the sky, our eagles came impassively to transport us to the next pit. So it went for all of them. Two pits had dead as well as living Beasts. Most of the living were just barely breathing. A few gazed at us hopelessly, and every time they did I felt I couldn't face their pain.

The hardest time of all was at the last pit before the canyon trap. Not because the Beasts were difficult, for they weren't, but because this was the place of our tragedy. I left Jetsam alone after the winged host had carried away this next-to-last parcel of limp Beasts. I was sure Jetsam's mind was filled with those terrible hours of noise, fire, darkness, pursuit, and death, and with his part in it. Mine was.

Finally he went slowly to stand before his own handiwork, the Remembering Tree, which stood as straight and as impressive as it had on the day we left it to cross the desert. When at last he came back to me, his face was white and his eyes glistened. But he said only, "We'd better go to the big trap. I'll bet it will be the worst."

And it was the worst, by far. For here the Beasts had not been tangled in the web but only held in the box canyon by the enormous net across its one open end. Also, the pits had held from two to five Beasts, but this place had eighteen of them. Including the king. Fortunately for us, all but two of them were quite incapable of any resistance. Those two, one the king and the other a particularly fierce fellow who had been a guard, were still on their feet and able to snarl when they saw us. The snarls were small, but they showed a lot of spunk.

The king, when he saw us, tottered slowly to the web fence and glared at us. "So," he growled, "here are the heroes! The winners!" His voice shook and his body shook, and he had to pause to get his breath. "Well, it's only for a while. We'll get back. You'll see!"

Jetsam tried to explain that we didn't want to win, only to have peace—and I must say he did a good job, considering his previous treatment from the Beasts—but the king refused to listen. And at the suggestion that he and his comrades were to be moved to another place, the king spat out a vehement "No! Never!"

We had a conference then, Jetsam and I, Hatch and Isia, to discuss how to proceed. It was impossible to go in and get the unconscious Beasts until we had somehow confined the king and the guard. After a lot of arguing, we decided to send Hatch and one of our eagles to get several of Arachne's large sticky webs.

When they returned, Jetsam took one web with him and climbed up a cliff that formed one side of the prison. He maneuvered into a position where he had a ledge to stand on and a stunted bush to hold on to. He called Hatch to him, and Hatch began diving past the king, making a great commotion. A few such rapid passes had the king confused. He moved this way and that to get away from the new irritation. Hatch worked like a sheep dog, pushing his unhappy victim always nearer to the cliff where Jetsam stood waiting. Finally the poor king, wild-eyed and trembling, stood just below Jetsam who at that moment unfurled the web and dropped it neatly over the Beast.

It wasn't quite so easy with the guard, who had watched the king's downfall and so refused to be baited by Hatch. The substitution of two huge, flapping, screaming eagles soon unnerved him, however. Jetsam made one unsuccessful toss, but his second try snared the guard accurately.

The remarkable quality of Arachne's web became all too evident when Jetsam and I tried to enter the prison. We couldn't. Whenever we touched or pushed the curtain, our hands stuck and became tangled in the tough but almost invisible fibers. It took some work to get our hands free. It would have been funny if it hadn't been so frustrating. Isia found a solution. He and some of his butterfly helpers alighted on the ground and very, very carefully grasped the net with their slender forefeet. At a command from Isia they slowly fluttered upward, lifting the web as they rose and folding it back over the cliff's face.

When I followed Jetsam into the new-exposed canyon where the Beasts lay, I was scared. I think Jetsam was too, because of the king and the guard who eyed us malevolently from their entanglements. The sixteen others were unconscious although breathing. With considerable pushing and tugging (and revulsion on my part because they stank as dreadfully as ever), we managed to get them into four heaps, netted and fastened with ropes so they could be carried away. It took much longer to get the king and the guard ready for transport, because they continued to struggle and snarl right up to the moment they were lifted into the air. The last thing the king said as he went upward was, "You'll see!"

"He's nervy, isn't he?" Jetsam said as we sat down to rest.

"Yes." I was too tired to say more. It was late afternoon now, with long shadows from the mountains covering much of the desert before us. I hated to leave the Remembering Tree for the last time, but I longed to return to the Place of Them.

"Wonder what will happen to those that got away—that—that killed Red." For he first time Jetsam could say the terrible word "killed."

"I guess Grandfather and the rest will handle that."

"I suppose so. Wish I could. No, I don't, not really. It wouldn't help."

We got up then and walked back to the Remembering Tree. The carving of Red was glowing in the sunset light, and I could almost hear him say, "Now, Maris, you mustn't be sad—I mean—we all do what we must—"

Our eagles came and we mounted their backs wearily. As we rose into the darkening sky I fancied that, looking down, I could still see the Tree.

36

AFTER THE EXHAUSTING HOURS OF BEAST BRINGING, BOTH JETSAM
and I were used up. We must have been a disappointment to our
waiting friends, for we could hardly respond to their welcomes.
We said little, ate greedily, and wandered off to bed in a daze.

The following morning we redeemed ourselves by telling them
all we could of our work. They responded by describing to us the
arrivals of the various netfuls of captives. Grandfather and his
brother, Dark Fire, had taken places at either side of the square,
each standing before one of the towers. Grandfather had stepped
forward when the first Beasts had been brought, had said something to them, then given a long call. Immediately a group of
masked figures had appeared, removed the nets, and, one by one,
carried the Beasts into Grandfather's tower. The second batch of
captives was dealt with in like manner by Dark Fire, the third by
Grandfather, and so on until the king and his guard arrived.

Both Grandfather and Dark Fire, our friends said, had come
forth to meet the two resisting captives. Both had tried to talk
with the Beasts, especially with the king, asking for peace and
reasonable cooperation for everyone's good. But the King had
become very agitated and snarled defiant insults until he suddenly
collapsed and was carried away as gently as if he had been gentle
himself. Because the guard kept trying weakly to claw his captors,
they had finally taken him away still in his bonds. When Jetsam
asked what was happening to the Beasts now, no one could answer. They had disappeared into the towers, the dead and the living, the king and his subjects, and that was all anyone knew.

Except that we were to assemble in the big room shortly after our midday meal.

The beautiful red-brown room and its warm rugs welcomed us as always when we entered it. And as always the mysterious people were present and not present, making the very air quiver. Because it was day, no fire burned in the great fireplace; but Grandfather and his hooded dark brother stood before it to greet us.

"You have done well," Grandfather said. "We thank you."

"We were afraid sometimes," Jetsam replied.

"Good." Grandfather's eyes smiled. "That means you had the courage to keep trying."

He asked if we had questions, and we said Yes. In answer to them he told us that the Beasts who had died had been buried, that the others would all live. Yes, they were being bathed and fed and rested. Yes, he believed most of them now wanted peace and were willing to try. Of course, to make this as sure as possible they were being given healing rituals, which included cleansing by the drums. When we asked about the king and the guard, he shook his head and gave his opinion that their change would take a long, long time. Maybe it wouldn't ever come. But then, he said, perhaps "shadows always have to be there so we never forget they exist." No, for the time being nothing would be done about the few Beasts still free. Either they had learned and would alter their ways, or eventually they would be handled in some new way.

"Do you have more questions?"

"I—I guess not," I said, wanting to ask about the moon but deciding not to.

"Not even about the ceremony for Red?" He looked at Jetsam.

"Well, you see, sir," Jetsam swallowed hard, "I decided that you knew about that. And that you'd tell us when you were ready."

"Yes. Thank you, Jetsam."

Grandfather had a kind way of dismissal, but it was dismissal all the same. Jetsam and I wandered into the square. Our seven companions soon joined us. We ambled toward the forest lazily, not talking much, until Botta stopped and raised a paw. We all stopped.

"What is it, Botta?" Mr. Green whispered loudly, only to be shushed by everyone.

"Can't hear a thing, Botta," said Jetsam. He was also told to be still. I couldn't hear anything either, but from the alert attitudes of the others I knew they could. When I saw Botta put his ear to the ground, I lay down and did the same, followed by Jetsam. At first I couldn't make out the strange rhythmic rumblings, but then it came to me that of course we were hearing, or feeling, the cleansing by the drums. It was being done for the Beasts underground somewhere.

That day and the next were unfilled. We were completely free to go wherever we wished except into either of the squat towers. At sundown on the second day we were summoned, dressed in our ceremonial robes, and led to the great square. And there, into the multitude of Them, came Grandmother, Dark Fire, and Grandfather, to seat themselves by blazing fires and witness with us a night of complicated and moving dances and rituals which we did not understand but became part of, in spite of mystery.

Just before dawn the drums and all the complex movement ceased. Arachne, Exi, and Grandan disappeared. Then atop the northern tower they reappeared, bearing something between them. They were flanked by two groups of masked figures with torches. This procession slowly came down from the tower and onto the square. There I saw that they carried a bier on which lay the small, still body of Red.

Tears stung my eyes. Beside me I heard Jetsam clear his throat and I could guess what that meant. And I saw Mr. Green—humorless, heavy, dear Mr. Calosoma Green so filled with awkward love —I saw him reach out a front foot in a gesture of longing and heard him say (softly, for him), "I miss you, Red, *terribly* much."

No covering was over Red. He was unadorned, except for his proud sword, which lay beside him. He seemed peaceful, and his gnome's face was no longer shy but held a wisdom as if his eyes had seen all things. The three newest members of Them bore his bier gently on their backs—Exi and Grandan on either side, Arachne at the rear. The bier was carried to the center of the square, to be met by Grandmother, Grandfather, and Dark Fire. Now the eastern sky was taking on the particular silver-blue porcelain color that precedes the coming of the sun. As the night diminished, everything grew still. Absolute silence filled the world.

In this hush the three great ones and our three new ones formed a circle around the bier. Arachne gave Grandmother a tiny packet. Grandmother lifted it over her head, shook it, and a most beautiful gossamer material cascaded downward. This the rest of them laid carefully over Red and the bier; then, lifting the bier, they wrapped it underneath also. They stepped back and stood looking upon what was now an opaline egg. Exi came to Jetsam and held his pincers forward and open; Jetsam placed in them the box holding the opal belonging to the butterflies. Slowly Exi returned to the center and placed the box upon the wrapped bier.

Suddenly Grandfather lifted his face toward the east and gave a far-reaching call. "Ei-yee-ee-ee-ee! Ei-yoo-oo-oo-oo! Ei-yee-ee-ee-ee!"

My spine raked by pinpricks, I turned with all the others to face the eastern sky. And at the exact instant the sun glinted beyond the trees, there came a great host of monarchs streaming over the forest. The monarch king led them as they fluttered down to surround the lovely egg and the six who were beside it.

The monarch bowed. "I am here at your desire. Greetings in sadness and joy."

Grandfather bowed to the monarch. "Greetings in sadness and joy," he replied. "For this hero whose trying caused the moon to come again, and for his brave comrades"—and he turned toward us for a moment—"we have given the Ritual of Death and Life. Our hope is that for each one, including Red, this ceremony may bring healing in some way." He waited in silence, as if to let his words penetrate our depths.

Red is all right, I thought to myself. Wherever and whatever he is or will be, he is all right. It is I who must be made well. There's a hole inside me that will have to be filled up. And an aching that will have to grow less.

"The sea awaits the coming of Red, as of all heroes," said the monarch, breaking the silence.

"Yes. Of course." Grandfather turned toward our company. "Isia," he said, "Isia, you know it is time for you to go with your people."

Isia stepped forward. "Yes, sir. I know." Holding his fine brilliant wings above his body, he stood in front of us with his luminous lidless eyes full upon us. "I'm sorry to leave you. We've shared a lot together, and you loved me even when I was ugly. But we'll see each other. Good-bye." He joined the monarch and his host surrounding the shining egg.

"Good-bye! Good-bye!" we called.

Now the butterflies had enclosed Red and his bier. With a fluttering and sighing of many wings they rose like a giant flower into the bright morning and bore their frail burden seaward. In my mind's eye I saw the vast ocean, both as I knew it and as I had glimpsed it from Prince Feathers's back, and I was happy that Red would become a part of its mystery.

"Good-bye," I said very softly.

37

When at last I turned from watching the empty sky where Isia and his people had faded away, the square was empty of everyone except our group of eight and Exi, Grandan and Arachne, who stood apart near one of the buildings. They nodded to us in a kind of solemn salute, then slowly entered the building. No sign was left to show that the night-long ceremony had occurred. The two towers stood solid and expressionless. The forest greens held their emotionless peace.

"Everything's gone!" I said stupidly.

The others looked at me with expressions ranging from tolerance to anguish. Mr. Green was obviously shattered by the loss of Red. He kept his head down, but he couldn't hide the tears that kept plopping into the dust at his feet. Carabus stayed very near Mr. Green, saying nothing but clearly concerned. Jetsam was pale and strained looking. Bront had closed his eyes and seemed to be meditating in the warm sunlight. The others—Locus, Botta, and Scuro—were restless and uncomfortable.

After a brief conversation, we disbanded. Scuro led Locus and Botta into the cool shadows of the forest to rest. Bront said he'd stay where he was. Jetsam and I wanted to console Mr. Green, but he said for us to go away and leave him alone. "Just let me get it *out* of my *system!* Let me *feel* it as long as I *can!*" So we left him, after Carabus indicated that he'd stay near.

"I've got to rest," Jetsam said.

"Me too," I replied.

I awoke after a short few hours of sleep in my room, feeling refreshed. I dressed in my own old clothes, somehow restored during my stay with Them to a state very like the one in which they had begun the journey. I was pleased, but not surprised. I went out into the great square. I could tell from the way the shadows fell that the day had moved into early afternoon. For a while I wandered about alone, then one by one the others came.

Jetsam looked better for his rest. He too had donned his own old clothes—which is to say, his no longer tattered trousers and a shirt like the one he had once had. He scratched his head in the way I knew so well. "You know," he said, "we've come to the end of something." I nodded. "Well," he continued, "don't you wonder what'll come next?" I nodded again, not trusting myself to speak. Flying into my mind instantly, and quickly gone, was a picture of my own home, the slightly bent gate and the long grass under the cherry tree, a light going on in the kitchen and my mother calling out, as I came in, "That you, Sis? Where've you been?"

So I said to Jetsam, "I don't want to wonder! Don't make me!"

He looked as if I had slapped him. I was as startled as he was. "I'm sorry," I said. "I didn't mean it the way it sounded. It's only that—well, I don't want it to, but I suppose it's got to end sometime—"

"That's what I was thinking too."

Without anyone's suggesting it, the eight of us straggled quietly into the forest. The sun lay in scattered splashes of warmth on the pine needles where we walked. The pines, firs, and spruces stood tall around us. Infrequently there came clear spaces in the forest where there were grasses and a few broad-leaved bush trees bearing small, round, reddish-purple berries. We stopped to rest in one such clearing, some of us nibbling at the berries.

Scuro, Jetsam, and I stretched out on the warm sweet earth while Locus kept working at the berries. The others found various resting spots. I looked over at Jetsam as he lay there in the sun, eyes closed, berry stains around his mouth. He seemed lean and strong, and his brown face was relaxed under its crest of black, unruly hair. I knew in that moment that he would go on to other adventures and that, while he would miss us, the pull of the future would be stronger than the memory of the past. I couldn't imagine

myself being able to go on in this way. And yet I think I was wise
enough to know that most of my life was ahead of me and was
going to be lived no matter what.

"What do you think will come next?" I asked.

"Don't know." Jetsam's voice was clear and almost happy.

Evidently others had been listening, because Mr. Green spoke
up at once. "Carabus and I want to ask Them if They can use our
services. With Exi and Grandan part of Them, there must be *some*
way we can serve." Carabus, I saw as I sat, was nodding his head
firmly.

Jetsam sat up too. He wrapped his arms around his knees and
eyed the beetles speculatively. Then he said he thought that was
just what Red would have done.

And so it was that all of a sudden I found myself saying a last
good-bye to two old friends, Mr. Calosoma Green and Carabus. It
wasn't easy to part from these two very different people. I said
some of the things you say at partings, and I kissed each of them.
Everyone gathered around in a busyness of good-byes, giving me
time to realize with a shock that I had already said farewell to Isia,
and to Exi, Arachne and Grandan.

While I was trying to absorb this loss, I became aware that
Botta and Bront were standing together in awkward embarrassment, glancing first at each other and then at us. I didn't feel like
saying anything, so I waited. Finally Botta cleared his throat.

"All play and no work doesn't make a good gopher," Botta said,
his bucktoothed, furry face wrinkled into a grin. "If you follow me.
Which you needn't. Probably won't. Anyway—"

With several false starts, unfunny jokes, and halts along the
way, Botta managed to tell us that he had decided that he could
be a better gopher if he went back to his old home near the Beasts'
kingdom. Some Beasts were still untaught, and maybe he could
help Arachne in some way. In any event, he was returning home.
And Bront wished to go back to his own country. Didn't we think
They would call him if he was needed?

We agreed that undoubtedly They would. So I was face to face
with another leave-taking. Somehow Botta, from my first sight of
him on that far-off day, had held a special place in my heart. I
hoped that I would hold on to his absurd humor as well as his high

courage. I tried to say this in simpler words as I hugged his warm, solid little body.

I had genuine feeling for Bront too, as I said good-bye. We sent our regards to Toad. And two more were subtracted.

"Which way are you going?" Jetsam asked.

"Straight on," I said. "Toward the sea."

"I'll go along for a while," he replied.

We moved on out of the clearing into the cool forest again. A slight breeze began to move through the trees, sometimes making them sigh very faintly. Jetsam and I didn't talk. There wasn't really anything to say. We ambled along, with Locus and Scuro playing hide-and-seek and let's-chase-each-other and what-monster-is-that.

A fresher wind suddenly asserted itself, and I saw Scuro stop still, lift his head, hold his breath, and swivel his nose. I began to sniff with mine. "Smell it, Jetsam," I cried. "Smell the ocean."

He admitted after inhaling several times that something was new and strange to him. Led by an eager Scuro, we increased our pace. Before long I could hear the familiar irregular beat of waves on a rocky shore. Then Scuro barked in excitement and we came onto a grassy, windswept headland against which great waves pounded far below. Not much beach was visible because this promontory thrust sharply forward. What we could see was mostly rocky tidal flats across which the swells surged, smoothed in some places by beds of kelp and seaweed, in other places shattered into fountains of white spume by half-submerged rocks. Each wave eventually spent itself against the shore, to be replaced by another. And another. And another. Endlessly.

I had forgotten how I had loved and lived with the sea for most of my years. Now it burst over me in a flood of sounds and scents and sights and feelings. My attempt to communicate this to Jetsam was not successful. He was too absorbed by his own responses to this enormity of water and space.

Scuro found a narrow trail down and started and was called back by me several times. Finally he sat nearby, whining a bit and sniffing the salt damp air. Locus, a little insecure in the face of the ocean, pressed herself against Scuro.

Knowing the sea as I did, I could tell that the offshore fog bank was moving in. I asked Jetsam if he wanted to try the path downward, and said that if he did we'd better start or it would be too late. After a moment's thought he said he did, adding that after all he couldn't go back.

Just as we stood poised at the cliff's edge ready to start our descent, something almost physical held me back.

"What's the matter with you?" Jetsam asked. "Let's go."

"Nothing's the matter! Don't push me. I just wanted to give you something, that's all." And I took from my pocket the gift of the Mantid. The desire to give this to Jetsam had come from somewhere inside me, and I could only carry it out. "Here," I said, holding it out to him. "It's yours now."

He accepted it with surprise and awe, his hands enfolding it carefully. "But—but—" he stammered, "it's the—the thing that helped us—"

"The Mantid's gift. It's yours. I guess you'll need it."

"Thanks," he said.

With that undramatic, almost noncommittal exchange, we went over the side. Scuro led off of course, followed by Locus, then me, with Jetsam last. It was a fearfully steep path, and narrow. It twisted itself back and forth and around so much that rarely could anyone see anyone else. I began to realize that I was colder and couldn't see so well. I stopped to look up. To my distress I was surrounded by the fog, which had come faster than I had supposed and was now blotting out everything. The sky was darkened. The sea had disappeared. The only things I could see were myself and a few feet of path ahead and behind.

"Scuro!" I shouted. "Jetsam! Locus! Where are you?"

The fog muffled my repeated calls into whispers. Why didn't Jetsam come? He'd been behind me and couldn't have passed me! Where was everyone? What would I do? My fear made me do the worst thing possible: I started to run uphill to where Jetsam might be. And my feet slipped on loose stones and damp grass, and I was sliding and falling through gray emptiness down and down and down. The time I was falling went on forever—an eternity of wet gray fluffiness with bits of earth speeding past. It came to an end as abruptly as it had begun. I landed hard on a soft something, heard a harsh grunt, bounced from softness to solid ground.

Eventually I opened one eye cautiously, and it took several

minutes for me to recognize that I was lying face down on the earth. I waited to see if I hurt any. I didn't, although my body felt stiff and tired as I stretched and sat up. All around me, like a basket or a cradle, was my beloved and familiar hollow halfway up from the sea. It was, as always in April, aglow with short, shining grass and minute pastel flowers. The sea sound was filling the air. The fog through which I had fallen was high now, blotting out the cliff's crest.

"Where have I been—falling through the fog?" I said aloud, almost as if I expected Scuro to answer. Which was silly because he couldn't, but sat there grinning at me, his tongue lolling out happily. Or could he? My mind seemed a bit muddled and I felt not quite myself. Or was I myself some different way?

"I must be crazy," I said. "We'd better get home or Mom'll be mad! It's late!" And I jumped to my feet. Then across the soft hollow I saw the pile of dirt Scuro had dug when he'd spied the beetle, and the whole thing came back to me in a rush of memories.

"You *did* talk," I said to Scuro. "And you could now if you wanted to. Only you won't. Because nobody'd understand." He wagged his brief tail and shook himself. "But you won't forget our friends, will you?" And he whined and started off homeward down our special way.

When we reached the beach, the tide was far out, and the wide wet sands gleamed under the gray sky. Scuro raced along the beach wildly, his lonely tracks disappearing like little bubbles. I turned around once and looked back. My footprints, too, had vanished. Far, far down the beach I saw a slender figure walking away from me. Was it he? Who could tell? I lifted my hand, half wanting to wave and half not wanting to. I didn't. I'm glad, now; for if I had gotten no response I would have gone on wondering why, if it was Jetsam, he didn't reply. If I had gotten a response, I don't know what I'd have done. As it was, I could let the distant walker proceed out of sight on the shining beach, could let him go into whatever awaited him.

I left the sea then, and went along the street toward home. The street lights came on, looking magical against the growing night. All the houses had lights shining from them. The neighbor dogs barked greetings, and fragrances of dinner cooking drifted into the street.

"Where have you been, Sis? You're late," my mother called, as I had expected she would, when Scuro and I came in. But before I had time to answer she said, "Better get washed up for dinner. It won't be long now." Her voice had laughter in it, so I knew things were better than when I'd left.

Nobody asked much about my day. Dinner talk was of my father's office and my brother's football team and whether, on to-morrow's family outing, we should have cold ham or cold chicken or both and whether we should take Aunt Helen with us or not. My father did say he hoped I'd had fun, and I said I had. My mother wondered if I didn't spend too much time alone, and I said I didn't and she dropped the subject. Their faces and their persons, each of the three of them, were very dear to me as I sat there with them, listening to them and their lives, but thinking of Locus, Exi, Mr. Green, Arachne, Grandan, and all the others I had to be parted from.

That night after my parents had kissed me good night and closed my door, I got out of bed and took from my shirt pocket the three seeds I had carried since we left the ant kingdom. Every-thing else I'd gathered, I realized, had been either given away or given back. Way back on my closet shelf was a tiny woven Indian basket with a cover. My grandfather had given me this when I was only nine years old, but it had always held some sort of secret for me. Into this basket I put the seeds, and hid it again.

"We'll use them," I told Scuro as I got back into bed. "Just wait. We'll use them."

He sighed and rearranged himself on his rug in the corner. I noticed then that the kitten—a shy little creature only recently come to our household and up till now afraid of everything includ-ing Scuro—was curled between Scuro's paws, purring in its sleep.